A Curious Earth

A Curious Earth

GERARD WOODWARD

W. W. NORTON & COMPANY
NEW YORK · LONDON

For information about permission to reproduce selections from this book, write to
Permissions, W. W. Norton & Company, Inc., 500 Fifth Avenue,
New York, NY 10110

For information about special discounts for bulk purchases, please contact
W. W. Norton Special Sales at specialsales@wwnorton.com or 800-233-4830

Manufacturing by Courier Westford
Production manager: Devon Zahn

Library of Congress Cataloging-in-Publication Data

Woodward, Gerard, 1961–
A curious Earth / Gerard Woodward. — 1st American ed.
p. cm.
ISBN 978-0-393-33097-7 (pbk.)
1. Loneliness in old age—Fiction. 2. Older men—Psychology—Fiction.
3. Widowers—Psychology—Fiction. 4. Ostend (Belgium)—Fiction.
5. Man-woman relationships—Fiction. I. Title.
PR6073.O634C87 2008
823'.914—dc22

2007046857

W. W. Norton & Company, Inc., 500 Fifth Avenue, New York, N.Y. 10110
www.wwnorton.com

W. W. Norton & Company Ltd., Castle House, 75/76 Wells Street, London
W1T 3QT

1 2 3 4 5 6 7 8 9 0

Never draw on a sleeping person's face,
The bedewed spirit beaded like an arithmetician
Might not recognise herself when she returns;
It is wise, by the same token,
To repaint a departed person's room; and
People about to kill themselves will start by redecorating, often.

Peter Redgrove

Going to Heaven!
I don't know when –
Pray do not ask me how!
Indeed I'm too astonished
To think of answering you!
Going to Heaven!
How dim it sounds!
And yet it will be done
As sure as flocks go home at night
Unto the Shepherd's arm!

Perhaps you're going too!
Who knows?
If you should get there first
Save just a little place for me
Close to the two I lost –
The smallest "Robe" will fit me
And just a bit of "Crown" –
For you know we do not mind our dress
When we are going home –

I'm glad I don't believe it
For it would stop my breath –
And I'd like to look a little more
At such a curious Earth!
I'm glad they did believe it
Whom I have never found
Since the mighty Autumn afternoon
I left them in the ground.

Emily Dickinson

Part One

I

Aldous Rex Llewelwyn Jones sat alone in his kitchen looking at the cupboard. In a previous life, when it had furnished the kitchen of his wife's sister, Meg, this cupboard had been a dresser; a tall structure of shelves and doors with chrome, half-moon handles, frosted-glass panels etched with art deco horizontals, the whole thing a garish, institutional yellow. When Meg died and the dresser had come to live at Fernlight Avenue, Aldous had taken a saw to it and cut through its waist, separating the upper section from the lower. The top half, with its glass doors removed, had become a bookcase for the music room, storing all of his son's music manuscripts. The lower half (two large cupboards underneath, two little square cupboards above, either side of two small drawers) served as a cupboard and worktop for the kitchen.

Here Colette could have chopped, sliced and peeled. She could have rolled pastry, kneaded dough, iced cakes. But Aldous couldn't remember his wife doing any of these things at Meg's old dresser. Instead it had accumulated odd items of junk until there was no space left – old copies of the *Daily Telegraph*, an empty, cracked lotus vase, a tennis racket with broken strings, a pair of scuffed, brown suede shoes, a large, wooden fruit bowl. The fruit bowl didn't contain any fruit. It had never contained any fruit. Instead it contained a tin of 3-in-1 oil, a bunch of redundant keys, a toy train and a set of knitting; the peacock-blue beginnings of a cardigan hanging on a pair of needles beside a fat ball of wool.

Colette had rediscovered knitting in the last years of her life. It had always been one of her skills. She had been good at it. When the children were growing up she had knitted all the time – baby clothes, bobble hats, mittens. As they grew older she had knitted less, until, at some point, she had put away the needles for good, or so Aldous had thought. Then suddenly, perhaps less than a year before she died, she'd felt the urge to knit again. Not something for the children this time, but something for herself. A big blue pullover to keep herself warm. She was weak by then, and could only knit slowly, with her horribly withered hands, shaky and hesitant. And yet the knitting that grew on the needles was as even and as regular as a well-tended lawn.

Now and then Aldous experienced a fleeting desire to finish the cardigan, to take up the needles where Colette had left off, to knit her last garment into existence. He was put off by a vaguely recollected previous encounter with the art of knitting. It hadn't been a happy one: dropped stitches, uneven rows, tangled wool, blistered fingers. He could imagine the travesty that would result if he tampered with what had been started off so beautifully.

By an accident of household geography, the cupboard was directly in Aldous's line of sight. This was why he spent so much time looking at it. Sitting in Colette's armchair by the boiler (although the boiler itself had gone, its alcove filled now with a bookshelf), there was nothing else to look at. In the winter he could spend a whole day in the armchair listening to the rasp and burr of the cooker's gas jets (his only source of heating), and looking at the cupboard. It was now his second winter since Colette had died. They were becoming colder, harder to bear. For the first time he considered that the armchair, the last and least comfortable in a long line of armchairs that had occupied that spot in the kitchen, might actually outlive him.

Aldous never felt the need to actually look inside the cupboard. Its contents had changed very little over the years. Slowly it had filled with objects and, once full, had simply retained them. If he opened the top drawer, for instance, Aldous knew he would encounter several sets of false teeth. They were his wife's, and his wife's mother's. Colette had had her last remaining four front teeth pulled, with difficulty, a few years before she died. The new structure of her mouth meant a new set of dentures, making the old palate redundant. As for Nana's teeth, Aldous really had no idea why they'd been kept. Opening that drawer could be like unlocking a casket of grins.

Also in the drawer was a shock of Colette's hair. Colette always cut her own hair. She once decided to have it short, so simply razored through her ponytail. The severed mane was still in its hairband (in fact a rubber band), and still retained its aroma of hairspray and cigarette smoke. Along with other things of his wife's that the cupboard contained − her books of Green Shield Stamps bulky and crumpled with her dried spittle, her batches of cigarette coupons, her sandals, a box of needlework dangerous with pins and hooks, a jar of buttons that had fallen from her dresses over the years − there seemed almost enough raw components to reconstruct her. If he could have somehow stirred all the contents together, recited some miraculous incantation over the mix, his wife might materialise as a wobbling tower of possessions and activities.

Instead Aldous made do with trophies. Mementoes. He wore her seventeen-jewelled Ingersol ladies' wristwatch on his left wrist. One of the first things she'd bought when she'd come into her brother's inheritance. A band of textured silver called ash, as he recalled, with a tiny clockface set into it. On his other wrist he wore the watch she'd bought him at the same time. Neither of them had ever owned watches before. It was one of the few things Colette left that had financial value, and mechanism. It seemed a waste to let its clockwork go unwound in one of those drawers, so he wore the time on both wrists, his wife's watch there as a pleasing presence, a pulse, a weight, a gentle grip on his wrist, a counterbalance to the weight of his loneliness.

Aldous now noticed something odd about the cupboard. From the small, left-hand, square door there seemed to be something protruding. Through the cracks green matter was poking out. It was as though it had been filled to capacity with green wool and then squeezed shut, trapping tufts. But Aldous hadn't opened the cupboard for weeks. Months, even. So he went over to the cupboard and pulled the handle. Its ball-and-socket latch was stiff, and came open with a sudden snap. A cloud of tiny flies drifted out, and Aldous was momentarily horrified by what he saw inside. The green things, it turned out, were the tips of leaves, and the leaves were at the end of long spindly tubers that had grown out of some potatoes that Aldous had put in the cupboard sometime before, and then forgotten about. The potatoes themselves were few and small, yet they had spawned a looping, arching network of growths – eyes emerging from spidery sockets and insisting through the narrow door cracks to put a leaf forth. When Aldous first opened the door he was shocked by the way the vegetable architecture of the potatoes had been stirred to movement, as though alive in an animal way, as though some knuckly arthropod had ensconced itself in the cupboard – a lobster or a spider crab. But when he finally realised what had happened, he felt strangely heartened. He took a Robert the Bruce kind of encouragement from the tenacity of nature. That a bunch of old potatoes could yen so strongly for the sixty-watt gloom of Aldous's winter kitchen. That they could put in so much effort, using every last drop of starch and moisture to attain the light . . .

All this time Aldous had spent looking at the cupboard, when in fact the cupboard had been looking at him, insistently, unblinkingly. It took a while for him to accept this fact, and the uncomfortable conclusion that resulted – that some old potatoes in his cupboard were more actively interested in life than he was.

2

With considerable effort, Aldous lifted himself out of his chair and walked to the windows at the back of the kitchen. These gave on to a view of the back garden.

It shouldn't have surprised Aldous to find that the same silent process that was at work in the cupboard was also at work here – or at least it had been over the previous summer. Growth. The accretion of matter. The conversion of sunlight into hydrocarbons, cellulose, starch.

Since Colette's death the garden had been left to do what it liked. What the garden liked doing, it seemed, was growing. The poplar and the plum tree had both sent up shoots in the area that had been a lawn; little delicate spires that, unleafed, were as straight and as vertical as tent poles. Other bushes had appeared as well, though not of any obvious species. They grew in untidy bursts amid the tall, dead grass. Some were still green with leaves, others had turned reddish brown, the leaves crumpled up on the shoots. The leaves of the previous autumn had formed a rotting, broken carpet where they'd fallen. It took the barrenness of winter to enable Aldous to see the extent to which the garden had become overgrown. In the summer the view was obscured by the low canopies of the apple and plum trees, which nearly touched the windows. Now, in winter, it was as though a veil had fallen, to reveal further, deeper veils. Layer upon layer of nature thickening, ramifying.

As with the potatoes in the cupboard, Aldous was taking a strange, inverted sense of pride in his neglect of the garden. Somehow it had become a monument to his own sense of isolation and loneliness. For Aldous, letting the garden grow without interference was like letting his hair or his beard grow. Weren't there people in India who did that out of religious devotion? Weren't there widows who let their hair grow down to their ankles, or shamans who let their fingernails evolve into waxy helixes of keratin? The garden was Aldous's own beard. His beard of mourning. That was why he couldn't go out into the garden and hack away, or why he couldn't bring himself to rip out those brave little potatoes. It would have announced to the world that he was happy with his place in it. Secretly he hoped that the potatoes wouldn't stop growing, that their pallid tubers would extend into the kitchen itself, envelop the cupboard, fill the room with their delicate branches, at the same time as the forest in the back garden soared over the rooftop and the ivy embraced all four brick walls. The garden was both his statement to the world and his protection from it. It quite pleased Aldous to think of himself expiring in a house that was invisible beneath foliage. That the firemen would have to saw through thick tree roots, ivy roots, take their chainsaw to a thicket of plum trees and poplar shoots, with gauntleted hands yank out the thorny necks of mulberries, before they found him, a skeleton with two wristwatches, potato tubers growing out of his eye sockets.

Aldous had not known loneliness like this before. The ear-pounding silence of a house vacated by all-but-one. The loping, bounding, empty spaces of its rooms. The coldness of its books. The way it echoed, but was alive all night with timbers settling, giving back what little heat they'd absorbed. And he'd wake after a cold night and glance with horror at how his breath had filled the windows with a champagne fizz of interior dew that dripped and spilled from the jambs with long, pathetic trickling noises, or else froze in a paisley pattern on the glass.

For company he kept the radio on all day – Radio 4, John Timpson and Brian Redhead in the morning, introducing the day with their grumbling and guffawing, their growly but good-hearted interviews with slippery politicians. The world's events reduced to an endless string of wisecracking sophistry. Nothing mattered. Miners on strike. The invasion of the Falkland Islands. The Pope in Ireland. A man phoned in on *Tuesday Call* to say the Pope was just another man, what was all the fuss about?

But even the radio became too much. He would have to

switch it off at some point, especially in the afternoon when some hammy actor would deliver a long monologue about having cancer. If he was lucky Aldous would drift off to sleep in the armchair by the boiler, glass of whisky beside him, to be woken, usually, by the sensation of having a cat jump into his lap. He would open his eyes to find nothing there. A ghost cat, or waking dream, or hallucination. But over the months the cat seemed to gain more and more substance, until he finally saw it on the floor in front of him, sitting in that perfect way they have, flanks folded neatly, tail curled economically round the front paws, staring at him, as if waiting patiently to be fed.

Up until the death of his son's cat Scipio, there had always been a feline presence in the house. In fact, there had been cats in the family even before there had been children. It was not surprising, therefore, that they should persist in some form, even in their physical absence. That was how Aldous tried to understand the appearance of this hungry little silver-spotted cat, who licked his lips (or whatever they have) continually, and stared with that odd, familiar expression – both intense and indifferent.

At first the cat had looked sleek and fat, but over the months it had started to deteriorate. It became thinner and thinner, its face taking on the gaunt, hollow-cheeked, big-eyed look of a cat from the tomb of the Pharaohs. Later, its fur began to thin as well. Little patches of blue skin became visible on its shanks. Every day there was less fur on the cat. The bare notches of its vertebrae, almost dinosaur-like, began to show through. Then the parallel corrugations of its ribcage. Although it never became completely hairless, its manginess revolted Aldous. That naked, secret skin with its tiny goose pimples and dainty scabs . . . Sometimes Aldous would feel, unaccountably, an overwhelming sense of guilt. As though he were solely responsible for the emaciated condition of this imaginary cat. The cat had done nothing to make him feel like this: it simply continued with its indifferent, supercilious looks, occasionally licking its nose, while any attempt to feed it caused it to vanish instantly. Aldous could usually make it disappear simply by blinking and rinsing his eyes. Nevertheless he was entranced by the verisimilitude of his visions, how a product of his imagination seemed to act so independently of it.

Aldous had never much cared for the cats that had lived with him, that he had spent so much time feeding, taking to the vets, hunting for when they went missing. Why, therefore, was his imagination so insistent on conjuring this creature into existence, when he could think of a hundred more favourable companions, not least his wife? Other widowers he knew of had been haunted by their wives, but Aldous had to make do with a hungry, dying cat.

Perhaps if he visited Colette's grave more often she could be encouraged to leave it, Aldous thought. But he didn't like visiting her grave, and had done so only once, on the anniversary of their wedding, and then only under pressure from his daughter Juliette, who went with him.

The grave was one among countless hundreds that were filling Ladore Lane Cemetery up to its tall iron railings. Colette occupied the same little corner that was dotted with numerous other members of her family – her mother and older sister Meg were two rows away, her brother Janus Brian and his wife Mary were on the opposite side of the path, facing their mother. Colette and Aldous's own son, Janus, was a few files further along the path and three rows back. They were like an unsorted deal at bridge.

It had been a rainy day. The asphalt paths were riddled with puddles. Juliette had a pink umbrella that kept jabbing Aldous in the eye. Even so, Aldous couldn't manage any tears. Juliette sobbed quietly as they laid brilliant purple and pink asters and chrysanthemums on Colette's grave, and she had wanted to linger about afterwards, talking with her father about happier times. But Aldous had just wanted to get away as quickly as he could.

Sometimes the emptiness of the house would become intolerable, and finding a reserve of energy in his body that was only there infrequently, Aldous would use his free bus pass to travel into London and wander the streets of the capital, just to be away from the house. Sometimes, to prolong the sense of escape, he would visit a theatre, see a play. In theatres he became conscious of how few people visited these places alone. He would be seated between couples whispering and giggling into each other's ears. Couples in front of him and behind him, couples at all points of the compass. Sometimes people went to the theatre, Aldous noted with surprise, in large groups, and if he was unlucky he would find himself adrift in a sea of friends who carried on their hearty and playful conversations through his body, over and around his head, so that he would shrink down into his seat to avoid the crossfire of their happiness.

In the snows before Christmas Aldous had seen a production of *The Winter's Tale* at the Young Vic. He'd never been to that theatre before, nor seen the play. He was very taken with its youthful audience. He couldn't quite understand why, but gone were the grey-haired retired grammar-school teachers of the RSC and the National, with their walking sticks and tweed skirts, or the blundering tourists who coughed and chatted through all the great speeches. Here the audience was young and exuberant and very adept at succumbing to enchantment. They giggled and gossiped in between the acts, but seemed entranced by the performance.

The play had taken Aldous entirely by surprise. It was an economical production. The actors were dressed in standard Elizabethan costume, the stage was bare but for a table and chairs, and later, for the pastoral scenes, after a surprise fall of confetti, a large horn of plenty spilling its contents was lowered. Aldous was startled to find himself recognising fragments of dialogue, particularly lines uttered by Perdita, the baby abandoned on a sea coast, found by shepherds and raised as one of their own. Time itself made an appearance, turned an hourglass on its head, and there was Perdita, a beautiful girl welcoming visitors to the shearing. '*Daffodils, that come before the swallow dares, and take the winds of March with beauty.*' The line brought a sudden shower of tears from Aldous's eyes, and he felt stupid. He could feel that sour tightening in his neck that presaged the need to audibly sob. This he managed to hold off until the statue scene. What had Shakespeare thought he was doing? This was utter madness. A woman presumed dead for sixteen years makes her reappearance, going through the masque of posing as a thing of alabaster? When the line came – '*what fine chisel could ever yet cut breath?'* – it cut into Aldous's own heart. A laughable plot, yet the eventual stirring of that convincing stone (how had she managed to remain so still, kneeling?) had been too much for Aldous, and the subsequent sequence of reconciliations (*'You precious winners all'*) had him calling out, as though drunk, 'That's lovely. That's lovely.' The few grey heads in the audience turned sternly in his direction, but the younger people laughed, which made Aldous feel warm, a feeling further enhanced when the interruption was taken good-naturedly by the cast: Leontes and Hermione both gave friendly nods at Aldous, and sweet little Perdita, all golden curls and lacy smocks, smiled sweetly at him.

It meant that Aldous fell into conversation with the young people surrounding him on the way out of the theatre. It turned out they were drama students. 'Perhaps you'll play Perdita one day,' Aldous said to the fair-haired girl in torn jeans who walked beside him. 'More like Lady Macbeth,' said a tall, whispily bearded young man, whose casual intimacy with the girl (he had his hand tucked into the rear pocket of the girl's trousers) Aldous found rather troubling.

'We're doing *The White Devil*,' said another girl, dark and gypsyesque in a red-spotted headscarf.

'Can I come and see you?' asked Aldous.

They went into a pub near the theatre. Aldous was pleased to find that he could impress them with his knowledge of Shakespeare. They seemed to find him mysterious and slightly dangerous and rather funny, and he didn't feel a need to act younger than his years, which was a talent he'd never had anyway.

'I think Shakespeare was most moved by the father-daughter relationship, far more than the husband-wife relationship. Shakespeare's marriages tend to be unhappy, but his feelings for his daughters are tender beyond compare. Think of Prospero and Miranda – how he saved her, carrying her as a baby – "thy crying self" – on to the boat and into exile. Think of Lear and Cordelia – "Why should a dog, a horse, a rat have life, and thou no breath at all?" Think even of Titus Andronicus and Lavinia . . .'

The students nodded thoughtfully.

Afterwards Aldous walked home alone, through the cold, empty streets, having extracted from the fair-haired girl a promise to send him a ticket for their *White Devil*. He had left his address and phone number on a beer mat. He didn't expect her to keep her promise, and he even had the sense that he'd slightly frightened her. But the exquisite, redemptive, mad power of the play stayed with him. Statues coming alive. That exquisite Perdita. Sheep shearing, lovemaking in the blizzard of the sheep-shearing shed, swallows and daffodils – snow on the pavement at Waterloo and on the silent streets of Windhover Hill, another day another dollar back to Fernlight Avenue.

Aldous didn't hear from the fair-haired girl about tickets. He even felt a little ashamed for having asked her, a total stranger, a young girl. What must she have thought? That he was some lecherous old devil in his shabby brown tweed coat, reeking faintly of whisky and cigarettes, wanting to paw the tight little jeans off an innocent sweetheart young enough to be his grand-daughter? On the other hand, Aldous thought, looking at himself in the bathroom mirror, there were supposed to be women around who found older men attractive. But where were they all? Aldous could, with reasonable modesty, assert that he was a good-looking man for his age. He still had hair, he hadn't run to fat, he was tall (when he remembered not to stoop), he had what one of his sisters-in-law had called (it embarrassed him to recall) 'come-to-bed eyes'. But no female, young or old, had given him a second glance for as long as he could remember.

The potatoes in the cupboard continued to grow. The green tufts had extended and unfolded into proper leaves, emerging from all four cracks around the little cupboard door.

3

'What do you think those are?' said Aldous, pointing at the cupboard.

Juliette was sitting on one of the dining-table chairs, which she'd turned round to face her father's chair by the boiler. She hadn't taken off her brown leather coat because the kitchen felt as cold to her as it did outdoors. Aldous too was wearing his overcoat and had the collar turned up. He had forgotten to light the oven.

'What *what* are?'

Aldous pointed again at the cupboard, smiling.

'In there. What do you think they are?'

He hoped the potatoes might deflect Juliette's anger, but he had overestimated their significance. The tiny little green leaves were nothing in the face of his daughter's grievances. Juliette hadn't even seen them.

'Do you think that by putting whisky in your tea you can hide the fact you're drinking it?'

'Yes,' said Aldous, 'I suppose so.'

'Well, it doesn't work. The whole house reeks of whisky. I could smell it even as I came up the path.'

'Could you?' Aldous was genuinely surprised. Surely whisky wasn't that pungent.

Juliette's visits were frequent but came at unexpected times. She was a journalist on the *London Evening News*, working shifts, and was as likely to appear in the early morning as she was late at night. She lived in Holland Park with a middle-aged political correspondent called Bernard. It was a long trek from west London to Windhover Hill and Aldous always thought he should be grateful for Juliette's visits, and he usually was, but sometimes he rather feared them.

'It's the feeble patheticness of it that really gets to me. The furtiveness – the way you wrap up whisky bottles loosely in newspaper before you put them in the bin. They open up again – it's almost like you want them to be found. And those whisky bottles I found just now, under the cushions of the settee – what was the point of doing that? You know how those cushions spring up when you sit on them. They were always going to be discovered. And now this feeble attempt to disguise your whisky by dressing it up in a costume of tea. I didn't realise at first, but now I remember how you've always got a mug of tea by your side, always with the teaspoon still in so that it rattles annoyingly . . .'

'Yes,' said Aldous, 'I don't even like tea that much. Now I'm on fifty cups a day . . .'

He laughed hopefully, but Juliette maintained her expression of tired contempt. Aldous hated being found out in his drinking, and wasn't sure how to react. The furtiveness itself was a kind of admission of guilt, so to make light of it now seemed hypocritical. But he felt he had no choice. The only alternative was to tell Juliette to shut up and mind her own business, but that would have upset her more than the drinking. He could tell her he was going to make a vow never again to touch a drop of the hard stuff – but she would have seen through it. Perhaps he'd handled this boozing business wrong right from the start. He never meant it to become a secretive, furtive thing, but once he'd made the choice to hide his drinking, it became impossible to turn back and drink openly. He'd created a taboo for himself which he was unable to break.

'So how much are you getting through?' she went on.

'I don't know.'

'A bottle a day?'

'Christ, no. Nothing like that. I'd be dead by now on a bottle a day –'

'Half a bottle?'

'No –' the negative was rather less forceful – 'I shouldn't think so – I don't keep track, how can you? It's not much anyway, in the evening, helps me to sleep . . .'

'Exactly what Mum used to say . . .'

'You still haven't told me what you think of that.' He pointed again at the cupboard.

'I don't know what you're talking about — what am I supposed to be looking at?'

'The cupboard — the little cupboard — left-hand. Can you see those things sticking out?'

Suddenly Juliette's eyes registered the little shoots and leaves sprouting around the cupboard door.

'What are they?'

'Why don't you have a look?'

Aldous was grinning broadly, as though presenting a child with a really special treat, as though the cupboard might be full of sweets and toys. Juliette walked over and pulled open the cupboard door. Another diffuse cloud of those tiny black flies, then a squeal of shock from Juliette as the webby, knuckly movement of the tubers seemed to pose a momentary threat.

'What the hell . . .' After the initial shock she peered closer. 'Potatoes . . .'

'I put them in there and forgot about them, and they've grown . . . They're amazing, aren't they?'

Aldous took Juliette's thoughtful silence as agreement, but when she reached in as if to yank the potatoes out of the cupboard he had to yell at her.

'What are you doing? Leave them alone!'

Juliette stopped, shocked by her father's outburst. She hadn't yet touched the plants. Aldous went on.

'I'm letting them grow. I want them to grow. I want to see how long they'll survive — and shut that door carefully, you might squash the leaves.'

Juliette sighed resignedly as she carefully closed the cupboard door on the potatoes. Like a tiny theatre troupe, they'd given their brief, silent performance, and now the curtain had fallen.

Juliette sat back in the chair that was facing her father, looking at her fingernails thoughtfully. Aldous looked as well, from a distance. Once they had been bitten down almost to the quick, but now they had regrown, were smooth and shiny with white, shapely fringes. Aldous was never quite sure if it was ditching her old boyfriend Boris and moving in with Bernard that had stopped her chewing her nails, or the death of her mother. Probably both. They had happened at almost the same time.

Juliette suddenly snapped herself out of her fingernail contemplation, as though they had done their job of strengthening her resolve.

'You've started to smell,' she said, with affected coldness.

'Have I? What of?' Aldous could only just suppress his shock at Juliette's observation. It had never been said to him before, and he sensed it came as the last remaining weapon in Juliette's armoury of admonition.

'You've just started to smell of . . . not washing. You smell really bad, Daddy, and I don't just mean the whisky on your breath, though that's bad enough . . .'

Aldous shrugged and looked away.

'Don't people ever say anything to you?' Juliette went on. 'I mean when you go in a shop or something? Or on a bus? I'm not trying to be horrible, but it really suprises me that people don't come after you with a spray or something when you go in places like that. I mean – you know, I can smell you now and I'm straining to control myself . . .'

'Well, why don't you shove off back to the perfumed-scented boulevards of Holland Park if it offends you so much?'

Juliette ignored him, making allowances for his hurt.

'You know what it reminds me of, your smell? It's the exact same smell that used to come off Janus Brian. That horrible, sickly, sweet, sweaty, grotty smell.'

'Don't start comparing me to Janus Brian, for God's sake. I'm nothing like as bad as him.'

The evocation of his wife's brother, Juliette's uncle, whose drunken decline after the death of his wife seemed to use up the last reserves of Colette's maternal energies in the years of her own decline, always made Aldous squirm with anxiety. He could not resist the awful temptation of seeing Janus Brian's brief, sickly, intoxicated widowerhood as a premonition of his own.

'I can't see much difference. What's the difference? It's just a question of time but you're following the exact same path. Those potatoes and your stupid delight in them are just the same thing. How long before I come round and find you unconscious with vomit all over your trousers?'

17

'You say this just because there are some old potatoes in my cupboard? Janus Brian never had potatoes. He never grew anything after Mary died.'

'Forget about the potatoes. Why don't you just try and do something with yourself?'

'Like what?'

'Like washing – that could be a start. How often do you wash? Do you ever wash?'

Aldous gave a shrug.

'It's so bloody cold in this house. The bathroom – you can't go in there. What am I supposed to do, carry saucepans of boiling water upstairs? What's the point? I can just shave in the front room next to the gas fire. That's enough for me.'

They both foresaw and declined to follow the familiar route this discussion was taking. The heating of Fernlight Avenue had been a lively topic of conversation for nearly thirty years, a problem never satisfactorily resolved. The coal fires that had once provided welcoming glows in all the rooms had long since been blocked up. Only the gas fire in the living room and the gas cooker in the kitchen provided a reliable source of warmth during the winter months. The upstairs rooms were cold, frosty places during these times, no warmer than caves. Central heating was always thought too expensive to install, electric-bar fires too expensive to run, paraffin heaters were cheap but lukewarm and fumy. Oil-fired electric radiators, bought through a catalogue, were once thought to be the solution, but in the end they only combined the expense of electric heaters with the feeble warmth of paraffin stoves. Juliette had suggested everything from night storage heaters to solar power. In the end she decided that Aldous actually liked the cold. Once, when the skylight in the loft was broken, and the hatch in the landing had been left open, snow had actually fallen into the house and settled on the landing carpet, without melting. Now Aldous seemed to be relishing the bad weather as a means of relieving him from the duties of being a normal citizen.

'It's the way you seem to be wasting your life. I can't stand to think of it, when I'm over the other side of London – you sitting here listening to the radio and falling asleep in a whisky stupor. I mean, what do you do all day? You just sit there, stagger down to the off-licence for a bottle of White Horse, stagger back, flop out in that chair and watch your potatoes grow.'

'No, sometimes I go out. I told you I went to see *The Winter's Tale* four times. When was the last time you went to the theatre? You don't have to answer, I can't expect all my children to be interested in worthless things like great works of art. You claim to like Shakespeare, well, you should have come with me to see this one. It was the most exquisite theatrical experience I've ever had. *Daffodils, that come before the swallow dares* . . . You've missed your chance, you know that, don't you, it'll never happen again. *What fine chisel could ever yet cut breath* . . . Do you know that line?'

At this Juliette's face finally broke into a smile, though it was partly a smile of defeat. Her father went on.

'Haven't you ever seen a play and felt as though it's been performed for you and you alone? That the actors are like your own memories made flesh . . .'

'Dad, I'd really love to talk about Shakespeare, but we have to talk about you and your drinking. It's no good trying to steer the conversation away like this and then try to belittle me as some sort of philistine. The fact of your drinking remains, we've got to do something about it.'

'Well, I've said I'm going to stop, haven't I? Why don't you just stop worrying about me?'

Juliette stood up again, walked over to the fridge and opened it. Empty shelves. A carton of sour milk. Some mouldy cheese.

'You're not eating, are you? That's another problem. Look at yourself in the mirror. You don't have any colour in your face.'

'There's no food in the fridge because I've eaten it all. Tomorrow morning I'm going out to buy some more.'

And so it went on, as it often did. Aldous fending off a welter of anguished criticism with half-lies and empty promises. It ended with Juliette in tears saying words to the effect that she was utterly disappointed in her father, whom, as a child, she had admired because he was a clever artist.

'I used to boast to my friends at school about you, how you could make paintings that, if you propped them against a wall and sat next to them, could make you think you were in the countryside. I was so proud of you. But you don't even paint now.'

Aldous put a consoling hand on Juliette's shoulder, who had crouched down beside Aldous's chair, a hanky held to her downturned face. He had never been much of a cuddler as a father, and found it even more difficult to be one now. The consoling shoulder-pat was the best he could manage.

'How do you know I don't paint? You wondered what I do all day – perhaps I paint all day.'

'But you don't, do you. You think I'm a philistine but what have you got to show for being an artist? If I had a talent like yours I could never stop painting.'

'But I'm not an artist, Juliette. That's what you have never understood, nor anyone else. I'm just a retired art teacher. I never wanted to be anything other than an art teacher.'

'But now that you've retired, surely you must want, I mean – now you can be an artist – you've got all this time and all that talent, but instead you just want to drink it all away –'

Juliette broke off, aware that the conversation was beginning to go round in circles. As she prepared to leave she brought forth from her father a few more empty promises (to stop drinking, to eat more, to do something about the heating, to start painting again . . .) and then, eyes dabbed and composure restored, she left the house.

Almost immediately Aldous took a long, desperate slug of Scotch straight from the neck of the bottle he'd retrieved from the open chimney and sat down again in the armchair by the boiler.

He spent a while looking at his hands. There was no doubt now that they were an old man's hands – raised veins, liver spots, wrinkles. And they were shaking. The first tremor of a drinker's palsy. For nearly seventy years the same hands at the ends of his arms. Were these really the fingers that had pushed those tin trucks round and round the kitchen floor, that had turned the pages of *Chicks' Own* and *Tiger Tim*, that had followed the lines of text of his first reading books? The same smooth, pale hands that had sketched his first nude at Hornsey School of Art, that had turned wet clay into a pot, that had eased through the strata of his future wife's silk to find her breast like a soft fossil, that had poked into the red, gasping mouths of his babies? It seemed hardly credible.

He took another swig of whisky, just as Juliette was returning to the kitchen, having let herself in, to retrieve her forgotten handbag. In mid-glug Aldous could do nothing but leave the bottle where it was, in his mouth, bottom up, and observe his daughter sheepishly through its warped glass. Having been through every emotion that evening Juliette was not prepared to expend any more emotional energy. She simply gave her father a long disgusted look, similar to those he had given her for childhood misdemeanours, and left, slamming the door with such fury he almost wondered why the house didn't collapse.

4

Aldous surprised himself with how angry he was. Juliette's comments had stung him – not the ones about his smell, but about his failure as an artist. The next day, restless with his anger, he took a bus down to London. It had been snowing, and the London streets were slushy. He wandered into the National Gallery for shelter from the cold, and then lost himself in its labyrinths of art.

Over a lifetime of visits Aldous had come to know the gallery pretty well, and its geography had altered little over the years, especially in the old, original building. Bits had been added on, galleries had been extended, paintings had been rehung and relit, but for the most part it was the same place: the same green flock wallpaper, the same tall doors with their shock-giving brass handles, the same Corinthian columns of lambs' fat marble. The gallery still had the capacity to surprise, however. All those years of walking along the tall, gilt-edged avenues of paintings was not long enough to know everything that dwelt there. And the day after Juliette's admonitions, still smarting from them, he came across a small, quiet painting he must have overlooked on a hundred previous visits, but which on this occasion grabbed his attention as much as if it had reached out and taken him by the lapels.

It was a painting by Rembrandt: his portrait of Hendrickje Stoffels, Rembrandt's housekeeper turned mistress. In it Hendrickje was rendered as an object of exquisite beauty, glowing at the centre of a typically gloomy space. She was dressed in a white fur robe, open at the neck, revealing a soft, shadowy cleavage. She had two strings of amber beads around her neck, jewelled earrings hanging from her lobes. Her hair was carefully crafted, set back, braided, hanging in ringlets and bunches. Her face was round, white and smooth, and she had a captivatingly open expression, which was probably the abject boredom of the artist's model but which translated as a girlishly unassuming acceptance of the strange, decadent, squalid and eccentric world of Rembrandt's widowerhood. Yet there was something more to Hendrickje's facial expression. She was depicted as an object of sexual desire, available and accepting, returning the artist's gaze with what Rembrandt would probably have seen as the reflection of his own desire. Mutual lust. But Aldous, held in the grip of this female gaze for an hour or more, felt strongly a deeper level of emotional connection between artist and model than mere sexual desire. And he couldn't break free from the painting until he'd decided what it was.

Aldous vaguely recollected the story. Saskia, Rembrandt's voluptuous and rich first wife, had died young, shortly after the birth of their only surviving child, Titus. Despair and lonely widowerhood had followed for Rembrandt, then a disastrous affair with Titus's nursemaid – what was her name? Then Hendrickje had come along as housekeeper, rivalries had developed, hair-tearing fights in the kitchen, the nursemaid kicked out but swearing revenge – didn't Rembrandt have her locked up? Eventually he hopped into bed with Hendrickje, who was denounced by the town burghers as a whore – but Rembrandt couldn't marry her because it would have meant losing Saskia's inheritance.

Aldous stared long and hard at the painting struggling to remember the facts. The label didn't give much information. There was something odd about the end of the story – Aldous could only half remember and vowed to get a book on the subject at the earliest opportunity – Hendrickje had ended up employing Rembrandt in order to shield him from his creditors. Something like that. There was something very touching in the story – this young, pretty woman of no great education or social standing, a daughter of the minor military, taking the sorrows and disappointments and ruins of a great artist's life on her pretty young shoulders. Defying the Church authorities. There was a tough, opportunistic chancer hidden somewhere behind that innocent smile.

What must she have thought of him, Hendrickje, the poorly educated girl from a poor family, suddenly in the house of the ageing artist, at one time the most celebrated painter in the country, married to the vivacious and wealthy Saskia, now a haunted, lonely figure struggling to raise his only surviving son of that marriage? Once sought after by princes and the wealthiest merchants as a portraitist, now struggling for commissions, his wealth fading rapidly, out of favour, too often steeped in his cups (look at that porous, shiny, bloated, red hooter of his, a drinker's nose if ever there was one), stumbling in his paints, unable for days or weeks on end to focus on a canvas long enough to achieve anything more than a few shadows . . . And what must he have thought of her when she first arrived in his household – another of the grabbing, mendacious, dour, puritanical nursemaids and housekeepers who turned his paintings to face the wall because they gave them the creeps? How long did it take him to notice her?

It wasn't until Aldous got home that evening and was sitting in the armchair by the boiler with a glass of whisky in his hand that he realised what that expression was on Hendrickje's face. With those wide, dark eyes of hers and that tangerine mouth, she was gazing at old, drunken, stumbling (though still with a steady hand) Rembrandt with one unmistakable emotion. Forgiveness.

Aldous fell asleep in the armchair, as quite often happened. Then, in the small hours, staggered into the front room and lay down on the couch to sleep properly. And when he woke the next morning it wasn't in the usual state of groggy inertia; instead he was filled with a furious, indignant energy.

He was still angry about Juliette's comments. It was true that he'd hardly painted or drawn at all over the last few years, certainly not since Colette had died, and probably not for a long while before that. It was also true that he'd never had ambitions to be an artist and had been quite content with his life's role as a teacher of art to thirty years' worth of Edmonton schoolchildren. And it was perhaps also true that he had used that career, and the family that it had provided for, as an excuse for his not becoming a professional artist. The little successes he'd had – the occasional picture at the Royal Academy, the winning of a competition now and then – hinted to anyone interested that there was a seething talent kept in check by the demands of family life, reinforced by the occasional sighing laments he expressed for a vocation that had passed him by, often echoed, teasingly by his wife. Whenever he brought home the latest landscapes and impastoed interiors he'd been working on in his free periods, she would express dismay at his wasting of his talents on talentless schoolchildren. 'Off to cast more pearls before swine?' she would say as he left for work in the morning, a sentiment that grew when the grammar turned comprehensive. Yet she would have been terrified if he'd chucked in his job with its reasonable and reliable salary.

But now that he was wifeless and jobless he could use none of those excuses that had served him all his adult life. He had no family to support, and none of the demands of the salaried schoolmaster. All he had was time and space – big bounding hunks of each, things he'd longed for all his life, but which now hung on his shoulders like great, fat, teasing gods. It occurred to Aldous that he might finally have found a way of driving them off. Poke them in the eyes with a paintbrush, throw some turpentine in their faces. He was going to do a painting.

Without washing, shaving, or stopping for something to eat (there wasn't anything anyway), he rummaged about the house for his painting things. His oil paints were heaped in an old cardboard box in a corner of the back bedroom. Mostly in tubes, they were an assortment that had grown over the years into a sizeable stock. There were some tubes that hadn't even been opened; others, half spent, had begun to ooze a brown gum from their necks. Others had leaked linseed oil which had darkened the paper of the labels, like newspaper that has been used to drain chips. Some tubes had been left with their caps off, and the paint within had hardened to an almost rock-like consistency, fossilised by the action of air. Some tubes had their caps incorrectly screwed on, so that air had got in anyway, and the caps themselves were welded fast to the tube, proving impossible to unscrew.

There were some brushes on the floor as well, filling an old pickled-onion jar like a bunch of very uninteresting flowers. In fact, here was everything he needed: an old bottle of white spirit, some rags scabby with dried paint, and even some unused boards primed and ready for painting on.

Aldous had decided that he wanted to paint the garden. There had been a fresh fall of snow in the night which had filled in the gaps of the previous snowfall perfectly. The garden was an extraordinary sight, almost like a drawing itself – branches against snow like lines vigorously sketched on to a sheet of white paper. Aldous had the idea that he would like to make a series of paintings depicting the garden through the seasons. The four seasons of the garden. For this reason he noticed the easel. An easel had been one of the gifts presented to Aldous by the school on his retirement. A spindly little thing of telescopic shafts and wing nuts that folded away into a neat pack. He'd never used it before, so he carried it downstairs with the rest of his equipment, busily ignoring the cold, remembering Monet's example – if you want to paint a snowy landscape you have no alternative but to go out into a snowy landscape and paint it. That was what a visiting lecturer at Hornsey had said when Aldous had presented him with a winter scene, where he'd simply overpainted a regular landscape with white to make it look like snow.

Aldous experienced the first of his time distortions as he descended the stairs. He suddenly felt as though he was watching a film about a man walking down a staircase that went on for ever – like in the film *A Matter of Life and Death*, the staircase that leads from life to the afterlife. The stairs at Fernlight Avenue seemed to go on endlessly, but when Aldous reached the ground floor and looked back up, the stairs were their normal length.

Aldous laughed to himself and carried his things out into the garden. How cold it was. The overspilling dustbin looked beautiful, a cottage loaf of snow on top of it. He set up the easel with some difficulty (it belonged to the same species of contraption as the deckchair), and then brought out two wooden dining chairs from the kitchen, one to place his materials on. At this point he began to remember the effortful nature of landscape painting. How one has to put everything into it, one's entire body, and mode of existence, so that painting and living are no longer separate activities, but are merged together. It cannot be done casually. Especially not in snow. Things have to be prepared and thought about in advance. The advice of his college tutors came back to him. How intent they were on the importance of looking rather than imagining. When Monet wanted to paint the snow, he took hot-water bottles with him to stop his fingers numbing up. Aldous couldn't complain. He was only ten feet from his back door. But by the time he'd squeezed out some paint on to a palette (an old enamel plate), his fingers were starting to tingle with coldness. He blew on his hands and sketched in some branches, made a suggestion of space beyond with some swipes of burnt umber. After a few minutes of dabbing with browns and whites, the structure of the garden was beginning to form on the board, but already Aldous's hands were numbing up. He would have to do as Monet, and fill a hot-water bottle. He went back inside, found the whisky bottle he'd been using the night before and took a swig. Then he went to the sink to fill a pan for the hot-water bottle. This was when he experienced the second of his time distortions.

No matter how much water poured into the saucepan, it remained empty. It puzzled Aldous greatly. He inspected the saucepan closely, wondering if there was a hole in it. He checked carefully that the water was actually going into the pan. The experience of filling the saucepan seemed to go on for hours. He looked very closely at the point where the stream of water from the tap hit the floor of the pan. Water scattered in all directions across the dry metal surface – in ball-shaped droplets, bouncing about like a game of marbles, then bursting like bubbles and, like bubbles, vanishing. Aldous spent some time rationalising this phenomenon. Water is air, he told himself. It is made of two gases – hydrogen and oxygen. I am simply watching water turning back into air. But after failing to fill for a long time, in an instant the saucepan became heavy and overspilling. Not only the saucepan but the sink below it. There was water spilling over on to the kitchen floor. It was as though the first second of saucepan-filling had expanded into a week, while the next half an hour had contracted into a second.

Curious, thought Aldous, who'd dropped the saucepan in shock, feeling a pain in his wrist. The kitchen was suddenly alive with noise and movement – the gushing of water, the rippling and splashing of it on the floor.

This is when Aldous experienced the third of his time distortions.

5

The house had been knocked sideways. That was how it felt. As though it had been flipped on to its side, the horizontal becoming the vertical, the floor the wall. It had taken Aldous entirely by surprise. For a moment his house seemed to have no more weight than a matchbox. It turned, spun, and the floor was brought up to Aldous's face. He felt himself clinging to it for support, in case the house should go through another ninety degrees and he find himself on the ceiling.

There had been a huge crash when the house flipped, as though a lorry had slammed into the front wall. Window frames shook, crockery and cutlery chimed. How long was it before Aldous realised that the sound was that of his own body hitting the floor, and that the house had not flipped – rather, he had fallen? A few seconds, probably, but it seemed to Aldous like hours. It was all a question of balance, and Aldous had momentarily lost his sense of it. His mind remained in the vertical long after his body had attained the horizontal.

With his right cheek hard against the cold lino, still damp from the overspilling sink, he had the same vantage point as the spiders he occasionally saw scuttling across the floor. His kitchen seemed like a Venetian piazza, a wide space divided by shadowy arcades and isolated obelisks. He amused himself with this floor-level view for a while, allowing the shock of the fall to sink in, before he tried lifting himself back into the vertical. But he couldn't. His body wouldn't respond. He couldn't even lift his head, or his arms, and was only vaguely conscious of where they were, somewhere underneath him.

He wanted to touch his own face, because it was hurting a little bit, and the wisps of hair that were hanging over his eyes were starting to annoy him. But he couldn't get either of his hands to work. He wondered why. It wasn't that he was experiencing any form of paralysis, he felt quite sure of that. Perhaps it was physically possible to break your spine falling over, but Aldous was quite sure that his was intact. This was because he could feel the rest of his body. He could feel his knees, because they were sore (he must have hit them against the floor on the way down) and he could feel his feet because they were awkwardly twisted. No, it wasn't paralysis. It was more as though he had just run out of strength. He didn't have the energy to make his body do anything, no matter how strongly he willed it.

Not a serious problem. He'd been overdoing the drink and not eating properly, as Juliette had pointed out. Of course his body should refuse to cooperate after such poor treatment. All Aldous had to do was wait a little while. Falling over was his body's way of saying 'That's it, I've had enough, I need a good lie-down and I can't wait another second. I'm going to lie down right now.' A strike, in effect. Aldous's body had gone on strike. A reasonable response to the pitiful wages he'd been paying it. All Aldous needed to do was to wait, perhaps half an hour, perhaps a bit longer. Wait until he'd recovered some strength, and then lift himself up.

There was a clock on the mantelpiece high above him, but Aldous couldn't turn his head to look at it. He had no sense of how much time was passing. All he knew was that, after what seemed like a very long time in the same position on the floor, he still had no strength, not even enough to move a finger, let alone turn his head. He still had the same view of chair and table legs. If only he'd left the radio on, Aldous thought. Every morning he had the radio on, but not this particular morning, when he was so intent on getting his painting started that he hadn't paused to switch on the *Today* programme. The radio would have given him a hold on time.

A fall. Aldous had experienced a fall. He always imagined that word as surrounded by quotation marks, because it wasn't a fall in the ordinary sense, of stumbling or tripping over, such as people of any age do every day. It was a fall with consequences. A fall in one's state of being. When old people fell they were never quite the same people again. It was as though the fear they felt as toddlers when taking their first steps, dizzied by the precipice of their own height, had finally proved to be founded, and walking had become a terrifying, vertiginous thing that risked dreadful plummets on to hard surfaces. Thereafter they might walk with a stick, or a frame, or be popped into a wheelchair.

It's what Aldous heard about almost every day on the local news – old Mr Peabody lying on the floor of his ground-floor flat for five days after a 'fall', discovered by the milkman, or the postman, or the Provident man. How long before the postman found Aldous? Five days wasn't too bad. There had been stories about old people dying in their beds and not being found for weeks or months, not until they were as shrivelled as mummies, their scalps coming away on the pillow, their carcasses busy with maggots.

At least that shouldn't be a problem for Aldous. Juliette would call before that could happen. Aldous now felt only too eager to prove his daughter's predictions correct. Yes, he had been drinking too much and eating too little. She had been right all along. She might even come round this evening, or at least phone, and if the phone wasn't answered she would ring and ring until late, and the silence might bring her over. On the other hand, they'd had a row. Aldous wouldn't have blamed her if she'd decided not to call round for a few days – to teach him a lesson. Perhaps she was going to stay away for a week. It had happened before.

The discomfort of lying on the floor was becoming intense. Aldous was more and more conscious of the pressure of his weight against the hardness of the lino, and he was beginning to feel a burning sort of ache at these points of contact. Though after a while a numbness came into his body. And it was cold down there. The oven was on, so the chill was taken off, but it wasn't enough. Normally he'd have had two gas rings on as well. And the floor is the coldest part of the room, because warm air rises.

Aldous began drifting in and out of sleep. From then on he had no sense at all of how long he'd been lying on the floor. The lights in the room were on, so it was difficult to know if it was day or night. At some point he managed to turn his head, and this was a great relief, both because it eased the pain he was experiencing in that part of his face, and because he had something else to look at. A different view. He was looking at the cupboard now. And if he strained his eyes he could just see the potatoes protruding from the door. There they were. His potatoes. Laughing at him down on the ground. Would you believe it? They'd actually burst into flower. Little white flowers, delicately petalled, very shy, unassuming.

Turning his head back, Aldous was surprised to see that there were people in the room. He could only see their feet. They were rather well-turned-out feet – a female shod in expensive-looking, glossy high heels and a male in carefully polished wet-look brogues. Aldous sensed, though couldn't quite follow, a conversation going on above his head. The couple were talking in an intimately flirting sort of way. In fact, it seemed that the man was trying it on. There were sudden bursts of giggling, a smacking sound as a wayward hand was slapped, and gentle, unconvincing protests – 'No, not here, not yet, get your hand out . . .'

Shortly he could make out more of the girl's words: 'I don't want to do it now.' 'Why not?' 'Not while there's that funny man lying on the floor. It doesn't seem right.' 'What funny man? Oh. Don't worry. He won't take any notice.'

Aldous tried to call out to them, but only a watery, faint growl came from his throat. Then the feet, and the speakers to whom they belonged, disappeared.

From then on there were frequent visitors to Fernlight Avenue. Feet everywhere, in all variety of shoes. At one point there seemed to be a crowded cocktail party going on, and people were stepping carefully over Aldous, and trying their best to pretend he wasn't there. 'Don't mind that old man lying on the floor, darling, but be careful not to trip over him.' 'Where does he come from?' 'I've really no idea, he came with the house, and we don't know how to get rid of him.'

It was during one of these parties that Aldous finally decided he would have to pee. There was really no alternative. The pressure had been building up ever since he fell. So he emptied his bladder there and then. The relief was immense, but the sensation of an expanding puddle of urine, of which he represented one shore, was unpleasant, particularly as it began to cool. The unevenness of the floor meant that it lapped against his face. Then came the desire to empty his bowels. Aldous was rather surprised that the pressure was so insistent, since when he went in the regular way, not a lot came out. Yet for some reason, in his horizontal and immobile position, the need to shit was irresistible, and so he succumbed. Not much was produced, but it was sufficient to make him feel distinctly uncomfortable. The cocktail-party guests all left in disgust.

Aldous found himself remembering an army story he'd heard once. This soldier. He'd told him about how he and his wife had got so drunk one night that when they arrived home they immediately stripped off ready for lovemaking. Unfortunately his wife experienced a sudden urge to vomit, so she went naked to the bathroom, got down on all fours and put her head in the toilet bowl, ready to puke. Their pet dog, some mangy mongrel, was so delighted by the sight of his wife's bare arse as she puked, that he went over and proceeded to mate with it. The soldier went in to the bathroom to find the dog fucking his wife and her moaning with ecstasy, thinking it was him doing her from behind. The soldier roared with laughter at the conclusion of this anecdote, thinking it really funny. 'For nine months I was expecting her to have a litter of human-headed puppies . . .' Aldous had only been in the army a few days when he heard this story, and was so shocked he could hardly speak. He'd never even heard anyone use the word 'fuck' before, and the yarn had created a strong mental picture that he couldn't get out of his head for days. It came back to him now, not only the woman being fucked by the dog, but the man's expectations for the subsequent pregnancy. Aldous imagined a litter of human-headed puppies, not-quite-centaurs, who grew up as ghastly hybrids, and yet no one took any notice. It was as if it was the most normal thing in the world, half-boys and -girls doing their doggy things and human things together and not noticing the difference. This gave rise to a long fantasy in Aldous's mind, that inter-species breeding was a hitherto unacknowledged biological possibility, and that humans had been mating with animals for centuries, and that all around us were the results, which accounted for all those people he'd seen with snake eyes, or spaniel eyes, or bird noses.

The fantasy went on as Aldous continued to drift in and out of sleep. Again he saw people in the room, but this time when he lifted his eyes he could see their heads, which were dogs' heads. Dogs dressed in posh clothes – suits and frocks, drinking Babychams with cherries in, spilling most of it because they didn't have lips.

And then suddenly the room would be silent and empty. And Aldous would stir, discovering strength in his body at last, enough finally to lift it off the floor. And then he found himself in the middle of a deep forest, a dense thicket of undergrowth, which he pushed through, realising that it was contained within the house, and that it consisted entirely of potato tubers all emanating from that little cupboard, all from those little dried-up potatoes, blossoming with demure white flowers.

Then he was at the back door, looking out of the indoor forest into an empty garden. Thick snow still out there, but not pristine any more. There were footprints everywhere. Someone had been busy. In the middle of the old lawn there was a snowman. Life-sized. Good piece of work. All the footprints clustered around it. Aldous opened the door and walked out. Carefully down the snowy steps, underneath the apple and plum trees and on to the twilit lawn. Good piece of work, this snowman, though it wasn't a snowman, but a snowwoman. He recognised her even before he got close. It was Colette, his wife, rendered perfectly in fresh snow, even with her snow-glasses on, slightly crooked, and a snow cigarette hanging from between her fingers.

'Christ,' said Aldous, 'you must be cold.'

And he reached out to touch her sparkling face.

And she was.

She was freezing.

6

The curtains on Faith Ward opened and closed with a constant swish-swish. Beds vanished without warning, reappearing later after a brisk tugging of fabric. It was rare for them all to be visible at the same time. Several were usually concealed. Sometimes most of them were. The room was constantly reforming itself, new permutations of space evolving as different curtains were pulled aside.

And you could only guess what went on behind them. A Morecambe and Wise buffeting of the material, cooed supplications or cajoling, a masked sister's head appearing, disappearing. After a while the curtains might open again, though this time less urgently. Or they would be left closed for hours, only to open slowly, incrementally. And the patient in the bed would be the same patient, though different in some imperceptible way. Sometimes the bed would be empty, and the patient gone for good. And you never saw how it was done.

The hospital was the North Tottenham, where Aldous had been born. He didn't understand why he'd been brought to this particular hospital. The East Edmonton, where his own children were born and where Colette had died, was much nearer, newer and bigger. The North Tottenham was a cramped, crumbling Victorian hospital that hadn't changed greatly since it had delivered Aldous into the world. The old neo-Gothic wards had been whitewashed and plasterboarded in places, and had had odd bits of high-tech gadgetry bolted on, but they were basically the same. In his ward there was still an open fireplace (though not in use).

The patients were mostly of that rough-diamond type Aldous knew so well from childhood. Old henpecked men with feeble moustaches who in the outside world probably wore waistcoats with a watch and chain. Wisecracking, Brylcreemed ex-squaddies with leering smiles and winking eyes. Triple-chinned gaffers reading Agatha Christie through bifocals. Then there were the very old – the hairless, toothless, Manila-skinned shadow-men who drifted about like spectres. Dead Souls, Aldous called them, after the book he was reading. When a nurse saw him with Gogol's masterwork she seemed really annoyed, that he should be reading something with such a depressing title.

The man in the bed next to Aldous was an ex-con. He had served 'a handful' (five years) for an unspecified crime which Aldous imagined to be bank robbery, even though that would probably have attracted a much longer sentence (two handfuls?). The man spent a lot of his time on the wheelie-phone berating his friends for not rushing to his bedside. He'd leave messages on their answering machines – 'Where are you now your so-called best mate's in hospital? You don't give a toss, do you . . .'

Sometimes he'd sit on the side of his bed and talk to Aldous, delivering long, grumbly monologues of woe. 'They were flocking to my bedside when I first came in, but now they don't want to know.' He was a big man, a former boxer with a broken nose and a bristly head, happy-go-lucky, a big drinker. He'd never have called himself an alcoholic – he just used to go the pub every night and some lunchtimes with his mates. Been doing so ever since he was seventeen; now he was forty-three. Twenty-five years of regular drinking ('I never get drunk, me,') and now his pancreas had packed up. 'Bloody silly organ. A joke organ. Named after a railway station. No one bothers about the pancreas. No one gives a toss about it.' But now not only could he not drink, he could barely eat either. 'Why me?' He'd been in hospital for over six months. In that time he'd got so used to vomiting he treated it as casually as yawning. 'I still can't get used to the idea, Rex,' he said (Aldous had reverted to using his childhood name in hospital), 'they told me I can never drink again. Not if I want to live. And anyway, I just can't. Half a pint of shandy and I'll be puking all over the pub. I thought it was your liver that's supposed to get fucked.'

Several others in the ward had the same condition. They

would tentatively eat bland, milky food, then vomit lazily and casually shortly afterwards. The ability to keep food down was talked about with great excitement. 'Hey, Ron, I've not thrown up for three days now. I might try one of them rice puddings this afternoon.' It was the vomiting that was keeping them in hospital. They couldn't go out until they'd convinced the doctors they could digest food properly. For this reason the sound of puking was greeted with commiserations and groans of disappointment, since it meant at least another week on the ward.

Not all the pancreatitis sufferers were alcoholics. Some were very resentful of the fact that the illness should be associated with alcohol at all. They formed a small clique who maintained a dignified distance from the drinkers, or ex-drinkers as they now were. One of them once confided in Aldous, assuming him to be one of their non-drinking number, 'It's like we've gone to the doctor's with a headache and been put in a lunatic asylum.'

It must have been Aldous's success in keeping food down that had marked him out as a non-drinker. In fact, he had an ulcer whose bleeding had caused severe blood loss. In the weeks before his fall, Aldous had had little inkling of anything like that, though he had wondered why his faeces were turning black.

This was how the big, beefy, blond ex-public-schoolboy doctor had explained it to him.

'You've just about run out of blood, young man. Don't worry, we can soon give you a refill. Should have seen your face when you came in here. White as a ghost – and your whole body – like a snowman.'

Like a snowman, thought Aldous.

There was something odd about the way the doctor talked to him. A reluctance to be entirely serious, as though he was talking to a small child. Then Aldous realised: it was how doctors sometimes talked to old people.

Aldous spent a lot of time watching the other patients. There was a young man in the bed opposite who arrived one evening from the Intensive Care Unit, wheeled through in his bed, curled up like a cat, with an assortment of tubes

37

coming out of him, and a family entourage following close by – wife, mother, sister, children, friends. They spent time settling him into his new location, untangling the tubes that dangled from his nose. But out of all that life-support equipment – bags of blood and nutrients, tubes for draining away poison, monitors – what were they most concerned about? The television. 'Plug it in, plug it in,' the patient said urgently and as loudly as he could manage, fearing that they might all leave without having set up the telly properly, and the family laboured to get the telly in the right place, hunting for the aerial socket, worrying about the reception – if he could get a good picture. When it was finally established, the patient settled back to watch until the small hours of the morning, his bed cast in its blue light.

Another pancreatitis sufferer would occasionally talk across the room to the ex-con in the bed next to Aldous, but so that the whole ward could listen in. This man was small, slight, young, though balding. He too had been in hospital for six months. One afternoon he talked about his time as an employee in a pickle factory.

'We had to stand beside these whacking great vats,' he said in his gentle voice made silky by six months of vomiting, but he couldn't remember the name of the pickle. 'You know, that one with cauliflower, gherkins, silverskin onions, in a yellow mustard sauce.'

'Oh yeah, I know what you mean – what was it called?' said the convict.

'Piccalilli,' said Aldous.

'Piccalilli,' the man went on, without acknowledging Aldous's help. 'We had to stir these vats with things like white plastic cricket bats, stirring the piccalilli. Didn't matter how you were feeling – you could have a hangover, headache, feeling queasy – you still had to stir the piccalilli round and round, cauliflower, onions, gherkins, yellow sauce . . .'

But mostly it was the dead souls Aldous watched. The very old with their sucked-in, bloodless faces. They could sit for hours without moving, staring at nothing, yet they were not mad. When spoken to they answered like intelligent people, in fact it was only when spoken to that they seemed alive at all. Talking to them was like slotting a penny into a very slow, quiet arcade machine.

They were often attached to bags of blood which hovered above them like ghoulish kites. Sometimes they had a tube coming out of their penis to fill another bag. Red blood fed in through the arm, urine harvested at the other end. Aldous was horrified at how people here were reduced to mere processors of fluids, things with input and output − red in, yellow out (though sometimes it was red out as well).

Most fearsome of all, for Aldous, were the visitors for these people. Almost without exception, one of their party would take it upon themselves to act as ward entertainer, believing (for no good reason) that they could ease the horror of illness by drawing ever more attention to it. If someone puked there would come from them a cheer, or applause, or quips about cooking or mothers-in-law. 'Are you showing him photos of your missus again? No, he's just seen a picture of Norman Tebbit in the paper − yuk-yuk-yuk.'

The urine-collecting bags were a particular focus for their comedy. They called them poodles. 'Don't forget to feed your poodle.' Even when the hapless grandads' withered pricks were exposed, as they inevitably were through the open flies of their pyjamas, the comedians would draw attention to them: 'There's one for the ladies − always was a big lad − you're getting the nurses all excited . . .'

'Oh Christ,' Aldous was thinking, 'what if the comedians should come for me?'

But they never did. Somehow he'd managed to build an invisible barrier around his bed. Perhaps it was the copy of *Dead Souls* he hid behind. They couldn't make jokes about that. It was beyond them.

Still, Aldous hoped he wasn't going to be in hospital for long. So far he'd been there for two days and his blood transfusion was nearly complete. New blood. Rich and oxygenated. Amazing stuff. The haemotologist had told him all about blood, and what it did. How it was like the red London buses, ferrying oxygen passengers all around the body (but not just oxygen, countless other things as well − hormones, minerals, antibodies . . .). Aldous vaguely knew all this already, but having nearly died from its loss, blood had suddenly become a much more interesting thing.

'A few more hours and it could have been curtains,' the haematologist said. 'You can thank your lucky stars your daughter found you in time.'

'I do,' said Aldous.

It wasn't just the bleeding that had caused Aldous's collapse. It was a lack of iron as well.

'You seem to be suffering from severe anaemia,' the haematologist said.

'Do I? That's iron, isn't it?'

'Yes. That's right. Your blood is very low in iron. There should be enough iron in your body to make a small nail. I'm afraid you've got scarcely enough to make a . . .' The doctor struggled to think of a sufficiently small iron object, but all he could manage was 'paper clip'.

They both laughed.

The anaemia wasn't a serious problem. Aldous was prescribed iron tablets and a visit from a dietician, who recommended daily greens.

The doctor had other concerns.

'How are your waterworks?' he asked.

'Fine.'

'Passing water regularly?'

'Not exactly, but that's better than passing too much, isn't it?'

'Not necessarily,' the doctor said thoughtfully as he leafed through the notes at the end of the bed. 'It appears that you haven't passed water since you've been in here.'

'Really?'

'Just a moment.'

The doctor went in search of the ward sister, whom he consulted at the far end of the room, before returning.

'It's nothing to worry about, Mr Jones, but we need to be reassured that everything's working properly. If you don't pass water in the next twenty-four hours we may have to consider assistance.'

'Such as?'

'Inserting a catheter.'

40

Aldous felt deep horror.

'You mean a poodle?' he whispered.

A drain. A plastic tube attached to a bag. He would be at one with the old men. A dead soul.

Aldous found himself unconsciously pulling everything that was in reach closer to himself – dressing gown, bedclothes, book, newspaper . . . He remembered visiting his old friend Lesley Waugh in the High Wycombe hospital where Lesley had spent his final days. 'I can't stand it, Rex,' he'd whispered when they were alone for a moment, 'I can't stand these nurses fiddling with my penis . . .'

Though in his fantasies Aldous might yearn for such interference, the cold reality of medical manipulation, the insertion of plastic tubing to somehow siphon off the stale gold of his piss, he too found horrifying.

'Perhaps,' said the doctor, noticing the colour drain from Aldous's face, 'perhaps if you were to take in more . . . I'll get the nurse to fill your jug for you . . .'

Input, output, thought Aldous.

A little while later a plastic jug was delivered, brimming with tepid water, and from it a nurse filled a small glass beaker. So Aldous drank.

Visitors for Aldous were few. In fact, only his daughter Juliette visited, which she did dutifully every day, managing the difficult drive from Holland Park after her long shifts on the *London Evening News*. Her anecdotes of workaday journalism kept him entertained – how she'd had to interview the newly installed Bishop of Westminster – 'just because I was born a Catholic – the atheism bit didn't seem to bother them' – and how that interview had been a long exchange of non sequiturs. Equally entertaining were her tales from the shop floor of the newspaper office, the tetchy, secretive print unions, the old hacks who were wailing with anxiety at the prospect of leaving Fleet Street. 'Some of them have been drinking in the same pub every lunchtime for forty years. It's like they're being kicked out of their home . . . What have they got to look forward to, being dumped in some gleaming skyscraper on the Isle of Dogs with hardly a pub in sight?'

The only other visitor was a social worker, a freckled woman in late middle age who did the rounds of all the old people brought in after 'a fall'. She had been nice enough, holding and patting Aldous's hand while he recounted, as though it was an amusing anecdote, his experiences of life on the floor. Then he realised the agenda behind her gentle questioning – she was assessing his care needs. For a horrible few moments he wondered whether he might never be allowed home but end up in some geriatric ward to suck gruel with the dead souls for ever. 'My daughter looks after me,' Aldous reassured the social worker. 'She just happened to be away when I had my "fall". She's normally there every day . . .'

Then, one evening, after having produced, with great patience and careful effort, a weak piddle of urine into the bowl of the ward lavatory, and having returned to the bed after announcing his achievement with quiet triumph to the ward sister, Aldous found a young woman sitting beside it, dressed in a white fur stole, amber beads around her neck, gleaming earrings hanging.

Actually, not so. The white fur turned out to be a crumply, artificial fabric Aldous had never seen before, and the jewellery was of polished steel and jet. The young woman turned as Aldous approached the bed, bending a long neck, and as she did so he recognised Myra, girlfriend of his son, Julian.

Aldous checked himself quickly, to make sure he was properly covered, pulling his dressing gown cord tighter. Myra looked deeply embarrassed, frightened even.

'I wanted to say sorry,' she said, after Aldous settled in the bed.

'Sorry? What for?'

Myra looked deflated. She'd hoped Aldous's foreknowledge would have saved her a difficult explanation.

'When you fell over – lying on the floor like you were – I came over. I'm really sorry I didn't do anything to help you – I was in a bit of a state myself. I did ask you if you were all right, and you said you were. I asked you if you wanted any help and you said no thanks. I thought you were just having a lie-down, you looked really comfortable, and I wasn't seeing things properly.' Myra's monologue was heading for a tearful climax. 'And then yesterday Juliette phoned me up and told me you'd been on the floor for three days . . . When I told her I'd been round to Fernlight Avenue she flew into a rage – why didn't I tell her you were lying on the floor? Why didn't I call an ambulance? How could I be so stupid, especially with me thinking of training as a dental nurse? You'd think someone going into dentistry might have more common sense, and so on and so on . . .' The tearful climax was never reached, and Myra settled down into a sulky silence as she relived Juliette's scolding.

Although Aldous could hardly believe Myra's account either – that she'd ignored his horizontal crisis – he couldn't let her suffer any further.

'It's OK, Myra. I've been on the floor a lot lately. It's quite normal for me to be on the floor.'

'It was because I was so wound up about the thing I'd come to talk to you about. You won't remember, but I spent about half an hour pouring my heart out to you while you were lying there. I must have been mad now I think back on it, not to have realised there was something wrong with you. And now I'm doing it again. I've been here for five minutes yapping on and I haven't even asked you how you are. You look great. Really pink.'

'I've had a blood change.'

'That's good.' Then, as if struck by an unforeseen problem, she looked around her in the ward. 'Juliette's not coming this evening is she?'

'She'll be here a bit later. She's been very good with her visiting. Why? You're not frightened of her, are you?'

Caught off guard Myra was about to say yes, but checked herself just in time.

'Frightened? No, I was just feeling guilty about you. I still can't believe it.'

'So what were you telling me while I was lying on the floor?'

'It was about me and Julian. I don't know if I should tell you now that you're in here, you might have another heart attack.'

'And I haven't even had the first one yet. But what better place to have a heart attack? Tell me about you and Julian.'

'We're splitting up.'

It was hardly heart-attack news. In fact, Aldous was surprised to learn that the split had not yet taken place. Ever since Julian moved to Ostend Aldous had sensed the relationship had begun to die. Julian rarely came home now, saying he was far too busy to find the time to get up to London. But Aldous knew this wasn't true. He knew that Julian's working days were bunched together so that he had nearly one whole week off in every four. He knew he could cross the Channel for free and then it was just a couple of hours up from Dover. It was why he'd based himself in Ostend in the first place, when Dover, or even London, would have been just as convenient. Whether it had been to escape Fernlight Avenue or Myra, Aldous couldn't be sure, but now it seemed like both.

Myra had tried settling in Belgium with Julian. She didn't like it. She didn't like Ostend.

'It's just a boring town. The seafront's not even pretty, just boxy hotels and concrete casinos. No one speaks English – if they do they pretend they can't. It's a terrible place. There's nothing to do there. There are giant pedal cars that you can ride up and down the seafront (Julian loves them, of course), but that's about it. Why does he like it so much? I can't work it out. OK, he's got a nice apartment overlooking the water-front, but what's his view of? The sodding ferry terminal, with the ferries – *his* fucking ferries – coming and going.'

The last time Aldous had seen Julian and Myra together had been the Christmas before last. It had also been the first Christmas in his life that Aldous had tried to ignore, refusing to buy a tree, decorations, food or presents. Juliette and Bernard had seemed truly shocked, even disgusted, to find the house ungarlanded, and Bernard drove all the way back to Holland Park to fetch their own tree and decorations, spending a good two hours afterwards blowing, pinning and sticking Christmas into position. In the process they made Aldous feel like a crim-inal. Or like a traitor; to what cause, however, he couldn't tell. He supposed he'd somehow betrayed the childhoods of his grown-up children. That's how they seemed to take it, and they would hardly speak to him until they'd rigged up the house with paper chains and balloons, and festooned their father with prickly tinsel.

Aldous was amused by their annoyance, and rather touched by it as well. It meant he must have pulled off the huge gaudy illusion of Christmas successfully in the past. But what had they really expected now, at his age, living alone – that he should bother to go out and buy a bag of tinsel and paper bells and tape them to the cobwebby cornices of Fernlight Avenue's high rooms? That he should lug a spruce back from the Parade and spend a solitary afternoon restoring the crushed bulbs of the Christmas tree lights?

Even Julian and Myra, who'd arrived on Christmas Eve and whom he thought were supporters of his indifference to Christmas, turned out to side with Juliette and Bernard in the end. But whereas the mood did seem to brighten (he had to admit) once the decorations were up, Julian and Myra seemed sullen over the turkey, and remained sulky and withdrawn for the whole day. Julian had eaten very little, though he drank a lot – mostly some sort of whisky sour that smelt too much of almonds for Aldous's liking. And then he had fallen asleep. Myra went over to her mother's in the evening without even bothering to wake Julian up to say goodbye.

'I'm sorry to hear that,' Aldous said from his hospital bed, which always felt like an island when people visited. 'Why are you splitting up?'

'Julian's not interested in me any more. I'm not interested in him. I don't like where he lives. He doesn't like where I live. He expects me to get the ferry every fucking weekend, but he never comes to see me in London. He sends me free tickets but then always seems surprised when I turn up. Always makes out he's forgotten. He once put me up in a hotel because he had a friend staying. Must have been a bloody good friend (bloke, I should add). He hangs around with all these weird types. Writers and poets. English. There's a whole load of them out there. They're all part of some funny, English-run college – for the advancement of British Culture or something – I don't know. It was set up by people like Turner and Ruskin – you've heard of them? – they're always going on about them. But you wouldn't believe there are so many English poets and writers out there, Americans too, hanging on. There's this bloke, has Julian told you about him? – he's called Herman

Lorre, a right pain in the arse, but everyone fucking follows him around like poodles, they love him. He calls himself a poet. I went to one of his readings once (Julian dragged me there), and I've never heard such a load of pornographic rubbish in all my life. Herman Lorre is supposed to be a sexologist (can you believe there's such a thing?) and was a big name in America in the sixties, telling everyone to have sex with each other, like they did then. Full of every kind of bullshit imaginable. He claims he had sex with Hitler in the 1930s. He wrote a book about it called *Inside Hitler* or something. Never been published.'

Aldous didn't like to interrupt Myra when she was in this ranting mood. She was very good at ranting. Her voice became more melodious and fluent as the rant developed. A long-neglected Irish lilt crept into it.

'The truth is, I'm a bit worried about Julian. He's drinking too much. He drinks bottles of these horrible green and blue liqueurs that make him go all sweaty and sleepy, and then he's driving one of those enormous ferries across the Channel. Well, not driving exactly, but he's in charge of bits of the ship, I can't remember which, he never really explains what he does on board, but I wouldn't be surprised if it's something important like making sure those giant doors are shut. Julian says the cross-Channel ferries are unsinkable but I don't believe him.'

Myra paused, again looked furtively around her.

'What time did you say Juliette gets here?'

A dead soul shuffled by the bed, his arm linked through a nurse's, who also carried his poodle.

They remind me of those boil-in-the-bag meals we used to get for Janus Brian, Aldous thought. Myra had forgotten about looking for Juliette's approach and was instead taking in details of the ward as if for the first time. There came a retching, gagging noise from the far end as someone reproduced that evening's bland, fat and acid-free meal. This was greeted with respectful silence from the other patients. Myra looked uncertainly at Aldous, not sure whether to make light of the distant vomiting or not.

'It can put you off your food at first,' said Aldous, 'but then you get used to it.'

Myra suddenly said: 'Why don't you go over there and see if you can get him to pull himself together? He doesn't listen to anything I say any more. He's got no respect for me, especially not since I started training as a dental nurse. I don't know what he's got against it – it's no more boring or stupid than being a sailor. His hero Herman Lorre is actually married to a dentist. He might listen to you. When you get better. But you're nearly better now, aren't you? Go over there with your new blood and sort him out before he sinks a ship.'

7

Aldous didn't take Myra's suggestion that he should go to Ostend seriously until he came out of hospital a few days later to hear the suggestion echoed by Juliette.

'I really think you should visit Julian in Ostend, you know. Who am I describing? *Austrian physician . . .*'

'Freud,' said Bernard, with unnecessary decisiveness.

'Wrong,' said Juliette, gloating. 'I knew you'd leap in with the obvious and wrong answer, like you always do. *His interest in animal magnetism led to his development of hypnosis as a therapeutic treatment.*'

Lots of cogitative oohs and aahs from both Aldous and Bernard.

'*1734–1815,*' Juliette added teasingly.

'So definitely not Freud,' said Aldous.

'No, and we're on the Ms anyway, and Freud wasn't even a physician, which makes Bernard's answer doubly stupid.'

Aldous didn't mind Juliette and Bernard's obsession with quizzes, but he sometimes found it a bit of a strain. Shortly after Colette died it had become a consoling routine that he would visit the couple at their Holland Park flat every Sunday after lunch, and the quizzes had become a regular feature of those visits. The routine had tailed off in recent months, partly because Juliette and Bernard had both taken on extra work at the newspaper, which meant their Sundays weren't always free. Now, her father out of hospital, Juliette thought it was a good idea to make a special effort and revive the tradition.

The quizzes had started as spontaneous games that helped to while away an afternoon once the conversation had started to flag, but as the months had rolled by Juliette and Bernard

48

had started to take them more and more seriously. A complicated system of rules slowly evolved, and scores were meticulously kept. The source of questions was a large encyclopedia. Each participant took it in turns to read out a random entry; whoever correctly identified the entry won the point. The first time they had tried it they were so enthralled the quiz went on for five hours. Aldous had kept up at first but began to flag in the last two hours. Bernard won by 392 points to Juliette's 293. Aldous finished on 187. He wasn't sure that the quiz might not have gone on for ever. It only stopped when he declared his intention of going home. Once, when one of Juliette's friends was staying, the friend had taken to the quiz in a spontaneous way, making up her own rules, not realising they had already become so well established. Aldous felt some sympathy for her as Bernard spent half an hour detailing the rules of their Sunday-afternoon quizzes, covering everything from time limits, adjudication procedures and cumulative question distribution. 'I hadn't realised how important it was, sorry,' said the visitor, nervously.

'Will I have to give you yet another clue?'
'Yes.'
'If you don't get it after this you must be really, really stupid and I'm going to laugh at you for a whole week.'
'You'll do that anyway.'
'*His researches led to the development of mesmerism.*'
It was the constant need of Juliette and Bernard to prove the stupidity of the other that Aldous found most tiring. They had frequent competitive conversations, arguments even, where they hotly disputed some technical point (usually, being journalists, to do with the workings of the English language), and although playfully conducted they could be distractingly noisy. Once, when answering the door to him, Bernard greeted Aldous not with the expected 'Hello, Aldous, how are you?' but with 'OK, what is it – *All I see are trees* or *All I see is trees*?' Aldous didn't know and the question (Juliette for singular, Bernard for plural) was never satisfactorily settled.
'It depends whether the observer believes he is seeing one thing (a group of trees), or many things (lots of individual

49

trees),' said Juliette. 'After all, you wouldn't say "ten miles are a long way to walk", would you?'

'But they are,' said Bernard, 'a hell of a long way . . .'

'Perhaps it can be both,' said Aldous, thinking it was the only possible way of bringing the matter to a conclusion. Bernard was disgusted.

'Both? It can't be both. What use is grammar if you can apply the rules however you feel like it?'

'Language isn't logical,' said Juliette, a hint of weariness in her voice. The debate had continued for an hour after Aldous's arrival.

'No, but you should be able to apply some sort of consistency to it.'

Bernard was from the North. From Leeds. His father had been a small businessman who had made a fortune canning fruit in the sixties, but had been savaged by the unions in the seventies. He'd thought he'd built a happy little family in the cannery, but it turned out he'd raised a nest of vipers. Their greedy wage demands and continual strikes put him out of business. Bernard had been on the workers' side and so had set himself against his father, and they hadn't spoken in nearly ten years. And he brought something of that adversarial political obstinacy to his arguments about language. Juliette often found that her only means of escape from these arguments was the drawing of attention to the Yorkshire accent in which Bernard expressed his views.

'Like people saying con-sistency, with the stress on the first syllable when it should be on the second. What's con-sistent about that?'

'Mesmer,' said Bernard, with surprising calmness.

Aldous laughed.

'No. Is there really someone called . . . ? How silly.'

'First name?' demanded Juliette, weakly.

'First names, as you know, are only required when there is another distinguished person sharing the same surname. You're not telling me there's more than one famous Mesmer, are you?'

'You'll be telling me hypnotism was invented by Dr Hypnot in a minute.'

'Juliette, stop pretending to yawn. Everyone knows that when you start losing a quiz you pretend to be tired.'

'I am bloody tired. And I'm fed up with this bloody quiz. I'm fed up with asking questions from this stupid encyclopedia. Can't we just give it a rest and have a proper conversation?'

'No,' said Bernard, as though answering a ridiculously simple question.

'Well, I'm going to have a conversation with Dad. Dad,' (closing the huge encyclopedia and letting it thump on to the floor) 'what do you think about going to Ostend? When you're strong enough I think you should go.'

Aldous squirmed slightly in his chair and fiddled with the collar of his overcoat, which he hadn't removed since his arrival.

'Myra said exactly the same thing – did I tell you she came to visit me?'

Juliette nodded slowly, narrowing her eyes.

'She seemed to think Julian needed a stern talking-to from his elderly parent . . .' Aldous went on.

'About what?'

Here Aldous paused, suppressing a giggle.

'Here's the funny thing – about drinking too much. Yes, it is ridiculous, isn't it, me of all people. The only thing I could help him with is showing him how to drink whisky until you've got no blood left.'

Aldous was testing out a new persona as the confessional drunk, one who is open and apologetic about their drinking, at the same time as bragging about their helplessness in the face of it. He could tell instantly from Juliette's scowl that it didn't work, and he abandoned it immediately.

'Though actually I could act as a living (just) warning to him: this is how you'll end up if you carry on like this, et cetera . . .'

'Exactly,' said Juliette, giving not quite the response Aldous had been hoping for, 'we don't want him turning into another Janus, for God's sake.' She paused, before adding quietly, 'You don't think he could really be another Janus, do you? He does look very like him. I was thinking that the last time he came over. Since he's grown up it's like Janus is alive again.'

The memory of Aldous's oldest son, whose promise as a musician gave way to a life of pointless, drunken anger, violently curtailed, often made an appearance in conversations like these. Since his death it seemed they had been constantly watchful for his reincarnation in some form or other.

'No, I don't think so. Drink doesn't affect Julian in quite the same way, and he's not talented enough to be as unhappy as Janus.'

'All the same,' said Juliette, 'I think you should go there, when you've got your strength back. It'll be good for both of you.'

Aldous was reluctant at first. He had a strong sense that his son, although politely accepting of a visit, wouldn't be pleased to have his ailing, aged parent intruding on the crowded, bohemian lifestyle he described in his occasional letters, which made it seem as though the spirits of Dada and Futurism were alive and well in the garrets of Ostend.

He felt he would get in the way.

It wasn't the first time Aldous had contemplated a trip abroad, however. The previous year his other son, James, had invited him out to the Amazon for his wedding, and Aldous had very nearly gone. His cancellation at the last minute encouraged Juliette in her urging of Ostend. If he could come that close to travelling into the Venezuelan rainforest, he surely couldn't back out of a trip across the Channel to the flat, safe landscapes of the Belgian coast.

At first Aldous had thought himself immensely fortunate to have two sons living abroad. By coincidence their emigration had followed within days of Colette's burial, and they had left in a cloud of invitations and promises, both insisting that he come out soon to visit them. Then, when the dust had settled, these invitations were somehow forgotten. Julian and James were too busy adjusting to alien environments and Aldous too distracted with grief to think of inviting himself. It was a shame, because in the months immediately following Colette's death, Aldous had felt reasonably fit. His health and state of mind had gone through peaks and troughs, and although the peaks were never very high, they were enough to make him feel he could have managed a trip abroad.

Then James's wedding invitation had arrived, and Aldous

grasped at it with alacrity. James was marrying a tribeswoman from the village in which he was carrying out an anthropological study. This union wasn't an entire surprise. James had been doing fieldwork in the village for several years, on and off, originally as a research assistant to his then girlfriend Marilyn. His relationship with Marilyn had been a stormy one. Aldous hadn't followed the events in detail but Marilyn had eventually abandoned James to the jungle and had gone back to her parents in the States. James, meanwhile, had fallen for a tribeswoman called Mashami. James sent letters written on tissue-thin airmail paper describing these events, letters that arrived months after they were written, stained and smudged. One contained a photograph of Mashami which amused Aldous for weeks. A beautiful almond-eyed, bare-breasted native, she had zigzags painted across her conical bosoms and things like cocktail sticks piercing her face symmetrically.

Aldous began to have serious doubts about the trip when the details gradually emerged of what the journey out there would involve. The flight to Caracas Aldous believed he could manage, but another flight in a small plane, then two and a half days in a small motorboat up the Orinoco River, then a day and a half's trek through the rainforest with all its dangers and discomforts Aldous felt were too much to endure even for his oldest surviving son's wedding. Instead, he formed a perfect picture of it in his mind's eye from the descriptions that came from James in his letters shortly afterwards.

Mashami had wanted to be married in a Western-style wedding dress, and so one was brought to the village all the way from Caracas. En route it had fallen into the Orinoco, and there into the jaws of a small crocodile. Retrieved with difficulty it was delivered to the village sopping, muddy and torn. This did not diminish Mashami's delight in the garment, as she had never actually seen one before, only heard them described. The stains and rips were to her all part of the design. And Aldous long had this picture of the couple in his mind: James dressed in the best he could manage for formal Western clothes in that environment, his pretty Indian bride dressed in her shredded wedding dress, while the village headman bedecked in feathers and shells officiated, then a feast of mashed plantains and baked armadillos, and furious dancing to follow, fuelled by the hallucinogenic snuff that was the mainstay of all Icabaru celebrations, according to James.

A quiet, lingering regret stayed with Aldous when he read this account, that he should have missed the event.

But no invitations had come from Julian in Ostend, at least not until a week or so after his conversation with Juliette on the subject, when a letter arrived.

Dear Dad,

Sorry to hear you've been ill. Your letter from hospital was most entertaining and informative. I liked the bit about the living skeletons – Dead Souls (great book!!!). There are quite a few of those here, not in the hospitals though. Honestly, you should see the waves crashing on the concrete walls on those special Channel-breezy days, when the seagulls get hurled inland like spit. Or in the summer, when the beaches here fill up with people, and when the female folk take to sunbathing with nothing on their upper quarters (the main reason for my purchase of a refracting telescope, I can see the beaches from my window!!!).

I'm writing a novel about the end of the world and lots of poems about sand.

So you MUST come over here and visit me. I have asked you a hundred times. I can provide you with free ferry tickets, and can even sail you across myself. The sea air would do you no end of good, this place is, after all, the Bournemouth of Belgium. And you can stay in my flat, there's plenty of space.

Love,
Julian

It wasn't true that Julian had asked Aldous to visit a hundred times. He hadn't even asked him once. Aldous detected the firm but persuasive influence of Juliette behind this letter. However, it wasn't until receiving this official invitation that Aldous realised how much he would like to go to Ostend. And he replied to the letter within minutes of reading it.

Dear Julian,

Would love to come over. How about the week of 16 Feb? Please say if not convenient, otherwise I'll see you then.

Love,

Dad

Aldous normally left it a month or more before replying to Julian's letters, who left an even longer pause before replying himself. Aldous would have liked to reply by return of post every time, but he didn't want to inundate his busy son. It takes time to accumulate enough thoughts and gossip to fill a letter, after all, and even a would-be writer like Julian couldn't be expected to have anything to write about so soon. For this reason Aldous stripped his letter of news and left just the bare facts. A desire and an intention. It was like sending a telegram.

Julian telephoned a few days later, telling his father that the dates mentioned in the letter were, indeed, not convenient. Aldous pulled a face that he would never have produced in front of his son – a sort of retching, disgusted snarl – but maintained a composed voice on the phone, expressing sympathy for his son's predicament. How awful to have an ageing, convalescent parent descend on you, when you've gone through all that trouble to put twenty miles of salty water between you, and when you've got ships to sail and poems to write . . . And then he began, as he so often did on the phone, to listen to the tone and lilt of the voice itself, rather than the words it spoke.

Julian's voice had undergone so many shifts in register in the last few years it was hard to keep track of what he sounded like. It seemed only a matter of weeks ago that he had spoken in the piping trebles of childhood's wild valleys. Then that awful snap came into his voice, when the latch of his speech was broken and out crept all the groans and vibratos and basso profundos of adulthood. Then a long spell of plebeian locution, rich in expletives, fricatives, glottal stops and velar plosives that didn't particularly bother Aldous, though if he'd spoken in the same way to his own father he couldn't even guess what might have happened, he might even have been killed (accidentally). The Sea Training College at Gravesend had given volume and depth to Julian's voice, roughed out its cockney twang and endowed it with great musicality. But officer life on board the *Emperor Vespasian* (in fact just *Vespasian*; it was only Aldous who called the ship – which he'd never actually seen – *Emperor Vespasian*) seemed to have steered Julian's voice in another direction – still deep, but the faux working-class burr had begun to fade and a strange new theme was emerging: the middle-class aesthete's lisping eloquence, its over-pouted consonants given a Flemish tinge of staccato plosives spoken over-carefully. And it was in this voice that he spoke to his father (to his father's surprise) about a more convenient date for his visit to Ostend.

'The 23rd of Feb would be better for me, Dad. I've got a week off work that week,' he drawled.

Aldous took a moment, before he put down the phone, to notice with mild distaste that the mouthpiece of the instrument, with its watering-can-like matrix of holes, was discoloured, caked with a light yellow deposit, rather like earwax. Yet this part of the device never came into contact with the human body. Indeed, it had only rarely come into contact with the human voice. Yet this much had built up. Could his breath really be so filthy? The telephone had never been cleaned. It was probably mostly Colette's breath held there on the mouthpiece.

Everything changed when Aldous put down the phone. It was as though he'd fired the starting pistol on the rest of his life. Processes were set into motion that he had longed to see happening; the procurement of a passport, the packing of bags, the closing down of the house, and the colonisation of his thoughts by foreign soil. Ostend. He thought about it a great deal. He felt stupidly excited, so that he began to lose concentration, like a child waiting for the advent of a longed-for summer holiday. He worried more about his health than at any time in his life he could remember. He became morbidly obsessed that he might die before he made it across the Channel. His fall and his brush with the dead souls were still with him.

He tried to find out about Ostend, but as far as he could tell no books about the town had ever been printed in Britain. There were very few books about Belgium at all. He could find no pictures of the town. This made his desire to see Ostend before he died all the stronger.

8

The last time Aldous had been abroad it was as part of an army of invasion, landing in Normandy a few weeks after D-Day. By then Paris had been liberated and the front line was approaching the German border, but Aldous was to remain in rural northern France, repairing and manning the repeater stations that provided telephone communication across Europe. The only sign that the war was still going on was the constant stream of men and heavy artillery flowing east along the old roads, but away from these, the countryside had seemed almost mystically quiet. The theatre of war had moved on, leaving behind an overwhelming sense of frailty, of the near-collapse of age-old structures. Villages shot to bits, churches nibbled down as though by stone-eating locusts to scarcely more than the idea of a church, burnt-out panzers, little children riding bicycles too big for them, cafés with their tables on the pavements, but all of them empty. It was just as though a great gale had blown through the land taking everything valuable with it. What remained was crooked, displaced, broken.

At the same time it had been strangely beautiful. The wasp-filled orchards, the dark, prickly forests, the villages that had seemed populated entirely by girls. A sense of a terrible burden having been lifted, the decisiveness of those tanks and platoons rolling towards distant battlefields where their victory now seemed inevitable. But all the time Aldous wondered – as he tramped from station to station eventually as far as Amiens (torn and faded posters for Dubonnet) – how could this ever be a real, normal place again? How could it ever recover from the awful violence of its recent history? And in his mind, in the forty years since then, it had remained such a place – broken, sick, desperate.

When he did finally make it, passport clutched tightly in hand, on to the *Vespasian* with its rusting, pockmarked white paint, its bolts and never-been-used lifeboats, he experienced an unexpected sensation of fear, reliving exactly those anxieties he felt the last time he crossed the water – for what might be waiting for him on the other side of the Channel. He had to look around him for reassurance, some reference point that would drag him away from his memories of the war. The contemporary civilian melee of fellow travellers – lazily hedonistic and gauche in their anoraks and cardigans – dispelled such anxieties almost instantly.

The white cliffs were disappointingly small and rather grey in the misty February weather. He felt almost cheated when he thought about how everything that had happened in his life had taken place behind those cliffs, within the limited terrain they encompassed, how all those apparently vast landscapes – the Welsh mountains, the Cotswolds, the Chilterns – were in reality small things, tucked away in a small place.

Aldous wondered at the smoothness of the ride, but they were not even out of the harbour. Passing a red lighthouse at the end of a long stone pier, the ship seemed suddenly to plunge like a submarine about to dive, then lift again, then plunge. Aldous was caught off balance and only just managed to lurch to a slatted wooden bench without falling over. A reminder that they were crossing the open sea. The second reminder being the blast of Channel air that ripped down the starboard deck taking an old man's hat with it, and lifting the skirt of an attractive blonde woman momentarily up above her waist, revealing black knickers crookedly hitched and low-hanging. The skirt was pushed down with blushing and laughter. A family ran past, three young children screaming with delight, pursued by a worried-looking father like a man chasing three balloons caught on a breeze. And everyone on the open decks had hair like eighteenth-century French aristocrats, piled up on top of their heads, given vertical hold, backcombed by salt blasts. The long hank of one man's comb-over writhed and undulated on the crown of his head like a cobra. A woman in a plastic headscarf rattled past, the plastic rasping like a kazoo as the wind rushed beneath it, her set hair not budging an inch. Another woman clutched her Skye terrier to her bosom with a tightness that had the dog gasping and growling, though it was as much the wind it was trying to bite. Aldous leaned over the stern rail watching the trailing paleness of the wake, the seagulls floating in the warm currents from the funnel.

What did Julian do on board this ship? Aldous wondered. His son was on leave this week but he felt that he should make his way to the bridge and introduce himself – 'Your first mate's father . . .' Was Julian even a first mate? Were there still such things as first mates? He couldn't remember. Out on deck he looked up an impossibly steep flight of steps, beyond which he could see more steps, other levels chained off to the public, projections, funnels, vents, rotating radar booms, things hanging and swinging. He felt like a marchpane on the lowest level of a wedding cake, looking hopelessly up the Doric tiers to the top.

Eventually Aldous's ears started to ache from the pressure of the gales assailing them, and he went inside. Stepping through the door he may as well have stepped out of the world and into a new one – one that was still and quiet – although imbued with an air of stunned confusion. He noticed people lying on benches or on the floor, moaning ecstatically. One Japanese woman was nursing another Japanese woman, who was lying with her head in her companion's lap. They were kitted out in traditional Japanese costume, like extras from *The Mikado*. The supine woman was holding her hand over her eyes as if to shield herself against bright light. Her companion was feeding her a lollipop, or at least trying to, since her hand was constantly pushed away, as if the lollipop was unwanted medicine.

There was a faintly sulphurous zest of vomit in the air. The entire cohort of passengers seemed to be toiling under the weight of a great burden. They moaned, seemed crushed. An elderly man was crawling along the floor on all fours, his much younger wife lying face down on a bench, her hands clasped over the back of her head. It was as though it was four o'clock in the morning after the most debauched party anyone could ever imagine. Within minutes of being in their company Aldous began to share their feelings of nausea. He had to save himself by exiting on to the deck again.

This time he didn't mind the endless thudding of the Channel wind, though he gripped the railings so that his knuckles were white. The view was across the bulwarks to the big crumpled, creasy tarpaulin of the sea. Incredibly, out in this brilliantly racing wind, a man was reading a newspaper. He had folded the broadsheet down to the size of a brick, but turning the page involved a sudden unwrapping and rewrapping which the man performed somehow between his legs, as though straddling a sheep for shearing, until, hey presto, the newspaper was once more a brick, displaying the next four columns of newsprint.

Aldous gasped. Pockets of vacuum forced the air out of his lungs and made him speak involuntarily. His mouth felt dry, as though he was having the spit sucked out of him by the wind. At the same time he felt intensely alive; vigorously, bravely, valiantly alive. Being in that wind was like having the world take you by the shoulders and shake sense into you. He had found his grip and he was using it. People seemed to love things all the more in a gale — did anyone ever pay so much devoted attention to their newspaper as the man who was now having another go at that stressful origami? And people loved their hair especially, they were attentive to it, feeling it, securing it, holding it. No one could kill themselves in this sort of weather surely, even though it would be the simplest thing — simply a matter of letting go one's grip on the boat and allowing oneself to be carried into the air.

As an experiment Aldous opened his mouth wide into the wind. The wind gathered itself into a large apple in his mouth that vanished each time he tried to take a bite. Such heavenly frustration. As Aldous flexed and reshaped his mouth he noticed he could alter the pitch of the wind as it vibrated in there. He could actually talk without using his voice, the wind funnelling around his mouth, standing in place of his own breath. He could make audible sentences, though there was no one to hear. He found himself saying, without quite knowing why, the phrase 'I love you, I love you, I love you' with his wind voice — to the wind, to the boat, to the sea, to that blonde-haired woman with the black knickers, perhaps to all of them. It made him laugh and the laughter, in combination with the tugging Channel gale, helped unseat that which he'd guarded so carefully before, had guarded so carefully all his life, but which this time was taken from him in a second – both sets. With a short rasp and slurp his false teeth were out of his head and snatched away by the wind, uppers and lowers both. He made a grab at them but was far too late. For what seemed like an hour, they hung in mid-air in front of him, glittering, whiplashing strings of spittle dangling, from them. They had rotated to face him, still in their pairing, smiling at him out of the sky, a grin without a face, receding, laughing at him, until they'd shrunk to two little white dots, enough to make (so he imagined), a visible splash as they entered the sea a hundred feet below and a quarter of a mile behind him.

9

God. A week in Belgium with no teeth. And Aldous full of topsy-turvy lust, an oceanic, wave-crashing desire for female contact.

Of course, it wasn't until the moment of separation from his teeth that he realised how strong this urge was, and how the wind had robbed him of any realistic chance of satisfying it. He'd had a vague picture of Ostend as the Belgian capital of sexual permissiveness, something to do with its role as a port, and the slightly grubby innuendos that peppered Julian's letters from the city. He imagined loose but pretty women tempting him with beckoning fingers into smoky salons, pawing at his lapels, loosening his tie, lowering the big soft Ws of their cleavages on to his face. How could this ever happen now when all he had to offer them in return was a shiny, gummy, old man's grin?

It had occurred to Aldous, a few days before leaving, that this trip to Belgium might provide him with the opportunity of sidestepping into Holland to visit the Rembrandt Museum in Amsterdam, which occupied the house in the Breestraat that the painter shared first with Saskia, and then with Hendrickje Stoffels. Perhaps he would also visit his birthplace in Leyden. And of course the Rijksmuseum with its countless Rembrandt treasures, though he had never much cared for its centrepiece, the *Night Watch*, a giant portrait of slightly dopey-looking Amsterdam yeomanry. He had an urgent longing to see these places before he died, to tread the same soil as Rembrandt, visit the same spots beneath rotting trees from which he had sketched the canals on his long solitary walks in the early days of his widowerhood.

But there had also been the hope that some of the old

master's sexual magnetism would somehow rub off on him. That he would learn just how the great painter managed to capture and retain the heart of that little angel Hendrickje, when he was by then already ageing into a chubby, lumpy old man. Rembrandt in his fifties had a pug nose and a blotchy drinker's complexion, he had greying lambswool curls and an overhanging paunch. But did he still have his teeth? Aldous tried to remember. Most of the later self-portraits showed Rembrandt with mouth closed. But there were several younger portraits that showed him smiling, laughing even, and in these there were rows of dainty pearl-like teeth. He may even have been rather proud of them. Teeth were not easy things to paint. Aldous could remember some early instruction at school on the difficulties of rendering teeth. *Always do portraits with the mouth closed.* Aldous wondered if he should do his own self-portrait when he got back, to celebrate his toothlessness. *Self-Portrait with No Teeth.*

The first sight of Ostend from the sea didn't please Aldous. A soulless strand with square, modern buildings, concrete piers and sea defences, though in the mistiness there were more promising glimpses of older architecture – a crocketed spire, pitched roofs.

The Vespasian docked – a three-point turn that used up half a mile of seawater. Then the long disembarkation – the extras from *The Mikado* tottering down the gangplank in their tiny shoes, still moaning in post-nauseal distress, intensified, it seemed, by the calm waters of the inner harbour.

Aldous showed his newly acquired passport and stepped on to the mainland of Europe. Julian wasn't there to meet him. He'd said he would be. He'd said he'd be at the ferry terminal. Aldous wasn't entirely surprised at not being met, and he even felt rather childishly excited to be alone and lost in a foreign country. The signs were incomprehensible. He decided he should follow the Japanese women, who seemed unexpectedly confident and sure of where they were going. He followed them out of the terminal and into the adjacent railway station, where they boarded a train for Berlin. Aldous was left to find his own way out of the station and right into the heart of the

64

town, or so it felt. Busy traffic, roundabouts, an expansive plaza with statues, opening beyond to avenues of shops and cafés, and to the right the tilting masts of moored yachts and fishing boats.

Aldous had not expected to be steeped so immediately in a foreign culture. He had anticipated a longer process of transition: queues through customs, his baggage searched by hostile guards, being herded on to a bus and driven to some induction centre or other. The reality was that he had stepped off the boat straight into a city. And the city, though distinctly foreign, seemed in no way threatening or difficult to navigate. In fact, he immediately felt he could find his own way to Julian's apartment without even having to ask anyone, or enter into the fraught business of hiring a taxi. He had the address on a piece of paper – *64 Residentie Regal, Albert I Promenade, Oostende* – and there was very evidently the beginnings of a seafront and promenade to his right, past the listing yachts and along the harbour side. Thankful that his suitcase wasn't too heavy, he made his way in this direction. He passed fish stalls selling pretty tubs of seafood and wafer-thin dried fish, hanging like torn curtains. Handwritten signs advertised something called *Warme Wallocks*. On his left were restaurants – Albatross, Mar-y-Sol, Le Dauphin. There was an aquarium, and, at the end of a short pier, a very slender lighthouse, like a matchstick. Oostende was a holiday town, now wintering. This fact surprised Aldous. From Myra's descriptions he had imagined a grim industrial port full of modern concrete and cranes. But all Aldous could see now, as he approached the promenade, was hotels and cafés, touristy shops selling beach paraphernalia, even in this brisk February weather, and fish stalls. The buildings were nearly all modern – low-rise apartment blocks – but they weren't ugly-modern, like their British equivalents. There was none of the rancid cement and blank, sod-you façades of British post-war architecture. Everything here seemed rather dainty and cosy.

The promenade itself had a broad strand that stretched as far as Aldous could see, and overlooked an enormous sandy beach, mostly empty, except for a solitary woman gathering shells. Grey waves crashed lazily in the distance. On the strand there were strolling couples or groups dotted about, but overall a sense of great empty space waiting to be filled. Then there appeared one of those go-karts Myra had told him about, an extraordinary contraption, just like a car stripped down to its chassis, seats and a steering wheel resting on a frame and four wheels. A family of four sat in this one and pedalled in a rather stately manner along the strand.

The Residentie Regal was a swish block of flats facing the promenade, one of an almost continuous sequence of such blocks overlooking the sea. Aldous counted nine storeys as he looked up at the block from the strand, presuming his son's apartment, number 64, to be on the sixth, and spent a while trying to guess which of those windows belonged to Julian. From street level nothing could be seen of the interiors, though a row of wine and whisky bottles lined up on the sill of one room did make Aldous wonder – could that be where his son lived?

As he approached the building itself, crossing a small road lined with parked cars, his first obstacle in this new land presented itself to him. As far as he could tell there was no way of getting into the building. There was an entrance – glass doors at the top of the small flight of steps – and through the glass Aldous could see an entrance lobby – all smooth granite and marble, lit by a solemn-looking chandelier with a stack of mailboxes to the left – but there seemed to be no way of opening the doors. Aldous was pondering the confusing array of unnumbered doorbells to the left, some sort of intercom system he supposed, when he was drawn back to the street by the sound of a commotion – a shrieking that seemed to come from the sky. He looked up and saw what looked like a puff of smoke – a little white cloud unfolding from a window in the upper floors. Perhaps the sixth floor, where Julian lived. Only, it wasn't smoke, Aldous quickly realised, but paper, sheets of paper. Pages. They came again, another puff of billowing pages. Someone was hurling loose leaves of foolscap out of a window. In among these buoyant, dithering things was heavier material that fell faster and landed with a thud on the pavement and in the road, only feet from Aldous. Books.

Passers-by on the strand had stopped to look. The go-kart

family halted in their stately procession as the drifting paper reached them, a slow, flapping blizzard. The breeze was carrying some pages further away, on to the beach itself where they intermingled with seagulls until you couldn't tell which was which. Aldous picked up a page that had settled near his feet and read

SEX AND THE ANCIENTS

Chapter 3: The Quest for the Clitoris

The journey to the clitoris is, for most people, a long and winding one. A journey that is beset by hazards and dangers, where the signposts are missing and the locals give misleading directions. The roads have been blocked and the paths are so overgrown they can be easily missed. The lone traveller is likely to find themselves in a dark forest or a gloopy marsh, and may soon be lost beyond all hope.

And yet our ancient ancestors, whether they were the Egyptians, the Sumerians, or even − God help us − the Celtic Britons, were as familiar with the clitoris as they were with the nose on their face . . .

Suddenly the shrieking arrived at ground level as a woman emerged from a lift in the lobby and exited the building, giving Aldous his chance to enter. The woman was exceptionally tall and angular. She looked as though she could be folded away like a trestle table. Her hair was bright yellow, and so sculpted it seemed more like a hat. Her mouth was big and pouty, and when she spoke she stuck her muzzle out, sulkily. She was jabbering in a language unknown to Aldous, though occasionally she burst into a brittle, sweary version of English.

'What the fuck he do to me?' she shouted. 'He can go to bloody hell!'

She said this to two other people who trailed after her like attendants, black-bobbed, black-clothed women.

'He can go to fuck!'

Noticing some of the fallen pages on the pavement she tried to kick them, and then picked some up, spat on them and tore them in half, attempted to throw them back into the sky, gave a final shriek and then trotted angrily away as the soiled pages landed for a second time.

Having watched all this from the entrance, Aldous now entered the building letting the door close behind him. Immediately there was an enveloping warmth and a sense of being cut off from the outside world, although the interior was rather brown and gloomy.

Emerging from the too-smooth lift on to the sixth floor, he followed golden arrows towards number 64. As he walked down a shiny corridor he noticed someone emerging from what he estimated was number 64 ahead, a far too vivid man – young with bright orange hair and fluffy orange beard, wearing a lime-green tracksuit and red training shoes. The man was remonstrating in Flemish (Aldous presumed) with someone in the flat. The someone inside the flat should have been Julian but wasn't; he had an old man's voice, deep and growly. Orange beard walked towards and past Aldous, with a slightly baffled look on his face, and then another bearded head emerged from the doorway. This time it was Julian, though Aldous took a moment to recognise him. His hair was much longer and darker than he remembered. And long hanks of it swung free as he leaned out of the door to call after orange beard.

'She's probably gone back to the Troonstraat, your dad says.'

'I don't care – I'm going to pick up the pieces first.'

Being in between the conversants, this exchange passed through Aldous as if he wasn't there. Aldous saw that Julian's eyes focused very briefly on his approaching father, but that they registered no recognition. His head disappeared into the flat again. The next thing to appear was a paper aeroplane, the exact shape of Concorde, which glided smoothly across the corridor until it crashed gently into the wall of the balcony, crumpling its nose. When Aldous arrived at the doorway, he found Julian waiting in it, cautiously, as though in ambush.

'So it *was* you! My God. It's Monday. Fuck!'

'Hello, Julian. Have I called at an inconvenient time? You've forgotten I was coming, haven't you?'

'I'm really sorry, Dad, I was going to meet you – I hadn't forgotten . . . well, I hadn't forgotten up until last night, and then all this happened. It's a right mess actually . . .'

'Can I come in?'

A child, engineer of the paper plane, popped his head out of an interior door, then hung from the door handle, watching.

'Of course, but what's happened to you? You look terrible, if you don't mind me saying. Your face, it's gone . . .'

'Gone what?'

'It's just gone. That's why I wasn't sure it was you.'

It was startling how quickly Aldous had adapted to life without teeth. He had been without them for less than three hours, and he'd almost forgotten he ever had them.

'Only a bit of it's gone,' he said, examining himself in the long, horizontal art deco mirror that hung in Julian's hall. 'I lost my teeth on the ferry. They were carried away by the wind and are now resting on the bed of the English Channel, laughing at lobsters.'

As he said this the strength drained out of Aldous's voice, because he was beginning to take in what he was seeing for the first time – his toothless self. Aldous's false teeth were very rarely out of his head. He often slept with them in, and when he took them out for a rare scrub-up he didn't look at himself in the mirror, as he was doing now. Was that old crone really him? No, that was the man he used to see leaning on farm gates in the 1920s, with a collarless shirt and broken fingernails, or underneath market crosses in dusty, gone-to-seed, bypassed country towns – it was the sort of yokel's face that gave sage advice about when to get the hay in, the best time to plant potatoes. He knew what Julian meant now about his face having gone, because it seemed to finish at his nose. The chin had become an odd, nose-shaped thing in itself, a bulkhead of fleshy, whiskery gristle that puckered and trembled. It hadn't occurred to Aldous before how sensitive chins were to the registering of emotions – they shiver and clench and throb like little hearts.

'Something's come up, Dad,' said Julian, steering him into a tiny, mint-green kitchen that smelt of warm grease. 'I've got someone staying with me.'

To Aldous's surprise, Julian was laughing as he said this. Nervous laughter, perhaps, but mostly, Aldous thought, an invitation to find the situation funny. Aldous accepted the invitation, and laughed back.

'Herman Lorre has fallen ill,' Julian went on. 'His legs have stopped working. His wife says he's invented the illness to deflect her rage at his marital infidelities and to stop her throwing him out of their house. But she did anyway. Pushed him out in his wheelchair, calling his bluff. And he wheeled himself here, all the way across town in the dead of night. A cold, windy night as well. Isn't that incredible? Such strength and power and resilience in the man. He arrived here at four in the morning wearing nothing but a T-shirt and a pair of boxer shorts.'

This information was all conveyed in an urgent whisper, since the subject of the monologue was in the next room. Aldous found himself a little irritated that he was expected to know who Herman Lorre was. He did, thanks to Myra's visit, but to express his irritation he spoke as if without this knowledge.

'This man is a friend of yours I take it?'

'Yes. Isn't it incredible? The greatest sexologist of the twentieth century is staying in my little flat.'

'Yes,' said Aldous thoughtfully, 'that's quite an achievement for an able seaman. Tell me, is Mrs Lorre about six foot tall with blonde hair that looks like a hat?'

'Yes, she was here a little while ago. Astrid – she's a dentist would you believe – hey, perhaps she could fix you up with some new teeth – on the other hand, perhaps wait till things have settled down a bit.'

'It takes ages to make teeth,' Aldous said, gloomily.

'She might be able to get you a temporary set – but anyway . . . You probably saw what just happened. She got very angry because Herman sent me round to get the manuscript he's been working on. *Sex and the Ancients*. It's going to be a complete classic. The greatest work on the history of sex yet written. The world has been crying out for this book for two thousand years. Anyway, Astrid took it as an affront, brought the manuscript round herself and threw it out of the window. Ten years' work scattered to the wind. Astrid's son by her first marriage – you just saw him – has gone off to collect the pages. The poor bloke's torn between his mum and his stepdad. He admires them both enormously. I said I'd help him but then you –'

'Please, don't let me stop you. The greatest sex book in the history of the world has to take priority over your father's little visit. I understand that.'

'The thing is I don't think Herman can be moved at the moment. He's taken up residence on the settee, where you were going to sleep. I'm really sorry but – how can I put this? – there's no room for you here. Unless you want to sleep on a hard floor in the same room as Herman. The man's crippled – otherwise I'd ask him to leave. I'm pretty sure Astrid will cool down in a day or two and take Herman back. He can't stay here for long, and they're always having these rows. In fact, I thought they were going to make it up just now – Astrid was all sweetness and sympathy when she came round, but it turned out to be ironic. Still, you never know – she's a very fickle woman, her moods change hourly – she might even take him back tonight . . .'

Julian thought for a moment.

'I know a really nice hotel, just a few streets away. The Hotel Eden. I used to stay there before I found this place. Full of character. You'll really like it. You can stay here during the day of course, and in the evening as well, but you'll be better off sleeping at the hotel.'

This confidential business over, Aldous was permitted his first viewing of Herman Lorre, who was sitting in and filling most of a two-seater brown leather couch. Next to the couch was the folded chrome and spokes of his packed-away wheelchair. Herman's legs were naked – white, veined and almost hairless. They were stretched out and cushioned on a black cuboid coffee table. His torso was clad in a beige safari shirt, buttoned tight over the dome of his belly, which projected so far forward it was impossible to tell if he was wearing anything around his loins. Herman was using his great stomach as a kind of living lectern on which to rest the book he was reading, with what seemed to Aldous exaggerated concentration. He couldn't glimpse the title of the book but could see on the cover a motif of Egyptian hieroglyphics.

'Herman, this is my father.'

Herman had a head made huge by its all surrounding bush of hair, mottled grey, swept back down to his shoulders, his big shapeless beard and moustache concealing most of his face below the eyes. His voice was surprisingly soft given his gruff, tangled appearance. A curious blend of public-school English, West Coast American and Eastern European.

'Pleased to meet you.' He held out a white, freckled hand which Aldous took and shook, horrified for a moment by the limpness of the thing, the way it seemed to collapse in his grip. 'Forgive my uncomely appearance,' Lorre went on, 'but since my legs stopped working, my life has become a series of uninhabited islands.'

Not knowing how to respond, Aldous allowed a silence that was broken by Julian.

'Out of the blue. It can't be good to lose your legs.'

Herman roared suddenly, a roar that was only just identifiable as laughter.

'But I've still got the damn things,' he called to Julian who'd returned to the kitchen, 'they're still here, taking up space in the world. I sometimes think,' directing his remarks now at Aldous, 'that I'd just like the bastards lopped off at the hip, then at least I wouldn't have to think about what to do with them. My wife thinks they still work, but you can stick pins in them, I won't feel a thing.'

'Really?' said Aldous. He looked hopefully around the room for a sharp instrument, then said, 'I once had a cat who couldn't feel anything in its tail.'

Herman grunted at this remark and returned to his book. It was almost, Aldous thought, as though he was offended in some way.

While Julian was in the kitchen, Aldous took the opportunity to examine his surroundings. Above the couch on which Herman was sitting he was very touched to see an artwork of his own hanging – the large tie-dye and batik Ophelia that he had made a few years ago, which showed the drowned woman from above, floating between huge lily pads, her fingertips metamorphosing into seaweedy fronds. Elsewhere the flat was rather conservative in its decor. From the low ceiling hung a cobwebby chandelier, ridiculously out of proportion to the room, so low that hanging crystals brushed against the top of Aldous's head as he passed beneath it. There were two black armchairs, a fussy little mahogany table supporting an owl-shaped plant holder, but no plant. The walls were a sombre brown. On the windowsill an enormous oriental vase sat between rows of wine bottles, and to one side was a tripod-mounted telescope directed towards a dizzyingly magnificent view; the pepper-coloured beaches of Ostend with the grey sea beyond, looking quite blustery now, and to the right the ramshackle pier with its matchstick lighthouse, then a glimpse of the ferry terminal, with the red funnel of the *Vespasian* just visible.

Looking directly down, Aldous could see the scattered white pages of *Sex and the Ancients*, and the orange-haired stepson of Herman scampering across the beach trying to gather them, and failing hopelessly.

Aldous felt very reluctant to sit down. He wasn't sure why. The two black, shiny armchairs were ready to take him. But sitting down would put him on a level with Herman Lorre. Aldous wanted to make use of his legs, so he stood.

The child who'd thrown the paper dart suddenly dashed into the room and sat in one of the chairs, grinning with great excitement, but apparently taking no notice of Aldous.

Julian returned to the room but was sent away almost immediately by Herman who said, 'Julian, get me some frigging fried eggs for Christ's sake.'

'Of course, Herman.'

Sure enough, within seconds there came from the kitchen the thud of a gas ring coming to life, and the meek tap-tap-tapping of eggshells against the rim of something.

'I've got to eat,' said Herman, while Aldous circled the room, looking at the books that filled some shelving that didn't quite look as though it had been designed for books. 'Disputing with one's spouse always gets the appetite going don't you find?'

Aldous could only laugh politely in reply.

He was just wondering whether he should go into the kitchen and help with the eggs, which he could hear seething in the distance, when Julian appeared with them on a plate. There was nothing else, just three fried eggs looking a little underdone round the yolks but nice and frilly at the edges. Herman ate them, resting the plate on his belly, chopping into the yolks with the edge of his fork, clumsily shovelling the eggs into his mouth. Yolk ran down his grey beard. Aldous found this quite disgusting.

'So you, Father of Julian, what do you do?'

'I used to be an art teacher.'

'An art teacher? An artist? But that's a good thing to be. You don't have to say it like that as though you were apologising for something. Julian, you never told me your daddy was an artist.'

Julian looked embarrassed. Aldous felt he knew why. Julian thought his father's paintings were old-fashioned and dull. Landscapes and still lifes. The artists of Ostend were probably steeped in the legacy of Mondrian and Duchamp. Julian was embarrassed by his father's painting, when once he'd been proud of it.

'I used to be an artist,' Herman said, 'for a while. A couple of years when I was holed up in New York after they found acid down my pants. I was banged up in a hole in the Lower East Side next door to de Kooning. Auerbach upstairs, Rivers over the road and Pollock up my backside every other night. Did a hundred and fifty canvases in two years, one for every book of the Bible, and then one for every book of the Koran, and then for made-up books of both. *Christ Preaching to the Dalmatians*. That was my masterpiece. De Kooning's wife gave me that title. Another one was *Zebra Samba*. Which was also the title of a book of poems I published at the same time. The poems came from the jazz trumpet I played twice a week at a dive in the Bowery. Weldon Kees and Lucille Jones, Buck Hartnell and Clayton Sax, all those great guys. In the evenings we'd lie on our backs with our legs in the air and psycho-analyse each other . . .'

Herman paused, scooped up some bits of yellow on his plate and, to Aldous's great relief, dealt with the yolk that hung from his beard.

'I don't really know about all that,' said Aldous, aware that he sounded rather pathetic, 'I just taught art to schoolchildren for nearly forty years. I had a son who was a musician. A very good musician.'

By this time the man with the orange beard had returned, clutching a crumpled bundle of pages to his chest.

'I have caught the greater part of it,' he said, 'but there were pages that had blown nearly half a kilometre down the road, and some that had actually gone over the sea. I was not going to swim for them. I had to come back or I would have dropped these.'

Herman threw his head back so that it rested on the shoulder of the settee. His arms flopped out sideways as though the strength had all of a sudden left his body.

'Thanks, Piet,' he said weakly, 'just leave them on the table.' The soiled pages of *Sex and the Ancients* was delivered with some difficulty on to a black dining table at the opposite end of the room. Piet then spent a long time shuffling through them, smoothing out the crumpled ones, wiping mud stains away, sorting out the page order. The child went over and helped him.

Presently Julian offered to take Aldous round to the Hotel Eden, and to get him something to eat.

'Quite a character, isn't he?' said Aldous as they descended in the lift.

'Herman? Yeah. The trouble is he has an entire university packed into his head. It can sometimes be hard for him to think about ordinary things.'

'Yes,' said Aldous, 'I can see that.'

The Hotel Eden was a spartan establishment in a narrow road a few streets back from the sea. The concierge was a harassed waiter from the next-door café, and Aldous was given a key attached to a steel ingot to carry in the tiny lift up to the fourth floor. The decor was long-faded bourgeois grandeur, rendered unintentionally charming through neglect. The corridors were panelled with dark wood, and smelt damp. The doors to the rooms were heavy and squeaky and were opened with big brass knobs. The bed was hard and hairy. The window opened on to a tiny wrought-iron balcony, then a narrow, shadowy street.

'Homely, isn't it?' said Julian, his hands in his jeans pockets, stooping to check himself in the small mirror that hung over a kicked-about writing desk.

The foreignness of the place really began to strike Aldous

when he started to think about food. Julian took him out of the hotel and they went in search of a restaurant. It soon became apparent that Julian knew nothing about these establishments. He'd been living in Ostend for over two years and still he hadn't bothered with the local cuisine. 'I usually eat on the ship, or in the staff canteen at the ferry terminal.'

They lingered for a while outside forbiddingly dark and empty eateries, trying to decipher the Flemish menus.

'I went in one of these places once. They gave me a huge knuckle to eat.'

Aldous felt doubtful.

'They look like they serve hard, chewy food. I don't think, in my condition, that I could quite manage biting anything very hard.'

They tried to avoid the cold gaze of motionless waiters, until they happened to find themselves outside the one restaurant Julian was familiar with. A garish, glitzy, gold-and-silver place, which stank of burning fat, called FastBurger. Father and son's mood changed from one of solemn anxiousness to relaxed cheerfulness as they entered the little glass-and-chrome outpost of American fast-food culture.

'They've really taken to the "fast" element of fast food, haven't they?' said Aldous perusing a menu that was in the shape of a Formula One racing car. The burgers were all named after speeds, from the Mach 2 Double-Decker down to the tiddly portions of the 50kph cheeseburger.

'It represents a contrast with the Belgian culture of slowness,' Julian said. 'Belgian youth are very conscious of being fast while previous generations have been slow. It's a defining thing.'

In fact, the pace of FastBurger was as slow, if not slower, than the town outside. Their burgers were a long time in preparation and even longer in delivery, brought over with foot-dragging reluctance by a nervous-looking, cross-eyed girl.

'Good food,' said Aldous biting into his bap, 'lovely and soft.'

'Dad, I'm going to a party tonight, I'm sorry I forgot to tell you. Do you want to spend the evening in your hotel, or at my place with Herman Lorre?' (Aldous noticed how Julian always referred to the sexologist by his full name.) 'He can be a bit much to take on a first encounter but he's great when you get to know him.'

'Why don't I come to your party?' said Aldous taking out a cigarette from its pack, a Rothman's. His burger was still only half eaten.

'You wouldn't want to come to it,' said Julian after a shocked pause. 'It'll be full of young people. They'll be loud and noisy and drunk.'

'I should hope so,' his father said, taking a puff then resuming the burger, while the cigarette smouldered in his other hand. 'Do you want one of these?' He pushed the folded-open pack of fags towards his son.

'I think I'll finish eating first.'

'So where's this party?'

Aldous didn't care if his son didn't want him to go. He was going whether he liked it or not. He could see that Julian was squirming with the embarrassment of the whole thing, first for having made the outrageous assumption that his father wouldn't want to go to the party, then at the thought of his father being there – old and grey and lumbering among the slim, shiny, bright young things of Ostend's bohemian elite. Julian seemed even a little depressed at the prospect. But Aldous hadn't made this journey across the sea, the first expedition in peacetime on to the European mainland, his first venture beyond the white cliffs in forty years, to spend his evenings alone in a dark wooden hotel, or in laconic confab with a clapped-out sexologist and historian of perversion, though that was mildly preferable to the first option.

Aldous had convinced himself that he had, since his fall and that dreadful time of incarceration in the hospital, been reborn as a social being. A man of a gregarious nature. Someone who thrived on, and was sustained by, human company. What would Colette have thought of his transformation? She would hardly have believed it. Aldous pestering his own son to take him to a young people's party! But she would have understood (or would she?) that Aldous now saw human contact as the only thing keeping him from death.

Once Aldous had impressed upon Julian his desire to go to this party, Julian did a reasonable job of appearing delighted at the idea. 'Yeah, come to the party, they'll really love you . . .'

So after their slow meal at FastBurger, Aldous returned to the Hotel Eden to settle himself in, Julian promising that he would return later to pick him up.

10

Aldous spent a while alone in his room. He opened the windows to let in the chilly sea air and the voices of the street which conversed loudly and musically in the guttural, glottal syllables of Flemish. He heard one noisy group of youths pause in their boisterousness and exclaim, 'Hotel Eden!' and then chuckle loudly. Their curious Continental locution with its unexpected emphasis gave Aldous a special thrill, as did the distant sound of crashing waves and the distressed wail of a foghorn. For the first time in many years, in many many years, Aldous felt he was in the middle of a great adventure, even if in reality he was only in the middle of this unremarkable town, on the cusp of the Eurasian continent, on its lip. But still there was the secretly thrilling notion that from here he could travel by land all the way to the coast of China. Looking at himself in the room's dusty mirror he saw an old man getting rapidly older, who'd felt the clean, scrubbed hand of death on his shoulder. But it had failed to take him this time. He'd gone on a journey across water, and was alive.

He left the hotel to walk for half an hour before Julian arrived. The tide was in and it had become stormy on the seafront. Giant cauliflowers of seawater repeatedly grew and were harvested behind the sea wall. In the darkness their curled blossoming was especially magnificent. He saw a big ferry all lit up like a Christmas tree steering into the jetties, sagging in the big waves, listing this way then that way. Another deckful of vomit rolling in the aisles. Aldous felt sure, though it was difficult to tell, that this was the *Vespasian* returning to dock having already made the journey back again. He retreated into the calm and relative warmth of the town centre. There were trams here. He hadn't noticed them before, little trundling red-and-white cars, single deckers, not like the London trams that Aldous remembered and lamented. But they were trams all the same, the most visible evidence that life was conducted differently here.

In a modern part of the town there was a cinema showing a pornographic film. The English title was given as *Ladies Blue 2*, and the poster was a slightly grotesque montage of body parts squashed into the shape of an enormous two – a mouth here, and eye there, a nipple in between, a sort of pornographic mince. It shocked him, for a moment, to consider this open display of sexual material, though he also felt a pang of nostalgic recognition – remembering the dives he'd visited in Amiens and Paris during the war, always the reluctant escort of some lusty corporal who seemed to regard Aldous as a means by which such visits were made respectable. He'd seen everything. Live copulation onstage, hideously unerotic, like watching pigs rooting about in a trough, some little Frenchman's buttocks quivering and oscillating, the splayed, bruised thighs of the girl who was all silks and camiknickers. It had all been such a sorry spectacle. But the prostitutes, they had been something else; not the hollow-eyed hags in fur draperies he'd sometimes noticed late at night in Stamford Hill, these were plucked, porcelain-faced, leaf-lipped chiselled beauties. The French could do that, somehow. Beauty was a vein that penetrated every social strata, unlike Britain where centuries of perpetual serfdom meant that beauty and wealth were intricately linked. He'd never made use of the prostitutes, though the opportunity had been there many times. Aldous noticed a different species of whore in Ostend. They seemed small, frozen, haunted. But they were not unat-tractive. They wore absurdly tight pink hot pants, clinging low-cut tops revealing overspilling cleavage. Aldous seriously considered taking his opportunity and was, on being approached, about to engage in negotiations, relishing the fact that for the first time in forty years he was able to do as he pleased in this regard, when a paralysis of the mouth came over him, partly to do with having no language, and no teeth. The girl slid her arm through his. She was crazily small, her head barely came up to his chest. She was hardly more than a child in size, though Aldous could see she was nearly middle-aged. He continued walking. The girl walked with him, pressing herself against him. He became acutely aware, even through his thick overcoat, of the sensation of a small, conical breast flattening out against him. That warm feel of collapsing softness. He looked down into the face that was gazing up at him, but all he could see was forehead – smooth and exposed, flaking and encrusted around the hairline. He was aware of a face somewhere beneath it, a face that was talking to him beseechingly, but not in English. All he could get a sense of below the forehead, foreshortened to nothing, was lashes and lipstick.

How to extricate himself? A sudden panic at the thought of attachment. That he was becoming entangled. That he was allowing himself to be led by the hand down a road of regrets. He quickened his pace, expecting that the increase in speed would cause the grip of the whore to slacken, that she would detach and fall behind. But it didn't happen. She hurried along beside him, her black, shiny heels tapping quickly against the steady, dull thud of Aldous's soft shoes. She went on talking incomprehensibly. Looking down, beyond the foreshortened face, Aldous could see the crescent of her left breast. Then she tilted her face towards him, opened her mouth wider than seemed necessary and said: 'Française?'

'No,' said Aldous, delighted to have understood, 'I'm English.'

'Française?' the girl said again.

'No, English.'

'You like Française?'

A little taken aback by the question, Aldous replied, 'They're OK.'

To his relief Aldous discovered unexpectedly that he was outside his hotel. EDEN flashed in vertical red neon above them.

'I'm going now,' said Aldous, carefully unlinking himself. 'Bye-bye.' He waved carefully. The prostitute broke into shrill English, calling after him as he passed through the hotel door, 'I am very middle class!'

All the way up the wooden stairs, across the creaky, squeaking landings, through the thudding, latchy doors, Aldous pondered on what had just happened. He felt an unexpected sense of regret, and at the same time, relief. When he settled back into his room he opened the shutters and stepped out on to the tiny balcony overlooking the narrow street. She was down there still, sauntering up and down, slipping her hands through the arms of any passing man, even those already accompanied by wives or girlfriends. He could even hear her little voice – 'Française? Française?'

'I still can't get used to it, Dad,' said Julian when he arrived in Aldous's room an hour later.

'Used to what?'

'Your toothless gob.'

'Strange,' said Aldous, 'I keep forgetting about it. It's only when other people react, like you, that I remember.'

Conscious now of the little prostitute patrolling outside the Hotel Eden, Aldous felt rather anxious as they left the building, but she was not in the street when they emerged. The whole place had become deserted after the raucous bustle of earlier in the evening.

They found a bar, and Aldous noticed a drink called 'Bitter' on the wall menu. Hoping for a pint of something that resembled Watneys Red Barrel he received instead a sherry glass of green chartreuse that tasted like liquefied Polo mints. He drank it anyway.

'I was just wondering what your mother would have thought of this,' said Aldous, adopting a conversational mode he'd always promised himself he would avoid, but which he just couldn't resist when the opportunity arose. He didn't want to harp on about Colette, but a conversation was, he felt, a means of recreating her momentarily. As long as a conversation could be engineered, that is. Julian was reluctant.

'I think she'd have hated it.'

'If they didn't serve Gold Labels . . . I don't suppose there's a single bottle of barley wine in the whole kingdom of Belgium. Do you want a cigarette?'

'Not really,' said Julian, taking one and lighting it.

'Myra came to see me while I was in hospital,' said Aldous, feeling the moment was right to raise the subject. 'She said she thought you were drinking too much. She wanted me to give you a stern talking-to. I'm hardly one to judge, I know. I've lost all sense of proportion regarding alcohol. You know how they say time slows down as you get older – or is it speeds up? One or the other. Days whizz by so that it's Christmas every other week (God, what a prospect). Well, a similar thing happens with alcohol. Alcohol slows down as you get older as well, so that it takes more and more to get you pissed. Whereas when you're young it flashes through your body like lightning, doesn't it? You can feel it going into your blood, you can feel all the little blood cells getting drunk (blood's an amazing thing by the way, Julian – it's incredible what blood does. Remind me to tell you about blood later) and then you can feel it here –' he touched the front of his head – 'it gets you right in the frontal lobes. I remember in the army – that was the first time I ever drank much. And then you think, "What's the point, how much time have we got left on this earth, do we really want to spend it feeling dizzy?" On the other hand, do we really want to spend it sober? You know there's a theory that senility is nature's way of stopping you from worrying about death? Alcohol does the same thing. What's the difference between senility and drunkenness? There can't be much. Senility is natural drunkenness. Drunkenness is artificial senility.'

Julian swigged his Belgian beer.

'If this is meant to be the stern, parental lecture on the perils of drink, it's not really hitting the mark.'

Aldous continued as though he hadn't heard.

'They call senility second childishness. Childishness is innocence. Senility is innocence. And so, by extension, if drunkenness is senility, it is also a state of innocence. If you are apprehended by an officer of the law and he says, "Are you drunk?" You should reply, "I am innocent."'

'I'll remember that. The trouble is, being drunk, you wouldn't have the presence of mind to say something like that.'

'Really? I find I have extraordinary presence of mind when I'm drunk. I could think of saying anything. How about this, which I've just thought of . . . What were we talking about?'

'I don't know.'

'Myra. Myra came to see me in hospital. Are you two still together?'

'I don't know,' said Julian in a helpless, I've-had-it-up-to-here voice, 'it's difficult to sustain love across water. She won't come to live here in Belgium, and I could never go back to England, never, never.' Aldous didn't show his hurt at these emphatic nevers, since they were expressed as a given, something that was beyond doubt, something that Aldous must surely already know. 'And she wrote to me, she keeps writing these letters, they're full of nostalgia for a past that's just a couple of years old. For when Mum was alive. She keeps talking about those days when Mum was alive as though it was some sort of Arcadian golden age, as though it was her childhood.'

'Perhaps it was in a way. You're both still very young. The trouble is you don't realise how young you are, neither of you. You're much younger than you think.'

'Last time she was here she tried to jump out of the window. I had to pull her back. She was drunk and it took her a long time to work out how to open it. I stood behind her watching. She was sobbing and sniffing to herself, but thinking with her hands how to open the window. Then she worked it out and the window swung open – you've seen those big windows in my flat, haven't you – and she started climbing out. I had to pull her back in. As soon as she was in she didn't scream or shout, she just made for the window again. Methodically, determinedly. Each time she got to the brink I pulled her back. I think she might really have jumped if I hadn't stopped her.'

'People are fond of throwing things out of your windows, aren't they – themselves or books?'

'Occasionally she phones up from England to tell me she's taken an overdose. What does she expect me to do, catch the next ferry?'

'What do you do?'

'Well, actually, it only happened once. I phoned up and got an ambulance sent round. She got her stomach pumped. They do that routinely if they suspect an overdose. I think she was just drunk. They stomach-pumped her just because of my phone call. A good way of getting back at your enemies. Wait till they're drunk then phone an ambulance and say they've taken an overdose. They'll go round and stomach-pump them on the spot, ask questions later. Make a note of it.'

'I will,' said Aldous, 'but I'm really surprised about all this with Myra. I never thought she was unhappy like that. What's the matter with her?'

'The psychiatrists (you automatically get to see a psychiatrist if you're taken in with an overdose) think it's all to do with her runaway father. Probably true. He sounds a right bastard and he's not interested in her.'

The party was in the basement of a big block of flats. It was dark and windy as they approached the building, and Aldous was tipsy on absinthe. He put his hand through Julian's arm to steady himself, but fell over anyway when walking down some unlit steps that led to the basement flat.

'The steps are too square,' said Aldous, still with a damp Rothman's burning in his mouth, as he hauled himself up Julian's sleeve. They passed through what seemed a warren of right angles to get to the flat, which was dimly lit, crowded and noisy. Aldous thought the music was horrible, electronic bleeps and insect-like synthesiser buzzings. The mechanical rhythms evoked a factory floor for Aldous. He felt as though he was descending into the engine room of a vast ship. There were people dancing, a highly preened selection of males and females, though Aldous found it hard to tell them apart – men with strongly defined cheekbones and staring eyes outlined in black danced in a strutting peacock fashion. Some men were dressed as eighteenth-century dandies, with long lacy cuffs and gashed breeches. The women wore over-frilly dresses with lashings of gauze. Aldous was delighted to see that there was a ballerina in the room; wearing pink tights and a fluffy tutu, she'd hopped right out of a Degas pastel. Her hair was lifted into a lopsided ponytail sprouting from somewhere above the temple. Silhouetted against the bright disco lighting she danced a twitchy, jerky, electrocuted dance that was nothing like ballet. When she turned around Aldous was a little disappointed to find that the ballerina was actually a heavily bearded male, who wore the solemn, expressionless face of George V.

The party couldn't have been further removed from Aldous's realm of experience, and yet he felt himself strangely welcomed. The expressions of preening disdain seemed undirected at him. He was smiled at, endearingly, as one might smile at a beloved grandparent. He was hugged and petted. Cuddled. He felt slender female hands travelling over his lapels, or twirling his grey hair. A girl in a sequinned bodice with eyes so heavily blacked-up she looked like a burglar, danced a close-up, pelvis thrusting dance that bumped seductively against Aldous's hips.

I can do this, Aldous thought, detecting no formal pattern in the dancing that was going on around him. It was all simply movement back and forth, side to side, up and down. He couldn't remember the last time he'd danced. And so he danced. His dancing seemed to endear him to the partygoers even more.

Then suddenly, quite without warning, he was face to face with the most beautiful woman he had ever seen. A black woman whose hair was rendered into a thousand little bell-pulls, black plaited ropes, hundreds of them, that stirred against each other all the time. A black woman with huge black woman's lips, but painted a glossy deep mauve, and behind the lips – teeth like glazed ceramics, good pieces of hard-wearing pottery, tough, shapely. And behind the teeth – a tongue as pink and as bright as a baby's. She smiled a lot, this woman, and somehow Aldous could only see her as an after-image when he closed his eyes. When he looked at her directly there was too much to see. He could only look at her a piece at a time. She was like looking at the sun. And she could dance as easily and as spontaneously as a bird flies. Utterly unselfconscious, utterly unlike the ballerina. Arms up and crossed above her head, pale brown armpits exposed, the faintest trace of whiskeriness darkening them, wooden beads clicking in bunches around her neck, they could have been shells. Aldous didn't want to think of this woman as primitive, but he couldn't help it. She was more animal than human, and more human than animal, both at the same time. It was as though she'd stepped out of the withdrawn tide of prehistory, dripping and glossy with its mud. She wrinkled her fantastic nose, pouted her plummy lips and then smiled again. Those teeth. Surely more teeth than in a normal human being. In the after-image

86

Aldous got, he saw hundreds of them, like tesserae on some wonderful mosaic, a Roman pavement depicting one vast smile across a whole piazza. This woman, Aldous soon realised, was her mouth. It was the most expressive part of her face. Not her eyes (though they were expressive enough). This woman's mouth behaved very like an enormous cyclopean eye – it winked at him, it stared at him, it wept, it blinked and above all it seemed to see him.

It was this one huge mouth/eye that seemed to draw him into a darkness beyond the darkness of the room, to a lesser room beyond, a room that was as soft and dark and sweet as the woman herself. A room with a big squashy bed in it, on to which they fell, the black girl beneath him. He approached her face. It was as big and as solid as a cliff. He kissed her. Her lips were warm and slightly greasy, and they left a taste and a texture on his own lips. Then the tongue arrived, jabbing at him, as firm and as damp and as insistent as a child's finger. Aldous felt stabs of terror and panic alternating with ecstasy and delight. He felt as though he should make his position clear, stand up and say something like, 'You may be suffering under a misapprehension, my dear. You may not have noticed in all this dark, but I am actually an old man with no teeth . . .' The tongue was hers though. Unspeaking, it probed, nudged, dwelt. Beneath him Aldous was aware of a shifting, quaking landscape. Volumes of soft flesh, perfumed layers of thin, crisp clothing. Buttons, buckles and straps. The girl was giggling, her beads were rattling. Metal jewellery somewhere was jangling. The girl squirmed, giggled. Something gave. And Aldous was staring at a large, prune-coloured nipple, so close he could, without his glasses, read its every wrinkle, ruck and goose pimple. He put it into his gummy mouth and pulled on it gently. It seems to expand in his mouth, to fill it. His gumminess seemed perfectly adapted to this activity. The woman shrieked. He couldn't tell whether with pain, or desire, or laughter.

II

'I want you to bite as hard as you can, sugar-pie,' said the dentist.

Aldous bit down into the thing that seemed to fill his mouth to capacity.

'Harder, keep going, keep going, nearly there . . .'

Soft wax. He felt it pressing against his upper palate. The faintest hint of a gag reflex.

'Like biting into the biggest sandwich in the world – am I right?'

And the most tasteless, thought Aldous, unable to speak. When the impression was taken there was a surprising amount of effort required to remove the wax. The dentist tugged at it and for a moment Aldous felt that a part of his head was going to come away. Then it was out, leaving behind it a big sticky nothingness in his mouth.

'A nice impression,' said the dentist.

'Did I tell you,' said Aldous, eager to talk again, 'that this is the first time I've been to the dentist in over forty years?'

'Yes you did, sugar-pie. What you've been missing in all those years.'

'I had my teeth all out so that I would never have to go to the dentist again. If they'd been like you perhaps I would have kept my teeth.'

Astrid smiled.

'You're a real old-world charmer, aren't you? A real old-order gentleman. Now, let me just have another look.' She dipped for another peek into the wet cavern of Aldous's wide-open mouth.

'Good gums,' she said, checking the wax tablet that bore the imprint of those gums against the real thing, as though they might not match. 'Never no problems in forty years? No blis-

88

ters? No inflammation? That's fabulous. And the same set all that time? That's fabulous again. You must have been so sad to lose them.'

Aldous had been, at first. In all those years he'd saved them, caught them, rescued them several times. But now he couldn't help thinking that his loss of them in the English Channel had been fortuitous. Necessary, even. He'd let them be taken by the air and now here he was in a chair in a foreign city being treated by an extraordinarily beautiful woman who seemed to regard him as a friend. And a few days ago he couldn't have said he had any friends at all.

Astrid had augmented breasts that made her, in her dentist's white coat unbuttoned down to the third degree, slightly comical. Like something from a *Carry On* film. She was a seaside postcard in want of a caption. Julian had told him about them. They were filled with a substance – silicone. Herman Lorre had arranged for the operation.

'It's very kind of you to do this for me, Astrid, and at such short notice . . .'

'No problem, sugar-pie. I had a slot, that's all.'

'I mean, with all your difficulties at the moment with Herman. I'm sure you weren't – I mean I wouldn't have been surprised if you hadn't wanted anything to do with the father of one of his friends.'

'Why? It's got nothing to do with Julian. Herman is just using the poor boy, just like he uses me and everybody else. He has that power over people to make them do whatever. Almost like a hypnotist. And this means he will do nothing for himself. Never ever ever.' The last sentence was said with throwaway, breathless resignation.

Astrid talked while she moved around the surgery, adjusting apparatus, filling in forms, putting things in small plastic bags. There was a constant clicking and tapping of small metal instruments being rearranged.

'But the main problem with Herman is that he has been unable to get an erection since 1972, and this is something he can't tolerate. Think about it, a man who spends most of his life lecturing the world on how to have the best sex, who describes fourteen different kinds of hard-on in his book *The*

Compleat Lovemaker, from the young man's cudgel to the old man's bratwurst. And now he is writing that silly book about how the ancient Egyptians screwed around. But he is the desperate man. That is why he made me have these . . .' She cupped her bosoms together. 'But even these are not working.'

Aldous wondered if he should tell the joke he heard while he was in hospital.

An old man goes to the doctor and says, 'Doctor, I'm worried. When I was twenty and I got an erection, I couldn't bend it with two hands. Now that I'm seventy I can bend it with two fingers. What's happening to me?' The doctor looks at the man sympathetically and says, 'I'm sorry, it's just your age.' 'But Doctor,' the old man says, 'where am I getting all this strength from at my age?'

Astrid had surprisingly bad teeth, not horrendously bad, just a little uneven and the crowns were poorly matched in shade.

Aldous's new teeth were to be shipped to London and might even be waiting for him on his return. In the meantime Astrid fixed him up with a temporary, emergency set. This meant trying out countless sets of uppers and lowers. 'A laughing stock,' Aldous thought, as Astrid arranged the sets before him.

Funnier still, the thought of his new false teeth travelling alone across Europe to the family dentist's in Windhover Hill. Will they come by sea, or air? he wondered.

'So are you and Herman getting back together again?' Aldous said, after Astrid eased out another set of teeth.

'No we're bloody not. Not until he come clean about his legs. If he will just admit that his legs are a fantasy he has made up to make himself even more dependent on me than ever, then I will have him back and we can wheel his wheelchair into the La Manche once and for all.'

'How can you be so sure he is faking his legs?'

'How I can be so sure? Because how is a man like that able to go out at night and fuck himself with any number of women? You think they sit on him while he's in that wheelchair. No, that's one big lie that wheelchair . . .'

'But I thought you said he hadn't −' Aldous's mouth was plugged with another set of dentures, he had to wait for them to come out before he could continue − '. . . had an erection since 1972.'

'That's what I said, sugar-pie. But you think you need an erection to have sex? You think a little thing like that will stop Herman Lorre? There are all sort of ways, sugar-pie, all sort of ways.' Astrid was cradling the latest dentures, fresh from Aldous's mouth, still dripping with his spittle. 'You know what, I think we've found the best match. Try again – open.'

Aldous was enjoying the Hotel Eden. He liked his tatty wooden bedroom, and he liked the breakfast room where he found breakfast was, to his surprise, something he could delight in. A large bowl of strong black coffee and a pile of sweet bread rolls. He was dreading having to confront a plate of fried meat and eggs every morning. And in the evenings, if he wanted it, there was a meal provided. He could deal with the first course which was always tomato soup, and which he smothered with white pepper to make palatable, soaking up the crimson mulch with more bread rolls. The main courses were a little more problematic. There were pallid-looking heaps of cold fish, mounds of aromatic, yellow rice, eels baked in vinegar, frank-furters with watery onions that repeated on him all night.

But most evenings Aldous went to Julian's flat, to sup with Herman Lorre and whoever else might turn up there. People always seemed to be coming and going.

Aldous had spoken little with Herman Lorre since the day of his arrival. Most of the time he was there, Herman Lorre was spread out on the couch with a typewriter on his stomach, tapping away at the keys, filling the flat with a foul-smelling stench of the Mexican cheroots he continually smoked. Every day someone, usually Julian, was sent to Herman's home to fetch something, usually a book. He drank constantly, Cinzano Rosso with ice and lemonade and sometimes, if Julian thought of it, a slice of lemon. Aldous quickly became used to Herman's self-absorption, his doglike obsession with his own bodily exist-ence. Every now and then he would rub some part of his body and then sniff his hand. Then tap tap tap, another sentence added to the great work. Or he would reach for a book from the small library that had accumulated next to him, and look up some reference or other. 'Hey, you know the Aztecs used to mix semen into their bread? This is going in the book, man.'

Then some more tapping, a pull on the blue-smouldering fag, squinting to keep the fumes out of his eyes, then another scratch and sniff. A long sniff, sometimes, a long, important sniff, a connoisseur's sniff, as if discerning the precise vintage of his own body.

Not since 1972, eh? Aldous chuckled to himself, running a tongue over the unfamiliar polymers of his new teeth. But Herman surprised Aldous by speaking directly to him, though without looking at him.

'Aldous, I just had the sweetest, prettiest, most life-affirming shit I can remember.'

'Did you?'

'Right in your son's bathroom. That's where it happened.'

'Oh good.'

'Julian tells me you made that thing up there.' Herman gestured with a flick of his thumb over his shoulder to the batik Ophelia that was hanging on the wall behind him.

'Yes, I did.'

The sexologist mumbled something, a faint sound that seemed approving.

'In that case,' said Herman, 'I will need to ask you about your sexual technique.'

'Really?'

'Uh-huh. This is too important to keep to yourself. You need to share it with the world. A man who can make a work of art like that has something to tell us all. That body, the curves, and all made with tie-dye and wax? It's a triumph of erotic art. So come on. Tell me.'

'I find it rather difficult to talk about.'

'It's easy.'

'But where should I start?'

'That's a good question. Where do you start? Tell us. On the back of the neck like the Japanese? Or the shoulder blades like the Egyptians of the third dynasty. Or with the thighs, like the Sumerians? You know what? I was a sexual consultant for UNESCO when the United Nations was trying to draw up a charter of universal sexual rights. Of course it didn't get anywhere. Not when I told them it would mean the legalisa-tion of buggery and sex with children. There is not one sexual

92

practice that you can think of that is not the norm in some part of the world. Quite a thought, isn't it? Brings a new meaning to the term sexual politics. It's just a question of matching your desires with your nationhood.'

'Did you really have sex with Hitler?'

Herman laughed.

'When I said that most sex practices are the norm some-where, most of them were the norm for the whole inner circle of the Nazi Party. The most rapaciously sexual group of people there has ever been, in my opinion. You haven't read my book, *Priapus in the Third Reich*, because it has never been published, but in it I state that the Holocaust was driven essen-tially by latent sexual jealousy the Nazis had for the Jews. Hey, where in God's name did you get those teeth?'

'Your wife.'

'Astrid? You've been talking to Astrid? What did she say about me?'

Aldous hesitated, wondering whether he should tell Herman.

'I bet she told you I was impotent. What's that line she has – hasn't had an erection since 1972? That's what she always tells strangers. You didn't believe her of course . . .' Herman fixed Aldous with a from-under-the-eyebrows stare, which caused Aldous to shake his head helplessly, '. . . because we've only been together since 1977. The woman has a desperate need to humiliate me, it's her only way of coping with my past. She had the most frigid upbringing you can imagine – Daddy was a Lutheran preacher in Copenhagen, descendent of Kierkegaard, though he'd never read him. Her mother was Swedish, and had been a big movie star in the 1940s, same generation as Garbo, knew Garbo in fact, before she left for America. I met Garbo twice in California, but that's another story . . .'

Tap tap, puff puff. Conversation with Herman was not so much conversation as the submitting to a monologue divided into instalments. Since it required so little effort on Aldous's part he was coming to quite enjoy it.

'I heard you were a great hit at the party the other night.'

'Did you?'

'A big hit. A really big hit. Lots of people talking about you. And you made great friends with Agnès Florizoone. Now she really is an extraordinary woman, you are a very lucky man.'

'Agnès – what was that name you said?'

Herman gave Aldous the from-under-the-eyebrows stare again.

'Florizoone? You mean you didn't even know you'd met Agnès Florizoone . . . ?'

'Is she the . . . you know . . . ?'

'She is a beautiful black woman who is also one of the most original and interesting artists in Ostend.'

The woman whose taste was still on his tongue (even after Astrid's best attempts to wash it away). Aldous still had a hauntingly vivid memory of that party and his encounter with her, but he didn't have a clear memory of how the encounter had ended. He could only recollect a vague sense of confusion and embarrassment, perhaps of their being discovered together, the lights thrown on, or of Agnès (only now did he know her name) suddenly changing mood and backing off. Something hadn't seemed right, and though the beauty of the experience had remained, Aldous had felt disinclined to mention it afterwards, or to talk about it with anyone, even to the extent of enquiring who exactly this woman was. But now, it seemed, Herman was telling him.

'Yes,' said Aldous. 'Has she spoken about me?'

'She was on the phone an hour ago. She's coming over later – apparently you had some arrangement, you'd fixed a date?'

Aldous had no memory of fixing anything.

'You asked her to show you the town. That's what she said. But if you take my advice you should ask her to show you her studio.'

Aldous was so delightfully distracted by the news that he was to encounter the woman again, he could hardly take notice of what Herman was saying.

'Really?' he said, abstractedly. 'She's an artist, you say?'

'One of the finest proponents of erotic art I have ever seen. In which case, in view of that randy tie-dye thing, you should get along really well. I mean *really* well. One day I'm going to write a book about her work. She's a photographer mainly – but her photographs, they take erotic art to a completely new level. The randiest, horniest, lustiest work you'll ever see . . .'

Her beauty was still transfixing. The great puffy lips, the nose wrinkled with smiling, the meticulous braids of her hair, each finished with a little yellow-and-green bead. This time she was wearing a big, floppy peaked hat made of fluffy wool, and a long black shiny coat that wasn't quite leather.

'Show him your studio . . .' Herman called from the couch as they left the flat together, Aldous hardly knowing what was happening, and being led away, rather like on the night of the party itself, having submitted himself to a power beyond his control. It was something about the nearfulness of Agnès that entranced him. He would think of her as something in the distance and then find her right next to him. He would imagine her as something to be watched through binoculars, something to be observed from afar, or on the television, but in fact she was real, and close, so close that she had actually been in his mouth that night, filling it. And she hadn't come round to Julian's flat to say, 'How dare you take advantage of a drunk young woman, you lecherous, filthy, formerly toothless old, old, old man. You should have spat me out as soon as you realised what was happening.' No, his feeding on her nipple had been taken, it seemed, as acceptable. Or had she forgotten? Had she perhaps not even noticed in the haze and confusion and noise of the party? Perhaps, having had no teeth at the time, his suction was the less noticeable. Perhaps the loss of his teeth had rendered him invisible.

'I'm not spoiling a great conversation, am I?' said Agnès, as she led him out of the building, into a wintry late-afternoon Ostend. 'I could see how much you were enjoying talking to Herman Lorre.'

It was the first time Aldous had noticed her voice. It was husky, like the wind in the trees. She spoke English almost perfectly, with only a slight Belgian accent.

'They say he's a great man,' said Aldous.

'No doubt about it. It's hard to believe one man can know

so much. Or have done so much. It's sad about Astrid, but what can you do when you're married to a genius?'

'Throw him out, would appear to be Astrid's answer.'

'How has he been since he's moved in with Julian?'

'How's Herman been? He seems to be having the time of his life. My son waits on him like he was in a cocktail bar, feeding him endless Martinis and plates of fried eggs. He runs errands for him, goes out to buy him packs of those disgusting cigarillos, washes his clothes for him.'

'Julian's very devoted to Herman. Herman says Julian is a very good writer.'

'Really?'

'Yes. He says Julian has written a book that is longer than *The Magic Mountain*.'

Aldous presumed *The Magic Mountain* was a novel.

'Look. We are in the main square of Ostend. That clock on the town hall – you see? It has signs of the zodiac instead of numbers.'

'So it has,' said Aldous, peering carefully, 'which means the time is a quarter past Pisces. What a peculiar thing, why have they done it?'

'I have no idea,' said Agnès, laughing after a thoughtful pause, and as she did so she put her arm through Aldous's, to his delight. An extraordinarily beautiful sensation to have this young woman linked to him physically in this way, to feel the gentle pushing and pulling of her body as she walked beside him, sometimes leaning away, at other times haphazardly colliding with him. It was as though they'd known each other for years.

They left the wide town square, with its pavement cafés and bandstand, and walked along one of the long, straight shopping streets.

'Why do you wear a lady's wristwatch?' asked Agnès, reminding Aldous of that instrument's much less weighty grip on his body. Thankfully, before Aldous had time to answer, Agnès was distracted by their arrival at another of Ostend's attractions.

'And this building here is the most interesting museum in

Ostend, if not the world. In fact, it is the world's only museum dedicated to ice cream.'

Appropriately enough, at that moment, there was a tremendous hail shower that pinged and rattled all around them, so they took shelter in the museum.

'I often come here. I find it a very relaxing place.'

Galleries of freezers, some so misted up you couldn't see inside them, others revealing, like crude lumps of glazed ceramics, an array of frozen-forever gelati, sorbets, slices of Neapolitan, chocolate bombes, amarettos, and other exotic European ice creams. The English cabinet gave a woeful display – an Arctic Roll, a Wall's Viennetta, and a 99. Though, according to Agnès, these were considered delicacies by the Belgians.

'They love the sweetness of the British, like with your chocolate. You know British chocolate isn't real, don't you? – just vegetable fat and sugar dyed brown. And so you pump tons of fat and sugar into your ice cream. But while this makes it technically revolting, it also makes it unique, unlike anything produced in Europe, so here we go mad about it.'

Agnès still had her arm linked through his. Every so often she leaned her head on his shoulder, as though infinitely grateful for its soft pillowiness.

'Hey,' she said, after they'd left the British Ice Creams, 'that ice cream reminds me of you.' A big curled, conch-like scoop of bright white Greek ice cream, lemon and coconut flavour. 'You're such a big white thing, aren't you,' Agnès giggled, 'such a big white cuddly polar bear of a man.'

They wandered among the shops of Ostend, dodging rain. Lightning flashed a few times. They lingered outside shoe shops. Agnès, it seemed, was fascinated by shoes, pointing at the little pumps and stilettos and sandals, squealing with delight at their cutesiness. It was as though they were looking at a shop window full of puppies and kittens. Never in his forty years of married life had he lingered outside a shoe shop, discussing shoes. The ones that delighted Agnès the most were those with the least substance – nothing more than a sole and a heel with a couple of spaghetti-thin straps. They were also the priciest. Agnès went into such squeaky raptures about these shoes that Aldous offered to buy her a pair. She protested at first, but soon relented. Aldous found himself being very insistent. He wanted, suddenly, nothing more than to provide this beautiful woman with shoes. Inside the shop the staff seemed concerned. It was as though something improper was happening. An old man buying a young woman shoes. What business was it of theirs? He also noticed how Agnès was different in the shop. She treated the staff with a curious disdain, she put on airs and lorded it over them, curtly demanding other sizes, complaining at the least blemish on the shoes. The shop staff stared and were slow and reluctant in their response.

'What was going on in there? I thought you were a bit rude to those shop people, Agnès.'

'Me rude? Aldous, don't be a baby. Couldn't you tell what was going on? You couldn't, could you? Oh, that makes you even more sweet.' She squeezed herself against Aldous, as though he was a teddy bear. 'They were troubled by our – what shall I call it . . . ?'

'They thought I was too old for you?'

'No, that's not it. I think it was more to do with . . .'

'Oh, you mean they thought you were a prostitute?'

'No!' Agnès unlinked herself and stood still, offended. 'Aldous – how could you be so . . . No, they were troubled by my colour.'

Aldous thought for a moment.

'Oh, you mean, because you're black?'

'And you're white. Haven't you noticed those looks we've been getting all afternoon? Practically every other person gives us the look. In the Ice Cream Museum why do you think that attendant got so shirty when we were looking at the sorbets? He wasn't worried about us melting the ice creams, he was worried because we were different colours.'

Aldous realised for the first time that Agnès was the only black person he'd seen since his arrival in Belgium.

'Oh, they're just – they're probably just confused.'

'By what?'

Aldous wasn't sure.

'They've probably never seen . . .'

'A black person before? That's a typical middle-class white

response – trying to excuse even the worst racism. But I don't even want to talk about it. I love this city. I don't let a few shoe shop people and Ice Cream Museum staff spoil my love for it. Aldous, wouldn't you like to live here for ever? Become a true citizen of the world? Then we could go for walks together every day.'

Aldous agreed it was a great city. It was the finest city he'd ever visited. He didn't want to live anywhere else.

'I have to go back to England to pick up my new teeth.'

'Why? I prefer you without the teeth. With the teeth you're a crocodile, without the teeth you're an elephant. Now which would you rather be, a crocodile or an elephant?'

Agnès looked at him with an isn't-it-obvious smile on her face. Though the question didn't seem at all obvious to Aldous.

Agnès showed him many more sights of Ostend – the cathedral that was all crocketed pinnacles but which in fact was modern (Aldous impressed Agnès by telling her this before she had a chance to tell him), a clock made of flowers, a Napoleonic fort. They even hired a two-seater go-kart and took a stately ride along the strand which made Aldous a bit breathless. The journey brought them to the vicinity of Agnès's studio, which was above some dreary-looking shops close to the seafront at a point where the opulence of the city centre gave way to slightly shabbier suburbs.

'Now you did promise to show me your studio, Agnès, and Herman would be very disappointed if you didn't let me have a look . . .'

'For sure,' said Agnès. 'Julian told me you were a very great artist. I'd like to have your thoughts on my work.'

It continually surprised Aldous that Agnès was an artist, and he had to keep reminding himself. Somehow she seemed too happy. Too carefree. Apart from that one discussion about racism, which she herself had quickly steered away from, she seemed to have no seriousness about her at all. She seemed startlingly uncomplicated.

'Well, I was only an art teacher,' Aldous muttered as he followed Agnès up the narrow stairs to her studio, wondering, as they ascended, how he should respond to the work he was about to be presented with. The randiest, raunchiest work ever to be seen on planet Earth, or whatever it was Herman had said about it. A beautiful young woman shows you a collection of explicit, erotic photography – what is the correct response? Should he enjoy it? Should he be shocked by it? Embarrassed by it? But in the end he was none of these. He was simply puzzled by it.

The small space of whitewashed bricks was stacked with framed images, some hanging on the walls. The images were all black-and-white photographs of what appeared to be rather desolate landscapes and still lifes. A derelict petrol station, the moon rising between factory chimneys. There was a photograph of a bowl of apples, and next to it another photograph of the same bowl of apples, but in the second picture the apples had all been eaten, and were just a heap of cores. All the photographs were beautifully lit and composed, and full of the finest detail. There was a picture of a path worn into a carpet, where every loose thread seemed visible.

'Very . . .'

Aldous struggled for a sincere adjective. To his surprise Agnès supplied one for him.

'Sensual? That is what most people say. It is what I try to do.'

'I was going to say lonely,' said Aldous, suddenly inspired. Agnès was taken aback.

'Oh. No one has ever said that before.'

'But there's no one in them. All these photos, not one person.'

Agnès shrugged, smiling.

'The point of these images is that the things represent people. For instance, that carpet makes me think of someone's skin . . .' She pointed to the photograph as though it explained everything, and carefully watched Aldous's face as he looked at it, for a sign that he had cottoned on. He decided to see the carpet as skin as well, and immediately the curious tension that had developed since they entered the studio was gone.

'I see it now,' he said. 'And those chimneys, I suppose they stand for . . .'

'Exactly. It is about how the world is constructed in the image of our own bodies . . .'

Agnès wandered over to a sink where there was a small electric kettle, which she filled.

'Tell me about your art, Aldous. Are you a painter?'

'Well, like I said, I was only –'

'An Ivon Hitchens type of painter I imagine you to be. Or who is that other great English artist? Paul Nash? Graham Sutherland?'

'Well, I'd be very flattered if anyone put me in the same bracket –'

'What artists do you like?'

'Rembrandt,' said Aldous, with a sudden decisiveness, 'although I don't paint like him at all, when I paint at all, that is. But I'm very interested in him, always have been. In fact, I'm hoping to visit his house in Amsterdam before I leave, if it's possible, but I'm only here for a week.'

Agnès looked thrilled.

'The Rembrandt House Museum? I have been there many times. It is easy. Change at Antwerp. I will take you there.'

12

It had become a routine for Aldous and Julian to meet for lunch at FastBurger (a Mach 2 for Julian, a 50kph cheeseburger for Aldous), and to have an evening drink at the same bar they'd visited on Aldous's first night in Ostend, which was on the main square, the Wapenplein, with its zodiac clock (ten to Sagittarius). Aldous had taken a liking to green chartreuse, and would knock back three or four while Julian drank Continental beers from tall, tulip-shaped glasses. Aldous insisted on paying for all the drinks.

'I was just wondering if I could claim my pension if I lived here . . . Any ideas, Julian? There must be some expats in Ostend old enough to be claiming pensions. What about Herman? How does he manage? Does he claim a pension from somewhere?'

'I think Herman still gets a pension from the College of the Arts – he worked there for a long time actually. And he still gets some royalties from his books. *Let's Have Sex* is still in print in the States, though it's sad – almost everything else he's written has gone out of print. Herman's very angry about it inside because he thinks of himself as a poet first and foremost – but if he's known at all it is as a sexologist. You won't find his poetry books anywhere.'

'Well, I'm going to look into it. I think I could do it. There's a man who writes to the local paper in Windhover Hill, always complaining about something, an old-age pensioner – but he lives in Spain, in retirement. A lot of OAPs spend their retirement in Spain now. I don't think I could take the heat myself. Ostend would be much more convenient, and if you could get me free ferry tickets I could nip back and forth across the Channel –'

'Dad – I don't know how much longer I'm going to be working on the ferries. I don't know about Ostend either. I'm starting to feel like I've been here for too long already –'

'But why? It is a wonderful city. It seems to me it has got everything – it's beautiful, it's got atmosphere, interesting museums, and this extraordinary community of artists and writers. So many creative people, and they all seem to know each other . . .'

Julian tugged thoughtfully at his beard.

'At the same time it is a very small and enclosed world. If you live in the midst of it for too long you can begin to feel trapped –'

'I know, I'm just thinking ahead, too far probably, and too fast. It's just that I can't really stand the thought of going back to that empty house in Fernlight Avenue. You know, sometimes I don't see anyone for weeks on end, apart from your sister, and she doesn't really count . . .'

Aldous wanted to say 'I've got no friends, Julian, not a single friend in the world', but somehow couldn't bring himself to. As though there was something rather shameful in the admission. It was like he'd reneged, unwittingly, on some fundamental clause in the human contract.

Aldous drained his glass of green alcohol and fiddled about in his pocket for a piece of paper and a pen, making do with the back of his ferry ticket.

'What are you writing?' said Julian, craning his neck.

'A list of all the people I've met here. I don't want to forget them. I've got Rudolf, he was a nice chap, Geert, she was so funny, with that cigarette holder, and who was that girl with the tattoo on her neck? – Carmen, that's it. And then there was Willy, I don't really believe he's a neurosurgeon, do you? How could he be? And what was the name of that young man with the plaited beard and the sunglasses . . . ?'

'August.'

'August – how could I forget? I want to be able to remember them for next time, everyone's been so kind to me. And that woman with the white miniskirt –Monique. And Agnès, of course – do you know Agnès?'

'A little bit. She teaches at the College of the Arts – runs a photography course. You must know her better than I do.'

'She really is a remarkable woman. Very interesting . . .'

Aldous had not told anyone he was going to Amsterdam with Agnès. This was partly because he didn't quite believe it himself. He had arranged a day and a time to meet her early at Ostend railway station (in fact the last day of his stay – he was due on the ferry home the next morning), but he had a nagging suspicion that this was one step too far on his road to paradise, that the arrangements had been too casual and were not to be taken seriously. It had been a joke, really. He couldn't expect this young woman to drag herself away from her studio at this ungodly hour just to take a near stranger, an old man, on a trip to Amsterdam.

And so the arrangement had remained a secret, and Aldous, after an early breakfast in the wooden breakfast room, made his way to the station with no great expectation of seeing Agnès, which made his thrill at finding her there waiting for him all the greater.

She was standing in the enormous mock-Gothic booking hall looking very elegant in a long white coat with a furry collar turned up. Her face broke into the familiar, all-consuming smile as he approached. Aldous felt as though he was in a film. That he should rush up to her and embrace her. It was fortunate that he didn't do this because as he came nearer, a tall figure standing beside Agnès, whom Aldous had presumed was a stranger, one among many in the bustling hall, turned and faced him. A grey-bearded figure in a safari hat and safari shirt, grey hairs tumbling above the top button, dressed as though for a sunny day, and red-skinned beneath the silver hairs, as though sunburnt. He held out a hand, which Aldous took and shook, trying not to show reluctance.

Perhaps a friend she had happened to meet at the station, who was en route to somewhere else? A nuisance colleague from the College of the Arts who, being fanatical about Rembrandt, had insisted on coming along as well? Just some over-friendly stranger who'd got talking to her while she was waiting?

'My husband Georges,' said Agnès. 'This is Aldous Jones, friend of Herman's.'

'Oho! A friend of Herman's.' The man had an accent Aldous couldn't quite pin down – Australian? South African? But perhaps it was the safari hat that made Aldous think of those places. 'That man's a real dyed-in-the-wool, snout-in-the-trough, head-in-the-clouds pig. You agree with me, don't you?'

The handshake was unreasonably tight, a nasty, vigorous assertion of the man's existence.

Surely not. Surely not. This delicate, sweet young woman hitched to a brutish, overfed, crude, loud, bombastic fool like this. A man who looked like he would be happier patrolling the townships with a bullwhip and a dogwhistle, not savouring the delicate chiaroscuros of Rembrandt's portraits. Yet the man claimed to be an expert on Rembrandt.

'I'm an expert on Rembrandt,' he said. 'I have made this journey many times. I will show you.'

They made their way to the waiting train, while Aldous tried desperately to understand the situation. Agnès had sprung the surprise of a husband on him. A husband who was an expert on Rembrandt. Surely she would have mentioned him the other day when he'd first talked of his passion for Rembrandt, unless she'd wanted to hide the fact of her marriage from him, in which case, he supposed, it must be an unhappy marriage. Her husband was an older man. He looked to Aldous nearly as old as himself, though looking again he was probably a decade younger. Agnès must have a thing about older men. But where did that leave Aldous? Was it, after all, just a friendship? Or had Agnès been intent on having an affair from the beginning? Perhaps she was well known for her flings with older men, and perhaps this was why her husband had invited himself along. Perhaps he was jealous of Aldous. The thought thrilled Aldous in an odd way. No one had been jealous of him since before the war.

They had to climb up a sort of ladder to board the train. Inside there were corridors and compartments, evoking a more glamorous era of travel for Aldous, since such things had largely disappeared from the railways in Britain. The train was bound for Berlin and yet it was nearly empty. The three of them had a compartment to themselves.

Aldous and Agnès sat opposite each other by the window, and Georges took up position beside Aldous, rather to Aldous's surprise. But Georges wanted to talk Rembrandt, and did so almost continually from the moment they sat down. He had a book with him, in Swedish, on the subject of the artist, and an unpublished manuscript, in German, of a book he'd written about the great man. From what Aldous could tell, this was a most tedious and turgid examination of the artist's works. Like so many art books, a long and uninteresting analysis of the paintings in terms of their compositional balance, their handling of form and colour. 'Rembrandt was an incomparable master of the brown end of the spectrum. My word, he could handle brown like no other man.'

Aldous watched Agnès carefully. She was an utterly different person from the flirtatious, vivacious, affectionate, carefree young woman who had, arm in arm, shown him round Ostend. That had been only the day before yesterday. Now she was quiet, almost silent. Sometimes she smiled at Georges, but Aldous saw them as ironic smiles. When Georges spoke to her (they conversed in Flemish, to Aldous's fury), she gave curt replies to gruff questions. It was possible that she was even frightened of the man. There was no trace of affection between the two as far as Aldous could tell. And this provided him with a shred of comfort.

Georges talked incessantly. He would sometimes nudge Aldous quite hard in the ribs to draw his attention to an illustration in the book that was open in his lap, then drone on, sometimes reading from the text, translating as he went, about the painting. Aldous feared the man was going to read the entire book out loud.

He tried catching Agnès's eyes, and on the rare occasions that he did he would smile and wink at her, as though he was sharing a joke. To his delight this sometimes brought a smile in return (though not a wink), and Aldous felt he was saying, 'It's OK, I understand, you've got a ridiculous, humourless husband who you can't shake off. We'll have to put up with him for the moment but once we're in Amsterdam perhaps we can give him the slip . . .' He yearned for Georges to absent himself to the toilet so he could say this out loud to Agnès, but although Georges drank cupfuls of hot black coffee from a flask, his big, strong bladder retained it all with ease.

Aldous looked out of the window whenever he could. He saw landscapes by Ruisdael and Hobbema drift past – shimmering poplars, flooded plains, goats trotting along muddy tracks. Then suddenly a sweep of pristine motorway bisecting rectangular fields, oblong houses of white concrete, a power station with red-and-white-striped chimneys, rows of pylons that stood much straighter and stiffer than the graceful, relaxed English pylons, and which seemed to have horns.

Looking through the glass of the carriage window at all this foreignness, Aldous was aware that he was also looking through the reflection of Agnès's face, and that it bore the same expression of distracted longing that was on his own.

'From the 1630s onwards, Rembrandt's structural conception is increasingly determined by the single figure, and his use of the posture becomes critical to his expression of inner action –'

'Do you think,' said Aldous, interrupting Georges in mid-flow, half an hour into their journey, 'that it is only possible to truly understand Rembrandt's paintings when one has reached a certain age?'

Georges paused, eyeing Aldous carefully.

'What do you mean by a certain age?'

'Well, you and I, we're both men of advanced years – mine somewhat more advanced than yours – don't you find that the power of Rembrandt's paintings is something that increases the older you get?'

Georges looked back at his book, as if the answer should be written there somewhere.

'I agree,' Agnès called from her seat opposite, and smiled conspiratorially with Aldous.

Georges gave one of his gruff Flemish outbursts, and then resumed his monologue.

'Multi-figure compositions in this phase show a dynamic weakness, often falling away on a diagonal from the centre . . .'

They arrived at Antwerp where they were to change trains. Even though they had exchanged hardly any words, Aldous felt that he'd formed an alliance with Agnès against her husband. He was the object of their silent mockery, a joke that they could share together. But the more he thought about it, the harder it would be to lose the man. He kept guard over them, was very watchful of Agnès's every move. It seemed she could do nothing without asking him (at least that's what Aldous took those incomprehensible exchanges to be – requests accepted or denied). A long day stretched before him in ruins, what had been a blissful prospect now one of unremitting tediousness, chaperoned everywhere by this gormless brute, subjected to his vacuous and endless lectures on art. The only relief being the brief eye contacts and exchanged smiles with Agnès. Why was she so terrified of the man?

They wandered through an underpass and emerged on to a vast concourse. Aldous declared a need to go the lavatory. He was fearful that Georges would accompany him, but to his relief that amazing bladder still held tight. Georges and Agnès said they would meet him on Platform 8.

In the Gents' a sudden nausea took hold of Aldous. An hour and a half of hopeful thinking suddenly deserted him, and he saw the situation in all its bleakness. He found that he was shaking uncontrollably, and couldn't go when he stood at the urinal. He washed his hands anyway, took some deep breaths, and emerged again on to the concourse. The sight that met him there finally did for him. In the near distance, outside a chocolate boutique, Agnès and her husband in a deep, sickly embrace. Not just an affectionate cuddle, but a passionate, open-mouthed session of kissing, Georges's big white hands stirring all over Agnès's back and rump, while she yielded to it, arching backwards as though waiting to be swept up and carried away. The sheer horror of it. In all the time he'd been planning his escape with Agnès, they had been waiting to escape from him.

Aldous ducked into a shop before they could see him. It was a newsagent's and bookshop. It had another entrance on the other side which, via an escalator, emerged on to the street. He walked a couple of blocks and then took refuge in a bar, carefully wiping tears away before he ordered anything. He spent an hour drinking green chartreuse, before wandering back to the railway station and catching the next train to Ostend.

Part Two

13

Aldous opened the small left-hand cupboard. The flies that drifted out seemed slightly bigger this time, as though they'd grown.

He consoled himself with the thought that the potatoes were dying anyway, and reached in. His hand was met by what felt like small, cold, bony, other hands. He pushed further until he touched the potatoes themselves. Their unexpected softness shocked him. It was like touching an old lady's cheek. Nevertheless he steeled himself, gripped and pulled. They were resistant – the stupid, pathetic things – resistant! They clung on to hinges and latches. Tubers snapped. He could almost hear the feeble whining of their distress as he brought out a handful and thrust them into a rubbish bag. Then silence. It was like drowning puppies.

He spent a while unpicking the torn-off shoots from where they'd grown through the cracks of the door. Then he wiped out the metal interior with a Brillo Pad.

It wasn't his first act on returning to London. In fact it had been more than a week since he'd crossed the Channel back to Fernlight Avenue, and for much of that week he had lapsed into a perilously depressed state, just as he'd been prior to his fall, and his spell in hospital. The emptiness of the house had consumed him, as he had feared it would, and he'd moped about, listening to Radio 3 in the dark afternoons and drinking whisky, all the way to midnight and beyond.

He made a show for Juliette's visits. Made believe he was a new man, that he'd made a fresh start. He wasn't sure if he convinced her. He told her at length about his adventures in Belgium, placing particular emphasis on his encounters with Agnès, to the extent that Juliette became visibly bored whenever her name was mentioned. At first she'd been interested, asking him what sort of woman she was, telling him off, to his surprise, for describing her as 'coloured' ('What do you mean – purple? orange? green?') and had asked for details of their encounters, which Aldous preferred to leave ambiguously vague. Perhaps they had made love in the full sense of the word and perhaps they hadn't. He developed an openly teasing way of talking about his experiences.

'You know, I've often wondered what a coloured – I mean a black woman – looked like, I mean beneath her clothes . . .'

'Have you? And now you know, is that what you're saying?'

Aldous's reply would be a tantalising giggle.

At other times he would express an urgent longing.

'I'm sorry, Juliette, but I've just got to get back to Ostend. This matter can't rest any longer. It's got to be done . . .'

Juliette would wearily deliver the required response. 'Why do you have to go back to Ostend so urgently?'

'Because I've got to see a certain woman again . . .'

'Why "a certain woman"? You say her name happily all the time, every other word it seems like. Why are you being coy all of a sudden?'

Then, in a sterner mood, Juliette said, 'I had a long talk with Julian on the phone the other day.'

'Did you?' said Aldous lazily, but cautiously.

'Yes, and he told me all about this Agnès woman. You know she's married, don't you?'

'Of course,' said Aldous, with a brisk 'that's obvious' inflection in his voice. Though he was deeply hurt at having the fact put so plainly before him.

'Well?'

'Well what?'

'You never said she was a married woman.'

And then Aldous would change the mood entirely by casting the whole thing as a childish game.

'Don't take any notice of what I say, Juliette, it's just the foolish prattlings of an easily seduced, half-drunk old man . . .'

But it didn't stop him from restating his desires the next time he saw Juliette.

'It's no good, Juliette. My heart lies on the other side of the Channel, on the grey shores of Belgium. I must return . . .'

Then, alone in his house, the hopelessness of the project would strike him. Agnès was in Belgium, a kingdom he could never truly enter. She was married, young, black. She had been fooling with him. He had misunderstood. The whole thing really had been a joke, but it had left Aldous right back where he'd started – alone, wife-haunted, potato-watched.

But then, a week after he came home, two letters arrived at the flat. The first one read:

Dearest Aldous,

I am so very sorry about what happened on the train to Antwerp, and sorry that we lost you. I think you made it back to Oostende. We miss you and hope you will come back soon. You are a very kindly man.

We had a very good day in Amsterdam, looking for you all the time. We are so sorry you never got there. Perhaps another day soon.

I am enclosing a small gift for you.

Yours truly,

Agnès

PS Please do not write to me.

The gift, in the accompanying parcel, was a guidebook to the Rembrandt House Museum. A delightful publication, full of colour photographs of the house and reproductions of Rembrandt's works. Aldous spent a whole day reading it, cursing himself for having thrown away the opportunity of visiting the place.

The other letter read:

Dear Mr Jones,

Some teeth have arrived for you from laboratories in Bruges, Belgium. Please make an appointment at your earliest convenience for a fitting.

Yours sincerely,

J. Collins, FRCDS

Perhaps it was the 'dearest' that did it, rather than the strangely disappointing 'kindly', or the rather clumsy postscript, but Agnès's letter brought the whole wave-crashing, book-throwing, randy-talking week of Ostend back to life for Aldous. In his formless, empty house he felt as though he'd been exiled from his own existence, cut off from his own future, which he now felt lay on the shores of the Belgian coast.

At the same time, return seemed impossible. Shortly after receiving Agnès's letter, Aldous phoned his son in Ostend. The telephone was answered by Herman Lorre who seemed to have already forgotten Aldous.

'Julian, no, he's out on the high seas . . .'

'This is Aldous.'

A pause.

'Yeah?'

'Julian's father.'

'You want to leave a message?'

Aldous hung up, feeling infuriated at the snub of indifference he'd received at the hands of the self-obsessed sexologist. He could imagine him lounging on the leatherette settee, typewriter on his tummy, answering the phone, paying only a tiny portion of his attention to the voice, still thinking through some subtle nuance of the sex lives of the Incas. What was he still doing there anyway? Had he taken up permanent residence?

By a remarkable coincidence, Aldous was watching a television programme one evening when a much younger Herman Lorre appeared. It was a documentary about the sixties, specifically the flower-power movement of 1967 onwards. Aldous was taking little notice, until some archive footage showed a heavily bearded, long-haired and spectacled man sitting cross-legged on the floor in a circle of studenty-looking young people with wispily long hair and minstrel-like clothes. Aldous recognised the figure even before the caption appeared: *Dr Herman Lorre – counter-culturalist.*

'Dr Herman Lorre,' the straight-laced, English voice-over explained, 'has rewritten the American constitution in the form of what he calls a prose-poem, in which he describes it as a citizen's inalienable right to have sex with whomsoever he or she chooses. He believes in the abolition of marriage and the sanctity of the orgy.'

Then came Herman's voice, a semitone higher than the one Aldous had heard in Ostend.

'Today's kids will not accept the two-thousand-year-old patriarchal order that is currently screwing up our world. I call on the US Senate and the House of Representatives to ratify my constitution as a blueprint for a new social order that will put love and peace at the heart of our society.' Herman Lorre said this direct to camera, pointing and jabbing his finger with the kind of aggressive thrusting that rather undermined the tone of his speech. Aldous was strangely moved by this image of the younger Herman Lorre. His hair was a darker grey, his beard almost black, and black chest hairs frothed from the open V of his flowery shirt, looking as if they might painfully entangle with the beads and chains he wore around his neck. A younger man, though still much older than his student acolytes, he looked all the more absurd in his young person's clothes.

Aldous didn't really know what to do with the cupboard once he'd cleared the potatoes. After he'd cleaned it he thought about the other compartments. The larger cupboards underneath. He opened one quickly and closed it after a brief survey of its contents. It was like opening the door on a crowded party of the dead. He glimpsed wickerwork, newspapers, chipped ornaments, a bicycle pump, wads of fag coupons bound with rubber bands. The drawers yielded an archive of even greater density – teeth, hair – it was as though the past might bite him. Interference with these remote regions of the cupboards was for another time. The eviction of the potatoes, their newest resident, cleared sufficient space in Aldous's life for something else to happen. But what?

He spent a week re-establishing the old routines of his pre-fall days. He travelled the red buses with his free bus pass. He began exploring parts of London he'd never visited before. South of the Thames and east along the Old Kent Road; Lewisham, Woolwich, Erith. He once took a bus all the way to Dartford, and found he was at the end of London Transport's realm. Beyond Dartford he had to pay, so he got on a train and began exploring the north Kent Coast discovering, in Whitstable, a forgotten enclave of Victorian seafront. He began visiting Whitstable frequently. The slow progress through south-east London and then the long journey through the Medway towns on the dirty, clumsy electric trains (born of the first wave of electrification, they were now almost museum pieces, one of the last remaining survivors of the early days of British Rail) meant that the trip there and back could occupy a whole day. When there he would wander along the shingle beaches, watch the whelk fishermen boiling their vats of molluscs, drink a couple of pints in one of the pleasantly shadowy pubs. He managed to treat his visits to Whitstable as an occupation. Something he was required to do, almost as if he was going to work. A hard day's work treading the margins of existence, throwing stones childishly into the grey abyss of the estuary. He bought a sketchbook, the first sketchbook he'd bought in years, and began filling it with drawings of crooked masts, dead fish, living lovers, or the tall breakwaters that sectioned the beach into countless domains of piled shingle. It was a good occupation.

In all his life in London he had never thought of it as being a place within easy reach of the sea. Now he was beginning to think of Whitstable as a place to be associated with good fortune, especially, when, one evening on the train back home, he met a very old friend.

He was sitting opposite him on the train. He was wearing headphones and listening to a Walkman, tapping in rhythm, and occasionally humming to himself in accompaniment to the music that he was listening to. Aldous didn't recognise him at first, and was rather irritated by him and his antics. He had never seen anyone older than a teenager wearing headphones before. Then, when their eyes happened to meet, the man said (too loudly because of the headphones), 'I say, it's Aldous Jones, isn't it?'

It took a while for Aldous to remember and recognise Cliff Ashbrittle, fellow student at the Hornsey School of Art. He had aged rather badly, Aldous thought, losing most of his hair (the remaining shreds were bright white) and his face had become hollow and lined, the skin having that crisp, dirty-yellow look of very old Sellotape. Overall, he had a rather skeletal appearance. He was wearing a mushroom-coloured raincoat over a respectable shirt, tie and navy blue jersey.

The pair exchanged histories between Erith and Abbey Wood. Cliff no longer painted. He'd changed direction after the war.

'I sort of drifted into the actuarial business. Then I became an accountant. Finished up as Chief Auditor for Bromley Council – making sure the cheques went to all the right places,' (a squeaky laugh), 'moved down to Herne Bay when I retired. Pop up to the capital quite a lot. Here – must just listen to this bit . . .' He turned his attention to the music that was still feeding into his ears from the headphones, closing his eyes and conducting with one finger. When the passage was over he opened his eyes and removed the headphones – 'Haydn Quintet. One can never get enough of Haydn, can one?'

Aldous nodded, as if in approval, though in fact he couldn't stand Haydn, the fool who'd failed to notice the signs of genius in his pupil, Beethoven, and who'd dashed off all those symphonies with stupid names.

'I'm going to a recital this evening, in fact. Purcell Room.'

Cliff was very pleased with himself and how his life had turned out. When Aldous explained that he'd been an art teacher for nearly forty years, the response was commiseration rather than congratulation. It seemed that Cliff felt a sense of triumph for having escaped the underpaid, self-delusory world of fine art and getting a proper job in the real world. Chief Auditor for Bromley Council. He was married to someone called Grace, whom he mostly referred to as 'She Who Must Be Obeyed', had four successful children, a host of grandchildren. Like Aldous he was fond of solitary expeditions into the capital for what he called 'cultural reconnoitres', or else a visit to Harrods Food Hall to restock on olive oil. Here he took the trouble to write down and hand to Aldous a little note describing the exact brand of olive oil, in case Aldous should want some as well, since it was the best olive oil available in London. Yet as far as Aldous knew, olive oil was some sort of foul-tasting medicine or embrocation that one avoided like the plague unless one was vitamin-deficient.

As they pulled into Charing Cross Cliff offered casually generous invitations – 'Give us a ring, we'll meet up sometime, come down to Herne Bay if you like, I'll see if I can get She Who Must Be Obeyed to do her Tuscan jugged hare . . .'

Aldous didn't warm to Cliff Ashbrittle. As far as he could recall, they hadn't been particularly friendly at college, and he may have even rather disliked him then. And he was irritated now by his smug self-satisfaction, by his eagerness to boast of his material success, and his lame aesthetic sensibility.

And yet he's all I've got, Aldous said to himself. And the next day he phoned him up.

'How was the Haydn?'

'Oh, heavenly. Absolutely heavenly.'

'I was thinking of coming down to see you actually.'

For the first time Cliff stammered, seemed uncertain what to say. He mumbled something about practical difficulties – children staying over, builders in. Then he found a way out.

'I'm coming up to see *Ulysses*, the film version, at the Hampstead Everyman on Tuesday. Fancy coming along?'

So they sat through two hours of Leopold and Molly Bloom in black and white and afterwards discussed the film without saying anything about it, Aldous failing to admit that he hadn't read the novel, and then feeling annoyed at his resultant sense of guilt.

Over the following weeks Aldous met Cliff regularly, sometimes as often as once or twice a week, always in order to do or see something – a play, an exhibition, a film. Their friendship never progressed beyond polite cultural chit-chat and hazy reminiscence. Aldous would sometimes insist that they went into a pub after whatever event they'd been to, but Cliff looked very uncomfortable in the pub environment, almost as though he'd never been to one before – not seeming sure of the protocols of ordering at the bar, or what he actually liked to drink. The conversations became tedious, Cliff soon running out of things to say about whatever show they'd seen, and reverting instead to the safer territory of domestic matters. Aldous could almost see defiance in the way Cliff talked about the new gravel drive he was having laid down, or the estimates he'd had for replacement windows. 'I'm sorry, old chap,' he seemed to be saying, 'I'm going to talk about this stuff whether you like it or not – call me boring if you must, but in the final analysis the fabric of one's home is just more interesting than Shostakovich's Thirteenth Symphony.'

And you know more about it, Aldous could have added.

Though Cliff did alert Aldous to something that might be of interest to him. Home-improvement grants. Local authorities were dishing out money to homeowners, paying for new roofs and windows. Cliff was planning to get an application in. 'You still have to pay a proportion, but the council will pay for the bulk of the costs.' Aldous thought about the rotting window frames in Fernlight Avenue, the patchy, crooked slate tiles on the roof. The brickwork that needed repointing. In the last few years these things had begun to weigh heavily upon him. Up until quite recently he could have managed them by himself, crawling about on the roof, replacing cracked and lost tiles, redoing the guttering, fixing the windows. But these days it was becoming too much. If he climbed a ladder to roof level now he got vertigo. He had lost the agility and mental sharpness to deal with heights, and the diagonal world of roofs seemed lethal. Without his continual tinkering the roof and everything external to the house would do nothing but deteriorate slowly, tile by tile, sill by sill, until he would be forced to call in the builders, and then, as an old man, to be at the mercy of cheeky, chirpy rogues who'd botch up his fabric and diddle him out of thousands. The other appealing thing about the home-improvement grants was that the builders were responsible to the council as much as the homeowner. According to Cliff the council only contracted out to their regular, trustworthy builders, and if anything went wrong it was the council who did the chasing up and sorting out.

But even this subject was not enough to sustain the friendship. Any more intimate subject matter had Cliff looking at his watch and remarking on the time, saying he had to be back for She Who Must Be Obeyed. This was usually after Aldous had begun gloomily relating the decline of his son Janus, or the death of his wife, or asking Cliff questions such as, 'What would you do, Cliff, if you went home and found She Who

Must Be Obeyed flat out on the floor with her head in the gas oven?' or 'Have you ever felt totally betrayed, I mean utterly and absolutely betrayed by your children, Cliff?'

'Well,' said Cliff, to this particular question, 'I did once lend George the princely sum of two thousand pounds to help him buy a flat in Penge – interest-free, mind, interest-free . . .' He leaned over to Aldous and tapped the side of his nose with his index finger, then laughed. Aldous laughed as well, but at the absurdity of the gesture, rather than what was being said. 'And have I seen any of that money in the last eight years . . .'

'No,' said Aldous, 'you haven't, have you?'

'But then I feel it has been money well spent. He's got two houses now, one of which he lets out. And a beautiful family. Two boys.'

Aldous couldn't blame Cliff for his failure as a friend. He knew he was being hard work for the man. Aldous had disrupted Cliff's life as a solitary bon viveur with his long, troubling questions.

'What would you do, Cliff, if She Who Must Be Obeyed dropped dead tomorrow? Would you get married again?'

'Well, I don't know, I . . . er . . . it's rather hard to say.'

'My advice is that you should, if you can. The trouble is – how do you find someone? That's the difficulty.'

Then Cliff came up with a useful suggestion.

'Have you thought of evening classes?'

'No. I know everything I want to know already.'

'But there's a place in London – the Central London College – where you can study almost anything. Really. You can do ten-week courses in conducting, or Egyptology. Or wine appreciation – though perhaps . . .' (Cliff looked suddenly embarrassed.) '. . . I'm going down next week to enrol. Why don't you come along?'

It was good of Cliff Ashbrittle to go to these lengths to divest himself of Aldous's care. He could have just not answered his frequent telephone calls, or have made any number of excuses not to come up from Herne Bay. Instead, he introduced him to what seemed to Aldous the most unexpectedly wonderful institution he had ever come across in London.

The Central London College was an unremarkable Edwardian building on the fringes of Bloomsbury, so out of the way that it took Aldous, who'd previously thought he'd known the area pretty well, having spent much of his life wandering between the British Museum and the Courtauld Institute beneath Russell Square's sprawling planes, quite a while to find it.

And now Aldous realised why, once and for all, he loved London. Did the citizens of High Wycombe ever get the chance to attend night classes in conducting? Of orchestras? Because that was on the prospectus, just as Cliff had said. Along with classes on counterpoint and harmony.

'I might try my hand at Spinoza for Beginners,' said Cliff, as they leafed through the programme together, 'or maybe Astrophysics Level 1, or Beyond the Googolplex, that sounds intriguing. What do you think, Aldous – see anything there?'

'What do you think "Conversations with Stones" is about?' asked Aldous.

'That sounds a bit what they call New Age, I think . . .'

Whole continents of language were available for study – Hindustani, Gaelic, Hebrew . . .

'A chap once said to me,' Cliff began, 'if you studied everything on offer here it would take you a hundred years.'

Aldous was still in the section on languages, and it was in this section that he found, to his surprise, something he did want to learn, something he wanted to learn very urgently, but would, for some stupid reason, not have thought of had it not presented itself to him in the prospectus. In among truly obscure tongues (Zapotec, Nooksack) there it stood – Tuesday evenings from seven to nine, tutored by someone called Erich van Hoof – *Flemish for Beginners*.

14

Aldous's fellow students seemed, at first sight, rather unpromising as a source of future companionship. They were mostly elderly, his coevals, uninterested in adventure and sex, a bunch of retired, smug, owner-occupiers with crisp, white, cloud-puff hairdos and cheese-biscuit moustaches. Many of them knew each other already, and it soon became clear that the old people of the suburbs were using the Central London College as a social club, signing up for the courses with little regard for their content, taking whatever subject happened to be available on their particular night, as long as they hadn't done it before. This became all the more apparent when the tutor, by way of breaking the ice, asked them one by one why they were keen to learn Flemish. The answers were mostly along the lines of: 'It's the only class on Tuesday evenings that I haven't done yet,' or: 'Everything else clashes with my beekeeping for beginners.' (The person who said this, Aldous later found out, did not keep, and had no intention of ever keeping bees. She lived in a gardenless maisonette in Forest Hill.)

They came prepared with their own food for the break – flasks of tea, Tupperware boxes of sandwiches and fairy cakes. They would sit at tables in the surprisingly elegant canteen, scoffing these items and looking disdainfully upon those who'd been foolish enough, like Aldous, to actually spend money at the counter, which they considered outrageously overpriced and substandard. They would exchange banter with their counterparts from other classes – 'How's the wine appreciation going, old chap?' 'I'm doing the History of the Bicycle this term.' 'You should come over to Great Victorian Explorers, if you can find the way that is, heh-heh . . .'

When Aldous was asked by their tutor why he'd chosen to

study Flemish he'd caused a ripple of fruity laughter by replying, 'In order to declare my love for a Belgian woman.' After the laughter had died down he added, 'I'd also like to visit the Rembrandt House Museum in Amsterdam one day, and to be able to talk about Rembrandt in his own language – which may not have been exactly Flemish, but I understand Flemish is actually quite close to the Dutch that Rembrandt must have spoken – is that right?'

Their tutor gave the slow and thoughtful nod of someone who didn't know, and in many ways he was a rather disappointing teacher. He was too young, for one thing, and had trouble commanding a sense of authority, seeming at a loss to explain any technical questions that were thrown at him. He also seemed permanently exhausted from his day job as a tour guide, herding people around the sights of London and beyond. But he was strikingly handsome in a very Aryan way – blond hair, blue eyes, fine cheekbones – and all the older ladies in the class would gaze at him in fixed fascination. This despite the fact that he had made himself look rather absurd by growing a handlebar moustache.

'Ladies and gentlemen,' he would address the class (still in tour-guide mode), 'today we are going to make a journey through the land of prepositions . . .'

A great deal of the teaching involved pair-work. At one time this would have horrified Aldous, but his more sociable self now relished the chance of one-to-one contact with another person. On the first evening students were asked to pair up and interview each other, using as much basic vocabulary as they could.

Aldous was paired with one of the evening-class stalwarts, a little round ball of a woman wearing owlish bifocals, whose bulk had so restricted the movement in her chest that her voice came out as a rather undignified squeak.

Aldous asked her questions in stumbling Flemish, and the woman jabbered her replies in endless, squeaky English, even producing photographs to illustrate the biographical details she was giving – a creased black-and-white photo that appeared to show an entirely different woman: slim, bluntly pretty, and dressed in a Wren's uniform. By the end of the exercise she and Aldous were conversing in fluent English. I've never spoken so much English since I started learning Flemish, Aldous thought.

The following week Aldous avoided sitting next to the ex-Wren, even though seat places seemed already to have become fixed. It made his avoidance seem deliberate and obvious. Instead he managed to position himself next to a woman new to the class that week, a woman who appeared much younger than the other regulars, perhaps in her late forties or early fifties, it was hard to tell. She had blonde hair cut in a slightly prickly bob. Her eyes wore a constant smile. She was heavily made up, unnecessarily it seemed to Aldous. Her foundation was caked around her cheeks, the little downy hairs clogged with face powder, and her lips were pillar-box red, which gave her smile a piercing, stabbing quality.

This time they did a role-playing exercise, where Aldous had to pretend to be a lost visitor to Brussels, and his partner, whose name was Maria, had to direct him to the railway station.

Maria spoke what seemed to Aldous fluent Flemish.

'I've been on this course twice before,' she said. 'Unfortunately Flemish for Beginners is the only course in the language available anywhere in London. There is no advanced Flemish. So I just keep coming back, and pick up a little more each time.'

Aldous asked her why she was learning it, and she gave one of those twinkly, stabbing smiles that jolted his heart.

'My boyfriend was working in Brussels, for the Common Market, the EEC as we have to call it these days.'

'*Was* working?'

'He still is, but we're not seeing each other any more. At least I don't think so. He comes and goes. So do I. It's funny, but while we were properly together I kept meaning to come to classes like this, but I only finally enrolled once we'd started drifting apart. So I'm learning Flemish and will probably never go to Belgium again in my life. Anyway, I should be learning French, or Walloon. Nobody in Brussels would understand a word of this. You have a very kind face. What have you done all your life?'

The words came out in a long musical recitative, a spontaneous outspilling of thoughts. Somehow she seemed both curious about and indifferent to the world in one go. There was no hint that she had interpreted Aldous's interest in her boyfriend as the first parry in a duel of courtship.

'I was an art teacher.'

'That is a very good thing to have been. I wanted to be an artist once, but the easels were so expensive – and the paints . . . my flatmate is doing an evening class in soft sculpture. She made a whole person out of old cushions – gave me the fright of my life when I came in late one night and she'd left it sitting on the sofa, looking as though it was watching the TV. I wanted to do the life-drawing classes here but I got terribly embarrassed when I realised the models would be nude. I was all jittery about seeing a strange man with no clothes on. A woman would have been even worse. My friend Helen did the class and she told me the model was an old man with no pubic hair and a ring through his whatsit, so I think I made the right decision, don't you? Do you know where I can buy easels cheaply?'

'You don't need an easel,' Aldous laughed. 'I'd never used an easel in my life, until I was given one as a retirement gift. And I hate the thing. It wobbles about all over the place, you can never get the angles right, you can't lean on it with any weight, it just collapses without warning in the middle of a brushstroke, like I will one day soon . . .'

'That's what I'd really like to be,' said Maria, 'the sort of artist who's so good they don't need an easel. I suppose you're like a writer who doesn't need an expensive fountain pen with just the right shade of tortoiseshell casing and comfortably worn-in gold nib in order to write. I expect a real writer can write with just any old cheap disposable biro, or even an HB pencil without a rubber on the end. And they write on anything – backs of envelopes, margins of newspapers.'

Aldous found himself in a conversation he didn't want to end. He searched his memory for anecdotes to prolong it.

'If Picasso didn't have paints to hand, he'd draw with what he could find – lipstick, children's crayons. I once saw a film of him in which he'd made a collage out of the leftovers from the meal he'd just eaten – a beautiful fish skeleton was the centrepiece . . .'

'Must have ponged a bit. Perhaps that was all part of the experience. Paintings never smell much, do they, except when they're wet. That lovely smell of linseed oil. Do your paintings smell?'

'I've never noticed, actually. Perhaps I'll give them a sniff when I get home.'

'You must have a lot if you've been painting all your life – or have you sold them all?'

'No, I've sold hardly any. A few friends and relatives have taken some, but not many.'

'So your house must be bursting with paintings . . .'

Aldous thought. Yes, it should be, but apart from a stack of oil paintings that took up a corner of the back bedroom, and a portfolio bulging with works on paper, there didn't seem to be a lot. Where was it all, his lifetime's work?

Aldous and Maria carried on talking like this for most of the lesson, ignoring or forgetting the various exercises they were set – '*You are in an ice-cream parlour in Ghent. You have spilt ice cream on your waistcoat. What do you say to your dear one?*' Maria's conversation was constant and free-ranging, and years ago might have rather annoyed Aldous. Instead he found it soothing and stimulating, and something he could respond to, be equal to. He was hoping that they might continue talking to each other in a nearby pub but, as soon as the class was over, Maria made a hasty and busy exit. There was a frantic minute of packing things within other things (like many women, Aldous observed, she had a handbag that seemed to contain smaller handbags within it, some of which contained even smaller bags), a brief, valedictory chit-chat with old acquaintances, and then she was gone.

Yet she also stayed with Aldous, she fluttered in and out of his vision, her brisk yet fragile chatter still buzzing in his ears, and as he watched the hideously distorted reflections of himself in the bent glass of the Tube train windows (two Aldouses slowly peeling away from each other), he felt her sitting closely at his side.

When he got home he felt a desperate urge to record the events of the evening, but didn't know quite how to. Writing always struck Aldous as something of a chore. Whenever he wrote he was always bogged down by his materials – in just the way that Maria had said a real writer wouldn't be. The pen would feel uncomfortable and slippery, the paper too smooth or too scratchy. The lengthy preparations necessary to avoid this feeling – the long search for suitable instruments, the clearing of a space to write, the donning of reading glasses – often dissuaded him from even beginning. And that was how he felt when he got home. A desire to write something down but a reluctance to arrange the materials for so doing. In the end he took the rolled-up and slightly flattened *Evening Standard* he'd been carrying around for most of the day and wrote, above the masthead, in blue biro:

Met Maria, CLC

The newspaper, dated, served as a page of a diary. Aldous laid it on the arm of the couch in the front room.

15

A week now seemed to Aldous like an interminably long period of time. A whole seven days to fill before he had a chance of continuing his conversation with Maria. He realised that the only way to make the time move reasonably fast was to fill it with activity. Tomorrow he could go to Whitstable. On Thursday he could go to Foyles and look for a Flemish–English, English–Flemish dictionary. On Friday he could go to Whitstable again – no, not Fridays, he had to remind himself, Fridays on the train back from Whitstable were quite horrible, loaded with yobbish children on their way up to town for a night on the tiles, or 'the piss' as they called it. Something else for Friday. Saturday, something to do on Saturday? Sunday to Juliette's for lunch and a quiz marathon – then Monday, he needed something for Monday.

Aldous read through the book Agnès had sent him, the guidebook to the Rembrandt House Museum. The information it gave was very detailed. Four steps up from the street to the front door which opened into a spacious entrance hall (Voorhuys), floored with black-and-white marble (there was an illustration – it was rather like a bigger version of the chessboard tiles in Aldous's own hall), a room designed to impress wealthy clients. The walls would have been covered in the artist's own paintings – and other paintings from his collection that were for sale. This hadn't occurred to Aldous before – Rembrandt's house was also a kind of shop from which he ran a lucrative art-dealing business. Downstairs he would entertain clients, sitting them in one of his Spanish leather chairs, plying them with wine from an earthenware cooler, getting his assistants to bring in paintings for viewing, while upstairs he had his studio, and his vast collection of still life objects. What an extraordinarily gratifying life it must have been in that house on the Breestraat – in the early years at least.

These thoughts led Aldous back to his own project for a series of garden paintings, 'The Garden Through the Seasons'. Here was something that would fill the time. Although he hated to consider it as merely something to kill the time, there was no denying that painting, with the extended periods of concentration it involved, could make the hours pass like nothing else.

He was rather surprised to find that his painting of Winter, which he'd begun on the day of his fall, was still out there, in the garden, and had been for nearly four months. So was the easel, tipped up, on its side, like a ballerina fallen in mid-pirouette. Aldous must have seen it in the weeks when his only visit to the garden had been to dump a black sack full of rubbish down by the alley door but somehow its presence hadn't registered. The chairs were still there too. Their seats were littered with twigs and there was a big elongated oval of bird shit down the back of one.

Aldous sat in one of the chairs. He felt strangely as if he'd been sitting there all the time since he'd put it out, just sitting there while the winter melted away around him and the bright grass of spring emerged. The painting, barely begun, was on its side at the foot of the Ellison Orange. An outline of wintry fruit trees, bending under the weight of snow. Some suggestions of a wilderness beyond. What should he do with it? One idea was simply to take up the same painting again, but to paint out the snow and redraft it as a Spring painting. Aldous thought of this for a while, but decided he would start a new painting for spring, and leave 'Winter' until it was winter again.

So the 'Spring' project occupied him on some of those days he had left over in the week. He went down to the art shop in the Green Lanes (the only art materials suppliers within many miles), and bought a canvas, exactly the same dimensions as his old painting, and rather boldly made the first marks of spring. Spring, it turned out, was a much more demanding subject than winter would have been, because the garden seemed to change daily, even hourly. He felt sure that the buds on the evening cherry tree had swelled noticeably since the morning. In a few days' time the blossom would break out, and the painting would have to change all over again.

On one of the other days he hung around the Rembrandt room of the National Gallery, drawn as always to the portrait of Hendrickje Stoffels. The small, compact face. The kindly, conker-brown eyes. The fur stole. Housekeeper as princess. He found some books on Rembrandt in the local library, bought some books from Foyles (pleased to see that there were none in there by Georges Florizoone (if that was his surname, Aldous never actually knew), and spent long hours reading about the painter, though the books frustratingly concentrated on the paintings, with only tantalising glimpses of the life behind them.

What fun he and Saskia must have had in the early years of their marriage, hardly able to keep their hands off each other long enough for Rembrandt to get to his brushes and step back behind the canvas. They would have been like children at a dressing-up box, Saskia in the get-up of a warrior queen one minute (a steel breastplate and helmet for the portrait of Belloona), the next in a coronet of chrysanthemums and tulips for the painting of Flora.

And then she was gone. A long bedridden illness (his sketch-book seemed to show her fading away on what was to become her deathbed), never fully recovering from the birth of Titus, who was just seven months old when she finally expired.

The books Aldous read gave only sketchy summaries of life in the household after the death of Saskia. Aldous found himself filling in the gaps. He imagined a series of frumpy, grumpy nurses culminating in Geertje Dircks, that big lump of a woman plonking herself in the best chair by the fire, effortlessly disappointing Rembrandt, whose friend had soliloquised her beauty – 'She has a face from Amsterdam, gait from Delft, bearing from Leyden, voice from Gouda, stature from Dordrecht and complexion from Haarlem.' That may have been so when she'd married her first husband, a ship's trumpeter from Edam. Now she was stoop-shouldered, broad-rumped and her bosoms sagged dreadfully. She swaddled Titus so tightly he couldn't move his limbs, left him in his cradle for hours on end, ignoring his crying, and sat by the fire instead doing her clumsy, ugly embroidery. She had been employed on the assumption that she would act as wet nurse, but once in the house she said carelessly, as if it couldn't have mattered less, that she'd never had children and so had no milk. She spooned sweetened ewe's curd into Titus's crying mouth and, when he was old enough to stand, rigged him up in a rigid whalebone and leather corset to help him develop an erect posture (common practice at the time, Aldous read). She slipped iron and lead inserts inside to make it narrower. Swathed in several layers of unnecessary clothes – breeches, miniature doublet, stockings – Titus almost collapsed under his own weight, a solid little toddler unable to toddle, as heavy as a small man. If he wobbled he would just tip sideways like an old post.

And then Hendrickje arrived. Her role was to assist in the housekeeping, but she took complete charge of Titus. Almost her first act was to cry out with pity for the over-constrained child. She knelt down before him and began unbuckling the straps of his corset, exclaiming with horror as each new layer of binding was revealed – 'whalebone!' 'lead!' When she got to the core and found the child there, pale and shivery, it was as if she'd released a shy, uncertain butterfly from a cocoon of leather and iron. Titus walked falteringly at first but was soon galloping around the room, and then playing rowdily on the street with the other children.

The event caused a ferocious argument between Geertje and Hendrickje when Geertje returned from a shopping trip. They were at each other with such violence that Rembrandt, who had taken the argument as a piece of amusing entertainment at first, had to step in between them. Hendrickje, who still had the slimness and delicacy of figure that goes with youth, was no match for the big shapeless pudding of a woman that Geertje had become. Rembrandt had a large frame, but he seemed to become transparent when he stepped in between the women – they carried on arguing through him as if he wasn't there. It was the first of many such disputes.

Within the first day Geertje demanded that Hendrickje be dismissed from the household. Rembrandt refused. 'You're the one who said you needed help.' 'This isn't help, it's treachery.' 'Give the girl a chance.' 'Either she goes or I go.' When Rembrandt indicated the door, Geertje stood firm.

Rembrandt had made love to Geertje just once. He was dismayed to find that, as the climax of their passions approached, a curious snapping sound broke out. He looked up from the sweaty pit of Geertje's cleavage to see that she was idly breaking nuts with her teeth. After that she had taken to raiding Saskia's wardrobe. As the clothes were far too small for her, she tried letting them out but they still wouldn't fit. The only thing she could wear was the jewellery. Rembrandt found her draped in Saskia's pearls. He furiously made to tear them off her, but as he approached, his fist ready to rip the strings of stones from her neck, he faltered, perhaps because he saw a perverse, grotesque reincarnation of his wife in Geertje's square, pulpy frame.

But on this basis she seemed to think that he had made a proposal of marriage to her. When he dismissed her from the house she sued him for breach of promise. Rembrandt took his revenge by getting her imprisoned in Gouda, at his own expense, a gruelling incarceration that eventually all but did for her. It is the only real evidence of a cruel streak in Rembrandt's nature. How he must have loathed her.

Hendrickje had testified in favour of Rembrandt at the hearing brought by Geertje. Her first public act of alliance with the great artist. When, a few years later and pregnant with Cornelia, she was summoned by the Church Council to answer accusations that she was living in whoredom with Rembrandt, she apparently ignored the call. They had to summon her three times before she finally appeared. Of course, it could have been that she was afraid, but Aldous somehow thought not. Behind that sweet, gentle face there was something tough, resilient and defiant. And mischievous. Definitely something mischievous.

When Aldous next went to his Flemish class he was dismayed to find that someone had already taken the seat next to Maria. It was the buttery, ball-shaped ex-Wren. She'll yack at her all evening about World War II, Aldous thought, and I'll never get the chance to talk to her. And he was right. The Wren hogged Maria all through the break. Thinking Maria might want to be saved, Aldous tried lingering close by and waiting for a chance to ease himself into the conversation, but to his astonishment she actually seemed to be interested in what the Wren was saying. In fact, so transfixed by her was she that she took little notice of anything around her. Did this mean that the Wren was more interesting than Aldous, because he felt sure Maria hadn't seemed as transfixed when he'd been talking to her? And at the end of the class she performed again that vanishing act. Aldous wailed quietly to himself on the way home, dismayed at the prospect of a two-week gap opening up this early in his friendship with Maria: long enough for their first meeting, with all its unexpected intimacies, affirmations and concurrences, to have been forgotten. He would have to start all over again.

And so another week passed slowly. Three more trips to Whitstable and a few sessions on 'Spring' in the back garden (when it wasn't raining). He bought himself a Flemish Linguaphone in Foyles: a grey box folder with a stash of small gramophone records – a nest of 45s – and, to Aldous's delight, a collection of sticky labels. The labels were a set of simple vocabulary, mostly nouns, that Aldous could stick on things around the house – on the door (*deur*), window (*venster*), fridge (*koelkast*), floor (*verdieping*). On the front door he stuck a label that gave the Flemish for goodbye (*vaarwell*), and on the mirror, hello (*hallo*). On the stove he stuck the word for dinner (*middagmaal*). It was a curious experience, labelling the things of his life in a different language, but one that he found oddly satisfying. Now he spent long afternoons and evenings engrossed in the little vinyl 45s, sitting hunched beside the radio gramophone (*draadloze*) and doing his best to repeat the difficult phrases.

At the fourth evening class, Aldous did manage to manoeuvre himself into position and sit beside Maria, to the Wren's visible disappointment. Aldous felt like looking over his shoulder and poking his tongue out at the woman. Not that she would have noticed, being already deep in conversation with a tweedy chap in a mustard cardigan.

Aldous couldn't help reading much into the quick smile of acknowledgement Maria gave him as he took his seat beside her, in reality little more than a brief tightening of the mouth and eyes as she glanced in his direction, as though anxious not to lose track of an important point their tutor was making, but which seemed to Aldous to say, 'I'm so glad you made it back into your rightful place.'

But then he became rather frustrated. Maria was taking far too much interest in the lesson, when previously they'd talked almost as if the tutor hadn't been there. She had sat through the course twice before and knew it all already. She didn't need to listen. Aldous began to feel she was willingly allowing her attention to be drawn away from him.

The lesson was rather dull. Their tutor had brought in with him what the students referred to as a ghetto blaster, a nasty-looking piece of machinery, like a giant stag beetle, overspilling with buttons and dials. The sort of machine that looked as if it might spring up and punch you in the face. He was using it to play tapes of Flemish phrases for the students to repeat, in turn. Although it was his own machine he seemed at a loss for how to operate it, putting in the wrong tape (a sudden blast of Duran Duran), not knowing how to rewind or adjust the volume. He was eventually helped out by one of the elderly ladies, which drew syrupy chuckling from the class.

Without warning Maria turned to Aldous and beckoned him to lean close, as if she had something desperately urgent to tell him. But what she said was: 'Did you ever work in a turpentine factory?'

Aldous replied that he hadn't, saying it several times for emphasis: 'No, no I didn't, definitely not, no.'

Maria gave a satisfied nod, as though he'd reassured her on some troubling matter.

She said nothing more until the break, when Aldous finally felt able to follow up the turpentine question. His puzzlement seemed to puzzle her.

'Many years ago I worked in a turpentine factory – secretarial, of course,' she laughed. 'My boss there, I'm sure he was called something Jones, and he looked a little bit like you might have done many years ago. When did your hair go grey? It doesn't matter. You aren't him, which is just as well, because he was a horrible man.'

Maria was one of the ones who brought her own food for the break. A tartan flask and a Tupperware box. From the flask, which she unscrewed carefully, peeping inside as though unsure of what she might see, she poured a clear liquid, which turned out to be plain water.

'It's spring water, from the Dolomite Mountains. They say it's taken four thousand years to trickle down through the rocks. London tap water is recycled seven times before it goes back into the sea. I really don't understand how people can drink the stuff. Imagine, seven times down the loo and we're still drinking it.'

When Juliette had offered him water from a bottle, Aldous had sniggered at the credulousness of young consumers, always eager to spend money on ideas rather than things. The thing itself comes free from the tap, but the idea of purity could only be bought in bottled form. That Maria subscribed to this same notion changed everything. She made bottled water accept-able. Aldous was aware of this fact and felt a little embarrassed at Maria's power to influence his thinking.

From the Tupperware box came what to Aldous looked like smaller Tupperware boxes, but which Maria said were Japanese rice biscuits. Almost see-through grey squares with little shreds of dark stuff that was seaweed.

'Do you always eat transparent meals?' said Aldous.

Maria threw her head back and laughed. This gave Aldous a perfect view of her upper teeth. There was a peculiar asym-metry about them: the left molars had all been filled, the right ones were untouched.

'I'd never thought of it like that. You do say funny things. That's why I like you.'

'But it's you that says funny things. Fancy asking me about a turpentine factory.'

'But you do bear a striking resemblance. Perhaps your father worked in a turpentine factory – or one of your brothers?'

'I don't have any brothers – as for my father, he died over forty years ago. Long before you were old enough to work anywhere. Long before you were born, even . . .' Aldous added the last comment daringly, knowing it couldn't possibly be true. She slapped the back of his wrist for being cheeky. But she wouldn't tell him how old she was. In fact, Aldous found it very hard to find out anything about Maria. Her age remained a puzzle, though she would sometimes drop hints, and present him with little conundrums of dates and events that perhaps could, if he wrote them down and added them up, have revealed the answer − but which usually turned out to be annoyingly paradoxical. If she talked about her parents it was only in a very generalised way − 'My father was a typical father, a very fatherly man. Oh, he was very much of his time, and my mother, both products of their time and place,' but which time, and which place, remained obscure. If Aldous pushed further − 'What did your father do − I mean, what job did he have?' − the most she would reveal would be something like, 'Oh, he was in business, from time to time. A lot of travelling.'

For his part, Aldous found himself haemorrhaging history from the tiniest cuts of her questions, relating the whole story of his family, from beginning to end, the happy early years leading up to the decline and fall of his wife and oldest son, stopping only when he realised the narrative was having a bad effect on Maria.

'I didn't mean to make you cry,' he said, as Maria dabbed at her eyes with a tissue.

'It's not your fault,' said Maria. 'It's not your fault you've had such a sad life.'

'Don't say I've had a sad life, that makes it sound as though it's been completely wasted . . .'

'No, I'm sorry. I mean − it does all sound rather tragic.'

'Tragic is much better than sad. I'm happy with tragic.'

'That's such a funny thing to say.'

'What about you, Maria, I'm sure there must have been some sad moments in your life . . . ?'

Aldous again felt he was being daring, tiptoeing as he was into the private halls of Maria's hidden past.

'No, my life has been one of unutterably boring happiness.'

These conversations mostly took place in the refectory of the Central London College. Maria would sit at one of the knocked-about tables, back straight, knees and legs together, nibbling at her Japanese crackers, sipping her four-thousand-year-old water, smiling and twinkling and breaking into bubbly laughter at almost anything Aldous said. Aldous had taken to buying things from the counter, feeling sympathy for the two elderly ladies who ran the place, and who were boycotted, for no obvious reason, by most of the night-class students. Aldous would return from a grateful encounter with them carrying a styrofoam cup of browny-grey coffee and a cellophane-wrapped slice of fruit cake, feeling frowned upon and pitied by the rest of his group.

After five weeks Aldous asked Maria if she'd like to go to a pub after the class. Maria declined, very nicely. She said that she didn't drink. Also, that she had to be home to attend to her iguana.

'It's really my flatmate's, but she's away nearly every night at her boyfriend's house, the other side of London. So poor old Cicero is entirely in my careless, unmotherly hands. I don't know why but every time I return to the house I expect to find him dead. He never is, of course, but sometimes it's hard to tell. You have to poke him to see if he moves. I'm not a natural nurturer, you see. All my pot plants shrivel up and die. I wouldn't dare to keep a cat.'

'One wouldn't think that to look at you,' said Aldous.

Maria gave an I've-heard-that-one-before laugh which made Aldous feel foolish.

'It's the same reason I can't do anything creative. Can't draw, can't paint, can't cook, can't write. I could never even get the hang of knitting. I haven't produced any children. I can't save money. I am absolutely uncreative.'

'But I'm sure . . .' Aldous struggled to think of a way in which Maria's active life could be interpreted as creative, '. . . I mean, you were born, weren't you – that's being creative, isn't it?'

'Being born isn't something you do. It's something that's done to you.'

'I don't know about that, Maria. People aren't like pot plants – you water them and they grow up into nice big flowers (or not, in your case). It takes a lot of effort to become a person, a lot of hard work.'

'Well, it's nice of you to try, Aldous. Lots of people have tried before to find something creative about me. But being born and being alive as a creative achievement – it's scraping the barrel, isn't it, you have to admit . . .'

Aldous shrugged, helpless in the face of Maria's self-deprecation.

On the sixth week he said to her, 'It's strange, isn't it, a class like this?'

'Yes,' said Maria, 'very strange.'

Aldous didn't know if she meant strange in the same way. To his surprise, she did, and went on to offer a perfect delineation of his own thoughts.

'All these people coming together at this time in their life, to study an arcane subject like Flemish, taught by a handsome young part-time tour guide. Then, when it's over, off they go, never to meet again. Ships in the night, as my mother used to say.'

By week seven Aldous was becoming anxious about the approaching conclusion of the course.

'Will you do the course again?' he asked her.

'I think not,' she replied. 'This is the third time, and I've learned nothing new. Time to call it a day. I don't even need this silly language any more. And if you do go to Belgium, everyone talks English. What about you? Does that Belgian fancy woman of yours speak English?'

Aldous had kept the idea of Agnès alive in Maria's mind, seeing it as a potentially useful resource – a bargaining tool, excuse, something he hoped would present him in a more attractive light. The trick had been to make her real without giving too much information about her. Occasionally Maria would interrogate Aldous:

'So how in goodness' name did you come to have a Belgian fancy woman, do tell me?'

'My son lives in Ostend, I pop over every now and then to sample the nightlife and the bars . . .'

'Gosh, I bet you've got all sorts of fancy women over there . . .'

The most interesting moment was when Aldous revealed that Agnès was black. Maria just couldn't contain her shock.

Had she been drinking her mineral water at the moment of revelation she might have sprayed it everywhere. Watching the progress of expressions on her face, Aldous felt he could actually see the process by which instinctive shock and distaste was hurriedly and clumsily replaced at first by moral uncertainty, then acceptance, and then even approval and admiration.

'I have the most awful confession to make, Aldous,' she said, a little while later. 'I live a mile from Brixton and yet I don't have a single coloured friend. Does that make me a racialist?'

'It depends what you mean by "coloured". What colour do you mean precisely? Purple? Green? Blue?'

But his principal question – how would they continue their friendship after the course had finished – remained unanswered.

And then, in week eight, a calamity befell Aldous. Maria was absent. He felt horribly panicky at the coffee break. He realised he'd become so consumed by his friendship with Maria that he'd hardly spoken to the other members of the class. He found himself in a crowd of virtual strangers. The only person he knew at all was the ex-Wren (and he didn't even know her name). On the off chance that she might know Maria better than he, he sidled over to her and quizzed her. Did she know why Maria hadn't come? Did she know where Maria lived? Of course, the ex-Wren knew nothing about her, and neither did anyone else in the class, but she could see Aldous was worried, and shamed him by offering sympathies and condolences. 'Don't worry, I'm sure she'll be back next week . . .'

But she wasn't. There was only one more week to go and then the course was over. If she didn't come in week ten he risked never seeing her again. He cursed himself for not being bolder in his attempts to take the friendship beyond the classroom. He didn't even have her phone number, or address, and she didn't have his. All he knew was that she lived a mile from Brixton. She'd told him the precise district but he'd forgotten. That part of the world was unexplored territory to him. He remembered only that she came to college by catching a bus to Brixton, a Tube to Victoria and then another bus from there. Brixton station would be her entry point into central London. Aldous began preparing himself for a long vigil at that station, hoping to be there for the few seconds each week that she must pass through it. He could try asking the college authorities for her details, but knew, as a former teacher of evening classes himself, that this information was never given out.

When, in the final week, she did show up, he almost ran to greet her.

'I thought you weren't coming back,' he said, feeling stupid.

'I wasn't going to,' she said, without smiling, 'but then I thought I should come and say goodbye to everyone.'

That 'everyone' was very annoying: a little, pointless swipe at their friendship.

Aldous could tell something was wrong. It was as though she was rendered in matt, when before she'd been gloss. She smiled and laughed as before, but this time there was a sense of grinding effort behind the performance.

'I was thinking, we should meet up sometime, outside, in London somewhere, perhaps,' Aldous, in trying to sound casual, had stumbled slightly.

'Yes,' said Maria abstractedly, 'I'll miss our little chats . . .'

Aldous felt another swipe. Little chats? Is that all they were?

Though Aldous persisted, he couldn't draw any firm commitment from Maria, though he made sure she had his address and phone number. He had little chance to talk to her at the break because she had been true to her word and was, indeed, saying goodbye to everyone, even to people she'd hardly spoken to in the ten weeks of the course.

'Goodbye, my dear,' said the ex-Wren, 'I do hope you're feeling better.' (Maria had answered queries about her absence with casual remarks about feeling under the weather.)

She was about to do her vanishing act when Aldous caught up with her, and physically took her by the wrist, almost yanking her round to face him. It was a frighteningly easy thing to do, as though she carried no weight. For a split second Aldous enjoyed the hunter's sense of catching his prey, but the mild shock on Maria's face dispelled any pleasure instantly. She had the innocent delicacy of expression that made Aldous think of a fawn.

'You will promise me you'll phone,' he said.

'Of course,' she replied, 'I've said I will.'

An embarrassed pause, Aldous unsure of how to conclude. Maria did so by giving him a kiss on the cheek.

'Cicero will be waiting. I'm sure he's alive but I must hurry . . .'

The moisture of Maria's kiss took a long time to evaporate.

16

Having been prepared for disappointment, Aldous hardly knew how to cope with success. Maria phoned him the next day.

'How funny to hear your voice on the phone,' she said, sounding a little more like her old self, 'you sound quite posh.'

She was phoning, as Aldous had hoped she would, to propose a meeting.

'I thought, why don't you take me to see those Rembrandts you're always talking about? You know how hopeless I am with art, perhaps you could show me how to appreciate them . . .'

So they arranged to meet, on Saturday, at the National Gallery.

She was waiting for him sitting at one of the benches in the entrance hall, among the mosaics and the fat pillars of veined marble, looking far more formal than she did at the class. She was wearing a black knee-length skirt, a pink blouse with a gold necklace, white tights, sensible office shoes. She could have been a secretary who'd snatched an hour from work, though Aldous knew she didn't work in an office. She had no work at the moment (Aldous had not found out how she subsisted), but she had been a secretary in her life, several times. Aldous passed over the unbecomingness of her clothes, the utter lack of colour sense they displayed, their failure to register a shred of artistic sensibility, and went straight to the woman, who exchanged cheek kisses with him, his far more firmly planted than hers.

'This place is an absolute maze,' she said, grappling with the fold-out map she'd been examining when he'd arrived. 'It's like trying to find your way through a small city, and there aren't even any street names . . .'

She had already had a look around and had been impressed by the vast Monet *Water-Lilies* – 'I felt as though I could jump right into it' – and had found the *Virgin of the Rocks*, 'only because I asked the way'. But the Rembrandts had been beyond her, occupying a region deep in the recesses of the gallery, so it seemed to her.

'They can be quite hard to find, if you don't know the way,' said Aldous, very happy to be in such a position of power – a guide through a labyrinth of images. To his utter delight, Maria took hold of his arm as he guided her, as though she really was in some alien, slightly dangerous place.

It was a long journey to the Rembrandts because they were distracted by many paintings on the way. *The Rokeby Venus*, *The Judgement of Paris* . . . Maria would suddenly grab Aldous's sleeve and ask him to explain some mythological scene, and Aldous was thrilled to find that he usually could. They paused at one of Aldous's favourite spots, where landscapes by Turner and Claude hung side by side, stipulated to do so in Turner's will, to prove that he was no mere imitator of the French master. *The Embarkation of the Queen of Sheba* and *The Decline of the Carthaginian Empire*, two magnificent seaport paintings. To Aldous's disappointment Maria preferred the Claude – 'Because it's clearer. You can see all the faces of the little people. On the other hand they all have the same face, which is a shame, but at least you can see them.'

'But don't you think Turner's is more full of a real sense of weather and what clouds and water actually look like?'

'Well, it all looks a bit scribbly to me – but oh,' she suddenly burst into laughter, peering closely at the Turner painting, 'he's done little children playing with boats – there down by the waterfront, while there are the great big boats sailing off, here are the little children – perhaps I like the Turner better after all.'

Maria disappointed him again in the Rembrandt room. She didn't like the gloominess of the paintings – his fondness for painting old people, dark interiors and cloudy days.

'Was Rembrandt a very unhappy man?'

'I think he got sadder as he got older. That's what the self-portraits seem to show. Though sadness is really too simple a word for it. Not sadness, but a mixture of things – fear, loneliness and the gradually dawning realisation that one is alone in the world and that in a fairly short time one will be dead and will never be allowed to see a beautiful woman or a sunny day again for eternity ever – for which there isn't a word, there should be.'

Aldous lingered over the portrait of Hendrickje Stoffels. If he had been looking for a living representation of Rembrandt's muse, he had failed completely in Maria. She was almost the exact opposite of the woman depicted in the painting – blonde where Hendrickje was dark; narrow, smiling-eyes where Hendrickje's were open and deep. Where Hendrickje was soft and cloudy, Maria was all sharp angles and dazzling colours.

'Don't you think it's amazing how a man of Rembrandt's age could paint a young woman with such tenderness – such sexual empathy?'

'Not if you'd met some of the old men I've met in my time.'

There was a hint of uncharacteristic smuttiness in Maria's remark that warned him that he should avoid letting her come into contact with Rembrandt's paintings in future. He steered her carefully out and found some Gainsboroughs, which delighted her.

'It's not your fault of course, Aldous,' she said as they returned to the bright air of Trafalgar Square, 'but I feel I understand no more about paintings now than I did before I went in.'

They watched a family feeding pigeons. Two parents and two golden-haired girls. As so often happened, what started out as a little bird-feeding comedy turned suddenly nasty as one of the girls became engulfed in pigeons: half a dozen lined up on her arms, two standing on her shoulders, four or more hanging off her hands, two jostling for position on her head, the girl frozen beneath, arms rigidly outstretched, her face red and wailing with genuine terror, the birds carrying on their scratching and flapping. The parents were unsure what to do, misreading their daughter's distress as excitement, while other tourists stood around, watching the spectacle but not doing anything to stop it, as if the ordeal was simply one of the rituals visitors to London had to undergo, whether they liked it or not.

When eventually the child was stripped of her bird costume

and escorted sobbingly away, Maria's sympathy was for the birds, not the girl.

'Those poor things got the fright of their life when that man shook them off. Such silliness – it's not as though they're dangerous, is it?'

'But the girl was only small – imagine what it must feel like to have what to her must have felt like a bunch of eagles crawling all over her ...'

Maria dismissed the scene and declared she was hungry.

'There's a Pizzaland in Cockspur Street. I've been told I should eat more ...'

Once or twice in his life Aldous had eaten a pizza. Colette had had a go at making them at some point, and as far as he could recall they turned out to be disappointingly dry, tough things of tomato paste and cheese criss-crossed by anchovies, horrendously salty, one of his wife's rare culinary failures.

But in Pizzaland neither Aldous nor Maria ate pizzas. Instead they went up to something which Maria called a salad bar, a little crock of plastic tubs, each brimming with some vivid thing: sweetcorn, beetroot, tomatoes – the whole spectrum of vegetable life seemed to be there. The fact that customers could help themselves to this assortment, and could take as much as they liked so long as it fitted into the ceramic bowl they paid for, was a delightful novelty to Aldous, for whom eating in restaurants at all was a very rare occurrence. In fact, apart from the FastBurger in Ostend, he could hardly recall the last time such an event took place. In their final years together, he and Colette had gone for pub lunches, when pub food was itself a novelty, but never to restaurants.

At the salad bar Aldous and Maria jostled politely with other customers, amused by the ingenuity these people were using to make the most of their allotted bowls – assembling volcanoes of celery and new potatoes down which the lava of thousand island dressing would run. Aldous and Maria were more restrained, Aldous more so than Maria, taking only a few tomatoes, some new potatoes, a hard-boiled egg and, on Maria's insistence, some spiced chicken wings, although Aldous doubted his teeth were up to those.

'This is a wonderful place,' said Aldous, marvelling at the

green carpets and mirrors, the mass-produced, low-budget luxury of the restaurant, all the pine and gold. 'How did you find it?'

'Have you never heard of Pizzaland before? There are dozens of these places all over London.'

'It's just so funny,' said Aldous, 'the way you pay for the crockery instead of the food. It's the sort of thing I've been waiting for all my life.'

'Are you sure you wouldn't like some pizza?'

'Absolutely – but you should have one. Go on, have a pizza –'

'No,' Maria laughed, 'I couldn't possibly think of eating a pizza –'

'Go on,' said Aldous again, enjoying this game of urging Maria to eat. 'Go on, have some pizza.' Then, suddenly fearing he'd overlooked some crucial piece of etiquette, he added, 'I'll pay for it . . .'

'It's not that,' Maria laughed again. 'I don't think my little tummy could contain it. Have you seen the size of them?'

They watched other tables where pizzas were being served – huge, thick, chunky monsters of bread and rubbery cheese that seemed almost to bounce off the plates.

'Though they do look absolutely delicious,' said Maria. 'But perhaps I'll just have some garlic bread.'

The phrase stopped Aldous in his tracks, and he was unable to respond to the suggestion other than with open-mouthed shock that such a concoction had even been thought of.

'Would you like some as well?' She added.

'No,' Aldous replied, firmly, decisively, trying to imagine what form the combination could take. When later the bread arrived, two angled slices of a French stick toasted and soaked in butter, he had to concede it looked rather nice. Perhaps Maria would even manage to change his opinion of garlic.

'There is something very sad about food, isn't there,' said Maria, as she tore off a piece of garlic bread with what to Aldous looked like unbecoming savagery, 'in that a meal must always come to an end. And once a meal is finished it can't happen again, not the same meal. It's very unlike reading a book or looking at paintings, isn't it? The book can always be reread, the paintings, like those ones in the gallery, you can look at those again and again, all your life, and they're the same paintings. But every meal is a unique experience that can't be repeated. I've had meals where I've felt nearly in tears towards the end because it's felt like an idyllic part of my life is about to pass away, when I want it to go on for ever.'

'I can't say I've ever felt that way about food,' said Aldous, frustrated that he wasn't able to agree with Maria, 'I've rarely had a meal that I would want to go on for ever.' Then, inspired, he added, 'Until now, that is.'

Maria gave him a brief smile,

'I don't think your salad could be made to last very long. It's a very sad salad, Aldous. You should eat more – yet you don't look undernourished at all . . .'

'I suppose we could extrapolate from your theory,' said Aldous with mock seriousness, wanting to make the subject, like the meals it referred to, last as long as possible, 'that puddings should be the saddest food of all.'

'Yes, and I suppose the very existence of puddings supports my theory. Why should you want a lot of sweet food at the end of a meal? It must be to counterbalance the sadness of the meal ending, to take away the pain of the meal being over.'

'You've really thought this through, haven't you? Why should you spend so much time thinking about food?'

'I told you, my doctor's said I'm not eating enough. But it is something I have always felt. Meals are like life itself, aren't they, really? They're a little story, in stages: the delicate infancy of the starter, the grand sprawling extravagance of middle age for the main course, and then the senility of puddings for old age. Then it's all over . . .'

'Rather like the seven ages of man,' said Aldous, wondering if Maria would understand the reference, 'sans teeth, sans eyes, sans pudding . . .'

She didn't.

'But you're still on the main course of life, Maria. You don't have to worry. It's me that should be worrying. I'm on to the last spoonful of trifle, nearly. Although, a few months ago, I thought I'd polished off the whole lot, that I'd licked the bowl clean . . .'

149

Aldous paused when he realised that Maria was crying. It was hardly perceptible as such, and she showed barely any sign that she even realised herself that she was weeping, except when she plucked a tissue from her sleeve and dabbed at the rapidly falling moisture.

'I'm sorry, I didn't mean to . . .' Aldous felt suddenly angry with himself for drawing attention to his age, and for talking about death, and the gulf of time that separated them.

'It's nothing, Aldous. I'm one of those stupid people who cry at the drop of a hat. Look,' she pushed her empty salad bowl away and leaned towards Aldous as if she was about to impart a secret, 'there is a very stripy building somewhere in London, I pass it whenever I get the bus from Victoria and it's the most astonishing thing – it has this tall tower, stripy all the way to the top, it's like something out of the *Arabian Nights* yet it's surrounded by ugly office blocks. I've always wanted to go and see it properly, but I can never seem to find it when I'm actually looking for it. You know London so well, Aldous, I'm sure you must know where I mean. Could you help me find it?'

Aldous realised she must have meant Westminster Cathedral. After they had finished at Pizzaland, Aldous offered to walk her there.

Walking along the street with Maria could be an adventure. She got very cross with the busy, bullying London traffic, and even hit a passing white van with the handle of her umbrella because she thought it had jumped a red light. 'When that little green man comes on it means it's safe to cross. That's what it means, so that van should have stopped . . .' She could get angry, very angry, about trivial things like vans, while the big issues of politics and life seemed a matter of indifference to her. 'Who is this Henry Mandela person they keep singing about?' she would say as they slalomed between protesters outside the South African Embassy, or, on seeing collectors for the families of mineworkers still on strike, 'You'd think they'd be glad the mines were closing down, it must be an awful job.'

All the way along Victoria Street, Maria was convinced they were going the wrong way.

'I may have no sense of direction at all, Aldous, but I'm

sure we are nowhere near this building we're looking for . . .'
Then the building almost seemed to jump out at them, perfectly
concealed, crouching like a monstrous tabby cat between the
towering glass blocks either side of it.

'Here we are,' said Aldous, proudly displaying the building
as though it was his own personal treasure.

Maria exclaimed with delight, squealing almost, and hugged
Aldous.

'I was beginning to think it was some weird fantasy of mine,
that there was this little fairy-tale building hidden in London.
It is like a fairy-tale palace, isn't it? Oh, it must be hundreds
of years old – why isn't it one of the most famous buildings
in London? It's much prettier than Westminster Abbey, or St
Paul's and yet it's completely forgotten about. Aldous, you're
an artist, you agree with me that this is the prettiest building
in London?'

'Absolutely . . .'

'And how many hundreds of years old, is it?'

Aldous was about to humour Maria by saying the building
was at least a thousand years old, but suddenly felt compelled
to speak the truth.

'In fact it's less than one.'

'What? It can't be. Don't be silly, Aldous.'

'I think it was begun after the turn of the century, which
makes it about eighty years old. They're still finishing off the
interior decoration.'

The anger crept back into Maria's tone of voice, but only
slightly, as she berated the dishonesty of the building – 'And
for a religious building after all . . . You'd expect a religious
building to be honest, but this cathedral is actually telling a
lie . . .' Then, with a lingering sigh, she added, 'Like me . . .'

'What do you mean like you?'

'Aldous, I need to tell you something about myself . . .' She
sat down on one of the benches by the brick-surrounded flower
beds, beckoning for Aldous to sit beside her. 'I'm really quite
ill.'

'No you're not,' said Aldous, as though they were playing
a game.

'No, really I am. You may think I don't look ill, and I hope

I don't, although if you'd seen me before I became ill you might notice a difference – I wasn't always this slender and pale, you know . . .'

'But what sort of illness?' said Aldous, suddenly taking the matter seriously. Maria's reply was very abrupt.

'Cancer,' she said.

Aldous couldn't say anything. Maria went on.

'I don't really want to tell you any more about it, not at the moment anyway. It's gone away for the time being. I had a lot of surgery and chemotherapy last year, and although the cancer has gone it has left me feeling very weak and delicate. If it comes back, which I pray that it will not, I don't think I could go through that same treatment again. So I will trust to nature and let nature take its course, and I will try alternative therapies and . . .' Here she looked over her shoulder at the cathedral. 'I've never been a religious person, and it seems to be a bit opportunistic of me to think of enlisting God's help, but it has made me very curious of religion and what it all means . . .'

Aldous looked at the cathedral as well. He realised, as he did so, that he had never looked at a cathedral in quite the same way before.

'My parents were both atheists,' she went on, 'and in some ways I now find that as puzzling as if they had been religious. It seems as strange to not believe in God as it does to believe. That's how I feel. Even more strange was the fact that my parents had given so little thought to the subject. My father's line was, 'It's a funny old thing, religion – you either believe it or you don't.'

Maria quoted her father in what Aldous presumed was a parody of his voice – deep, gruff, military.

Aldous, as though trying to snap them both out of something, said, 'Don't be ridiculous, Maria – you're not ill. Look at you – you're radiant, the most healthy person I've ever seen.'

'Thank you, but as I said, if you'd seen me before, you might think differently. Anyway, I'm telling you this because I value your friendship, more than I can tell you, and I believe it is the best thing if I am honest with you from the beginning . . .'

Aldous liked that word 'beginning', implying, as it did, the long narrative of their future friendship to follow. When he saw her off on the bus a little while later, after a hug and another kiss on the cheek, he felt, despite Maria's disturbing revelations, that their relationship was even more assured of a long continuance. He had a vision of it stretching before him like a long red path to the horizon. He dismissed the cancer as a chimera, a little moth that had blundered into her anatomy and that had now been shepherded back to the open window and the night to which it belonged. It might flutter anxiously against the glass, but it would not come in again. Of that Aldous felt quite certain.

On his way home Aldous bought an *Evening Standard*. And before he went to bed he wrote across its top:

Met Maria, National Gallery, Pizzaland, Westminster Cathedral.

17

It happened with frightening suddenness, much sooner than he expected. Two men standing on the doorstep, one a surveyor from the council, the other a local builder.

'I only put the forms in a couple of weeks ago,' said Aldous, 'I wasn't expecting you so soon.'

The surveyor gave a friendly nod, as if to say such promptness was all part of the service, though the builder, who turned out to be freer with information, nudged Aldous a little while later and told him, 'They're panicking about being under-budget. If they don't spend it all by November they'll get less for next year.' He winked, as if it was all a devious little game. 'Nice houses these,' he went on, 'we done three in this road already, done four in the next one, ten on Hoopers Lane.'

Aldous had noticed the scaffolding. Ever since Cliff had told him about the home-improvement grants he had become aware of an almost constant operation of renewal that was taking place piecemeal around the suburbs of London. Houses cropped of their roof tiles, their windows yanked out leaving bare, gaping holes. The coming and going of flatbed trucks and rusty yellow skips in which rose soufflés of bricks and window frames. Once, walking along Hoopers Lane, Aldous was woken from daydreams by the crash of roof tiles landing in the skip he was just passing. He felt the rush of air from the plummeting masonry against the side of his head. It was as though he'd just missed being struck by a meteor. The rooftop builders had hollered jovial apologies, trying to disguise the shock they felt at their own carelessness.

The restored houses stood out from their neighbours: ceramic roof tiles where the rest of the street's were slate, sparkling plastic window frames, pebble-dash and repointing. Aldous often noticed how these houses went in pairs, or threes, a little group of competitive neighbours not wanting to be outdone by each other. By such logic this plague of rejuvenation should spread to all the houses in the city.

It had been pressure from Juliette that had set his own renovation project in motion. It turned out she knew all about the home-improvement grants and had sorted out the paper work for him, Aldous merely signing the application forms. Even so he felt rather proud of the fact that these two inspectors had now called, as though it had been all his own work bringing them here. The two presented an almost comic contrast of types: the surveyor in his dark grey suit and tie, sensible moustache, clipboard in one hand, attaché case in the other, walking smartly and briskly about the place; the builder with his carefree stubble and sunburnt neck, check shirt straining to contain a pot belly, plaster-dusted jeans and paint-splattered trainers, shuffling and slouching through the house.

They were mostly interested in the outside of the house and wanted the view from the back. This meant guiding them through the kitchen and into the garden. The surveyor was respectfully silent as they passed through the dishevelled landscape of the house, though the builder seemed to be chuckling quietly to himself. 'Nice job,' he said, whenever they passed a painting, pausing for a second at the waterfall in the hall, and later at one of the busts of Ophelia. 'Nice job.'

Having strangers in the house made Aldous acutely aware of the state of his dwelling space. They were so out of place they could, in their ordinary clothes, have been strolling across the surface of the moon. Yet it was their task to understand the house, to explain it to Aldous. In spite of this Aldous soon found himself explaining the house to them, or to the builder at least, who was looking at Aldous's lotus vase.

'Never seen one of these,' he said. 'Where did you get it?'

'I made it actually,' said Aldous.

The builder showed an artisan's interest as Aldous explained the construction of the piece, the surveyor looking on good-humouredly, though clearly anxious to get down to the serious business of inspecting and recording. Aldous was pleased with the little mess of artistic paraphernalia that occupied the far end of the kitchen by the cooker – the jumble of soaked rags and squeezed-out tubes of oil paint, splodgy palettes and worked-on canvases, the latest bearing the construction marks of his 'Summer' painting, though that season was already fading, and he hadn't even got his canvas ready for Autumn. These things were lost to the visitors, however, who failed to notice them among the more familiar domestic junk of the kitchen.

In fact, the house was tidier than it had been for a long time, still bearing the traces of order that Aldous had managed to restore for Maria's first visit. He had spent a whole morning cleaning, frantically stowing dirty clothes and five-year-old newspapers, then riding the wild beast of the Electrolux all around the house as it gave its one long shocked intake of breath. Strangely, Maria, even in her twinkly finery, hadn't seemed out of place in the house, and she, for her part, had not seemed at all surprised by the house's odd juxtapositions. Aldous had wondered if this simply reflected her lack of observational interest. The only thing she seemed to notice were the Flemish labels that still adhered to odd things around the house. 'Oh, how sweet, look, Aldous has put *opgang* on his stairs, and – oh, how funny, he's put *vanvell* on the door. So that he will remember.'

She had come with two of her friends, the same age as her but seeming much older, and dressed eccentrically in rainbow woollens and floppy berets. Aldous was going to give them all an art lesson. In the front room he'd set up an arrangement for them to draw – a stepladder rigged with boards and tins of paint – representing certain aspects of linear perspective. He told them about vanishing points and how to construct lines that receded towards them. The paint cans illustrated the problems of ellipses. 'The closer to eye level, the narrower the ellipse. A circle viewed at eye level becomes a line.' He showed them how to draw an ellipse by imagining it as a circle drawn within a square. It was easy to draw the square in perspective, then it was simply a matter of fitting the circle inside. He was a little shocked by how difficult they found it, particularly Maria, who almost seemed determined to prove her earlier statements, repeated frequently, 'I have no artistic talent whatsoever. I am an utterly uncreative person.' He had to conclude that, in art at least, this was true. The simple geometries of

Aldous's stepladder set-up were beyond her. She simply didn't seem to know where to start. If Aldous put in a few marks to help her, she didn't know how to go on. She held her pencil as though it was the lever on an incomprehensible and dangerous machine. But the whole experience was a cause of great entertainment nonetheless. She seemed superbly happy, as did her friends, though they were hardly any more adept at drawing. In the end all three put down their paper and watched instead as Aldous did his drawing, gasping with delight as the picture formed.

'It's incredible, Aldous,' said Maria, 'you can look at something and then draw it, and the drawing is exactly the same as the thing you're looking at.'

'If I could draw like that I'd be happy,' said the friend, who seemed quite happy anyway.

'Yes,' said Maria, 'I really don't understand why artists get depressed. They should be the happiest people of all. Unless they keep making mistakes – like that painter Cézanne. He must have got dreadfully depressed when he couldn't get those shapes right . . .' (Aside to her friends:) 'Aldous takes me to the galleries, like I told you, and tries to help me with the pictures, but I just can't understand the Cézannes (I can't understand most of the paintings), but Cézanne just seems to get it wrong all the time – he'll draw a table all wonky, or the rim of a bowl all out of shape. Sometimes I think it must just be my eyes. But you, Aldous, you're such a better artist than Cézanne – you can get it exactly right. And if you're feeling a bit gloomy all you have to do is to do a drawing and it must make you feel wonderful.'

The students turned to him waiting for him to confirm or deny this theory.

'The problem is,' he said, after some careful thought, 'if you're feeling gloomy, the drawing is more likely to go wrong. Maybe you have to feel good to start with.'

The three of them made sounds of cottoning on, as though Aldous had supplied the answer to an exasperating riddle.

'Isn't he wonderful?' Maria said, 'I told you, he's got all the answers. And you can talk to him about absolutely anything – music, painting, philosophy, Shakespeare . . .'

'Do you know about engineering?' said one of the friends, eagerly.

'No,' said Aldous flatly.

'Oh,' said the friend, and looked at Maria reproachfully.

That afternoon at Fernlight Avenue had been an exquisite climax to a long, strange and happy summer of encounters with Maria. It seemed that once she had told Aldous about her illness (in which he still didn't quite believe), the air had been cleared and she felt happy to spend time with him. Though it was always at Maria's initiative. He had to wait for her to phone, as she would not give him her phone number. If he asked she would produce varying excuses – that she couldn't remember it, that she was in the process of getting it changed, that she was plagued by nuisance phone calls and didn't answer the phone, that her ex-boyfriend (the one in Belgium) was causing problems on the phone. She even told him there would be no point in his having her phone number, as she never answered the phone anyway, 'I absolutely loathe the things.' Eventually Aldous gave up asking.

It meant some periods of despair for Aldous, if Maria didn't phone. Though for a while at the height of summer she seemed to phone nearly every day, and they would meet at least once or twice a week. It had become a routine for them to begin and end their meetings outside Westminster Cathedral, some-times with a visit to the nearby Pizzaland in Victoria Street.

One day, as they were sitting outside the cathedral, Maria said to him, 'Can you show me what you're supposed to do in a church?'

'What do you mean?'

'Well, you know – whatever people do in a church – not just praying, but all those other things . . .'

So Aldous gave her instruction in the various rites and ceremonies of the Catholic Church, as far as he understood them.

'To pray, you have to begin by making the sign of the cross.'

'Why?'

'Well, it's a bit like dialling a phone number . . .'

'God's phone number?'

'Yes.'

'If you're not actually a Catholic, are you allowed to make the sign of the cross?'

'I don't think God would have any objection.'

He showed her how to genuflect, what to do with the stoop of holy water by the door. Maria was particularly fascinated by the votive candles, an iron grid set with little dish-like holders, each with a spike to take a candle, the whole thing oozing with melted wax. There were candles of every age, from the fresh, just-lit, almost entire candles down to those that were giving their last in a little puddle of transparent wax. It was like a burning bush.

'They're so pretty. What are they for?'

'Well, you light a candle, make a donation, and you can dedicate the candle to anything you want – usually to the memory of the dear departed – that's how I've always understood it anyway.'

'How sweet. It almost makes me wish I knew someone who was dead. You should light one, Aldous, for all those people who've died you've told me about.'

'There aren't enough candles,' said Aldous, rummaging in the dispenser, then, seeing the look of sadness on Maria's face, 'I'm only joking. I'll just light one . . .' He took a candle and dipped its white wick into the flame of another, set it on the little thorn of a holder. Maria watched him do this with something like awe, as though she was witnessing a miracle. As Aldous stood silently watching the little flame establish itself, she leaned towards him and whispered urgently, 'What are you doing now? Are you praying?'

Aldous nodded slowly, though he wasn't really sure if that was actually what he was doing.

'Am I allowed, do you think?' she whispered again.

Again Aldous nodded, and Maria took a candle and nervously lit it, almost burning herself in the process. Aldous watched her, her face lit from below by the quaking lights, and decided that he was praying after all.

'It's a bit like a wishing well, isn't it?' she said when they were outside.

And from then on, the lighting of candles in Westminster Cathedral was added to their routine.

As Aldous led the surveyor and the builder through to the garden he was conscious that he hadn't ventured beyond the small area of cracked concrete by the back door for a long time. The leaves were already beginning to turn. They stooped to pass through the tunnel formed by the Warwickshire drooper and the Ellison's Orange, then had to wade through the waist-high scrub that used to be the lawn, itself in danger of becoming a forest as the spindly sucker shoots of the plum and the poplar grew taller each year.

The surveyor had a small pair of binoculars which he drew out of his attaché case to inspect the roof and chimneys with.

'I think we can put the roof down for complete replacement of tiles. Three chimneys – do you have any open fires?'

'No.'

'In that case I suggest removing the chimneys altogether – one of them is quite badly cracked near the parapet.'

They walked back to the house. The surveyor and the builder inspected the brickwork of the back wall closely, conferring like connoisseurs over an ancient cheese, the surveyor probing the mortar with a pen. They seemed not to notice the sets of initials and other graffiti the children had carved into the wall by the back door. James had incised his with such deep under-cutting it looked like lettering for a Victorian tombstone. Two feet underneath, the shallow scratchings of seven-year-old Julian's efforts presented a poignant contrast.

'I would recommend pebble-dashing for the back of the property,' said the surveyor, almost apologetically. 'A lot of the brickwork is eroded here, and pebble-dashing would provide a great deal of protection.'

'OK,' said Aldous, absently. He was hardly thinking about the pebble-dashing, but pondering instead the surveyor's use of the word 'property' to describe the house, and wondering why he detested it so much. He decided, a while later, that it was because the word didn't describe the thing itself (the house) at all, but merely an abstract notion of ownership in relation to it. Why couldn't they call it a house, or a building? They were men of material things, men who made and built and measured, talking about a house as though it had no phys-ical existence.

It was an odd thing, but the last time Aldous had spoken to anyone at his bank, they had talked about 'financial products', as though the bank was a little workshop that made things. It was as though the abstract world of banking, which makes nothing, was trying to acquire the same qualities of physical durability that the building trade seemed anxious to lose.

Aldous said he didn't really mind what they did to the house. The builder and the surveyor looked rather bewildered by this. They were used to clients being very specific about what they wanted done to their homes. Aldous's indifference was a cause for embarrassment.

'Should add a few bob to the value,' said the builder, as they neared completion of their tour, having just poked pens into the spongy wood of all the window frames. 'As they say, every quid spent on a property adds five quid to the value, or thereabouts. Probably more in an area like this. I was going to buy a property in one of these roads once. Wish I had now, I'd have made what . . . ?' Here the builder paused to count up in his head the percentage profit he'd missed out on, but never seemed to finish the calculation. Instead the surveyor filled in.

'I'll expect you'll be wanting to sell soon, Mr Jones. In view of which, these proposed improvements will be a very wise investment. It is a very good time to take advantage of these grants.'

'Yeah – otherwise you'll have to remortgage the place,' the builder laughed. 'That's a funny thing, isn't it? Happened to a friend of a friend. He remortgaged the house so he could get the house done up. When he couldn't keep up the payments, the mortgage company took the house off him. Poor bloke. He said it was like the house had eaten itself. I know what he means. Still, my mum's just bought her council house. That's an even funnier thing, isn't it? What's that all about?'

The builder turned to the surveyor, as though he was solely responsible for council-house sales. The surveyor gave the ambivalent shrug of someone reluctant to take political sides. The builder went on:

'She's over the moon about it though. I can't understand it. Just a load of expense with the upkeep, and who's going to want to buy it off her when she comes to sell? If you've got the money to buy a place, you're not going to buy one on a grotty council estate, are you? I told her, in five years' time that old house won't be worth bugger all. It'll be a millstone round her neck, and there's one less house for poor people to rent. What does she care – all she wants is the right to choose the colour of her front door. People get funny about it, don't they, houses?'

'Yes, well, thank you, Mr Jones . . .' The surveyor spoke with the embarrassment of someone trying to excuse an eccentric elderly relative.

'I expect the kids have got their eye on this place, eh?' the builder continued as he was ushered by the surveyor towards the front door. 'That's another reason to sell up before it's too late. You know what'll happen. They'll shove you in a home and have to sell the house to pay for it. If you sell up now and give the kids their share, the state picks up the tab for your old folks' home. That's the way with this society – if you're at the top you're OK, if you're at the bottom you're OK, but if you're in the middle, you get hammered for every penny you've got . . .'

When the builder and surveyor left, Aldous felt a curious need to revisit all the places where they'd poked with their pencils and pens, to examine minutely the holes they'd made in the windows frames, the little patches of bright mortar they'd uncovered between the bricks of the back wall. They'd done damage to his house, in a little way, and their damage fascinated him. Soon they would do even more damage: strip the house down to a frightening degree, scalp it, deglaze it, holler about the place, bring mud in on their muddy boots. And he would endure it all because he would be doing something sensible. Securing the fabric of his 'property', increasing its value.

One room the builders hadn't visited was the front room, where Aldous went shortly afterwards. What would they have thought if they'd seen it? Almost certainly they'd have thought, 'Hello, doing a bit of decorating, are we?' The stepladder still life was still there, an impromptu sculpture. Would they have taken in the oddness of the arrangement, however – would they have noticed that, though a stepladder and paints were present, no decorating had been done, that the paint tins were empty or dried up, that the stepladder also supported plants and a vase. Because this was also a trace, of Maria's visit to the house. This was why Aldous had felt reluctant to dismantle it, even though it made watching the television difficult. Like a landing craft, it had settled right in the middle of his life.

What was more, the stack of *Evening Standard*s was starting to build up. A pleasing heap of newsprint, the front page of each bearing a brief inscription:

With Maria to Kew Gardens — lovely day
Maria, Pizzaland, the Courtauld Institute
Maria, John Soanes, Pizzaland
Greenwich, the Observatory. Maria let me hold her hand.

18

'I hope you're right when you said she'll eat anything,' Juliette
muttered warningly as she opened the door for her father. 'I've
spent hours on this osso bucco.'

'Osso bucco? Is that meat?'

'Yes. Knuckle of veal. It's braised veal marrowbones,
basically. If you're a vegetarian it's probably the cruellest you
can get without actually eating the animal alive. But I don't have
to worry about Maria because she's not a vegetarian. Right?'

'Well, I don't think so. But then I don't think I've ever
actually seen her eat a piece of meat. She always goes for leaves
and things like that. Green stuff.'

Juliette looked suspiciously at her father as he settled himself
in the armchair that he always liked to sit in because it had
flat arms on which he could rest his drink. Drinking was accept-
able on Sunday afternoons at Juliette and Bernard's flat, even
encouraged, as long as it was negotiated through the hosts
themselves. As long as they dispensed and provided, then Aldous
could drink as much as he pleased. It was before he properly
understood this convention that he once got into trouble for
taking a swig from a quarter-bottle of whisky he had in his
coat pocket. Juliette came into the kitchen just as Aldous was
putting the bottle to his lips, and a row ensued that soured the
whole afternoon, and ended with Aldous ceremoniously
pouring his own whisky down the sink, under Juliette and
Bernard's stern supervision.

Aldous could never quite square their disapproval of his private
drinking with their acceptance of his social drinking. Nor could
he quite understand the varied and extensive drinks cabinet that
had grown in their kitchen; an arrangement of shelves behind

glass, filled with exotic wines and spirits, mostly gifts from their foreign-holidaying friends, Christmas presents from the editor of the *Evening News*, bottles of schnapps, sour mash whiskeys with quaint Wild West labels, Moët & Chandon champagnes and many others Aldous couldn't identify. The most puzzling thing about this display, however, was that most of the bottles still contained drink, indeed many were full, unopened. Occasionally, towards the end of the evening, Bernard might open the glass doors and reach up for a bottle, pouring out a minuscule measure of an exotic spirit, as though the stuff was foul-tasting medicine and he didn't want Aldous to suffer unnecessarily. In reality Aldous was silently pleading for his glass to be refilled as soon as he'd knocked it back, but by then the bottle was safely back in the cabinet, on a high shelf. In this way, the bottles lasted for months, years even, a place where alcohol could be at rest. So different from the bottles in Aldous's house, which had their throats ripped out and their contents drained in a matter of hours, their carcasses carefully hidden beneath cushions or covertly wrapped and tipped into the bin. But a never-ending procession of carcasses nonetheless. At least, so it had been. Aldous was drinking less now.

'I still think it's a bit odd that she's making her own way here. It's a long way for her to come on her own, and it's nearly dark. Are you sure she knows how to get here?'

'Of course she knows. She's very independent. And she's very funny . . .'

'Really,' said Juliette, with flat irony. She may as well have said, 'I'll believe that when I see it.' Aldous missed this deprecating tone in her voice. Like he missed the glances Juliette and Bernard gave each other whenever he mentioned Maria's name, the eyes-to-heaven looks, the sad shaking of heads. Nor had he noticed the strained tones of polite acceptance when, a couple of weeks before, he'd suggested bringing Maria over for Sunday afternoon.

'I'd love you to meet her, and she's dying to meet you. You'll really like her.'

It was the presumptiveness of her father's tone that most annoyed Juliette. The fact that Aldous spent so much time bragging about her. She even warned him, on one occasion, 'You can build someone up too much, you know . . .'

'What do you mean?'

'I mean you can build someone up so much that they're almost bound to be a disappointment. They can never live up to expectations.'

Aldous had shrugged off this idea without really considering it. That may be true for mere mortals, he seemed to be thinking, but for true angels, different rules apply.

Then, when the bell rang that Sunday, he made downstairs to answer the door. Juliette pushed passed him.

'What are you doing?'

'I'm going to let Maria in.'

'It's my flat, don't you think I should let her in?'

'But she won't know who you are.'

'I think I might be able to explain.'

'And you won't know who she is, you've never seen her.'

'Just go back upstairs. I'll answer the door. Go and sit down and wait . . .'

There was almost a tussle on the stairs as Juliette persuaded her father to retreat, the bell sounding again, which made Aldous panic even more, worrying that if the door wasn't answered immediately Maria might think she'd got the wrong address and wander off.

Then, when Maria emerged into the living space from the stairwell, Aldous was all over her again, exchanging with her the now customary, and to Juliette totally out of character, cheek kisses (she couldn't remember him exchanging such familiarities even with her mother), and generally acting host, shouldering his daughter out of the way to take Maria's coat, explaining the flat to her ('the toilet's up these little stairs here, it's a bit awkward . . .'), and generally talking over and around his daughter and her partner, as though they were mere auxiliaries in some inordinately intimate hotel. It was Maria who had to initiate introductions.

'You must be Juliette. I've heard lots about you –'

'No you haven't,' said Aldous, shocked at what he saw as a rare lie from Maria, 'I've hardly told you anything about her.'

'That's not really true, Aldous, is it?' Maria laughed, hanging on to Juliette's hand after she had shaken it. 'He's always telling me about you. You're a teacher, aren't you?'

'Journalist.'

'Journalist. Well, I knew it was something to do with words. I'm sure your father said you were an English teacher.'

'Come and look at the view from the window,' said Aldous, as though suddenly unspeakably bored of the conversation, taking Maria by the elbow.

'Would you like a drink?' said Juliette.

'She doesn't drink alcohol,' said Aldous, calling backwards as he pulled Maria towards the window.

'I would love some mineral water, Juliette. Now what is it you want to show me, Aldous? Yes, it's a very nice view – a road and some cars. And trees. Very Londonish, isn't it? Is that a word? Londonish?'

'Look at the parking meters,' said Aldous.

'What about them?'

'Aren't they funny?'

'It depends what you mean by funny. I think they're quite sad things really. Little pointless stumps that everybody hates. Juliette – ah thank you – why does your father find parking meters so funny?'

She took the glass of mineral water Juliette had just delivered. 'Does he?'

'Oh for God's sake,' said Aldous, impatiently, 'how many times have we sat here laughing at the parking meters?'

'Oh, you mean the things people get up to with them. He means the way they kick and punch them, and shake them, when they've swallowed their change or when they've come back to find a penalty on the windscreen. It can be quite entertaining.'

'Actually I didn't mean that at all,' said Aldous, slightly sulky. 'It just struck me that parking meters are very funny things to have outside your house.'

'Oh poor you,' said Maria turning to Juliette with sudden realisation. 'Do you have to pay the meter to park outside your own house, I mean flat?'

'We've got a residents' permit,' said Juliette. Then, wanting to get off such a trivial subject, she said, 'And where do you live Maria, south London, isn't it?'

'Yes, go on, Maria,' said Aldous, 'tell them about where you live. Listen to this, Juliette, it's really funny.'

Maria sat down on the arm of an armchair, adopting her little girl on her best behaviour pose (knees together, back straight and a bright twinkly grin on her face), and performed a well-worn monologue on the subject of her locale.

'I live about a mile past Brixton (thank goodness!) in a road called (you won't believe this) – Asylum Lane. Though the asylum has long since been knocked down, we think most of the lunatics are still there.' Here she paused for laughter which didn't come, to Aldous's visible annoyance . . .

'Did you hear that?' he said, 'She lives in a road called Asylum Lane – she really does.' He laughed. 'And most of the lunatics . . .' He couldn't continue for laughing.

'Yes, that's right,' said Maria. 'Well, my flat mate Jocasta (she makes people out of cushions) says that when anyone comes to visit us, we should call them Asylum Seekers, and if any canvassers call when there's an election, we should claim Political Asylum.'

'How handy to live in a road with a funny name,' said Bernard solemnly. 'Must save you a lot of time on jokes.'

Things settled down a bit during dinner. Juliette was not entirely convinced by Maria's apparent delight at the main course's arrival, and she observed that very little of Maria's portion was eaten. On the other hand, if she was a vegetarian she was very good at disguising the fact. But then she didn't seem the sort of vegetarian who would want to. Her talking was incessant and wearying for everyone except Aldous, who seemed to take pleasure in everything Maria said. Yet her chat was so full of well-intentioned observations, harmless anecdotes and naked self-deprecation that it was hard to find it objectionable. Juliette was almost more irritated by her father, who seemed intent on trying to draw Maria into private exchanges incomprehensible to outsiders. At least Maria was endeavouring to be inclusive in her monologues.

'Your father has struggled gallantly to make me understand art, Juliette, but I'm afraid he's had to concede defeat, as many have before him. My life is strewn with the corpses of people who've tried to educate me in one way or another. We're on to Shakespeare now, and I'm finding that an awful struggle as well –'

'Come on now, Maria,' said Aldous, 'you're doing much better than you realise, you enjoyed *A Midsummer Night's Dream*, didn't you?'

'Well, yes I did, but I wasn't sure that I was enjoying it in the proper way.'

'What do you mean "the proper way"?' said Aldous.

'I mean the way everyone else was enjoying it. I'm sure they were finding all sorts of pleasure in the words, but I was enjoying the actors' faces, and their voices, and the scenery and props. The language is very beautiful, but it just washes over me, like music, and then there will be laughter at something I don't understand . . .'

'Don't worry about that,' said Aldous, 'there are always people in the audience of every Shakespeare play who make it their business to laugh loudly and knowingly at long-forgotten Elizabethan puns. They're usually English teachers trying to show off to their A-level students –'

'I'm sorry, Aldous, but you were doing it too. Not as loudly as that wheezy man behind us, but you were still laughing. I know you weren't doing it to show off your knowledge, so there must have been something funny I was missing. No, you don't have to explain, Aldous. I'm not hurt at all, as I say – my life is strewn . . . Juliette, I've asked Aldous to try me with opera next. They sing in another language so it doesn't matter if you don't understand the words. So I might get on with opera. Though if we fail with that I don't know what we'll do. We're running out of art forms.'

Aldous and Maria tittered together and shoved each other, something they did frequently, to the greater annoyance of Juliette.

Maria became quieter when the quiz got going, and Juliette did feel a little sorry for her. At first she had fallen into the trap of believing the quiz to be a spontaneous, unstructured thing, a piece of childish fun which she herself could take control of and organise.

'A quiz? OK, I'll be question master. Silence. I'm the question master. OK, where's a question, here we are . . .' thumbing through the big encyclopedia. 'What is the capital of Afghanistan?'

After a slightly tense pause Bernard asked, in a quiet voice, 'Are you asking all of us or is this an individual round?'

'No, come on now, I'll only take the first answer.' Maria was enjoying her quiz-master role, for which she had adopted the style of a brisk, stern headmistress.

'We've done the As already, Maria,' said Juliette, apologetically. 'We all know that it's Kabul –'

'Kabul is the correct answer, Juliette has one point . . .' Maria was closing her eyes and holding up a finger to assuage further protests. She still hadn't understood.

'We usually start with a series of individual rounds, followed by an open round,' said Bernard, 'and it's usually two points for a correct answer. One point for a partially correct answer (at the discretion of the question master at the time). The question master's role rotates every twenty questions, and we start from the bookmark so that we don't duplicate questions –'

'Well, that may have been the way you've done it before, but I'm question master now, so there.' She poked her tongue at Bernard, to Aldous's glee, but even this level of defiance was useless against the well-established, solid routines of Juliette and Bernard's quizzes. In the end she had to concede defeat and submit to the rules. It soon became clear that her eagerness to be question master came from a desire to avoid answering questions. Maria's ignorance was exposed in the first few rounds, when she failed to answer what the others regarded as easy questions. 'Who wrote *Madam Butterfly*? Ask me in a few weeks and I'll probably know. The author of *Eugene Onegin*? Is that a novel? Aldous, can't you just whisper it to me?'

It wasn't Maria's failure to answer the questions that caused embarrassment among the others, it was the fact that they were shocked by her lack of general knowledge. Suddenly they all felt like hideous snobs who'd taken their own education and cultural refinement for granted. When they laughed they became worried that Maria might think they were laughing at her. Although she had jokingly shrugged off her ineptitude at the beginning, after several rounds with no points she was finding it harder and harder to maintain her composure. Finally, having suggested that Titus Oates was the founder of the Quakers, she gave up attempting answers at all. Then she became very attentive to her eyes. Dabbing at them carefully, examining them closely in a compact mirror, as though trying to extricate a speck of dust.

After a while Aldous began deliberately to answer questions wrongly, or to claim he didn't know the answer at all. It was a generous move on his part, one that would not have occurred to the others, least of all Bernard, for whom the deliberate losing of a quiz was an incomprehensible and pointless sacrifice. It was this attitude that caused him unconsciously to draw attention to the harmless subterfuge – 'Come on, Aldous, you must know the answer to that! What's got into you all of a sudden, have you had a stroke or something?'

Maria cottoned on after this, and made light of it.

'You don't have to come out in some sort of solidarity of stupidness, Aldous . . .' she said. But Aldous was keen to demonstrate that he was above all that sort of competitiveness. Quizzes were for people who had no other means of displaying their knowledge. The inverse logic was that only the truly wise could afford to get questions wrong. So from then on he gave the most ridiculous and absurd answers he could think of.

'Who discovered radium?'

'Fanny Craddock.'

And the atmosphere was considerably lightened. Maria had been rescued from the quicksands of her ignorance, and it seemed somehow that Aldous had won the quiz by default.

It was not enough to keep Maria, however, and she declared soon after this that it was time for her to leave.

'If I don't get home before ten o'clock my eyes start to dry up.'

Aldous managed to persuade her to accept a lift from Juliette. Maria was very reluctant at first, as if fearing the lift would take her all the way home, and so encourage an intrusion into her private space. She insisted on being taken only as far as Victoria, where she could catch the Tube.

Juliette was quite happy to do this, but became infuriated when her father decided to sit in the back of the car with Maria, leaving Juliette alone in the front, as though the car was a minicab.

She tried joking ways of expressing her annoyance, talking in exaggerated minicab driverese – 'Where to, guv? Don't forget to leave a tip,' and such like – a tactic lost on Aldous, who was busy in some private conversation with Maria.

But Maria seemed slightly irked by Aldous's relegation of his daughter to a menial role, and tried her best to include her in conversation, calling from the back of the car, 'You know, Juliette, when I said your father had failed to educate me about art, it's not quite true. I can appreciate his own paintings without any help at all. Your father is a very fine artist.'

Juliette mumbled a reluctant agreement.

'I have told him that he should turn his house into an art gallery. He could do it, couldn't he?'

'Yes,' said Juliette, not realising that Maria was quite serious. Her seriousness became apparent as she went on.

'I found this article in one of the Sunday papers about a couple who turned their house into an art gallery – just an ordinary house, not much bigger than your father's house, and they have small exhibitions of their work and of other artists as well. When I saw your father's house with all those paint-ings on the walls, and the size of the rooms, I thought you could easily turn it into a gallery, it's almost a gallery already, all you'd have to do is take some of the furniture out. I've told your father but he thinks I'm being silly.'

'I couldn't have a lot of strangers wandering all over the house, it would be like living in a shop . . .'

'But you could still have private quarters – that lovely back bedroom with the cherry tree outside, for instance, you could make that and the little room next to it into a self-contained flat almost, and then –'

'It's my childhood home you're talking about, you know,' said Juliette curtly. Maria didn't seem to hear, and persisted in describing her vision for Fernlight Avenue all the way to Victoria station where, after a flurry of hurried embraces and cheek-kisses, she departed.

'So you deign to sit in the front now, do you?' Juliette said as they started their return journey, Aldous craning over the seat back to watch Maria as she disappeared into the Underground entrance.

Seeing, at last, that his daughter was genuinely hurt, he tried to excuse himself.

'I couldn't leave Maria sitting in the back on her own. That would have been terribly rude.'

'But didn't you see how awkward you'd made her feel by leaving me alone in the front? After all, she could have sat in the front and you could have sat in the back.'

'I didn't think of that . . . but no, she automatically went for the back seat . . .'

'Assuming you'd sit in the front to help with directions. Honestly, Daddy, you made me feel like a taxi driver . . .'

Aldous gave one of his surely-you-can't-be-upset-about-such-a-little-thing sighs which had the effect of making Juliette feel embarrassed at her own pettiness, though she couldn't be charitable when Aldous asked, with bluntly inappropriate timing, 'So what did you think of her then?'

'She talks a lot, doesn't she?'

'Well, I like people who talk a lot.'

'You didn't used to.'

'Nonsense. I've always been fond of good conversation.'

'Good conversation is not the same thing as jabbering on endlessly about nothing –' Juliette checked herself, realising she'd gone too far. 'Sorry – but you must know what I mean. A few years ago someone like Maria would have really got on your nerves – I mean, she's very nice and everything – oh God, I'm sounding really bitchy now, aren't I? I suppose I just mean she seems a very unlikely sort of person for you to be friends with. She just seems a bit . . .' Juliette searched for a suitable adjective, but could only manage the slightly conciliatory '. . . daft.'

'The thing is,' said Aldous as Juliette steered nervously round Hyde Park Corner, 'you didn't know your mother when she was young. The word "daft" would probably have been a perfect description of her.'

'What's Mummy got to do with it?'

'I'm just saying –'

'You're saying she's like my mother, and that is supposed to make me like her?'

'No, I'm just trying to explain . . . You said she seemed like an unlikely friend, I'm trying to say why she's not an unlikely friend, I've always been attracted to women like that.'

'Like what?'

'You know – larger than life, vivacious, loquacious, mischievous, everything I'm not, you could say . . .'

'She seems very young . . .'

'She's very young for her age.'

'Which is?'

Aldous still didn't know exactly.

Juliette gripped the steering wheel as if for support, blew air out from her cheeks, exhausted with trying to understand her father's emotions. She knew she should be happy for him in his new friendship, and felt angry with herself because she wasn't. It was her father's use of the word 'attracted' that most bothered her, suggesting, as it did, more than mere friendship. She worried about how he would cope with rejection after having been married for so long. These days he seemed so vulnerable to damage. The tough, unshakeable figure of her childhood was now a smaller man, capable of being frightened and of doing stupid things.

'Shouldn't you put the wipers on?'

And yet still there was the sensible father, the one who'd taught her to drive, and who'd tried for hours to talk her out of dropping out of school.

Juliette switched on the wipers, sweeping away a world of distortions and replacing it with one of startling clarity. But only for a moment. The blurring and distortion returned drop

174

by drop. It was like the half-glimpsed but intolerably persistent visions of Aldous and Maria Juliette was now having, linked arm in arm as they walked through a Gothic archway, from darkness into the sunshine and a modest shower of confetti. Every time she saw them she tried to blink them away, but like the raindrops on the windscreen they kept coming back.

19

Aldous had kept the article about the house-that-was-an-art-gallery tucked behind the clock on the mantelpiece. Maria had brought it along with her the day she came for her art lesson (still the only time she had visited Fernlight Avenue): a clipping cut from the *Guardian*, a newspaper he had encountered so rarely its fonts and layout looked almost exotic.

'It's about a husband and wife who've turned their house into an art gallery. Just an ordinary house . . .'

But it wasn't an ordinary house, as Aldous had discovered when he read the article in detail after Maria had gone. To his surprise he found that it was in Whitstable: a tall, Victorian, weather-boarded villa overlooking the shingle with bay windows and big airy rooms full of sea-light. But Aldous was rather touched by the article. The two artists had met at art school, later becoming husband and wife. They'd become disillusioned with the cliquiness of the London art world and the money-obsessed West End galleries. As they approached middle age they realised their only chance was to take control of their own destiny and start an art gallery of their own, where they could display and sell their own work, and the work of their friends. They had no money to buy or rent anywhere so they used what was already available to them. They opened their own house to the public.

Aldous recognised the house from his many saunters along the pebbles of those beaches. It was close to the cafés and pubs of the town centre. There was an independent cinema nearby. A second-hand bookshop. Even a thing called a wine bar. It was not like Fernlight Avenue where there was nothing but other houses in every direction, with mock wishing wells in their front gardens, no café society but drab pubs and

Wimpy Bars. The thought of anyone making a special journey to visit an art gallery in a house in Windhover Hill was laughable. And Aldous did laugh. And when he next saw Maria after she had shown him the article, he laughed again, and he was surprised how disappointed she was by his laughter.

'I thought artists were supposed to have vision,' she'd said. Aldous was contrite.

'I didn't mean to laugh at your idea, Maria . . .'

'The wonderful thing is, because it's your own house, you don't have any overheads, so it doesn't matter if not many people come. It's not as if you can lose anything, except your time and a tiny bit of money on framing and technical things like that. And you're always saying how much time you've got on your hands. Think of the fun you could have. You could have opening parties and invite the local press, or even the national press, why not? And some famous people – I'm told arty people will turn up to anything, as long as there's free wine. You'll slowly build a reputation. You could give a leg-up to struggling young artists by staging exhibitions for them. Just imagine that front room with no furniture, the walls painted white and floor painted pale grey, just like those little galleries you showed me in Mayfair, and a few small paint-ings or just one big one on each wall, or perhaps a piece of sculpture. The back room, the one with the piano in it, you could have your own work on display there. You might even sell something and start making money – who knows – but that's not the important thing . . .'

'You forget one vital thing – the house is also my home. How am I supposed to live while all this is going on?'

'The people in Whitstable – I think they're only open to the public a couple of days a week, and by appointment at other times. You could do it like that –'

'But that's even madder. For five days a week I'm sitting in an empty art gallery with no furniture –'

'Then stay open longer. You'll have the upstairs as your living area. You don't see it, do you? You don't realise what's under your nose just like you don't realise the talent you have at your fingertips.'

Aldous was utterly charmed by the piercing clarity of Maria's idea, by the simple philistine innocence of it. Only a person with no appreciation of art could come up with such a bold plan.

By way of concluding the discussion Maria had made a suggestion.

'Aldous, just do one thing for me. Promise me you'll take me to Whitstable and we'll visit this gallery place and see what it's like and how it works.'

It had been a promise Aldous was very eager to keep. For months he had been pondering and planning the ways in which he might engineer a trip somewhere with Maria. He had thought of Whitstable before. Who knew where those shingles and breakwaters might take their relationship, hand in hand stepping over the shattered crab carapaces or sharing an oyster-and-shrimp chowder with spumante in one of those beachside restaurants? Whitstable might act as a stepping stone to an overnight stay further down the coast, which Aldous had tentatively begun to explore – Margate Sands with its funfairs and shell grottos, or Broadstairs with its old ladies and tea shops. Or why stop at the sea, why not weekends in Boulogne or Calais? But whenever he'd proposed a trip out of London, Maria had seemed keen but non-committal, and his suggestions were never taken up. So to have Maria herself suggesting a trip to Whitstable seemed to Aldous like a break-through.

But that had now been some time ago, and the trip to Whitstable had not yet materialised. Whenever he raised the subject, Maria always seemed to have some excuse or pretext to postpone it. Perhaps, Aldous worried, Maria could see that it might draw their relationship closer than she wanted.

Aldous had intended to use the occasion of their visit to an opera to draw from Maria a firm commitment to visit Whitstable, even perhaps an actual date. He had booked tickets for a performance of *Don Giovanni* at the London Coliseum. The prospect seemed to trouble Maria more than any of their previous cultural outings. At first she had protested about the price of the tickets, assuming it must have been enormous.

'I couldn't think of letting you pay for tickets to the opera, Aldous, you must let me pay my share . . .' She had her cheque-book open and pen poised. 'Tell me what I owe you.'

Aldous refused, preferring her to have delusions of his grandeur. She gave him a blank cheque in the end, which he laughingly tore up in front of her.

Then it was a series of nervous phone calls, asking him what she should wear, or for yet another summary of the plot. She assumed Aldous would have to wear a tuxedo and black tie.

'It's the Coliseum, Maria, not Glyndebourne. They let anyone in, you don't have to dress up.'

'That may be so for the men, Aldous, but I'm sure all the ladies are going to be wearing evening dress and jewellery. I'll look a complete fool if I turn up in my ordinary skirt and blouse.'

After several phone calls in this vein Aldous began to suspect that Maria was rather wanting to dress up. He suggested this to her and she agreed.

'Well, why not,' she said, 'it is an opera after all. I know you say it's all democratic and open but I bet you just can't see the signs.'

It was true that some people did dress up for the Coliseum. Among the throng in the foyer were men in bow ties and tuxedos. They usually had quivering, bullfrog throats and receding grey hair oiled down flat on their scalps. Sometimes they were accompanied by bare-shouldered women draped with nacre and gold, who were often also red about the face, as though they'd just stepped out of an icy wind. Aldous found such ostentation funny, all part of some painted-up, overdressed comedy of manners. He hoped Maria would feel the same once she'd stepped over the threshold, but until then he found himself forced to humour her.

Eventually Aldous and Maria agreed that it would be fun to make a night of it. She promised to wear an evening dress if he promised to wear a tuxedo.

'It'll only work if we both do it, Aldous. If one of us comes dressed normally, the other will look ridiculous. So you've got to promise.'

So Aldous made his way to Houseman's, the gentlemen's outfitter on the parade, where he hadn't been since the last round of family funerals. And there he was kitted out in black from head to foot, with a white shirt and a black bow tie. In the mirror he was confronted by an array of alarming people – has-been, late-night Las Vegas crooners; the manager of an Odeon; desolate, unemployed croupiers; card sharps; bouncers and other assorted heavies. In not one of them did he see anything resembling an attendee at a performance of *Don Giovanni*. Nevertheless he bought the outfit and felt an extraordinary thrill at the new self it gave him as he caught the bus and Tube down to Charing Cross later that week.

He checked in his raincoat at the Coliseum cloakroom and waited among the others milling around. There were at least two others in tuxedos, and he spotted several evening dresses. Even a woman in furs. Previously he'd imagined that musical appreciation in the audience must decline in proportion to their level of adornment. Surely these whisked-up ladies and buttoned-down gents couldn't have a clue about the opera they were about to listen to. Would a serious music lover ever dress so stupidly? But of course they would have the librettos off by heart. They'd know every twist and turn of the plot. It saved them having to think about the music. Now here he was joining their ranks, one of the overdressed, overpaid, overfed thickos in the front stalls.

And he was rather enjoying it. The anticipation of seeing Maria in some sparkling down-to-the-ground number, with bare shoulders and lifted bosom and perhaps a loop of butterfly emeralds around her neck was worth the sacrifice of one's status as a musical connoisseur. He'd almost felt a little ashamed when he'd summarised the story of *Don Giovanni* for her the week before (for the third time): 'I've got to know what's happening,' she'd said, urgently, 'I've just got to.' When told she couldn't disguise her disappointment.

'So it's just the old, old, old, old story?'

'Is it? Which one?'

'Boy meets girl. Boy meets another girl. Boy plays one girl off against the other. Et cetera, et cetera.'

Aldous found Maria's trite summarising of a great opera almost as distasteful as her dismissal of Rembrandt as dreary. He couldn't help it, but her philistinism did annoy him. He would feel quite happy if they steered clear of art galleries and concert halls for good. But she would insist.

Prompted by Maria's remark, the conversation had led on to a brief discussion of their respective sexual histories.

'But not all men are like that, I suppose . . . You for instance. You're not what they call a Lothario or philanderer or whatever you like to call it . . . How long were you married?'

'Ooh,' said Aldous, as though he had to work it out, which he didn't. To make himself sound more interesting, he sliced ten years off his married life, too soon to realise his mistake.

'But I thought you said your son was thirty-four when he died.'

'Yes.'

'So he was born ten years before you were married?'

'Did I say thirty-four? I meant twenty-four. Oh I don't know, I've forgotten. I can never remember birthdays. Or anniversaries. I couldn't even tell you the date of our wedding anniversary. What is the past? Dreams and dust. You still haven't answered my question . . . How many boyfriends have you had?'

'Thirty-four,' said Maria, rather wistfully.

Aldous went pale.

'You're pulling my leg.'

'Oh sorry. I'm still thinking of your son's age. Thirty-four sounds so young to me now. Twenty-four sounds like a child. It seems a rather peculiar thing to forget how old your son was when he died.'

'Perhaps I need to forget,' said Aldous, trying hard to sound hurt. Maria was convinced.

'Oh, I'm so sorry, Aldous, bandying about your son's death as though it was just a statistic. Let's not talk about this any more. Sex and death – it never comes to any good when they pop up in a conversation, especially not at the same time.'

And now Maria was late. Aldous was still waiting in the foyer of the Coliseum, and the crowd was beginning to drain into the auditorium – the auditorium that he wanted to show

Maria almost as much as the opera itself, that great cherub-encrusted proscenium arch, the charioteers and bare-breasted harpies bursting out of the woodwork.

The bell buzzed impatiently. Aldous went on a frantic, last-minute hunt in case Maria should have tucked herself away in a golden recess on another level. He went outside to see if she was stranded on the pavement, awestruck and immobile before the gates of high culture. But she wasn't there. St Martin's Lane was emptying as the pubs and theatres filled. What remained was a calm, unhurried flow of taxis and couples with nowhere much to go. When he went back inside, the last of the audience were filing through the doors, and then suddenly the building seemed empty. The shocking way theatres do this, absorbing a thick crowd of people in a matter of seconds, leaving ushers to deal with the remains. This evening it seemed like a sinister conspiracy. The three-card trick on a monstrous scale. The doormen and box-office staff seemed to stand there with blank, innocent faces: *What's that you say? A crowd of people? Hundreds of them? No, you must have been seeing things.*

Embarrassed, Aldous hung around for another half an hour. He wandered over to a vestibule where he found himself staring at a row of payphones. They looked smug and disdainful, as though they knew something he didn't: how lowly he ranked in Maria's hierarchy of companionship. Not even allowed to know her phone number, they seemed to sneer. Was she really so untrusting of him?

He waited for another half an hour, and then could stand the emptiness of the foyer no longer. He collected his rain-coat and carried it over his arm as he descended the front steps and lit (with difficulty) a Rothman's, thinking that he must look like someone doing a very bad impersonation of Cary Grant. There was a pub opposite, with windows overlooking the opera-house entrance. He went in there and drank for an hour, watching the door, just in case. He saw the foyer suddenly become thick with people again, at the interval, some of whom spilt out on to the pavement with their drinks and cigarettes. Then they too were gone, ingested by the great gold and red velvet machine of the theatre.

At about the time Don Giovanni would have been talking to statues, Aldous embarked on a brief odyssey through the West End, imagining that he was a tour guide taking a party of Japanese tourists on a journey through his own life, as far as it had been lived in the centre of London. 'This is where my father used to take me for a glass of pop and a finger bun,' he said, passing the spot where Lyons Corner House used to stand (now a frothy coffee shop), 'This is where he took me to see *A Midsummer Night's Dream*, with Peggy Ashcroft as Titania. This is the restaurant where I had a plate of kidneys and lamb chops during the war, National Restaurant, it was called, now it's called Wendy's Hamburgers, and it is tremendous to see the hoity-toity people of the Strand scoffing chips and things in here: and this alleyway beside it is where the nancy boys used to parade up and down, men with lipstick, blowing kisses and grinding their molars at you. Gave me a real fright the first time I saw them . . .'

Cheeky youths were making remarks that yanked Aldous out of his fantasy and dissolved his Japanese entourage. He couldn't make out the wording of the remarks, but understood it had something to do with his clothes. The tuxedo and bow tie. Yet Aldous felt so comfortable in these clothes that he decided he would wear them all the time.

'You want to go to heaven?' someone said to him. He was somewhere else now. He'd wandered back up past the National Portrait Gallery, through the side streets to Soho, passing through the Chinese quarter with its galleries of dead ducks and its salty aromas, to a sleazy area of strip clubs, peep shows and sex shops. The liquors of Chinese cuisine seeped across into this area, and the flesh on display seemed similarly glazed and stewed.

'You want to go to heaven?' came the same voice, from a man dressed just like Aldous, tuxedo and black tie. He was standing to the side of a doorway that was tucked between shopfronts, and gave on to nothing but a flight of descending steps, flanked by pictures of fierce-looking, semi-nude women. How odd that he should say that, thought Aldous, when he looks just like the Devil at the gates of Hell. The staircase even seemed to descend into a pit of redness. 'Right down these stairs,' the man said, 'you'll be in heaven. Fully licensed bar. Countless gorgeous girls. You look like a man who appreciates quality. You're a man about town . . .'

The accent had a rough burr to it. Greek Scottish. Aldous wasn't fooled. He'd heard stories about these places. They take you downstairs, you buy a beautiful girl a few drinks, and then find the bar bill comes to a hundred and fifty pounds. To Aldous's astonishment the man was so insistent he actually came over and took him by the arm, pulling him towards the staircase, forcefully enough to make Aldous wince as he pulled back. Freeing his arm and trying to laugh off the assault, he walked quickly on.

A small Chinese woman was eating a tangerine as she walked along in front of him. She walked with such casualness it was almost a parody, shaking back her long black hair, rolling from hip to hip. She peeled the tangerine and discarded the skin, letting it fall on the pavement. Aldous found this suddenly and unexpectedly annoying. He felt like calling out, 'Hey, someone could slip over on that!' Just like he'd heard his old headmistress call out on sports day to a black sprinter who'd done the same thing. Aldous stopped to pick up the woman's trash. Perfectly peeled, the skin had come away in one piece. He followed the woman, slowing down to her pace, or slower, so that he wouldn't overtake her. Carrying her skin like a lost slipper. She finished her tangerine and veered off the main street into a narrower walkway between grimy brickwork walls. Aldous was following hesitantly, wondering at what point he should go up to her and say, 'Excuse me, I think you dropped this,' and worrying that a shady alleyway might not be the best place to approach a small young woman on her own, when the woman stopped, glanced over her shoulder so casually that she didn't seem even to notice Aldous, or if she did she didn't think he mattered, because the next thing she did was pull down her loose black trousers, squat down by the gutter, and pee.

Aldous felt he'd been challenged. It was as though she'd said, 'You think dropping tangerine peel is bad? Well, let me show you what else I can do . . .' And in the most appalling of social solecisms Aldous could only choose between turning back or carrying on, as though nothing was amiss. And this is what he did, the woman still squatting. He stepped carefully over her trickle as he passed.

20

When Aldous arrived home that evening he closed the front door carefully, as though afraid of waking a sleeping giant. He didn't want the house to echo. When, for warmth, he bent down to light the oven, which he did, as always, by lighting a spill of paper first then reaching cautiously into the greasy, gaping throat of the machine, he felt as though he was feeding fire to an insatiable tyrant. As it gargled on the blue flames it gave a long, breathy laugh. An *I told you so* sort of laugh. *Did you really think you'd escaped? Did you really think you'd broken free? Well, you haven't. It's just you and me now. An old man and an oven. And eight empty rooms.*

It was the first time Maria had failed to show; the first time Aldous had been (he hated to use the expression, with its associations of teenage romance) 'stood up'. He was amazed at how quickly Maria could metamorphose from the sweet, saintly figure that had occupied his thoughts for so long, to an object of anger, even hatred. He was overwhelmingly angry with Maria. Angry because he believed her failure to show up had been because of fear. She was frightened of opera. He could put up with her hopeless efforts to grapple with Rembrandt or Shakespeare, even be charmed by them. But to be frightened away by the ladies in pearls, that was somehow unforgivable.

But it wasn't fear that had kept Maria away, it was illness. The letter came a few days later.

Dear Aldous,

I hope you will forgive me for not letting you know sooner, but I have become ill again. Friends are doing everything for me. They are sending me away to a centre for alternative treatments, in Berkshire, as I can't stand the thought of knives or rays.

Thank you so much for your friendship. I did so much enjoy our little jaunts. I hope you weren't too cross with me last week. I know I should have phoned you but I hope you'll understand why I couldn't. I hate to think of you hanging around in your tuxedo. I bought a dress specially. Well, if there's another opera, perhaps I'll wear it then. I hope you saw the opera anyway. I expect it was very good.

I will let you know how the treatment is going.

Best wishes for now.

Love,

Maria.

PS Could you please, whenever you've a spare moment, visualise me in white light?

What upset Aldous at first was Maria's use of the word 'jaunts' to describe the time they'd spent together. It just wasn't the right word, and demeaned the experience. Just as she'd once referred to their conversations as 'little chats'. It didn't do justice to their relationship. And now the added swipe of her lack of need of him. 'Friends are doing everything for me.' Who were these friends? And what were they doing exactly? Maria had managed to give the impression that she was someone alone in the world. Not friendless exactly, but without attachments. She had no parents and she had no children. She looked neither backwards nor forwards. Somehow she existed in a continuous present, bracketed off from the flow of generational time. So who was there in her world that was taking such care of her? Not those dippy, ditzy women in their colourful pullovers she once brought round for an afternoon's drawing lesson, surely.

It took a while for Aldous to deal with the hurt of Maria's independence, and begin to grapple with the valedictory tone of the letter. The awful sense it gave of a farewell. *Thank you so much for your friendship.* A truly horrible sentence. *If there's another opera, perhaps I'll wear it then.* Of course there would be another opera, in the normal course of things. There would always be operas. Did she really believe that there might be no more operas? Was that really a possibility?

Maria had left no contact details. He did not know where this 'place' was that dealt in alternative therapies. All he was left with was the promise of future communication, for which he could do nothing but wait.

And how was he supposed to live his life now? Aldous realised for the first time that his every thought and action for the last few months had been directed towards securing his friendship with Maria. Now all he had was an idea of her, in a white robe and bedecked with crystals, being wheeled about the corridors of some converted Home Counties mansion, subject to the endless chanting of pagan priests and the copious strewing of petals. The funny thing, Aldous now realised, was that whenever he did think about Maria, it was in white light anyway. It always had been.

For a week Aldous managed to hold himself together. He went nearly every day to Whitstable, drank pints of dark ale in a weatherboarded inn, and even brought himself to open up a conversation with a whelk fisherman. But the whelk fisherman turned out to be rather reticent.

'Do you have to go far to get your whelks?' he asked, as the fisherman (was that the right word, Aldous wondered, given that they weren't really fish, perhaps they should be called whelkmen, or molluscers) dipped a string bag full of muddy, inhabited shells into a tureen of simmering water.

'It depends,' the fisherman had said, 'sometimes you have to go three or four miles. Sometimes to the other side of the island.'

And that was as far as their conversation went. To the other side of the island. Aldous presumed he meant the Isle of Sheppy, dimly visible in the hazy weather as a low strip of projecting land.

The art gallery that was really a house (it was called Domicile), Aldous avoided, because it was a reminder of the trip to Whitstable that he and Maria might now never take. But he did bring along his sketchbook and a 6B pencil. He would sit on one of the benches, or on a breakwater, or on the sea wall, and sketch. He went to Whitstable one Sunday morning and found that the only place open was a café full of silent people dressed in black reading the *Observer*. The menu offered a bewildering array of variations on a cup of coffee – mocha, cappuccino, latte, espresso (the filthy black stuff he remembered from the war). His request for tea was met with a patronising smile, as though it was the symptom of a disability. And when it came, the tea was a scented brew that smelt of flowers. He drank the top of it and tiptoed out. No one seemed to notice him leave.

It was on returning from one of these Whitstable trips that Aldous once more bumped into Cliff Ashbrittle, on his way back to Herne Bay from an olive-oil-gathering trip to the capital. Hands were shaken and smiles and pleasantries exchanged. To Aldous's surprise, Cliff looked almost pleased to see him, and asked him if he would like to come to the Hampstead Everyman on Sunday, to see a Tarkovsky film.

And this was how Aldous and Cliff Ashbrittle came to be in Jack Straw's Castle on a cold rainy night in early autumn. Aldous had sat through three hours of the Tarkovsky film, a rather dreary picture in which little seemed to happen, and what did happen happened in pouring rain. He had not so much persuaded as demanded that Cliff come to the pub with him afterwards. Cliff was not a pub man, as Aldous had already half acknowledged to himself, and yet he didn't know what else to do with him. So they walked to Jack Straw's Castle, and there Aldous fed Cliff a series of pints of bitter laced (unknown to Cliff) with brandy. He then watched the etched, rigid façade of Cliff's personality slowly plasticise and elongate. For a non-pub man he was surprisingly hard to get drunk. But the laced pints slowly did their work.

'Cancer is a most unlovely thing,' he said, after Aldous had queried him about the illness, 'it really is the most unlovely disease. Both my mother and father were taken away from me by the disease, and it was my gross misfortune to have to watch the ebbing of the life from their fine . . . they were fine people. My father, fine man. Fought in World War I. Oh dear.'

'But is it really true that people can have cancer and yet appear healthy?'

Cliff seemed to chuckle with cynical anger.

'It is a most devious, cunning, vile little illness.' He shook his head, as if unable to believe the depths of duplicity this disease was capable of. 'Of course, it has no symptoms, you see, not at first. And by the time the symptoms appear, it's too late, often as not. Even then, they are vague. Weight loss. Tiredness. Then the surgeons have a poke around and find a tumour the size of a pumpkin. That's what happened to my mother. It's an indecent disease. The way it treats the body with such indifference. Sucks it up and discards it. The body is helpless before it. But then I don't really know if it's even the right thing to call it a disease. It isn't a virus or bacteria, not something that attacks the body, invades it, in such a way that the body can fight back. Somehow it seems to attack the body from the inside out. And I mean from the interior of the cellular matter, even the genetic, hereditary material. It's like a madness of the body itself. I'm not making sense, am I, old chap? I can see you don't really hold with what I'm saying. That's all right. That's quite understandable. I'm a sentimental old one-time artist, painter of golf courses to the nobility. Did you know Sean Connery once bought one of my paintings of St Andrews? And now She Who Must Be Obeyed wants us to sell up and move to a farmhouse in Umbria.'

'Good for the olive oil, I should think.'

'Bloody good olive oil out there. They sell it in gallon demijohns. They pipe the stuff in. Marvellous.' He leaned inward towards Aldous, tapped a finger against the side of his nose, which Aldous had begun to realise gave forewarning of a joke so obvious it needed no forewarning. 'Extra virgin,' he said.

'Extra what?' said Aldous, looking around him, as though Cliff was pointing someone out among the clientele.

'First pressing. The purest olives. Do you know hardly anyone dies of cancer in Italy? Why? Why do you think?'

'The olive oil?' Aldous joked. And was then surprised to find he'd given the correct answer.

'Absolutely. The same with Greece. They all live to a ripe, crinkly old age, quaffing down the extra virgin by the pint. Do you know what? I'm going to have another of these pints of ale . . .' He made the non-drinker's fumblings for his wallet, stashed away somewhere in the rolled-up raincoat beside him, and the confused stirring of loose change that were the signs of a man unused to pub life.

'I'll get it for you,' said Aldous, jumping up, to Cliff's evident relief. At the bar Aldous slopped another single into Cliff's pint. He was annoyed with himself because he couldn't get drunk. All the alcohol was doing for him was giving him heartburn and a headache. Somehow getting Cliff drunk made up for it slightly.

'So you're going to live for ever, are you?' said Aldous when he'd returned from the bar. To his amusement Cliff actually licked his lips when he received his pint.

'That's the ticket, old chap. Live for ever. Yes, that's what's on the cards for us. Eternal life for me and She Who Must Be Obeyed.' He quaffed, and his eyes watered a little through want of oxygen, 'Yet I do feel the most strange feelings of despair when I think of leaving our little Herne Bay hovel and moving into some Umbrian villa. And then there's the money of course. We could buy a monstrous palace in Italy, but do we really need it? And we'd spend the rest of our capital on the renovation costs. But you've seen the way property prices have gone in the last few years. If we hang on for a bit longer, our little hovel will be worth a fortune. We'll have something to pass on to the kids. Whereas I'm afraid that if we move to Italy all we'll leave them is a ruined farmhouse and a pile of debts. Grace doesn't see it like that of course. She says I'm being unadventurous. Ha ha, you have to laugh, Aldous, don't you, when your beloved spouse turns on you like a veritable she-cat. Oh, she can lash out, Grace, she can really lash out when she wants to.'

Aldous felt small bursts of resentful rage towards Cliff. It was something to do with the horrible fact that he seemed to have usurped Maria's position in Aldous's life. He was a very poor substitute.

'Do you know what I'd like to do?' said Aldous, 'I'd like to go to Kenwood House and have a look at the Rembrandt self-portrait.'

Cliff looked at his watch.

'At nine o'clock at night? I think they might be a bit shut.'

'Maybe we could see it through a window. It's just a short walk across the Heath.'

Cliff suddenly started laughing. A rather forced laugh, as from someone who's not as drunk as he thinks he is.

'Do you know what, Aldous? I've just thought of something ever so funny.'

'What's that, Cliff?'

'I've just thought . . .' He clenched his eyes for another bout of giggles. 'I've just thought, if I don't leave this pub in the next thirty seconds, I'm going to miss the last train back to Herne Bay, ha ha ha, hee hee.'

'Plenty of time, Cliff. Just walk down to the Tube and it's the Northern Line straight to Charing Cross.'

'But it's a Sunday, Aldous. Last train to Ramsgate leaves at ten to ten on a Sunday. No, don't look so concerned. You needn't be. Because the even funnier thing is – I don't give a damn. I don't give a tinker's cuss about the last train. And I've lived in Herne Bay for ten years and I've never missed the last train back. So this is a most momentous occasion, wouldn't you say?'

'But what about She Who Must Be Obeyed?'

'You mean,' Cliff tapped the side of his nose again, leaning over, 'you mean, She Who Must Be Told To Go And Take A Running Jump . . .' He only just got to the end of this sentence before he collapsed in another fit of giggling, falling sideways on to the upholstered settle. Re-erecting himself he continued: 'I'm going to have to impose on your hospitality, Jonesy old man. You're going to have to put me up for the night. You got me into this pickle, now you can get me out of it.'

'Perhaps a taxi,' said Aldous suddenly. 'A taxi could get you to Charing Cross in time . . .' The project of getting Cliff drunk was going horribly wrong. Not only could Aldous not get drunk himself, now he was faced with the bleak prospect of wheeling the inebriated aesthete home while he himself remained coldly sober.

'A taxi? If you think a taxi can get across London faster than a Tube, you don't know London very well. No, I'm absolutely set on joining you in your little plan to visit Mr Rembrandt. And I'm – well, let's have another drink.'

So they stayed in Jack Straw's Castle for another hour, until
the bell went for last orders, by which time Cliff had begun
to doze. He'd somehow propped a shoulder against the cushioned back of the settle and was snoring gently, and salivating
a little. The potman, retrieving empty pints with a set of
knobbly fingers, eyed him with amusement.

'Come on, Cliff,' said Aldous eventually, tugging at the shoulders of Cliff's tweed jacket. The action woke Cliff with a start.

'There's no need for that,' he said, interpreting Aldous's
touch as an aggressive act. 'I can manage, thank you.'

But outside the pub it was as though he'd emerged on to
a ledge above a chasm: he went rigid as he strove for balance
in the face of a cold breeze. The change in temperature affected
Aldous as well. All the slowly consumed alcohol of the evening
seemed suddenly to do its work in an instant, and the two
men, crumpled raincoats hanging from their shoulders, leaning
together for support, tottered towards the dark Heath.

'I must say you know how to dress for an occasion, Aldous.
Do you always wear a dinner jacket and bow tie to go to the
pub? Is it the done thing? You know I've never really understood the drunkard's mentality. All that singing and fighting.
I've never been one for the bar-room life, as you've probably
guessed. I'm much more an – Oh golly. I've gone blind. Now
I know why I never drink, if it sends you blind, I'm an artist
for pete's sake. I can't afford to lose my eyes.'

'It's just a power cut,' said Aldous from the darkness caused
by the sudden failure of the only street lamp for a long way.
They were on a mulchy path parallel to the road but separated
from it by a strip of dense wood.

'Of course, I know that. Do you think we should sing,
Aldous, like two proper drunkards? That's what drunks do,
isn't it, have a big hearty sing-song, with lots of lewd words
thrown in . . .'

'I'm more keen on screaming,' said Aldous. 'Have you ever
had a good scream, Cliff? A really good screaming fit?'

'No, I can't say I have. Aldous, I can't keep up with you.
Can you slow down? I'm starting to feel a bit funny in the
old tummy. I need to sit down. Then we can have a scream.'

'There's a bench further on . . .'

Aldous waited for Cliff who was staggering badly. He took him by the arm and helped him to the bench. Cliff sat down and doubled up, then leaned back, like someone who'd just run a marathon, taking in deep breaths. Slightly recovered, he placed the palm of his hand flat down on top of Aldous's head, and pressed. Aldous took it to be a gesture of affection, though he couldn't be sure.

'Do you know, Aldo, you never told me so why you were worried about cancer. What is this big interest? You must know someone. I'm not an insensitive old chap as I look, and I could see you were . . . you know . . . the old waterworks came on, didn't they? I don't like to see a grown man cry . . . specially not in a place of public demeanour – what's it all about?'

Aldous didn't say anything. All evening he had wanted to talk about Maria, but something had prevented him. Now, with Cliff so drunk, it seemed impossible.

'I know it can't be your good lady, because she's already accounted for in the death department – heavens, that sounded insensitive, but you know what I mean. It can't be one of your children, because that would be too awful. No one deserves to lose a child . . . a wife can always be replaced, as my father used to say, somewhat to my dear mother's chagrin, but a child . . .'

'Just a friend,' said Aldous, rather sharply. But it shut Cliff up, as Aldous hoped it would. At least for a while. 'Shall we go on?'

Cliff had recovered a little and so they continued along the path, silently at first. Then Cliff spoke.

'Aldous, did you notice anything odd about that man who just passed us the other way?'

'Only that he was stark naked.'

'It's very odd, isn't it. He must be freezing. But did you notice the other thing about him?'

'No.'

'Well, mistake me if I'm correct, but wasn't he, sort of, playing with his todger?'

'I didn't see.'

'Well, I think he was. At first I thought he was having a wee-wee walking along, but then I saw that he wasn't doing that at all. But then it is awfully dark.'

'Here's a good place, Cliff. You can see from here, right across London. A good place to have a scream.'

They had emerged from trees on to an area of open Heath. Before them the city seemed heaped like jewels at the bottom of a well. Red, white, yellow, blue, some winking, some moving, thousands of points of light, enough to illuminate the sky to thousands of feet above them, casting a glow on the clouds and blotting the stars.

'It's a sight, isn't it?' said Cliff.

'I've always thought there aren't enough hills in London. Not enough places where you can get a view like this . . .'

'All those little lives,' said Cliff, thoughtfully. 'You know, Aldous, I think I am going to scream. I'm going to scream and then I'm going to be sick.'

'OK. Why don't we scream together?'

'What should we scream?'

'Just scream, shall we? Just one big scream, see if anyone hears us . . .'

Cliff had a try-out, a deep, churchy sort of voice as though he was just about to sing a baritone aria. Instantly realising it wasn't up to the mark, he tried again, with a bit more force, more a shout.

'Not bad,' said Aldous. 'I'm going to take my teeth out before I have a go, it's bloody dark here. You should do the same.'

'My teeth are the genuine article, old chap,' said Cliff.

'Oh shut up and scream,' said Aldous, punching him gently on the arm. 'We'll do it together, right?'

They were rapidly sobering up in the bracing air, and now had to approach the task of screaming from a rational point of view.

'No words, OK. Just scream together on three.'

'I'm with you, Aldous.'

'One, two, three . . .'

Both men took a lungful of dark air.

Part Three

21

Page three of the *North London Advertiser* contained the following headline:

BLACK AND BLUE: sad pensioner's face tells story of modern thuggery

And the picture alongside was rather shocking: an old man's visage, the eyes like two big shiny black plums, swollen so badly they looked as if they could never be opened again. There were bags under the man's eyes, and those had swollen as well. They looked like two hammocks full of blood. The mouth of the man was undamaged, but it was set in a down-turned rictus of misery and hopelessness. 'Hapless' was the word that, for Aldous, summed up the face of the man in the newspaper. The embodiment of bad luck and misfortune. Someone bereft of hope and at the mercy of the merciless. The article went on to describe the sickening attack on the helpless victim. How they came at him from behind, knocking him flat on the floor and stamping on his head. There was one odd detail: they didn't steal anything. They didn't even take his wallet. They must have done it, the paper concluded, for the sheer thrill of beating a helpless, sad old pensioner.

It was all lies of course. The man hadn't been attacked at all. He had fallen flat on his face, drunk, just a few yards from his house. Aldous knew this because the man pictured in the newspaper was himself. He'd been drunk enough to fall over, tripping on one of the crooked paving slabs at the base of the lime trees in Hoopers Lane, but not drunk enough to lose his presence of mind when questioned about his misfortune. He'd felt instantly that he couldn't admit to being drunk – that

Juliette would get to hear about it, that the machinery of institutional provision would slowly grind into motion. Aldous Jones, too old to look after himself properly. Too old to be trusted out alone. Can't cross roads without risking death. Can't even walk along pavements safely.

He could remember his fall with great and unwanted clarity. He was on his way back home from another Whitstable trip, feeling a little disappointed that he hadn't bumped into Cliff Ashbrittle en route and so have an opportunity to apologise for the adventure that had ended so badly (on the upper deck of a night bus they'd fallen among brawling nightclubbers, then Cliff had been sick in the back of a taxi, adding to the blood – not his – that was already splattered down his raincoat). Cliff left Fernlight Avenue the next day after a night of furious snoring, ashen and scared at the prospect of explaining himself to She Who Must Be Obeyed. He clearly blamed Aldous for the whole sorry affair, and Aldous doubted that their shaky friendship would survive. Instead Aldous met an ex-*Times* journalist in the Goat and Compasses on the way home, a man with bright yellow eyes and bleeding gums, who'd once known Juliette's boyfriend Bernard. They'd exchanged stories about Bernard, and the pints had multiplied, with chasers, until, by the time Aldous made his way home, crossing Woodberry Road, he was feeling quite giddy.

'Oh no, I'm falling,' he could remember thinking at the moment of his stumble. His hands were in his pockets and for some reason he couldn't extract them. He had a cigarette in his mouth, and he wondered what would happen to it when his face smacked into the pavement. Would he swallow it? Or would it flatten into a charred flower in his mouth? He could remember the approach of the pavement as it came to meet him: all the details of its silica and quartz conglomerate sparkling in the light of the street lamps. Then the impact. Nothing at first, just the cold, gritty pressure of stone equal to his own body weight. Then an echo of the impact, with the weight multiplied infinitely, as though the whole planet had headbutted him, with pain following the same curve. For a fraction of a second it was as though he had suffered infinite pain. Just for a fraction of a second. Any longer and he would have been unconscious. And afterwards came a feeling of numb powerlessness. He lay there on the pavement, the whole front of his face feeling as though it was clamped in the jaws of a lion, for what seemed like hours, until a motorist stopped and came to his aid: a small, bearded man in glasses and a suit, an executive very late home from the office, perhaps (Aldous never found out). He helped Aldous into the passenger seat of his spick and span car. It was to this man that Aldous had first burbled something about being attacked by muggers, just by way of explaining his predicament. It turned out to be a big mistake. The man was outraged, and, once he'd delivered Aldous to casualty, went and informed the police.

The police weren't particularly interested, at least not once Aldous had said he hadn't caught sight of his assailants, and that there had been no eyewitnesses to the attack. They took down a statement, issued a crime number, and went away. But then the local press heard about it. The plight of pensioners was a recurring theme in the *North London Advertiser*. They were constantly being found dead in their own homes, or dying of hypothermia, or having their purses and wallets stolen (which usually seemed to contain nothing but two old ten-bob notes and a photo of a neglectful son or daughter). Aldous supposed the reason for this interest was that the paper was mainly read by pensioners, who revelled in the vivid depiction of their own suffering. So a journalist and a photographer visited the hospital, and Aldous's battered face was photographed in detail.

'Big cow,' said a child's voice. Aldous lowered the paper and looked at the other face in the kitchen, the face that was almost as puzzling as the face in the newspaper. It was a child's face. After three days he still found it a mysterious and trans-fixing object.

'Black cow.'

The child pointed at Aldous and giggled. Its mother cooed at the child in his own language, and looked apologetically at Aldous, smiling.

'He say,' the mother explained, struggling hard to find the words, 'your face . . .' she circled her hand over her own face to illustrate, 'like the cows.'

Then she laughed cautiously, inviting Aldous to respond like-wise, which he did, then made a gesture of covering his own face in embarrassment. This made the child laugh even more.

Aldous felt as though he was wearing a mask that he couldn't take off. A mask that was actually sewn to his face. His only escape would have been to have worn another mask on top of it, but instead all he could do was avert his face or cover it with his hands, or hide it, as he was doing now, behind the opened pages of the local newspaper.

The child was called Wahimi, which, in the language of the Icabaru Indians, meant 'powerful hunter'. Aldous had never thought he would actually see this child, who was his grandson, because he had always been led to believe that he and his mother were determined never to leave the jungles in which they'd been born and raised. At least that's what James had always told him. Mashami, his mother, wouldn't even accompany James on his regular visits to the downstream mission station for supplies, much less his visits to Caracas. James had been to London twice since the marriage, mainly to complete research papers at the SOAS Library and submit for continuation of his research funding. But on these visits Mashami did not accompany him. When she was expecting Wahimi he had insisted that she journey to Caracas to have the baby delivered in a modern hospital, but she refused, and the men of the tribe were adamant that she remain in the village. Mashami's brother, in particular, was insistent. One of James's papers, which Aldous had read with only partial comprehension, concerned the role of the mother's brother in Icabaru society. It seemed to point to the fact that the mother's brother had more rights over the child than its father. One day the child would inherit all his uncle's wealth and power. 'What do they get from their father?' Aldous wondered, and asked James on one of his visits. Nothing was the answer. Fathers were not much interested in their own children, it turned out. It was called a matrilineal society. 'Oh, so women have all the power,' said Aldous, but it wasn't so apparently. It just meant that wealth and power passed through the mother's lineage, but in the hands of their brothers. Aldous still didn't quite understand.

But James had done some sort of deal with Mashami's brother, and had persuaded him to let Mashami take her son to London.

'I told her,' James said, 'that I was not prepared to spend the rest of my life in the jungle. I told her that before we were married. And she agreed, and said she would come with me when it was time for me to leave.'

Wahimi was fascinated by cows. Still unused to the vast perspectives of the open English countryside, he had first seen them far off, and had assumed them to be small, cat-like creatures. (Perhaps the similarity of the Friesians' black-and-white markings to those of some of the cats in the neighbourhood fuelled this assumption.) Then, to walk through a field of cows, to find how as distance shrank they grew into beasts bigger than people, had been an extraordinary odyssey for him, as though he had walked among giants. He was not scared of them, because few animals represented any real danger in the forests of his homeland. The danger there came from snakes and insects. Big cats were so rare and shy they were never encountered, and the same was mostly true of apes and chimps. So it was funny and fitting that he should liken Aldous's bruised, speckled face to the big, jigsaw face of a cow.

Aldous folded the newspaper and grinned at Wahimi. The family had arrived at Fernlight Avenue while Aldous was in hospital. His stay had been a short one. He was kept in overnight and allowed to rest in the ward for most of the next day. It had been a very different experience from his earlier spell in hospital. Here, on the surgical ward, most of the patients seemed to have broken something, usually their legs. The man in the next bed was an enormous Negro who'd broken both femurs. Looking at the great bulk of the man, the thickness of the thighs now encased in plaster, the thought of the force needed to break those two thick bones clean in two made Aldous wince. He glimpsed the X-rays. And there they were, two thick bars of white with a shattered gap in the middle. Like two pencils broken in half. Aldous never learned from the man how this injury had been sustained.

The nurses had been much brisker and sharper with the patients than in the medical ward last time. Perhaps, Aldous supposed, in this little community of broken limbs and fractured ribs, most of the patients were seen as authors of their own demise, whether they'd fallen off ladders or crashed their cars. Aldous certainly came into this category, a fact which caused him a certain amount of guilt and anxiety since his fictionalised account of his injuries placed him at the other extreme: as a person whose demise was brutally authored by other people. The sympathy that came from the nurses Aldous accepted through clenched teeth – he felt as though he was stealing their milk.

They would hold and stroke his hand. Pat him gently on the head. They would coo and gurgle over him to such a degree he wondered if they thought he was simple. To be old is one thing, to be old and a victim is another. An entirely new category of person – someone vulnerable, helpless, unable to cope. Little more than a baby. What worried Aldous most was how eager people were to see him in this way. What, apart from the numerical accumulation of years, had happened to him to bring about this change. Had he somehow begun to look old and frail? Yet when he looked in the mirror the same grey-haired face stared back as had done so for the last ten years. Perhaps the tiniest extra wrinkle here or there, perhaps the slightest extra sagging of the skin. And these were enough, it seemed, to tip him over from late middle to old age.

'You'll be getting used to hospitals now,' said a tubby Scottish nurse, one of those no nonsense Calvinists who seemed to regard disease and illness as a form of dirt that simply needed tidying away.

Aldous didn't know quite what to say. He had only been in hospital once before in his adult life, and that was earlier in the year. He said so to the nurse.

'Oh, come on now, you'll have been in hospital many more times than that, or you're the healthiest man on earth.' She then went into a detailed description of the medical histories of the various men in her life – her father, her husband, her brother, all in and out of hospital as they got older.

'So what were you in for last time?'

Aldous hesitated. He wasn't quite sure, or had somehow forgotten. He said the awful words, 'I had a fall.'

As though a fall was, like a bad cough or an upset stomach, a peculiar type of illness.

'A fall was it? And now, did you fall or were you pushed?'

'No, I just fell.'

'But this time you were pushed. What'll it be next time? You know what they say – three falls and you're out.'

Aldous didn't like that Scottish nurse, and was glad when she finished her shift. He was discharged before she returned.

During his one night on the ward Aldous had felt a desperate sense of loneliness and sorrow. It had been only a fortnight since he'd received the valedictory letter from Maria, with its pathetic little postscript asking that she be visualised in white light. Now here he was, hospitalised himself, and through his own stupidity. He tried to atone by imagining Maria bathed in white light all through his lonely night on the ward. He imagined a life for himself dedicated entirely to waiting for the phone to ring or for a letter to come giving him news of Maria. He had kept himself together by reading up on the subject of cancer – but he didn't even know what sort she had. Lung? Blood? Bones? Liver? (Probably not liver, he surmised, as it seemed to mean almost immediate death – and probably not lung either, as she had never been a smoker.) The treatments and risks of each seemed to vary rather wildly. Most of the books seemed to be written in a gently optimistic tone, the underlying message being that cancer wasn't the automatic killer it had been in the past, and that while a real cure was not in sight, present treatments could, if one was lucky, effect an indefinite postponement of death from the disease.

The prospect of returning to an empty Fernlight Avenue without even the friendship of Cliff Ashbrittle to console him, and Maria an unreachable figure wavering somewhere between life and death, seemed unbearably bleak. But when he did return, delivered in the early evening by a taxi (which he had to pay for), he was greeted with a scene of extraordinary chaos and turmoil.

James and his family had arrived at midday after flying through the night, letting themselves in through the unlock-able music-room doors. By the time Aldous arrived they had managed to transform the house. Backpacks and bags filled the hall, spilling their rather grimy contents; there was a strange reek of earth and fruit and sweat; a little brown child with its shirt off running around the house, jumping down the stairs and landing on a heap of clothes on the floor. James was striding about the place with the same loping confidence that carried him through rainforests and alongside crocodile-infested tributaries. He looked remarkably changed, his hair cropped short but with a dark sheen of stubble on his face. His usual outfit was a baseball cap, shorts and a sweaty T-shirt that exposed rangy, muscular arms. And he wore dark glasses almost constantly. Four years of jungle gloom, he said, had weakened his retinas.

It wasn't until James eventually removed his dark glasses that he noticed Aldous's black eyes. Mashami and Wahimi apparently had assumed his bruises to be ritual facial markings, and had not commented on them. 'What have you done to yourself, Dad?' In front of James and his family Aldous felt unable to lie. He told them about his fall, and confessed to being mildly drunk (much easier than confessing to Juliette). Nevertheless, he tried changing the subject as quickly as possible. 'I still don't understand why you didn't tell me you were coming.' 'I did,' said James, 'I wrote you letters months ago.' But these hadn't arrived, as far as Aldous could recall. Not that he cared. He couldn't have cared less. He was just delighted to have the house filled with people again.

'What noise do cows make?' said Aldous, having carefully hidden the newspaper with the horrifying face in it (not least because it preserved in black and white his clumsy lie about being mugged).

Wahimi thought long and hard before replying, his little face grinning broadly, the slightly oriental eyes reduced to happy slits. His answer came as a joyous shriek,

'Miaow!'

Over the following weeks it astonished Aldous how quickly he became used to this unusual family living in the house. Mother and son at first spoke hardly any English, and though Wahimi was rapidly acquiring vocabulary and grammar, Mashami was struggling. James didn't help by conversing in their own language all the time, which made Aldous feel rather excluded. For the most part, if Aldous wanted to talk to either Mashami or Wahimi, he would have to use James as an interpreter. The family gathered for meals at the dining table in the kitchen, which Aldous would observe from his chair by the boiler. Having politely declined an invitation to join them at the table, it was now understood that Aldous did his eating separately from the others. This was not out of any sense of antipathy on anyone's part, but boundaries had to be established. Besides, Aldous ate very little, and certainly wouldn't have enjoyed the odd concoctions, full of unusual aromas, that Mashami made at the stove, a contraption it had taken a while for her to master. It was a faintly disquieting experience to observe this family at mealtimes. Their eating was done mostly with the fingers and involved loud sucking and sipping sounds. The food consisted of lots of stringy things that slopped about and hung over the lips of their food bowls. And on top of this, an incomprehensible conversation took place, which seemed all clicks and soft burrs, and slightly plaintive, dying falls. At first James would occasionally offer his father a brief summary of the conversation as it was taking place ('Wahimi is saying the stew tastes like monkey dung'), but now he seemed no longer to bother.

Often James had to go out for the day, researching at the library or looking for jobs. His main task, he said, was to finish and publish a book on his study of Mashami's village and her people, and then to secure a university post on the strength of it. Until then he had no chance of finding a place of his own to live. It looked like the family were to live in Fernlight Avenue for some time.

James's absences meant that Aldous was often left alone with Mashami and her son, his grandson (the word seemed so odd). Their company was both a delight and a puzzle. At first he felt responsible for them. This woman, after all, had spent her entire life in a tiny village in the middle of the jungle, walking around semi-naked, eating a diet consisting almost solely of plantain soup. There were three small holes in her face, two just below each corner of her mouth, and one below the centre of her lower lip. In her normal life these would have contained cocktail-stick-length pieces of wood. On the plane James had had to reassure her that they wouldn't crash into the upper layer of the Icabaru cosmos. And at the same time she seemed almost absurdly casual about the modern world in which she had landed. Before, the biggest building she had seen was the meeting house of her neighbouring village, a circular structure about thirty yards in diameter. Aldous struggled to think what her mind would make of an average skyscraper. Why didn't she walk about in a constant state of wonder? Even the trivial machinery of a light bulb must seem to her like the eye of a bright god. And everything did strike her as a miraculous wonder, but only on the first encounter. Thereafter it was familiar. The world of objects had only a limited capacity to surprise. The social world seemed much more difficult for her to grasp.

Aldous became aware of this the first time he left them by themselves. James had assured his father that it would be OK for Aldous to leave mother and son alone at home while he went out. Aldous wasn't so sure when the time came. James was down at SOAS, and Aldous was anxious to be out of the house for a while. Mashami beamed reassurances at him when he warned her that he would be out all day. By now she knew how the lights worked, how the cooker and the television worked, how the kettle and the bath worked (the latter not very well, lacking hot water, but that was hardly a hardship for these two, he reassured himself; in fact, it was a relief to be host to people for whom his house represented a pinnacle of luxury and sophistication – they were unlikely to complain about a lack of central heating, or colour television, or freezer). When he came to leave he felt quietly confident that they would manage quite happily on their own.

So he was not expecting the scene that greeted him upon his return: a police car and ambulance outside the house, neighbours on the streets, raised voices, fists being shaken. The police were doing their best to calm an irate father and a weeping boy. Another neighbour explained that Wahimi had been discovered torturing a cat, beloved pet of the weeping child.

'I'm sure there's a reasonable explanation,' Aldous said, hesitantly, while the father said that the child was an 'inhuman monster. Worse than an animal.'

Mashami and Wahimi were to be found cowering in the

house. She screamed at Aldous incomprehensibly when he entered, ran to him and, clutching his arm, dragged him into the music room, as though for his own protection. It took a long time to get a clear picture of what had happened. They had wandered into a neighbouring front garden. There they had found a sleepy-looking tabby cat which they had tied by one leg to a tree so that Wahimi could shoot arrows at it with a home-made bow. They had done this all quite openly, just a few doors down, and had seemed surprised when the owner of the cat came screaming at them in a rage.

James later explained that it was a common pastime in the village, tying small animals (usually lizards) to a stake in the ground, and using them for archery or spear-throwing practice. 'It's their way of developing hunting skills. Their very existence can depend on their skill with an arrow or spear . . .'

'Well, can you explain to them that hunting is not done in suburban London. They really don't seem to understand.'

There followed a long exchange between James and Mashami in Icabaru.

'She understands the concept of "pet", and she won't try to kill any more cats, but it's difficult to get across the idea of private property. In the village everyone lives together. There are separate living spaces but they are all under one roof, and are not separated by walls. She has trouble getting used to all these fences and walls. She says we all seem to live in boxes here, and she can't get used to the fact that she can't see what's going on in other people's houses.'

'Yes, some neighbours were complaining that she was peering in through windows.'

When he was at home Aldous was fascinated by watching the two of them. Their almost endless capacity for doing very little. They could amuse themselves for whole afternoons by picking up twigs and leaves in the garden and making little things. But what delightful things they made. Mashami crafted a wicker basket from a few fallen cherry twigs and some grass blades. Wahimi made another longbow from a piece of poplar and strips of lilac bark. They made necklaces from plum and cherry stones, empty snail shells and acorns. They scraped around in the dirt, digging up worms and centipedes. Aldous was horrified by the idea that they might eat them, and dared not look. They lit fires without using matches, and would sit around them, Mashami lying on her back with her knees raised and crossed, Wahimi dancing and rolling around in the grass. They were much more comfortable in the garden, in the open air and, while the weather was mild enough, spent nearly all their time out of doors, even if it was raining. The only time they came indoors was when James was at home, when they would sit uncomfortably around the table for their 'Western' dinner. ('Western' was one of Mashami's most frequently used English words, which she used to describe anything that wasn't encountered in her home village. Eating at the table was having a 'Western dinner', reading a book was 'Western sitting down'.) One day Aldous found the two in the garden playing with what looked like an odd selection of sticks and stones but which, Aldous discovered as he came closer, turned out to be bones. They had dug them up from a shallow grave in a corner of the garden, and had cleaned them with spittle. They showed the bones to Aldous with a great sense of pride and excitement, and were busy fashioning the materials into jewellery and ornaments. Wahimi was particularly pleased with the skull, a small streamlined structure which he had cleaned to a gleaming white. The long, curved teeth of the skull identified it unmistakably as belonging to a cat, almost certainly Scipio, but Aldous couldn't be sure as several cats had been buried in that corner of the garden. By this time Aldous was beyond being surprised or shocked by what these two got up to. In fact, he couldn't help feeling a little pleased to be revisited by Scipio, if it was him, albeit in skeletal form.

It was rather extraordinary the extent to which James and his family lived their separate lives in Fernlight Avenue. They had taken up residence in the front bedroom, being the only room in the house with a double bed (apart from the bed settee in the living room), while Aldous had moved downstairs to sleep in the living room, which he already begun doing anyway, because the upstairs rooms were too cold in the winter. James had bought a small TV and they would spend their evenings up there, once they'd finished their meals and left a cooling array of juice-filled bowls on the table for Aldous to clear away.

James made some swift, practical changes to the house. He had the telephone reinstalled in the hall by the front door, so that he could use it without having to disturb Aldous in the living room. He paid for a plumber to come and sort out the boiler and reinstate the hot water for baths. He bought a small blue car and so reclaimed the long-usurped parking space outside the house. He would take his family on long, rambling drives into the Home Counties to rediscover and share with his wife and son the haunts of his childhood – Suffolk churches and Buckinghamshire forests, Hertfordshire village greens and duck ponds. Sometimes Aldous would accompany them, and it became a curiously treasured experience to see Mashami wandering among the weathered tombs of an English country churchyard. By now she had enough English to ask Aldous simple questions, and for him to provide comprehensible replies.

'What this say?' she asked in her quiet, slightly husky voice, pointing to a tombstone.

'It says: "*In loving memory of Daniel Habgood, 1856–1931. Where there is much light, the shadows are deepest."*'

'What this mean?'

'It means a dead man called Daniel Habgood is buried here, and that they thought rather a lot of him.'

'Dead man? Here?' Mashami suddenly looked worried, and started backing away.

'Yes but he's six feet under. There's no danger.'

'All these . . .' She gestured at the rest of the graveyard. 'All these dead men?'

'I'm afraid so – why, you look a bit worried.'

'We must go away,' she said to Aldous, gesturing for him to follow her back to the safety of the road. It took James a long time, conversing urgently in Icabaru, to convince Mashami that they were in no danger. He explained to his father later about Icabaru funerary rites and the power of ancestral spirits. 'The dead remain a strong presence in Icabaru society – not as ghosts exactly, more like a higher level of village authority. They tend to be grumpy and even a bit vindictive, which was why she was scared. It's hard for us to understand . . .'

Aldous was experiencing, with the presence of this alien family, an entirely novel form of strangeness. Even as Mashami slowly became westernised, her thoughts revealing themselves piece by piece as each new day brought its fresh stock of vocabulary, she retained an unalterable core of what, to James's angry indignation, Aldous had called primitivism.

'But you can't deny it, surely. I mean from what you've told me –'

'Primitive isn't really an acceptable –'

'Why not? Surely, in its literal sense, of "first" or "original" or "at the beginning", it's rather a dignified thing, isn't it?'

'Well, firstly it's a mistake to think that Mashami's society represents the original form of our own. The two societies are different, but they are not at different points on the same path, the Icabaru at the beginning, our own much further along. "Primitive" is loaded with value judgements, implying that one is more advanced than the other. The truth is both societies work very well in their different ways. Their continued existence is testament to that.'

'Except you said Mashami's society is under threat.'

'Yes, from us.'

'So our society must be the more efficient.'

'I call consuming rainforests to grow hamburger meat a grossly inefficient use of resources. Our own society is under threat, but from ourselves, as the current arms race proves. The Icabaru have wars, very violent ones. But they affect no one else. Ours threaten the whole planet.'

How Aldous enjoyed these conversations, even though he came down in flames every time. They were an echo of the type of conversations that used to fill the house all day, spontaneous debates and discussions, the swapping and testing of ideas, the exchanging of views. Since Colette's death and the dispersal of his children, those conversations had, for the most part, finished and the house been silenced.

The 'otherness' that Aldous now lived with, day in and day out, was something he felt immensely grateful for. Mashami was a beautiful, delicate and graceful presence. And she was changing by the hour. When she first arrived she was dressed in ill-fitting jeans and a man's shirt, as though someone had kitted her out with the first garments that came to hand. The clothes sat awkwardly on her slender body, concealing that customary nakedness. She took a long time, and indeed never fully understood, the concept of bodily shame. She would walk naked from the bedroom to the bathroom, and not look shocked or embarrassed if Aldous happened to be within eyeline which, to his delight, he occasionally was. Odd how, when naked, she looked rather podgy. In clothes she seemed to have a wasp-waisted, almost skeletal figure. In reality she had a round tummy that quivered and bounced when she walked, a dimpled and puckered though very round bottom and pyramidal breasts that projected from her body with no downward inclination at all. She would walk into the kitchen with her shirt undone, coffee-coloured, gleaming nipples exposed, and show an utter lack of concern if notified of the fact, buttoning up slowly and with difficulty when she could be bothered, providing Aldous with a chance to peer over the top of the *Daily Telegraph* and notice the odd patterns of symmetrical scars that marked that area of her body.

Aldous was also pleased because this particular form of strangeness was so explicable. Whereas trying to explain the behaviour of Janus or Colette to anyone would have been an impossible task, Mashami could be explained with the simple phrase, 'She's an Amazonian Indian.' The neighbours even moved towards a gradual acceptance of her, including the owner of the fired-upon cat. If Mashami broke some rule of etiquette or other social norm, it was not with furious indignation that this was reported to Aldous, but with gentle admonitions and advice – 'She was picking Mr Morris's dahlias. I thought you should know, I'm sure he wouldn't mind if she asked.'

Mashami and Wahimi were a useful reminder that Aldous's life was not his own, and not his own in an exceptional way. His life now was connected to the lives lived in the South American rainforest. He was, technically, father-in-law to one of their children, and grandfather to one of their sons, an affiliation brought about by no actions of his own. That was the oddest thing about having children, they took the train of cause and effect into their own hands and you became a kind of passenger in the drama of their lives. How could he have ever thought that he might turn the house into an art gallery? Where would Mashami and Wahimi have lived if he'd got rid of all the furniture and turned the art-hung walls over to the public? And when he thought of that, he thought of the other thing he had to be grateful to Mashami for. Her powers of distraction.

Aldous felt rather proud of the fact that he hadn't gone entirely to pieces. Perhaps he was not as dependent upon Maria as he'd feared. Though he still felt shocked that she seemed to have so little need of him. He told himself he was a fool for ever thinking that they were that close. They were chums who gallivanted around art galleries and theatres, nothing more. Of course she must have friends of longer standing to whom she could turn in times of real crisis. His own friendship would have been a nuisance in this time of palliative need. He respected her desire for distance. And yet there was this ache. A fear of losing something irretrievably. A door slamming shut deep in his heart that would sometimes wake him in the middle of the night, choking him with sadness, for the big desolate spaces into which he feared being cast. Sometimes he woke from a pillow so tear-sodden it was as though he'd fallen asleep while the tide was coming in. Or the angel of dejection had visited, scattering her sad pearls.

His plan was that he would give Maria three months. If he hadn't heard anything by then, he would take steps to find out what was going on. He chose three months because, in many of the books he'd read, three months seemed to be the typical time span for a course of treatment. At the same time three months, even to an old man for whom the days flitted past like lights from a train, seemed like a desperately long time. And he was beginning to wonder how he was going to cope with the painful sense of not knowing, when James and his family arrived.

'Why don't I give them English lessons?' Aldous said to James one day, when it occurred to him that Mashami's progress, never very great, had ground to a halt. Wahimi was worse and was picking up little English. This was mainly because he rarely encountered English speakers of his own age. The few that there were at that end of Fernlight Avenue were usually whisked protectively indoors whenever he approached. James thought it a good idea, and so a little language school was established in the kitchen where, for an hour or so every morning, Aldous would help the two with their English, working through some beginner's English textbooks he had bought. The experience reminded him of his Flemish for Beginners class, and indeed he borrowed some of his old teacher's techniques (role-playing buying a ticket at the Underground, for instance), though the two's needs were even more basic than his had been. Mashami didn't even know the Western alphabet. (Why should she? James reasoned, when Aldous expressed his shock.) In her own culture there was no written version of the language, which meant the idea of writing was utterly alien to her. She'd seen James scribbling down his field notes and tapping away at his word processor since he'd been back, but to her these were mysterious, Western skills that she would never have thought to acquire herself. It was both charming and sad, Aldous felt, to see how giggly and embarrassed she was to hold a pen in her hand, how she grasped it in her fist at first, like a wooden spoon, and had to be shown how to hold it in her fingers. Then her childish delight in making marks on paper with it. But Aldous preferred to teach spoken English after this. With a pen in her hand Mashami couldn't help appearing like a fool. An idiot even. And Aldous knew that she wasn't these things.

In parallel, and almost without having made a decision, Aldous found himself learning Flemish again. The Linguaphone set with its stack of little 45s was taken out of its grey covers and Aldous picked up where he'd left off: in the music room, a dining chair pulled up beside the record player, playing phrases of Flemish and repeating them, trying to reproduce the accent without reproducing the rather fruity, slightly lascivious tone of the speaker. Often he could hear through the wall Mashami practising her English with Wahimi, the husky intonations of English words, '*Station, ticket, one-way, return.*' And Wahimi's happy squeak of '*ball, teddy bear, toothbrush* . . .' And he wondered if she understood when he explained that he was trying to learn another language. He rather suspected that she hadn't understood, but had accepted it along with television watching and telephone answering as just another incomprehensible Western practice. He tore off all the Flemish sticky labels that had marked the nouns of the house and replaced them with

English ones for Mashami's benefit. Now the door was labelled 'door', and the fridge was labelled 'fridge'.

But then, why was he learning Flemish, after all? In the absence of Maria his thoughts had returned to Agnès. He decided it was foolish of him to have forgotten her completely. So what if she was a married woman, what sort of difference did that make these days? In the post-sixties world that Herman Lorre had helped create, and which seemed to thrive in certain quarters of Ostend, marriage didn't mean much any more. He should have held her in reserve just in case something like this happened. It wouldn't have been an infidelity because he and Maria were never together in that sense. And now, if the worst happened and Maria didn't make it, at least he could think of returning to Belgium. He wrote a tentative little letter to Julian hinting that he might be ready for another visit. Julian's reply stunned him.

Dear Dad,

You're welcome anytime, like I said, but a few things have changed around here since your last visit. You remember that black artist called Agnès? She's moved in with me. She was having problems where she was living. Herman Lorre is back with Astrid, I think I told you that (this is after the second estrangement – he was chucked out again, lived with me for another month), but Agnès is here now so if Herman gets chucked out a third time he can look for somewhere else. He still talks about you, by the way – that Ophelia wall hanging just blows his mind.

I'm thinking of leaving the navy and trying to make my way as a writer. Herman Lorre says I've got a good chance and he's going to put me on to his American agent. He thinks she might invite me over to New York for a meeting. The thing is I need to work flat out to get a collection of stories together, or even a novel. It's not easy what with manning the *Vespasian* day in, day out, all hands on deck for ever and ever. So I was thinking of packing it all in, hanging up my sextant and dividers, or for a while at least, and coming to London to write for a year or so. Would you be all right with putting me up? What did he mean, Agnès was living with him? Did that mean they were sexual partners, or was he just providing shelter for a friend in need?

Aldous replied immediately.

Much as I admire your literary ambitions I think it would be a serious mistake to abandon your career in the mercantile marine at this point in your life. The life of a sailor is one to be envied, there is hardly a more noble or exciting profession, or at least I can't think of one. What about all those skills you've picked up in your training and in the course of your work? It would be a great pity to see those all go to waste. And I'm sure if you just hung on a bit you would have a more adventurous post, perhaps on oil tankers going into the Persian Gulf, or freighters crossing the South China Sea, or any other sea for that matter. And what's more, on those long voyages, you'd have lots of spare time (how much work can there be on one of those ships, it's not as though you have to unfurl any sails, is it, and someone else does all the steering). You could have a nice little cabin where you could write your short stories and novels. More importantly, you could still be based in Ostend, a fine city. You seemed very at home there, and I think it would be a pity for you to leave the lively social scene of that city.

Apart from that, James and his family are staying here, as I've told you, so there isn't a lot of room.

Yes, I remember Agnès. How delightful that she is living with you. I'm just wondering what Georges makes of it – i.e. her husband. Presumably he's not bothered at all?

Love,
Dad

Aldous was disappointed not to get a reply to this letter. Julian evidently hadn't thought the question a serious one. But Aldous had desperately wanted clarification. And he desperately wanted to rid himself of this awful new emotion – jealousy of one's own son. Instead, he had to make do with vagueness. With mistiness. Opacity. And another door closed on the life that he had slowly built up over the last few months. Maria, Cliff, Agnès, Ostend, they were all fading away.

Then, quite unexpectedly and unannounced, a new layer of distraction was added to Aldous's life. Builders arrived. A chirpy crew of three men of such varying ages Aldous wondered at first if they were different generations of the same family. They rolled up in an open, flatbed truck, asking James if he wouldn't mind shifting his blue Fiesta, and swaggered through the house with what would have seemed terrible arrogance had they been uniformed in any way, but their plaster-dusted boots and paint-speckled T-shirts gave them a sort of happy licence. They were used to trooping through people's lives and knew how even the sternest proprietorial defensiveness quickly crumbled under the onslaught of their jollity. They asked for cups of tea in a jokily demanding tone, passed inoffensive comment on the furnishings of the house (they were especially interested in the piano, though talked about it solely in terms of its monetary value – 'Nice piano, must be worth a bit, any idea how much?' Aldous decided to impress them in the only way they knew: 'Oh about ten thousand . . .' 'Is it really? Ten grand for a grand?') and generally hollered about the place.

Mashami and Wahimi were terrified at first, and rushed to hide in the bedroom, which didn't provide much of a refuge because ladders were quickly hoisted and scaffolding assembled, and soon builders were ascending and descending in an almost continuous procession past the window.

'I really think you must have a word with Mashami about her – you know – lack of care in covering herself . . .' Aldous said to James, who agreed. No casual, forgetful nakedness from now on.

The interior invasion of the house was short-lived. Before long the builders mostly confined themselves to the outside of the house, making occasional forays indoors for water or use of the toilet. The demands for tea grew fewer, flasks were procured, but there occurred from then on the sense of a house under siege. When asked what they were going to do first – roof, walls or windows? – the foreman replied that they would start from the top down, doing the roof first, then the windows and finally the walls. Transformations were taking place beyond what Aldous had imagined. To get the scaffolding up at the front of the house a lot of the runaway vegetation had to be cut back. The pyracantha was clipped to within a few inches of the walls, the acacia tree was heavily pruned on one side. It was only when the vegetation was removed that a serious crack was revealed in the brickwork below the front-room window. The builders looked at it as though they'd discovered carvings on the side of a creeper-strewn ziggurat deep in the jungle, and gave low whistles. 'That's the tree, that is,' said the chief builder. 'Roots. Still. That's something for later.' The crack did look nasty, a black zigzag between bricks.

'You don't mean . . . I mean, do you think . . . I mean, the house isn't going to fall down, is it?' said Aldous to the chief builder.

The chief builder thought a lot before answering, with a cheeky smile, 'Put it this way. This house will last *your* life-time.'

Aldous was depressed about the tree. So all those fly-by-night arborealists, those chancers with their vans full of saws, ropes and ladders who for decades had knocked with irritating frequency, offering to cut back the acacia, had been right after all. It had damaged the house. Either through desiccation of the foundations or by the insistence of roots under the brick courses, it had done exactly what they had warned against.

'You could consider this a good first step to getting rid of the tree,' the builder told him once he'd hacked off the branches that were obstructing his scaffolding. 'Big trees like this, that are right up against houses, they need to be taken down in stages, with a few weeks or even months in between. If you take it all down in one go, there's a problem with the ground becoming saturated – because there's no tree to take up the moisture, so then you get danger of subsidence, flooding, God knows what. Well, we've taken down the main branches on one side. When we've gone you could get a bloke to take down the rest of the canopy. It's up to you, but that crack can only get worse if the tree's left. It's not going to get any better.'

'Might it not be the case that the roots are actually holding the house up? If you take out the tree perhaps the gap will open up even more?'

The builder looked at Aldous pityingly.

'Trust me,' he said, 'trees spell trouble as far as houses are concerned.'

They left it at that. The house became a small, industrious community, extending out beyond the front garden and into the road, where the builders' van took up semi-permanent residence, joined sometimes by other vans, a skip, heaps of sand and gravel. The builders really did start at the top, right at the top. The first thing they did was dismantle the chimneys. Aldous was wondering how they were going to do this, then discovered that it was carried out with painstaking slowness. The pots themselves were brought down whole and uncracked, then came the bricks, also whole, to be stacked in neatly square piles in the front garden. Such care was taken with these things that Aldous was impressed. It was James who pointed out that old bricks like these were worth a lot of money, and that that was the reason for the care. The same couldn't be said of the slate tiles. Judging by the treatment they received at the hands of the builders, they must have been utterly worthless. They were hurled like playing cards from the roof into the skip below, where they shattered loudly. It was like a war between crockery-throwing giants.

One morning Aldous came out of the house to find a stack of orange roofing tiles, in bundles shrink-wrapped in strong polythene, waiting on the front path, as though delivered by fairies (very strong fairies). Then Aldous watched as these several hundreds of tiles were conveyed to the roof of the house not, as he'd imagined, on shoulder-borne hods, but one by one thrown along a chain of builders positioned on the scaffolding like figures in an Escher engraving. Over five hundred tiles were conveyed in this chain of throwing and catching, and not a single one was dropped.

There was a brief hiatus in the operations once the roof was done. The scaffolding remained in place, but the builders left while the new window frames were being prepared. These really were beautiful objects in their own right. Aldous marvelled at their intricacies: the delicacy of the mouldings, the wonderful fantasia of right angles they represented, the straightness and accuracy of the joints. In their raw state, unpainted and exposed, they seemed to belong to the lineage of church-window tracery.

The fitting of the windows meant a longer spell of interior invasion. Rooms had to be rearranged while the old windows were hacked out. The new windows were then slotted in and glazed. Over fifty separate panes of glass. (Not one broken.) In the kitchen door they fitted a pane of extra tough glass in the lower section so that a child could bang into it without any danger of breakage.

All that was left then was the pebble-dashing of the walls, which didn't take long. Another huge pile of sand and a cement mixer rumbling, then came the rendering of the walls. The dash was applied simply by throwing handfuls of stones at the wet cement from a bucket. The men did this in pouring rain which, they said, was the best sort of weather for pebble-dashing, as it helped keep the cement wet and adhesive.

During the several weeks it took to complete the work, Aldous became quite used to the chirpy calling and happy hollering of the builders, their occasional crashes and bangs, their flitting in and out of view through the windows; and they in turn seemed to have become used to the unusual household they were working in, and on. In fact, the builders seemed incapable of expressing surprise about anything. Had they uncovered a complete human skeleton when clearing a space in the junk of the back bedroom, Aldous imagined they would have just had a look at it, wiggled its arms and jawbone (*What's this? A human skeleton? How much is that worth then?*) and then casually tossed it aside. They didn't look surprised when they found Aldous hunched over the record player repeating phrases in Flemish, or when they saw Mashami (who had taken a liking to watching *Dallas* and *Dynasty* on TV, and had adopted the same shoulder-padded, power-dressing style of clothing) climbing the cherry tree.

In all this time Aldous had heard nothing from Maria. As the builders' work began drawing to a close he wondered what he should do. He didn't know if she was alive or dead. If she had died would anyone have thought to inform him? Would some relative or friend find his name jotted in her address book and phone him? He might never know. He didn't even know her full address. He had the road, but not the number. He began to think he would have no alternative but to go down to Asylum Lane and knock on every door.

He didn't have to. Maria phoned him.

22

'You're alive.'

'Yes, I'm alive.'

'I knew you would be. Are you completely recovered?'

'Well, it depends what you mean by recovered . . .'

'I'll take that as a "yes", then. That's good enough for me. So the crystals and the chanting worked?'

'Not exactly. It's rather odd, Aldous, and I'm sorry for not telling you sooner, but what they took away turned out to be benign.'

It took Aldous a few moments to understand what she was saying.

'You mean . . . You're saying you weren't ill after all?'

'Yes I was ill, Aldous, but it wasn't the cancer. I was just . . . under the weather.' Aldous tried interrupting with baffled interjections, but Maria talked over him. 'You don't understand, Aldous. When you've had cancer, feeling "under the weather" can be a very serious thing. Anyway, the doctors thought they could see something on the scan, so I was sent in for surgery and, like I said, it turned out to be benign.'

There was a fragility to Maria's voice that discouraged Aldous from asking too many probing questions. He summoned the resolve to congratulate her.

'That is very good news, Maria,' (he was aware that he sounded rather cold, and tried to amend his remark), 'that's a cause for celebration.'

'Yes, it is. Aldous, is that a child I can hear in the background?'

'Yes, my grandson. Just after I last saw you, they arrived out of the blue – my son's family.'

'Oh, that's wonderful.'

'Yes, it is, isn't it? So when do you think you'll be strong enough for a day out?'

'Oh. Well, you see, the surgery was weeks ago, and I've been fully recovered for a while. In fact, I've got a job. That's why I haven't been in touch, I've been so busy.'

It took a few moments for Aldous to take this information in.

'You've got a job?' Aldous said quietly. 'What are you doing?'

'For the last six weeks I've been doing some voluntary work in a special school. Part-time. I work with blind children, though we mustn't call them that. They are visually impaired. The poor mites.'

'How old are the children?'

'Young ones, primary-school age. From toddlers up to ten-year-olds.'

'That must be very demanding work. Very tiring. Exhausting.'

'It is, Aldous, very tiring and very demanding. But, like I said, it's only part-time. The staff there are very good to me. They know about my illness and they are very understanding.'

And you've been doing this exhausting, demanding job for six weeks, while I've been wandering alone around London, not knowing whether to pine or to mourn, thinking you could be dead or dying and that there was nothing I could do, when in fact you've been healthy and fit enough to do a demanding job like that, and you never once thought to phone me or write to me to tell me that you weren't even seriously ill? How Aldous had wanted to say this. But he was too shocked to say anything other than, 'Really?' And hoped that this would convey what he wanted to express.

He asked her when they were going to meet, and he was frightened of the hesitancy in Maria's voice when she replied. She gave a rare stutter as she tried to explain how difficult it was, and her explanation was full of contradictions. She claimed she found travelling around London exhausting, for instance, but at the same time she travelled to and from this job of hers twice a week.

'It probably sounds very strange, but I really felt London had changed when I came out of hospital. I saw someone being mugged last week. Not in Brixton, but in the middle of the West End. And so many homeless people, and builders everywhere . . .'

Eventually they did arrange to meet. Maria revealed that she had an afternoon free the following week. Then, the very morning of that day, she phoned to cancel. Something had come up. She explained so quickly that Aldous couldn't take any of it in. She promised to phone soon to arrange an alternative. Again, Aldous was left waiting.

While he was waiting James announced that he and his family were leaving. He had been offered a lecturing job at the University of Edinburgh.

'But you haven't even published your book yet. I thought –'

'No need. The article in *Man* was enough. Thanks for putting up with us. I know it must have been a God-awful strain having these crazy strangers in the house. The university can put us in temporary accommodation while we look for somewhere to live, so we'll be leaving straight away.'

And they were gone. A few days of frantic packing and running around, Wahimi squealing in uncomprehending excitement, Mashami thanking Aldous in sweet, husky English for all he had done. Lots of jokes about Scotland, about how Mashami was going to teach caber tossing and sword dancing to her people in the rainforest. Invitations to visit as soon as they were settled. As they prepared, Aldous could do nothing but spectate. He could offer them no information about Edinburgh. He had been there once on a long summer cycling holiday in 1937, and couldn't really remember anything about it, probably because he was so exhausted from cycling up the Great North Road.

The little blue Fiesta was packed to its ceiling and the family piled in and purred off. Aldous could almost hear the collective gasp of relief that came from all the surrounding houses as the car disappeared around the corner into Hoopers Lane.

Then all that was left was the builders. The day after James and his family departed, they packed up their scaffolding. Screw by screw, the great steel lattice was taken down and the house was exposed for the first time in several weeks. It looked uncharacteristically bright and bare. There was something brutal in the clean orange tiles of the roof, and the smooth white cement that sealed the corners. The windows, too, were unsettlingly perfect in their gloss paint, the white fingerprints of the glaziers still evident. From the back, things looked even stranger. Pebble-dash. It was as though the house was wearing a tight-fitting jersey. Everything within ten feet of the walls had been trampled down, the grass in the back garden was reduced to mulch, and in the front the debris of broken trees and bushes was heaped as though for a ceremonial bonfire. The builders had even left their traces on the road: a patch of beige marked the place where the heap of sand had sat for weeks, a band of tape that had once secured a block of tiles tripped several people up. There were several dents in the tarmac where the skip had been. The hacked-back acacia looked brutally asymmetrical, the pyracantha had been pruned to within an inch of its life. Passing neighbours all commented on how nice the house looked, but to Aldous it looked raw, naked and exposed.

And from inside, the world had become alarmingly visible. The new glass let the outside world in almost exactly as it was, no warping or blurring with dust, and the retreat of the foliage had allowed it to come right up to the windows, making Aldous feel, for the first time in his life, the faintest desire for net curtains. He resisted the desire.

In the newly empty house the telephone, on the rare occasions that it rang, echoed like cathedral bells. When it did ring Aldous would pick it up with the eager desperation of a man who's found a glass of water in the middle of a desert. Annoyingly, he'd begun receiving cold calls (as he believed they were called) from people trying to sell him things. In fact it was more than annoying, it was heartbreaking. Picking up the telephone and hoping for Maria's free-ranging gabble, and having instead the scripted platitudes of someone selling banking 'products'.

But eventually Maria did phone. She claimed to have phoned him several times without the phone being answered, at hours of the day when Aldous knew he was at home. Could he really have not heard something he'd been so longing to hear? But then he had taken to falling asleep at odd times. Since the departure of James and his family Aldous suffered unbearable pangs of loneliness, and had taken refuge in rapidly swigged whisky. Sitting alone in the armchair by the boiler, or in front of the misty black-and-white telly in the living room, he would awake to find it night instead of day, or day instead of night, with a burning pain in his bladder that meant he was half an inch away from pissing himself. And if he thought about it he had to admit it was true, he did sometimes wake to the sound of chiming bells, and would spend what seemed like hours admiring their ding-dong lyricism, before the truth struck him, and cathedral peals shrunk down to the shrill, jingling spondee of the telephone. Then he would stand, lurch over to the couch where the phone used to be, remember that James had had it moved to the hall, by which time the ringing would have stopped, and Aldous would collapse on to the couch in the very spot where the phone wasn't any more.

They arranged to meet at the Festival Hall, a building that Aldous had visited frequently in recent months. Cliff Ashbrittle had told him about the deals for pensioners that were on offer. Standby tickets could be picked up for a few quid, and might land him in the third row of a performance by the Berlin Philharmonic. He soon learned that, if he feigned partial deafness, a sympathetic box-office clerk would usually try and find him somewhere near the front. Aldous had very fond memories of the Hall. He'd once, with Janus, found himself in the same lift as Artur Rubinstein. Then there was the time he went with Colette to a performance given by Rudolf Serkin, when Colette had leapt on to the stage and pursued the pianist backstage for his autograph. At the same time there was something cold and clinical about the big white spaces. The deep carpets and huge brass door handles and banisters seemed to whip up enough static to give Aldous constant electric shocks and headaches. Outside, the desolate concrete abutments and wind funnels added to the sense of brutal bleakness.

Recently attempts had been made to make a social space of the interior. The main bar, which used to open only for a short while before performances and during intervals, was now open all day. There was a bookshop, a record shop, cafés and an art gallery. You could wander in and hang around for hours without spending much money, though it took Aldous a while to get used to this new inclusiveness. He kept expecting, whenever he was there, a man in a bow tie to come up and ask him to leave if he didn't have a ticket.

He had taken Maria there before. Together they had heard Beethoven's Ninth and Britten's Spring Symphony. Maria had declared that she had thoroughly enjoyed it, but Aldous had a strong sense that she was bored during the concert. It may have been the way she kept looking at her fingernails and tapping them on her programme.

She was late, but at last she arrived. Aldous was sitting at one of the bar tables, whose chairs made horribly edgy grating sounds against the stone floor at the slightest movement. She looked transformed. The previous Maria of prim clothes and girlish colour sense was replaced by something much more youthful and casual. She was wearing jeans and training shoes, and a long, studenty trench coat, with a canvas bag slung over her shoulder. But it was the hair that shocked Aldous the most. It was darker, having lost its fussy blonde highlights He had not thought of her old hair as something unnatural. It was as though a great and long performance had ended and now he was meeting the woman behind it.

She exchanged cheek kisses with Aldous. He had hoped for a closer clinch, a *thank God you're alive—yes, thank God I'm alive* embrace. He felt put in his place by the brisk little exchange that he got instead.

'I saw five beggars on the way here from Charing Cross,' she said once Aldous had supplied her with a drink. 'Don't you think it's appalling the way this country is going? I walked past Lincoln's Inn Fields the other day and it was like walking past a campsite. Rows of cardboard boxes, even proper tents, as far as you could see. And then there are all these empty houses. I'm sorry to go on about it. The world has changed. You're looking very different, Aldous, what's the matter with you.'

'Different? I don't know . . . in what way?'

'Well, you've gone a bit redder, if you don't mind my saying. And you look bigger somehow. Perhaps I've got smaller. I don't mean you look fatter, just bigger. It's like I'm looking at you through the wrong glasses, if I wore glasses. Or it's like someone has pumped you up, like a balloon.'

'You look fantastic,' said Aldous, feeling that Maria's appearance was a more important topic of conversation.

'That's good of you to say so. I'm feeling fantastic actually.'

A jazz ensemble were gathering at the nearby grand piano and starting to tune up. There was a burst of solo song as a young woman in a sparkling dress tested out the amplification.

> '*Tie me in a ribbon,*
> *Lock me in a box,*
> *Drop me at the bottom*
> *Of the deep blue sea . . .*'

'Why didn't you tell me you weren't really ill?' Aldous felt as though he'd blurted these words out rather clumsily. 'You've been walking around for all these weeks and I was still worrying about you.'

Maria didn't say anything for a moment. She looked down at her drink, thinking deeply for a few seconds, focusing her thoughts.

'That's just it, Aldous. I didn't want to worry you any more. When I think of all you've been through these last few years – your son and then your wife dying . . . you don't want someone like me who's threatening to drop dead any minute. I feel terrible for causing you this anxiety . . .'

'Perhaps it means I'm better able to cope with it, the fact that I've been through it before?'

Again Maria hesitated, as though she had not considered this possibility.

'But Aldous, you've told me many times about the despair you felt, you described it all so vividly, the agonies you went through, the waking up in the middle of the night to salty howling, as you called it. The way you turned to drink . . . And you still drink, Aldous, I know. I can smell it on you now. I'm not complaining, don't think that. But by your own admission you've coped poorly with loss in the past. You mustn't become attached to someone who's likely to disappoint you again.'

'But you haven't disappointed me. You've come back, you're well, like I knew you would be –'

'I'm not well, Aldous. I'm very weak. Although this thing turned out to be benign, it has shaken me: being in hospital again, having surgery. Knowing how close I could be to . . . At the moment I need strength. I need people who are capable of giving me strength, because I have very little strength to give to others.'

Aldous saw the implications of this reasoning – that he was a drain on her emotional resources – but chose to ignore it. Instead he spent some silent moments regretting all those outpourings of his heart, though he hadn't considered them as such at the time. He'd been too vivid in his descriptions of Janus's and Colette's decline and fall, too explicit in his depictions of his despair. He had frightened her when he'd meant, by some peculiar logic of his own, to entertain her.

'Drop me at the bottom
Of the deep blue sea . . .'

'Those blind children you look after – surely they take a lot of your strength?'

'You see, Aldous, it's as though you're trying to catch me out, as though you're testing the soundness of my arguments. Those blind children, as you call them, give me an enormous amount in return. I don't know what you would call it, but to see a little girl with literally no eyes in her head, learning a tune on a xylophone, and to see her smile and laugh as a result . . . Do you understand? That is like food straight from the table of the gods. It's like hearing the music of paradise. I get far more strength from that little girl on the xylophone than I do from Beethoven's Tenth Symphony. I'm sorry if that sounds a bit harsh, but it's what I feel. That's the sort of person I am.'

'But it was you that wanted to be taken to art galleries and concerts. I didn't force any of it on you . . .'

'Oh look, let's not argue about it. Argument is so destructive. I'm not accusing you of anything. I'm not saying anything's your fault. I'm not blaming Beethoven or anyone. I'm just trying to explain to you where my priorities must lie now. It is with these children. I've never done anything like this before. I'm doing something meaningful with my life at last.'

'I don't want to argue. Let's stop, shall we? Why don't you just tell me about these children? Surely you need very specialised skills to be able to work with blind children?'

'Not really. I don't teach Braille or how to use a white stick, if that's what you're thinking. They have specially trained teachers for that. I just provide some support for the main staff. We do a lot of singing and storytelling, just like you would with sighted children. The school is very understaffed, and they're always looking for volunteers to help. They especially want people who can play musical instruments . . .'

Maria went on to tell Aldous more about the school, and as she did so more of the old Maria returned, until by the end of their time together he was beginning to feel that the faint hostility and resentment had passed, and they had become friends again.

Then Maria declared it was time for her to leave. She had some urgent appointment to keep, or work to do, or something. As they walked out of the Hall together, Aldous asked her, 'Maria, you never told me what sort of cancer you actually had.'

'Didn't I?'

'No, I've read a lot about it, but I realised they are all very different, and I didn't know which sort you had.'

'Oh, well. I thought you might not want to know.'

'No. I'd like to know, if you don't mind telling me.'

'Well, it's ovarian cancer. Last year I had one taken away, this time they took the other one, and everything else as well, just to be on the safe side: ovary, tubes, uterus. Some women have it done anyway when they get to a certain age, so I don't feel that bad about it.'

She left him with this news at the entrance to Waterloo Underground station.

23

The cold callers were changing. The door steppers. Once a month an old woman known as Ruby (though Aldous couldn't remember how he knew her name) knocked and, with a cold, trembling hand, gave Aldous a magazine called *Awake!*. He knew that she was a Jehovah's Witness, and that these people were the subject of ridicule among most householders. Juliette and Bernard, for instance, were full of amusing stories of how they'd dealt with Jehovah's Witnesses: by telling them they were satanists, or anarchists, or communists, by debating them out of their depths and bamboozling them with metaphysics and quantum mechanics. Given twenty minutes Bernard reckoned he could strip any Jehovah's Witness of their faith. That's why they always ended up running away, he said. Eighteen minutes was as much rational argument as they could take before their world of thorny superstition went pop. He and Juliette laughed at Aldous for being taken in by the beguiling charm of a buttoned-up old crone like Ruby. When they saw the copies of *Awake!* scattered about the house they would pick them up and read snippets from the articles aloud, laughing incredulously at their childish simplicity ('*The Sony Walkman – music to your ears or deafness to your children?*' '*Soap Operas – are they the modern Scriptures?*') and Aldous would laugh along with them, just as he would laugh along with their ridiculing of his choice of newspaper (the *Daily Telegraph*). But at the same time, at the back of his mind, people like Ruby nagged at him, the people who'd sorted it all out, who had all the answers, even if, as Bernard would say, it was only because they'd chosen to ignore the difficult questions. It was as if they'd somehow regained the childish viewpoint that dismisses complexity and ambiguity – a trait shared, Aldous was increasingly coming to feel, by all people of belief, whether religious or political. Bernard's little partisan rants displayed the same quality: the luxury of certainty. Aldous did not possess it. Had never possessed it.

The man from Neighbourly Hands possessed it. He was quite certain that if people 'got together', as he called it, they could achieve wonders. He was another of the new breed of cold callers, selling not things but ideas. He called one winter evening, and Aldous had assumed he was another Jehovah's Witness. He thought this because the man's opening shot was an enquiry after Aldous's well-being. *'How are you?'* The Jehovah's Witnesses always began with a similar personal question – *'We're just in the area, asking people how they feel about life today.'*

But the man from Neighbourly Hands (Aldous never caught his name) had a more practical reason for enquiring. He was trying to set up what he called a 'grey-watch network' – a system whereby the elderly in an area were kept an eye on by their neighbours. Aldous had heard of a similar scheme to combat crime. Neighbourhood Watch, it was called. When Aldous asked if this scheme was an offshoot of that, the man seemed quite offended. Aldous gathered from his remarks that Neighbourly Hands and the Neighbourhood Watch were ideologically opposed, the latter being a Thatcherite attempt to edge society towards vigilantism and the privatisation of the police force, the former being a shift towards collectivisation and the fostering of community spirit. Out of boredom Aldous had invited the man in and had learned a great deal about Neighbourly Hands. Grey-Watch was only a tiny part of what they did. They operated a volunteer bureau, a legal advice centre, an education council and a skills-exchange service. Apparently, through Neighbourly Hands, you could get your plumbing done and instead of paying money, you could offer the plumber a service in return. 'Such as?' Aldous enquired. 'Whatever skill you could offer,' came the reply. 'So I could pay my plumber in, say, drawing lessons?' 'Absolutely'. 'Are you sure it would work? I mean, supposing the plumber didn't want drawing lessons – or supposing he could already draw?' 'Eventually we will have so many plumbers in our directory you're bound to find one who wants drawing lessons. The wonderful thing is, that plumber will then be able to offer drawing lessons in payment for something else – for his car to be fixed, or whatever. Imagine, a teaming, thriving web of skill exchange growing and spreading . . .'

'Yes,' said Aldous, happy to share the vision for a moment, though he couldn't help having doubts. Something would go wrong. Certain skills would be in more demand than others. Plumbers, for instance, would be in almost constant demand, while art teachers would be rather more limited. There would be an awful lot of plumbers taking piano lessons, basket-weaving lessons and courses in Esperanto.

When the man finally persuaded Aldous to name the skills he could offer, the list went on and on – painting (oils, water-colours, acrylic), etching, lithography, screen printing, lino and woodcutting, steel engraving, calligraphy, drawing (pencil, pastel, charcoal), pottery, ceramic design, signwriting, book-binding, art history from the Renaissance to Modernism (with specialist areas including the life and work of Rembrandt, Cézanne and Piero della Francesca). Aldous illustrated his list with examples of his work, taking the man on a tour of the house and showing him samples of pottery and printmaking on the way. 'I suppose I could do elementary piano lessons as well,' he said when they came to the Bechstein, and he treated the visitor to a rendition of the cadenzas of Beethoven's Fourth Piano Concerto, which, due to the few whiskies he'd had, sounded to Aldous like a flawless performance.

'Marvellous,' said the man, who'd been carefully edging towards the door, 'really wonderful playing, but I must . . .' He looked at his watch.

'I could probably do a few classes on Shakespeare appreciation –'

'That's wonderful – someone with your experience –'

'Did I tell you I worked in a secondary school for nearly forty years?'

'You did, yes, but the reason –'

'That must count for something, in terms of experience, I mean we've all got skills of some sort or another, haven't we? But we can't all be good teachers, can we?'

'Absolutely, but –'

'How about a lecture on the representation of parenthood in *King Lear*?'

'We don't really do lectures.'

'I think you should –'

'Well, it's an idea. And, Mr Jones, I really value your range of skills, and your teaching experience, and I'm so pleased that you're willing to share them with us, but the main purpose of my visit was to inform you about Grey-Watch. Just before I go, can I give you this?'

He reached into his document wallet and brought out a square, red piece of card. He handed it to Aldous.

'If for any reason you need help, require assistance of any kind, you know – perhaps you need something from the shops but don't feel you can make it down there, or you're feeling ill but can't get to the doctor's. Just place this card in the window, so that it's visible from the street. It will soon be spotted by someone in Grey-Watch, and they'll come to your assistance . . .'

Rarely had Aldous felt so disappointed in someone. He had taken this man on a tour through his life as a visual artist, had played to him the difficult bits of a Beethoven piano concerto, and yet in his eyes he remained the helpless, hapless pensioner, someone who might spend days on the floor before anyone noticed, or be found weeks later maggot-blown and fused to the carpet. Someone to be watched over, worried about.

And even when dismissed from the house, the man returned several times to occupy the uncomfortable dreams that bothered Aldous in his daytime dozes. In these dreams the man appeared just as he had in real life, except that from his mouth flowed a constant stream of glittering saliva, and he would plead with Aldous to help him deal with this outpouring, asking, in a muffled, bubbly voice, for pans and buckets in which to catch the syrupy liquid, but there were never enough of these.

But yet he remained true to his word, and had in fact seen Aldous as far more than a problem to be solved. Aldous's skills had been entered into the skills-swap register, and within a matter of weeks Aldous was bartering with a plumber on the phone. Aldous had a leaky stopcock and the plumber was interested in Rembrandt appreciation. The stopcock proved to be a difficult job, taking up most of a morning, but all Aldous had to pay for were the materials used.

Getting up from his knees and wiping his mossy hands on a damp rag, the plumber said, 'That's that. Now, when can we squeeze this bit of Rembrandt in? I can fit you in Wednesday week,' the plumber leafed through a smudged, crumpled diary, 'say from eight till nine?'

'But you've been at that stopcock for three hours,' said Aldous, worried that the plumber wouldn't consider he was getting sufficient return, 'I'll need to give you three hours on Rembrandt in return, surely?'

'Christ, no,' said the plumber grimacing. 'It doesn't work like that. A job's a job, whether it takes an hour or three hours. It all depends. But a class on Rembrandt – you don't want to stretch that out for three hours. Blimey. No, an hour will do fine.'

And so a fortnight later the plumber turned up for his Rembrandt lesson. He seemed to be a completely different man. He had changed from his torn and greasy work clothes into something clean and casual. He carried a little cardboard document folder. When he'd called to fix the stopcock he'd swaggered about the house, turning off valves in the street, grunting and whistling with exertion as he yanked at joints, wielding lengths of piping as though they were gun barrels; now he was all humility and edgy embarrassment. Uncertain of himself. Quiet.

He positioned himself at the kitchen table which made him seem like an overgrown schoolboy sitting at a desk, while Aldous sat in the armchair by the boiler, glass of whisky by his side, giving an ad lib talk on the life of Rembrandt while the plumber busily made notes on a notepad. Several times Aldous lost the thread of what he was saying, and would pause, look at his watch, wonder how long he had been talking for, hold his head in his hands and try to regather his thoughts, conscious of how disconnected they must seem. During these pauses the plumber said nothing, and made no sound at all. The few times Aldous managed to glance in his direction, he saw that he was staring rather sadly into space. Then Aldous would remember another thing to say about Rembrandt, and start talking again.

As the end of the hour approached, the plumber startled Aldous by interrupting him suddenly in mid sentence.

'Excuse me, Mr Jones, sorry to interrupt, but I was rather expecting we was going to talk about Rembrandt's paintings in this talk. I mean, he did do some paintings, didn't he? He is an artist, isn't he?'

'Haven't I said anything about his paintings, surely –'

'No, just about his love life. That's all I've had. Very interesting, actually. I never knew all that about his mistress . . .'

'I should have got a book out. I don't have one here, I just go into town to look at the paintings, or I go in the library. But if you go to the National Gallery, you can see them for yourself – there's one truly wonderful portrait of Hendrickje, she looks fabulously beautiful, hauntingly beautiful. In fact, I've been trying –'

'But when you say Rembrandt was an alcoholic, and that Hendrickje used to take care of him when he got too "pissed" to look after himself – where's your proof of that? Is it written down in a book or something – how do you know?'

'Oh – well, you only have to look into the faces of his self-portraits. His nose gets redder and redder, it evolves into one of those bulbous drinkers' noses. You could actually do a study of it: the shades of redness in Rembrandt's nose. And there's no doubt that in one of the self-portraits he's quite severely drunk. It's never been described as such – in the books it is always "self-portrait laughing", but anyone can see it's "self-portrait drunk".'

'But that story you told about how he fell asleep in his paints and woke up stuck to his palette –'

'And how she became his art dealer, and made him an employee to protect his work from his creditors and to allow him to trade again. Isn't that incredible? If that's not looking after someone I don't know what is. But I haven't got to the important part of the story yet –'

The plumber suddenly closed his folder and stood up.

'That's the hour done, Mr Jones, I don't want to take up any more of your time.'

'What? But I'm in the middle.'

'So sorry, but we have to keep to strict time limits in the

skills-swap system, otherwise things can get out of hand. It's been a pleasure hearing all about Rembrandt's sex life, Mr Jones. It is amazing, as you say, how the sexual urge can persist so far into old age. But I would have liked a bit more proof, like I said . . .'

'Well, it wasn't just about sex of course. There was much else besides. But the final sad thing is that Hendrickje died before Rembrandt . . .'

The plumber was on his way down the hall now towards the front door.

'Thanks again, Mr Jones.'

'He outlived her. Where's the justice in that?'

But the plumber had gone.

The very next day Aldous decided to try out the red card. He placed it in the living-room window. Nothing happened for four hours, and then a slightly dishevelled, rosily middle-aged woman called at the door.

Aldous explained how he was feeling weak in the legs and couldn't get to the shops. Could she help him? She nodded in a tired but warm sort of way, and Aldous gave her a list and some money. The list read:

    1 individual steak and kidney pie
    1 bunch bananas
    1 carton UHT milk
    1 loaf
    1 70cl bottle whisky (White Horse pref)

Sure enough, an hour later, she returned with a shopping bag containing everything on the list, including the whisky. She didn't even pass comment on it, she just handed over the plastic shopping bag (the whisky bottle making its plonking, glugging sounds), as though it was just another one of the staples of life.

The woman insisted that Aldous put the red card in the window whenever he felt unable to go shopping in the future, and so a few days later he did. This was more to strike up a friendship with the rosy woman than to save his legs, as he rather enjoyed a stroll to the shops now and then. She was his neighbour. She lived in the same road. She said she had lived in Fernlight Avenue for twenty years, yet Aldous had never seen her before. He shouldn't have been surprised. Each successive door down the road was one further remove from his known world. Beyond four or five houses, his neighbours merged with the other six million London strangers he lived with.

He gave the rosy woman an almost identical list to the one he gave her before, but this time she took rather longer to read it. She looked up pleadingly from the list, clearly troubled by the whisky, but unable to find quite the right words to express her concerns. Then she dutifully went off and returned with the goods, including the alcohol.

On the third attempt, however, she cracked. She didn't say anything, she simply returned from the shopping trip without the whisky. She handed the bag over to Aldous, beaming, and said, as an afterthought when she was turning to go, 'By the way, they didn't have any – you know, whisky. They'd sold out. Sorry.'

Aldous didn't use his red card after that and he never saw the woman again.

Other people came though. Another neighbour, who said she lived in the same road but whom he'd never seen before, enquired after his artistic skills. She was looking for someone to paint giant pictures of characters from *Alice in Wonderland* for an after-school club's mini pantomime and had found Aldous on the Neighbourly Hands directory. She apologised but she could only offer lessons in French Provincial Cookery in return. Aldous said it didn't matter and spent two amusing afternoons and evenings in a room at the back of the main library drawing and painting the Mad Hatter and Tweedledee for the benefit of fascinated, galloping children.

The experience exhausted Aldous, but delighted him at the same time. Staggering home paint-splattered, with the shrieks of happy children in his ears, he was taken back to the early days of his teaching experience, in those grim art rooms with their decaying still lifes and sheep skulls – the unexpected joy of opening children's eyes to the world around them.

Aldous believed that Maria would be impressed by his

involvement with Neighbourly Hands. It was just the sort of thing, surely, that she would approve of. They met infrequently now, though still at the Festival Hall, and each time Maria seemed edgier than the last, always making her sudden and urgent exit, as though she'd only remembered an important appointment at the last minute. With no time for proper good-byes or the settling of future arrangements, she'd be tripping away carrying her coat over her arm, her bag hanging open and nearly spilling. Aldous would be left feeling as though he was something that had fallen out of the back door of her hectic life, and he would wander the concrete walkways of the South Bank alone, or stand solitary on Hungerford Bridge and watch the fat, oozing waters of the Thames slide beneath him.

Today, however, Maria failed to make her blustery departure in the foyer, and they walked out of the Festival Hall together.

'I don't understand how our society can leave people to live like this,' she said.

They had wandered into the Bullring, a sunken concrete piazza at the centre of a roundabout, the point of intersection for several pedestrian underpasses. It had become, in recent years, a recognised symbol of the new underclass of London homeless. Cardboard City. Doss Central. Large boxes – big sturdy ones that had once packaged fridges and cookers – were now filled with people. Tipped sideways and lined with shreds of blanket, bits of string serving as door fastenings and washing lines, they appeared like hideous travesties of dolls' houses, or the type of childish den Aldous would have made when he was a kid.

The most shocking thing was the appearance of the inhabitants. These weren't the winos and tramps one occasionally saw wrapped in blankets under embankment bridges, faces black with dirt. Some of the residents of this shanty town were young, clean and pretty. A teenage girl with long hanks of stiff hair hanging down her back sat cross-legged outside a box, a short-haired, sad-eyed dog resting its head in her lap. By another box sat a man with long sideburns and gold-rimmed spectacles, sewing buttons on to a shirt. He was just one haircut and shave away from seeming respectable. He looked as though he'd been lifted out of an ordinary, secure life and deposited in this hellish settlement by the hand of some mischievous god.

'These people remind me of the Borrowers,' said Aldous.

'It is quite obscene,' said Maria, 'that this should be allowed to happen. I may not know anything about politics, but I know you never saw anything like this until Mrs Thatcher came to power. Is that a coincidence?'

'Some of these places look quite cosy,' said Aldous, stooping to peer into an empty one.

'How can you say that? Aldous, that's a shameful thing to say.'

By this time Maria was reaching into her purse and handing silver to a man who was holding out his hand and murmuring in vaguely threatening Glaswegian. He was wearing a camouflage bush hat to which a badge was pinned that bore the words *No Wuckin' Forries*.

It's not even a decent spoonerism, Aldous was thinking to himself before the whiskery man turned his attention to him. Aldous reluctantly handed over change, which the man inspected with indifference.

'I don't really understand this begging thing,' said Aldous to Maria as they continued slowly through the desolation, Maria forking out more money at every turn. 'How much are you supposed to give? A few pennies might seem an insult, but then what's the upper limit? If I lived on bread and cheese I suppose I could afford to give away most of my pension . . .'

'A friend of mine,' said Maria, 'gave his house to a beggar, and then went and camped on Hackney Wick. He said he couldn't bear the thought of living in a house while there were people sleeping on the streets.'

'And is he still there?'

'No. Winter came on so he went back home. But the house had burned down – no one's quite sure why. He's living with his parents now, I think.'

'So now there are two homeless people where before there was one.'

'You could put it like that, I suppose, but you must admire the sacrifice . . . Aldous, I don't have much cash left, could you give this poor girl some money?'

'I haven't got anything smaller than a fiver ...' Aldous fingered the note in his wallet and looked at Maria hopefully. Her response was a 'so what?' glare, and so Aldous handed the note over to a girl in a tatty anorak, who took it and pocketed it as quickly as if it had been some illegal substance.

'Thank God for my free bus pass,' said Aldous, 'otherwise I wouldn't be able to get home tonight. That's something else Mrs Thatcher wants to ban, isn't it? In which case I would be homeless as well.'

'Aldous, I doubt these people are on the streets because they haven't got free bus passes.'

'No, I suppose not. Oh, I expect it will all sort itself out eventually.'

'Just by itself? Is that your attitude to the problems of the world – it'll all sort itself out eventually?'

'Well, it does, doesn't it?'

'Not without people making sacrifices and doing amazing things. That's the trouble with you, Aldous. You are complacent. Head in the sand. We could all go up in smoke for all you care. I sometimes think ...'

'Think what?'

'I shouldn't say this, but I sometimes think ... I sometimes think you just don't care, you just don't care about anything.'

They were out of the cardboard city now, walking back towards the river, and Maria was weeping quietly into a tissue. Aldous had the feeling that she hadn't said what she was going to say, that what she was going to say was much worse than what she actually said.

'I do care about things, Maria. I care about you ...'

Aldous felt himself wince when he said those last words, realising just too late that it was the wrong time to say them. And he sensed immediately that he had annoyed Maria.

'Don't be so stupid, Aldous. It's typical of you. We're talking about the homeless and you manage to bring it back to yourself –'

'But I was talking about you –'

'About your needs, your wants.'

'But what have I just told you? I taught a plumber about Rembrandt for God's sake. I painted Humpty-Dumpty for the kiddies. I'm a volunteer now, like you, galloping about doing good . . .'

Now it was time for Maria's sudden urgent exit. The tissue was stashed, the watch consulted and she made her sudden retreat. She had become like some panto fairy disappearing in a puff of smoke. But she did give Aldous a longer kiss on the cheek, saying, 'You are a very sweet man, but you won't understand, will you?'

And she was gone.

24

The first thing that surprised Aldous about the blind school was the mobility of the children. They were walking around the classroom, sometimes even running, as if they knew exactly where they were going.

He remarked on this to the teacher and she laughed at him. What did he expect, she said, that they would all be walking into the tables and chairs and each other, or falling out of the windows?

'They must have evolved echolocation, I suppose,' said Aldous, 'like bats. That's what happens, isn't it?' He paused, noticing how the teacher was looking at him in an odd way. 'I've just said something really stupid, haven't I?'

She laughed.

'Not at all, Mr Jones. In fact, most people are surprised when they see our classrooms. I don't know what they're expecting, but what they see is an apparently normal classroom, full of desks and chairs and clutter with children milling around, just like any other classroom. But if you look a little closer, you'll see that what at first appears to be chaotic is in fact meticulously organised. Everything is in its place. That's the secret. Everything, down to the last piece of Lego. Our children know that everything has a place and they know where that place is. If, for instance, a child needs a spoon, she knows that if she takes a certain route through the classroom (we have a very sophisticated one-way system in operation), she will find a spoon at the end of it. If that spoon isn't there because someone has put it in the wrong place, then it may as well be lost for ever, as far as the child is concerned. And the same for every other single object in the room.' She turned to Aldous. 'And that includes the people.' She smiled. 'They will need to know where they can find you, and you will need to know where you must be.'

Walking into the classroom, Aldous felt, was like stepping into a pool of darkness – his very presence caused ripples of disturbance. He had to be careful not to step in the way of the children's designated routes through the room; he had to remember not to move anything without replacing it exactly where it was. And in his inexperience he did both things several times, causing a little boy to crash into his legs, and a little girl to lose her basketwork.

It had been very easy to enrol as a volunteer at the school. A letter citing his old headmaster as a referee brought a phone call within days, and now here he was on his first trial day, being shown the ropes. Aldous sensed an enormous hunger for voluntary help, and to his mild alarm he also sensed that the staff were pleased with how he was coping. The mild alarm was because he didn't feel as though he was coping well at all. Children collided with him all day. He frequently forgot that they couldn't see, and was momentarily puzzled when they wouldn't respond to a visual cue. He felt that he was walking against the current of blindness, having to adapt his whole frame of bodily reference to the culture of the unsighted. Nodding the head no longer meant anything and nor did smiling. 'You can't hear a smile,' the teacher said, when Aldous offered one to a little girl who'd done something clever. 'You have to say your smile.'

It was exhausting having to do everything with the voice and with touch. But the teachers seemed to think he'd got on splendidly. A few solecisms were perfectly excusable in a newcomer to this kingdom. But what Aldous hadn't been prepared for was the fear. The children terrified him with their hopeful, unseeing gazes. He was angry at his own stupidity in not having prepared himself for the moment of encountering so many blind children, and he felt angry with himself for feeling such a sense of horror. 'They really . . . they really can't see a thing?' he thought to himself, as though the words 'School for Blind Children' had merely been some sort of metaphor, not to be taken literally. And now here was the blunt, horrible, literal truth behind the title. Here were the blind children, victims of the random cruelties of God or nature (get the Jehovah's Witnesses to explain this little lot, he thought), with their sad, empty sockets. And yet they smiled so much. That was the other terrifying thing. They didn't seem hurt or upset at all by their condition. They didn't even seem to recognise that there was something wrong with them, that they lacked a faculty. (How odd, thought Aldous, they can't see smiles yet they produce them probably more often than sighted children.) But of course it was the eyes that upset Aldous most of all. Some were very obviously useless – rolled half back into the head, with only the whites showing or just not there at all, the lids collapsing into a hollowness where they would have been. They reminded him of the old teddy bears he sometimes came across in a forgotten cupboard, once the steadfast night-time companion of one of his children, now sitting eyeless in endless night. Mostly the children were physically perfect in every other way. It was as though someone had simply forgotten to give them working eyes, as though a neglectful production-line worker had forgotten to pin them on. *Hey – I forgot these* (running down the corridor with two white balls in her hands – but too late). Their eyes were like the hooks you find in the wall when you take a picture down – the root, fastening, stud, but without the thing it's meant to hold. In·others the eyes were perma-nently closed, which gave them a curious look as though they were perpetually squinting against bright light, or laughing. A few had what seemed like perfect eyes. One small girl in partic-ular, her hair in a pretty bob, had wide brown eyes which, at a glance, appeared coordinated and focused. It was only when some colourful but silent event passed her by that you realised they were dead to the world. A line from a poem kept repeating itself in Aldous's mind – *Why aren't they screaming?* Why weren't they wailing or weeping in despair at their eternal confinement? The world of visual treasures was within touching distance, and yet it may as well have been as remote as the galaxies. They would never be able to see it. And the most distressing thing of all – they believed they were happy. They believed they were normal. And when Aldous went home at the end of that first long day, he sat down in his armchair by the boiler and held a tea towel against his face and sobbed into it.

His first feeling was that he should never go to the blind school again. But he had impressed the staff and they were expecting him to come in for an afternoon the day after next. His determination to impress Maria spurred him on. He was a little disappointed she hadn't been there that first day. He had forgotten she worked there only part-time. When he had mentioned her name to the staff, they had spoken of her with great admiration and praise – she was so dedicated, they said, and so good with the children. But they couldn't tell him exactly when she would next be in.

By the time of his next visit to the school, he had recovered a little from the trauma of his first encounter, but he still felt a strong pang of unease as he approached the gates, which was dampened somewhat by the tiny nip of whisky he had on his way. Aldous told himself that the children's happiness should not be viewed as a tragedy, but as a cause for celebration. As one teacher remarked to him – they know nothing else. They've grown up without sight, they don't sense that they're missing anything.

This wasn't true. One little girl kept asking Aldous what a horse looked like.

Aldous struggled for an answer. He wanted to say they were brown and glossy, but these were meaningless words to a blind child. Why was she asking the question, he wondered, when for her the act of 'looking' must have been incomprehensible? But he soon realised that what she was really asking about was the size of a horse. She had a toy horse, which she called Thunder, a kind of three-dimensional jigsaw specially designed for blind children, full of shapes and textures, which she loved to fit together with Aldous's help (though she didn't really need it), but she had no experience of real horses.

'A real horse is very big,' said Aldous.

'How big?'

'Big enough for a man to sit on.'

'Like a chair?'

'No, much bigger than a chair. If I was standing next to a horse, the top of my head would only come up to its back. I would need a ladder to get up and sit on him.'

'But how big are you?'

'I'm this big,' said Aldous, suddenly snatching the girl under her arms and lifting her into the air. She shrieked with excitement, but Aldous found the sudden exertion rather a shock and nearly dropped her, only just managing to lower her safely.

'Again!' said the girl.

'In a minute,' Aldous wheezed, 'I need to sit down. Let's put Thunder together again.'

'That was fun,' said the girl.

Her name was Emma. She had closed eyelids that sometimes opened a crack to reveal crescents of white. In every other respect she was an ordinary little girl, who grinned with a mouth of lopsided teeth, who flitted around the classroom in a flowery frock (like many of the children, especially the girls, she was dressed in very traditional children's clothes). The permanent staff were teaching her Braille, but she could write with pen and paper as clearly as a sighted child. Aldous developed a kind of friendship with this girl. For some reason she latched on to him. She waited for him on his helping days and wouldn't do any of her activities until he'd arrived. She kept asking the staff (so they told him), '*Is Aldous here yet? Is Aldous here yet?*' Then, when he arrived, announced by the teacher and standing in his given spot, Emma would skip over with some pieces of Thunder and wave them at him. They played washing-up together in a sink full of plastic crockery, they did puzzles and games and read each other stories, but most of all they took apart and reassembled Thunder. It was always the first and last activity of the day. It amused Aldous how she pretended it was more difficult than it really was, in order to convince Aldous that his help was needed. She would claim she didn't know where a leg was, or the horse's fluffy mane, or how his tail would fit, when of course she knew perfectly well.

After three weeks Aldous had still not encountered Maria. It occurred to him that they had been deliberately scheduled to work on different days, and so were doomed never to meet. Of course it made sense, there was no point in having all your volunteers come in on the same day. The school needed to manage its voluntary resources efficiently. But Aldous grew increasingly frustrated. He found out which days Maria worked.

Monday, Thursday and Friday. He asked if he could come in on one of those days instead. His request was denied. It would be a serious disruption to the routine, he was told. The school is built entirely on routines. Yes, Aldous knew that, but it was no longer convenient for him to work on Tuesdays and Wednesdays. The teacher looked troubled. It would be most difficult for us – we already have enough staff for those days. If you changed days it would leave us understaffed on these days. And so on. One minute they seemed to be crying out for his services and now they were saying they wanted to pick and choose when he came in. It wasn't as though he was getting paid. He had a life elsewhere. He reminded them of this, and instantly realised he'd crossed some indefinable boundary, bringing the values of paid employment to the voluntary sector.

He wondered how he had got himself into this bizarre situation. A whimsical idea contrived to provide him with a chance of regular contact with Maria, and now here he was, not seeing Maria at all, and committed to a demanding, not to say exhausting, job. And it would have been such a delight to work with Maria, to see her on a weekly basis, have chats in the staffroom with her, or after-works drinks at a nearby bar, talking about the wonders of working with the blind.

And working with the blind children was providing him with a new form of tiredness, one that he had never experienced before. Walking up Fernlight Avenue from the bus stop one day, he found he had to sit on a front-garden wall halfway up the road. Fernlight Avenue was on a gentle incline, hardly worthy of being called a hill, just enough slope to mean you didn't have to pedal a bike on the way down. But on this occasion Fernlight Avenue had been transformed into an almost sheer cliff, every step requiring a huge, tugging effort. Things went dark for a few moments, the blood roared in his ears like a Tube train and his breath became short and raspy. After a few minutes he walked on, not fully recovered, and he had to sit down twice more before he got to his front door.

It must have been the physical and emotional demands of Emma and her little friends. He was getting old, he had to admit it. He had a red card that could signal that fact to the whole world. He had people who could do the shopping for him, if things got bad. And, indeed, when he got home he thought about putting the red card in the window, but after a few gulps of whisky he began to feel his strength returning.

The problem remained of how to see Maria. She hadn't phoned for weeks. The staff still refused to be flexible about when he worked days, and he was left, he felt, with no alternative but to just turn up at the school on one of Maria's days. He could bluff his way in, claim he'd got his days mixed up. Once he was actually there they wouldn't mind, and they'd let him help out anyway. He just wanted to show Maria how much he'd achieved – what a rapport he'd developed with the children. He wanted her to see how Emma's little face lit up when he arrived in the morning. She would know then how much he cared about things.

But as the day approached on which he'd settled to make this move, he felt rather nervous. He wasn't sure why. He didn't want to upset anyone, that was all. He took a quarter-bottle of White Horse along with him and swallowed a few mouthfuls as he neared the school.

From the moment he entered the building he sensed it had been a bad idea. On his normal days he was welcomed as someone vitally important to the school day, and the children swarmed around him. Now he was almost ignored. The school secretary threw him a look of puzzlement instead of her usual smile. The atmosphere had changed. The children, of course, were not waiting for him as they usually were, but were happily and busily engaged with their regular teachers and helpers for that day. One of whom, Aldous could see from the end of the room, was Maria. And (his heart filled at the sight) the child she was helping was the little girl in the flowery frock who loved horses, his Emma. But before Maria could notice, the headmistress breezed over looking concerned.

'Aldous, is anything wrong?'

'No,' said Aldous, craning his neck to see Maria, who was bending down and helping Emma with her puzzle, 'sorry, I was getting my days muddled up. I was on my way down here and thought it was my day for working, but it's not now, I realise, but I might as well help out a bit while I'm here . . .'

'Oh dear,' said the headmistress, 'what a predicament. Aldous, are you feeling unwell?'

'No, not a bit of it. I'm feeling fine. Shall I just mill around and do a bit of helping now that I'm here?'

'But everything's organised for the day – you know how it works. Well . . .' the headmistress was succumbing to Aldous's gentle pressure, 'I suppose it wouldn't hurt . . . Charlene and Tina could do with some help – but I'll have to rearrange the rota . . .'

She bustled off to do exactly that. Aldous took his opportunity and drifted over towards Maria. She looked up and noticed him, and couldn't contain her sense of discomfort and surprise.

'Aldous, what on earth are you doing here?'

'Hello, darling,' he said, stupidly. He hadn't meant to use this term. The whisky must have been having more effect than he thought. 'Hasn't anyone told you I'm working here?'

'You're working here?'

'Aldous. Is Aldous here?' said Emma, who'd just returned from replacing something on a table. 'Oh, let's do Thunder.'

'I've been working here for nearly a month, but they won't let us be here on the same days. I thought perhaps we could work together. I don't mind, it's silly, isn't it? Isn't this a wonderful place?'

'I can't quite believe it, Aldous. Why haven't you mentioned it to me?'

'You haven't phoned. I've been wanting to tell you but you haven't phoned.'

'Oh, you know how I feel about telephones, Aldous . . .' She turned suddenly to Emma and whispered something reassuring and sensible in her ear. The gist of it was that she would have to leave her on her own for a few minutes while she went and had a chat with Aldous.

'Will Aldous come back and help me with Thunder?' called Emma as the two departed.

'I should think so,' said Maria.

They removed themselves to a remote part of the school.

'Amazing little creatures, aren't they,' said Aldous, 'so helpless, yet so happy.'

'They're not so helpless, Aldous, and that's the whole point of a place like this, to encourage their independence – and why shouldn't they be happy? As far as they're concerned there's nothing wrong with them.'

'I know, I know. I should follow the party line on this but we're just fooling ourselves, aren't we? We're all fooling ourselves in this place. These kids are horribly deprived and they'll never be able to look at a sunset or a waterfall or even the faces of their husbands and wives, if they find any, their entire lives. Personally I can't imagine anything more horrific, doomed to a lifetime of darkness . . .'

'You're assessing their chances of happiness purely by the standards of your own life as a sighted person. Why don't you think about them from their point of view? Their happiness is an unarguable fact. They're not pretending to be happy or putting on a brave face, they really are happy, just like any other children. Anyway, you didn't come here to have a long talk about the quality of life for blind children, did you? What did you come here for, Aldous?'

'I came here to see you.'

'I thought so. Why did you want to see me?'

'To ask you to marry me.'

Aldous hadn't meant to say that either. It had just slipped out. But, having said it, he had to go through with it and endure the sequence of exchanges that followed.

'You're not serious?'

'Why not?'

'Shall I pretend I didn't hear it?'

'What's so wrong with it?'

Maria hesitated, regathering her thoughts. Aldous could see she was going through all the different ramifications of this conversation in her mind before choosing which one to follow.

'Aldous, I don't believe you said that with any seriousness . . .'

'All right. Well. What about you let me paint your portrait?'

'What?'

'Sit for me. I'll paint your portrait.'

'So now you've just forgotten about the marriage question?'

'You didn't seem interested.'

Maria seemed dumbfounded, confused, shocked, even. Aldous felt a curious sense of triumph at having at last been able to baffle her. She was so rarely, if ever, lost for words.

'Aldous. We need a good long talk about all this. You've confused and upset me terribly. Now is not the best place. Not with the children and the work that I have to do here. Let's talk afterwards –'

'That's another thing. I've not told you about how well I'm doing here –'

'I really need to get back to my group. We'll talk later.'

They made their way back into the classroom.

'Is Aldous back?' Emma asked Maria as she returned to the girl.

'Yes, Emma, Aldous is just here. Why don't you ask him to do Thunder with you. I've got to go over to Katie's group now and I'll see you later.'

She walked across the room to her group. Emma held out the head and one leg of Thunder for Aldous to take, and he was about to, but the feeling of great weakness, tiredness, dizziness came back to him.

'Aldous, do Thunder with me.'

But Aldous was searching for a chair. He sat down heavily. Emma was only a few feet away, and she knew that Aldous was near, but wasn't sure in what direction.

'Aldous, do Thunder with me?' She held out the horse's head and leg offering them to emptiness in different directions. But Aldous found himself unable to make any reply. He watched Emma as though from across a great gulf of distance, or as though she was something on a television screen, turning left and right. Stop asking, he kept thinking to himself, just stop asking – not because he didn't want to do Thunder, but because he didn't want the little girl to go on calling into the darkness for ever.

Eventually Aldous noticed that all the staff were watching the scene – the little girl pleading for Aldous's help, Aldous silently refusing it, slumped a few feet away in a chair.

'Aldous, where are you?'

I'm over here, Emma, Aldous tried to call, but nothing came

out. Stop calling, I can't bear it, I'm coming. But there was no strength in his legs at all. He pulled at the arms of the chair in a desperate effort to propel himself in Emma's direction, but the next thing he knew he was on all fours on the floor, his arms shaking with the effort of holding his body up.

Staff approached with anxious, concerned looks on their faces and rescued Emma.

'Aldous is just having a rest at the moment, Emma, let's do Thunder together.'

'But he's here. I can hear him laughing. Why isn't he answering me?'

'I don't know, Emma. I think he's very tired.'

Aldous wasn't laughing. There was a sound coming out of his mouth, but it wasn't laughter. He wasn't sure what it was. He lay down on the classroom floor, and tried to get some sleep.

25

Aldous had never been sacked before, but the blind school had been very nice about it. He had feared a more humiliating stripping-down in front of the whole school and Maria, but when Aldous had been roused from his great lassitude, it had simply been a quiet chat in the headmistress's office, and all the apologising seemed to come from her. She was sorry that it wasn't working out for him, it was probably their mistake for burdening him with too much too soon, they were so sorry, etc. Not at all, don't mention it, Aldous found himself replying. Though there was one bit of their conversation that bothered him. The headmistress said something about not realising he had 'such a problem', and a couple of other times she referred to his 'condition'. What did she mean? he wondered. Then afterwards he realised. She must have thought he was drunk. Drunk on duty in a school for blind children. But he hadn't been. Not seriously. Just a few mouthfuls of whisky to take the edge off his nerves – certainly not enough to land him unconscious on the floor. Yet she must have smelt the spirit on his breath and assumed he was blotto. As if he would career through a blind school blind drunk, in front of Maria . . . the thought was too appalling.

Yet a few days later it was confirmed. Not through any official communication, but through Juliette. Maria had taken the inexplicably crass step of telephoning Aldous's daughter and pouring out the whole episode to her in every last detail. Of course, he had already told her about the work he was doing at the blind school. She had been very interested and impressed, both she and Bernard, by his energy and commitment to a worthy cause. He hadn't mentioned anything about Maria working at the school as well. To double the humiliation,

Juliette confronted Aldous at her flat one Sunday afternoon in the presence of Bernard, when they were all settled down for a game of Trivial Pursuit.

This game could have been invented for Bernard and Juliette, and indeed they seemed a little disappointed that they hadn't thought to invent it themselves. So obvious, they said, so simple. The people who patented it had become millionaires. Why didn't we think of it? It appealed to them because it gave a physical reality to what before had been abstract and piece-meal. Their old quizzes had used encyclopedias and scraps of paper to keep scores but there had been nothing in the room they could point to and say, 'That is our quiz.' But now there was: a stout green box of curiously satisfying dimensions and weight, a game board that flapped open four different ways, quaint little pie-shaped playing pieces, and a stack of question cards that looked as though they would provide a lifetime of questions. It was as though their life of quiz-setting had been officially sanctioned.

'Maria phoned me last night,' said Juliette, just as Aldous was inserting the first wedge into his pie.

'Maria phoned you?' It seemed incredible to Aldous that Maria would even know Juliette's number.

'She told me you got the sack from the blind school for being drunk.'

'That's not true. I wasn't. But why on earth was she phoning you?'

'Because she hoped I could talk some sense into you, I should think. I don't really understand. I had no idea she worked at the school as well.'

'Oh. Didn't I mention it?'

'No, you didn't. And then she told me that you'd asked her to marry you.'

'Oh for God's sake, this is very personal. She's no right telling you all this. I was only joking about the marriage thing. I don't even know why I said it.'

'Well, she seemed to think that you did mean it, and she's worried about your state of mind. She gave me these phone numbers for you – one of which is Alcoholics Anonymous.'

'I don't need it –'

'She said you were reeking with whisky at the blind school, and that you ignored a little girl who was asking you to do something, and that you lay down on the floor and went to sleep.'

'I was tired –'

'It sounds very like being drunk to me, not to mention this asking Maria for her hand-in-marriage lark.'

'Look, can we just get on with this game? It's my turn to roll.'

'Well, I think it's important to talk about it, isn't it? Maria has really worried me. She said the headmistress was very cross –'

'She was very nice about it, they all were.'

'Maria said that the headmistress was angry, disgusted and appalled by your behaviour, and that she had been in two minds about reporting you.'

'Who to?'

'I don't know. The police perhaps?'

'Well, like I said, the headmistress was very good about it, she could understand that I was just tired.'

'You've misread the signals, like you always do. You haven't read between the lines. She was obviously being pleasant to you because she didn't want to upset you and possibly provoke you into causing more trouble in the school, and upsetting those poor little kids.'

'I didn't upset any of the kids. Well, Emma was a bit puzzled, but that's all. Look, I've landed on an orange square. What subject is that?'

'Sport and Leisure,' said Bernard with relish, as it was known to be Aldous's weakest subject. There was a pause in the conversation as he extracted the question card, made a show of hiding it behind his hand, and read the question.

'Which golfer has won the US Masters Championship a record six times?'

Aldous groaned, and then made a lot of fuss about how boring the question was, how stupid the game of golf was, and how any knowledge of the subject was an indication of a wasted life. And then he gave the correct answer.

'Jack Nicklaus.'

Bernard eyed Aldous suspiciously as he replaced the card and doled out an orange wedge (it was his job, always, to distribute wedges).

'I once knew someone who made his living out of painting golf courses. Have I told you about him?'

'Yes, many times,' said Bernard.

Unfortunately the question was not enough to bring the preceding conversation to an end. Juliette went on.

'Maria has made me very worried, Dad. I don't like to think of you blundering about after women who aren't interested in you. Maria said she'd been ill, and that you were making her feel worse. And your drinking, it's getting out of control again, isn't it –'

'Look, forget about me and Maria, OK? We were just friends anyway – I don't know why she's gone and got everything out of proportion. I suppose I've just been a bit stupid. OK, I've been drinking a bit. But not any more, OK?'

He rolled the die rather vigorously, so that it spilled off the table and tumbled across the carpet, out of sight beneath a chair. He was angered by Maria's flighty and unpredictable tactic of enlisting his own daughter into an alliance against him. It broke some carefully and painstakingly erected boundaries in Aldous's life. It did more than break them, it trampled them into the ground so you'd think they'd never been there. As a result he felt vulnerable and exposed. Was this what Maria had wanted? For him to feel childlike and stupid before his own offspring? To be told off like a little boy who's eaten too many sweets? Somehow it pierced him that Maria could perceive his daughter as someone with that kind of authority, or that such an alliance was even possible. He'd struggled over countless months to build his relationship with Maria, to secure the priv-ileged intimacies, the sharing of joys and fears that can only come once the guy ropes of secure friendship are firmly in place. Yet here she was, able to form such a closeness with Juliette on the strength of one long-ago dinner party, and some shared notion of common sisterhood.

'Anyway,' said Juliette, who'd retrieved the die from under the chair, 'me and Bernard are thinking of buying a house.'

'Are you?' Aldous said with exaggerated disinterest, thinking the news irrelevant in the light of what had gone before, and besides, Juliette and Bernard were always talking over the prospect of buying a house. He shook the die and was gentler with it this time.

'Not round here, of course,' said Bernard, 'we couldn't afford a house in Holland Park.'

'No, I don't suppose you could. *Roll again.*'

'So we were thinking of somewhere closer to home. Windhover Hill, that area.'

'So you can keep an eye on me?'

'So we can be closer . . .'

'Mind you,' said Bernard, 'we'll need to act fast. Do you know what your house is worth now, Aldous?'

'Yes, people keep telling me. Eighty thousand or so.'

Bernard laughed scornfully.

'There was a house in Fernlight Avenue on the market last week for a hundred and twenty thousand.'

'That's ridiculous,' said Aldous.

'And the rise shows no sign of slowing down. This time next year it could be a hundred and fifty thousand, or even more.'

Aldous had landed on Arts and Entertainment, but he got some silly question about children's TV, which brought his winning streak to an end. He was thankful, he'd got fed up with rolling the dice.

'If we get somewhere nice with lots of bedrooms, you could always move in with us . . .' said Juliette.

'Very nice of you . . .'

'You could have your own self-contained room, we could even put a cooker in there . . .'

'You'd expect me to do my own cooking?'

'Well, no . . . But we might be out or something. Anyway, it's just an idea.'

'And a very sweet idea too. But I've got plans for Fernlight Avenue. Everyone keeps telling me I should sell it and move into a tiny bungalow. Everyone tells me I must be rattling around in that big empty house. But for what I've got planned, it's barely going to be big enough.'

'What do you mean? What have you got planned?'

'I am turning 89 Fernlight Avenue into an art gallery.'

259

Juliette and Bernard looked at each other in a shrugging sort of way, then at Aldous. They hadn't understood.

'I mean a proper, functioning art gallery, with exhibitions, open to the public.'

'Open to the public? People can just walk in?'

'On certain days, yes. It won't be open every day – or maybe it will, I haven't decided yet. It's something I've been thinking about for a long time. There's a couple of artists in Whitstable who've done the same thing, and it's a big success. I'm going to clear out the ground floor of everything except the piano, and I'm going to move upstairs. I'm going to strip the floors and walls, paint the floorboards grey and everything else white, put spotlight lighting in the rooms and hang an exhibition. My own work in the back rooms, a guest artist in the front room. I'm going to get the London press interested, have an opening with free wine and nuts and photographers . . .'

Despite the attractiveness of the idea, Aldous's enthusiasm and apparent commitment to a very public act was so uncharacteristic of him that Juliette's initial reaction was to tell her father off for being ridiculous. It just didn't seem in keeping with a man who, for most of his life, had avoided social gatherings whenever he could, and who looked on the display and sale of his own art as, for the most part, something rather sordid and seedy. The thought of her father transforming his house into a commercial art gallery, for the promotion of his own and others' work – it was almost impossible to take seriously. And she also vaguely remembered that it had been an idea of Maria's. Perhaps her father had taken up the idea as part of some hare-brained plan to impress her. Despite the slightly sleazy slant this possibility gave to the scheme, Juliette could do nothing apart from appear encouraging.

'That sounds like a fantastic idea,' she said, at the same time as trying to think of a way of steering the conversation back on to the course she had originally planned for it. The news about her and Bernard's search for a house was meant to lead on to the greater news that she was pregnant. It was this news that she had hoped would make up for the stern talking about drinking and Maria. She had been heartened by how starstruck Aldous had been with James's son, Wahimi, and how saddened he seemed when he was taken away to Edinburgh. Now she hoped her own news would offer Aldous the prospect of hope, of something to live for. It irked her slightly that he seemed to have done that for himself in this rather defiant manner. There was something about the way her father told of his gallery plans that was deliberately callous. *Sod you, I'm doing this whether you like it or not*. That's what he seemed to be saying.

'I should warn you,' Aldous continued, 'if you want anything from the house you'll have to come round pretty soon and get it, because everything else is going straight in the skip.'

'Everything?'

'Everything that I haven't taken upstairs, yes. And that will be nearly everything – all the furniture, all the books, all the junk. The piano is staying, the gas cooker is staying. I might get rid of it later and have a little kitchen upstairs. The downstairs kitchen I want to turn into a sort of office, and place for members of public to sit down, while they write out their cheques, or view paintings from the collection. Rembrandt had just the same sort of set-up in his house – a little room set aside for clients, with a display of paintings for purchase on the walls.'

'So you're going to live upstairs?'

'Yes.'

'Don't you need some sort of licence? I mean, can you just turn your house into an art gallery?' Juliette directed this question more at Bernard than her father, as if she wouldn't have expected her father to have thought about this.

'You could have some problems with house insurance, certainly,' said Bernard. 'In effect you'd be turning a domestic dwelling into a kind of shop. You might need planning permission, which is unlikely to be granted for a residential area like that, almost certainly there would be objections, not least on the grounds of access. They might feel that an art gallery would mean an increase in cars – where are all these visitors going to park? It's hard enough parking in Fernlight Avenue already – you always get some nasty little note tucked under your windscreen wiper – *would you mind not parking in our space*, etc, etc . . .'

'There, Dad. It's not going to be as easy as you thought, is it?' There was almost a sigh of relief in Juliette's voice. She was more bothered than she first realised by the proposed transformation of Fernlight Avenue. If it happened, she imagined it would feel like losing one's own natural habitat. Even though she had not lived there for years, it had remained much as it was when she'd been a child-in-residence. There'd been one or two spurts of redecoration, the lifting and replacing of carpet with lino, the daubing of walls with uncoordinated colours, but the house still hosted the same clutter of objects that she'd grown up with. The thought of these being uprooted and dispatched to the brooding incinerators in the Lee Valley disturbed her almost more than the suspicion that her father, through these actions, was exhibiting the signs of some sort of breakdown.

'Do you take me for a complete halfwit?' said Aldous. 'Of course I've thought all this through. I've even had meetings with the people in Whitstable about it.' (This wasn't true.) 'I'm not turning the house into a shop, I'm simply running a business from my own home, which is quite different. There's no obligation to register a change of use. The council would only object if I changed the frontage of the house and put up signage encouraging customers and so on. So I can't have 'Aldous's Art Gallery' in big flashing neon lights outside, and as long as it appears to be an ordinary house, I can do what I like inside.'

Bernard looked sceptical.

'I wouldn't be so sure,' he said, but couldn't articulate his doubts beyond pulling doubtful, inscrutable expressions.

Juliette's pregnancy went unannounced that evening.

26

Clearing the ground floor of the house was a more arduous task than Aldous had anticipated. He had assumed that when he hired the skip he also hired a person to help him fill it, but this was not the case. The skip descended with the clanking of chains and grinding of hydraulics, giving out a cathedral chime as it touched down outside the house. A man with a bulging and exposed midriff descended from the lorry cab with the same sense of carefully lowered weight, and waddled over with a chit for Aldous to sign.

'You're not staying?' said Aldous as the man waddled back to his lorry.

'Staying?' said the man, amazed.

'To help me with the stuff?'

'What stuff?' the man said, as though that would have made any difference.

'The stuff I want to put in the skip.'

'No,' the man said, smiling through his very curly beard, 'we just do skips. We don't do people.'

So Aldous had a rather hopeless first day. He couldn't move any of the furniture, as he'd planned. He did his best instead to fill the skip with portable things, but there weren't a lot of these. Most of the books he was saving to take upstairs. There were several old bicycles which he wheeled out and then, with some straining, lifted over the rim of the skip. There was all the stuff in and on the kitchen cupboard – those wads of ciga-rette coupons and false teeth – which he stuffed into a bin liner and carried out. At the end of the day he'd barely covered the floor of the container, but the exertion was enough to leave him shaking and gasping in the armchair that evening.

The skip wouldn't have been big enough to take the furniture anyway. The thought occurred to him that maybe he could sell it to a house-clearance firm. He phoned several, and each dutifully sent a man round, most of whom walked carefully on damaged back muscles and crushed spines, talking casually about boxing and the weather, while passing dismissively over Aldous's furniture.

'Has it got a fire safety certificate?' said one of them, prodding the dusty red armchair Aldous had sat in for a decade or more.

Another looked at the put-you-up bed settee where Colette had spent her last hours in the house.

'Bit of wear and tear on the arm. Sorry, couldn't take it.'

'You can have it for nothing,' Aldous pleaded with the fifth of these men, 'the whole lot.'

'Including the piano?'

'Apart from the piano.'

'Sorry. It's not worth it. We have to pay a fee to get into the tip these days.'

'I'll pay it for you.'

'Sorry.'

In the end Aldous did find someone willing to take the stuff away, but he had to pay him three hundred pounds, ten times the cost of the skip. Two young men showed up and performed the task in what seemed like a few minutes. Furniture was reduced to a series of large shapes, a person at each end, nodding and bobbing their way out of the house to be fed through the rear doors of a removals van. Carpets and lino were rolled up and carried out, shoulder-borne like floppy girders. Aldous parted with far more than he'd intended, especially in the kitchen. The feeling of being able to make these big heavy things float out of the house as if by magic was very seductive. He got rid of the dining table (he hadn't meant to) and every piece of furniture in the kitchen up as far as the fridge. It wasn't until the men had gone that he realised they'd also taken the TV, which, being rented, wasn't his to dispose of.

Having emptied the ground floor, Aldous was now faced with the more complex details of his project. The painting of the walls and floors did not present a problem. The installation of proper gallery lighting was a slightly more difficult prospect, especially since Aldous had a mild fear of working with electricity. But he hoped that the consultation of a few manuals might enable him to manage the task by himself. He wandered around the lighting departments of several stores and found a tracked system of spotlights that would do nicely for one of the rooms, a circular rose of spotlights that would do equally well for another. He bought them, and they sat in their allotted empty rooms, while Aldous read up on working with wiring and pondered the layout of his gallery.

The hall's chessboard of stone tiles provided a pleasant and startling floor at the entrance to the gallery, and with the walls freshly painted white, this part of the house would be almost complete. He imagined one of those thick ropes with brass, hooked ends to cordon off the stairs. Perhaps the name of the gallery elegantly written on the wall facing the front door. There needed to be something else in there as well, perhaps a table with a visitors' book, leaflets, catalogues and so on. He thought about the doors to the living room and the music room – Galleries 1 and 2, as he now tried to call them. Should they have doors, or should the doors be taken out of their frames? The latter option would make the place look more like a gallery – the former option would still retain the sense of an enclosed, domestic room. The fact that the gallery was also an inhabited house was, he supposed, part of the charm of the Whitstable gallery.

Then there was the problem of how to attract people to his gallery (he wasn't sure what to call them – clients? patrons? customers? visitors?). He bought copies of all the local papers and all the art magazines he could find, and looked up their advertising fees. He was horrified by the cost. He contacted printers and enquired about their rates for printing brochures, catalogues, flyers, leaflets, invitations. Again the costs came as something of a shock. He wondered how much he could manage himself on a silkscreen or a lino block.

When Juliette and Bernard came to visit Bernard joked that Margaret Thatcher would have been proud of him.

'Starting up your own business, being very enterprising, getting on your bike. Looks like a lifetime of reading the *Daily*

Telegraph has finally done the trick. Thatcher will probably give you a grant if you ask her nicely.'

Such money was available, Aldous had heard. The next week he went to the jobcentre to enquire about it. He was given leaflets about the Enterprise Allowance Scheme – money for people setting up their own businesses – though he was a little disappointed when he was given the figures: forty pounds a week for a year, plus a certain amount of free advice and training. He was slightly relieved to discover, after several hours of interviews and investigation, that it was not available to people of pensionable age.

The visit of Juliette and Bernard had been difficult, because they were unable to conceal their initial shock at the barren state of the house. In fact, Juliette had to reach into her handbag for a piece of tissue and hold it against her sudden tears.

'It's not that bad, is it? I'd ask you to sit down, but I haven't got any chairs.'

'It's all right,' said Juliette (the tears had quickly gone), 'it's just a shock, that's all. I mean, how can you live like this?'

'It's OK. I've got a bed upstairs . . .'

'But where do you eat?'

'Upstairs, if I have to. One thing I'll have to get sorted out before I open – some proper heating for this house once and for all.'

'Proper heating means central heating,' said Bernard. And the conversation had followed a wobbly course of business and domestic advice falteringly given and grudgingly accepted.

Then Juliette announced her pregnancy, and Aldous was conscious afterwards that he hadn't responded as he should have.

'You? Pregnant? Oh no,' (laughing), 'you can't mean it.'

'Why not?'

'No, it's wonderful. I don't know why I'm laughing. But what are you going to do with it?'

'What do you mean?'

'I don't know.'

'We're going to bring it up to be a fairly normal happy adult. What a strange question. Most people ask what we're going to call it, or when it's due, or whether we hope it's a boy or a girl.'

'I was going to ask all those things.'

'Aren't you a little bit pleased?'

'Of course I am. It's the most wonderful piece of news I've heard for ages, well, for ever, really. If there was a chair I'd definitely sit down. In fact, shouldn't you be sitting down?'

Aldous was rather disappointed with himself afterwards, feeling somehow that he'd failed a deeply important test of parenthood. He hadn't shown appropriate delight in the news of an impending grandchild. But then, he'd never been that keen on babies – their mad movements and ridiculous faces, their shocking lack of knowledge about anything. According to something he'd read recently, they didn't even know the world was made of separate things outside of themselves – they thought everything was part of a continuum with their own bodies (although, on revisiting that thought, Aldous wondered if that wasn't a rather sophisticated way of looking at the world). Whenever he encountered a baby he wished he had some device that would propel it instantly a few years into its own future. Not far, just enough to give it some independence and intelligence, so that it was no longer the crab-like vulnerable thing unable to lift its own head that he remembered in the maternity wards of his middle age. He made a mental note to himself (forgotten almost instantly, as most of his mental notes were these days) to buy Juliette and Bernard some sort of congratulatory gift, and so redeem himself a little.

Aldous was surprised to find, the next time he went to visit Juliette and Bernard in their Holland Park flat, that they too had transformed their place. Everything that had been on the floor, that was not furniture, had either been raised up a level, or had vanished altogether. So Bernard's collection of LPs, which had once sprawled impressively down one side of the living room, was now much shrunken and placed on a shelf. The records that couldn't fit there had been shut up in a cupboard. The little jungle of leaves that had filled a corner of the room was also gone, the rubber plant responsible was too big to go anywhere else and so was thrown away. Juliette said it made her feel rather sad, because the plant had been a present on the occasion of her marriage to Bill Brothers, and had been growing appreciatively ever since. Bernard looked rather smug when she said this.

The transformations were all in preparation for the arrival of the baby, even though that was still six months away, and it would probably be another six months after that before it was mobile enough for rubber plants to present a hazard. Space was being cleared in the world well in advance of its arrival. When he pointed this out to Juliette and Bernard they successfully returned the point by referring to his art gallery. He had cleared out a space without any idea what he was going to put in it. And this was a problem, Aldous had to admit. He could fill it with his own paintings if he wanted to, but this would make it merely a vanity project. No one would be interested in visiting an art gallery that only exhibited the work of its owner. What he desired most was that a reasonably well-known artist could be persuaded to mount a small exhibition in his front room, an artist who would have his own connections in the art world. After nearly forty years as an art teacher Aldous had no connections in the art world whatsoever. Four decades of cack-handed dullards passing through his classrooms, not one of them had flowered into an artist of any note, or, as far as he knew, any kind of artist at all. The thought irked him if he dwelt too long on it. As for colleagues from his student days, they had more than likely gone down the same road as dreary old Cliff Ashbrittle – their talents long since relegated to occasional weekend dabbling while they lived their lives of smug retirement from uninteresting jobs. On the other hand, well-known artists were probably contractually bound to exhibit in the galleries that already represented them. Perhaps he should aim for lesser-known artists. Perhaps he should visit some of the London art schools, or wait for the summer degree shows and do some talent-spotting. But the summer was a long way off. He wanted to get his gallery launched as soon as possible. And it was at this point that Julian phoned.

'Hi, Dad. I hear you're starting an art gallery.'

'That's right.'

'Who are you exhibiting?'

'Well, me in one room, and another artist in the front room.'

'Who've you got for the front room?'

'No one at the moment. I'm still in negotiations.'

'Who with?'

'Why are you so interested?'

'Oh, no reason. It's just that, well, you know Agnès is an artist, don't you?'

'Of course I do.'

'Well, she'd be really interested in having an exhibition in London – I mean, if this place is going to be a proper art gallery and so on. Juliette was saying you're going to have a press launch.'

'That's right.'

'So what do you say? The thing is, Agnès's been doing some really interesting work recently. In fact, it's the most exciting work I've ever seen – kind of science meets photography meets erotic art.'

Aldous didn't know what to say.

'I'll think about it. Tell you what – let Agnès send me a proposal, slides and a written supporting statement, and a CV ...'

There was clear disappointment in Julian's voice.

'What do you need all that stuff for? You've seen her work, you know who she is.'

'If this is recent work then I haven't seen it. Anyway, I'm not sure I want a photography exhibition.'

'But Dad, these photographs are like nothing you've ever seen before –'

'What are you, her agent all of a sudden? Just because she's your girlfriend doesn't mean she's got an automatic right to exhibit in my gallery –'

'What's got into you, Dad? I've never heard you talk like this before.'

How Aldous would have loved to explain, and how impossible it was to do so. He was unable to say to his son something like: first you snatch my girlfriend (or possible mistress at least) from under my nose, then you expect me to give over half my new gallery space to her.

But a week or so later a package did arrive from Belgium. A bulky package of photos and written material, catalogues, slide cases, it even included a slide viewer.

Aldous glanced at the supporting statement, saw that it was written by Herman Lorre and headed 'Horny Science

269

and See-Through Sex – the recent work of Agnès Florizoone', and felt instantly an inability to read any more. He reached instead for the box of slides and the viewer. The images that shone out of this box confused him at first – black-and-white pictures, like very hazy charcoal drawings, full of smudges and scratchings-out, interconnected things writhing in and out, over and through each other. Yet they fascinated him. Suddenly an exquisitely drawn piece of anatomy would appear – the curve of vertebrae, for instance, or the networked outlines of capillaries feeding some hazy organ. All at once he realised what they were. They were X-rays. But were they real X-rays, or drawings of X-ray plates? It was hard to tell. And there was something peculiar about the bodies depicted. They looked to have multiple limbs – perhaps they were Siamese twins.

Then he came across one image that explained all the rest to him. It behaved like a key to the whole thing. The image was, or at least appeared to be, an X-ray of two heads facing each other. Two ghostly, translucent skulls in profile, the jaws with their rows of teeth (the fillings showing up as solid white blobs) slightly open. The skulls looked like they were talking into each other's mouths. Aldous realised that although the skulls looked as though they were an inch or so apart from each other, the heads which contained them must have been so close as to be touching. The parts of the head lost to the X-ray – the nose, the lips, the tongue and hair, the muscle and flesh of the face – would have filled that inch or so that kept the skulls apart. And the open mouths made sense – this was an X-ray of two people kissing. Aldous returned to the slides he'd already viewed. What had previously been abstract intertwinings were now perfectly clear as X-rays of two people making love. That skull in profile with the mouth open wide was in fact an image of a woman performing oral sex, the male member reduced to a ghost outline barely visible filling the space between the sharp-looking teeth, and the other pictures were of the most explicit scenes of copulation, which, had they been photographed with normal equipment, would surely have ranked as hardcore pornography.

Aldous turned to Herman Lorre's explicatory essay. The

drawling mid-Atlantic, mid-European tones of the bearded libertine rang out from the text. From it he learned that Agnès Florizoone was *'our heretofore foremost maker of horny iconography, the laureate of the hard-on and eulogizer of the erogenous zones . . .'* and he also learned that the images were indeed real X-rays of people having sex. *'Whole spectra of new meaning are given to this most intimate of human relations when the gaze of rational objective science is cast upon it. The act of sex is literally stripped down to its bare bones. The result is part horror show, part divine epiphany. Are these figures devils or angels, saints or demons? Look again if you think these images are clinical and cold. Look at that phantom of a phallus entering the tree-like canopy of a woman's vagina, you might mistake it for a picture of a soul ascending to paradise. And if you look carefully and long enough I guarantee you will begin to feel the same erotic charge as you might from more traditional representations of the sexual act . . .'*

A week later Julian phoned again.

'Did you get the slides?'

'Yes I did.'

'What did you think?'

'I didn't really know what to think.'

'Were you shocked?'

'Not shocked. Amazed, I suppose, might be the word.'

'Amazed in what way?'

'Well . . .' Aldous paused, feeling that only now was he finally reaching an opinion on the pieces. 'I thought they were absolutely beautiful. At the same time they were ridiculous and absurd, and they were also slightly sick and disgusting. They were also intelligent and perceptive, philosophically provocative . . . just amazing.'

'Yeah, they are aren't they. That's just what I thought of them – amazing.'

'How did she get these images – I mean – did she go to a hospital or what?'

'No, she got hold of this old airport equipment – you know, for the baggage checks – don't ask me how. I think she's got friends at Schiphol Airport. So that's how she got the images.'

'And you managed to find some people stupid enough to have sex in an airport X-ray machine?'

'Well, no. That was a problem, we couldn't find anyone willing to do it, not with the health dangers associated.'

'So who are they?'

'Well, like I said, we couldn't find anyone – so we . . .'

It took a while for Aldous to twig.

'You mean it's you and her? You X-rayed yourselves?'

Julian's reply was a sniggering laugh.

'Are you mad? You know what X-rays can do to you? If you ever want to have children –'

'Dad, it was just one afternoon of exposure. We got all we needed in one shoot, so to speak. Nothing to worry about.'

'Now I know why you're so keen for an exhibition in London . . .'

'So what do you think, Dad? You said yourself you thought they were amazing . . . If you want to talk to Agnès she's away at the moment. But I think if you showed these in the gallery it would get the whole thing off to an explosive start. The national press are going to be interested, there might be censorship issues, it could get really exciting, and a lot of publicity . . .'

'Yes,' said Aldous, 'but I'm just trying to imagine – how big are these things?'

'They're mostly six foot by four, that sort of size.'

'I'm trying to imagine them, these great big startling images of X-ray sex, alongside my quiet little landscapes and still lifes – they're going to make my paintings look ridiculous. Either that or Agnès's will be made to look ridiculous.'

'No, you'll both look magnificent. The contrast will bring out the best qualities of each . . .'

Aldous was hesitant and concluded the conversation by telling his son that he needed more time to think about it. Really, he needed to see the images themselves, in the flesh, as it were. Under normal circumstances it would be the natural next step, a trip to Belgium, a business trip this time, to visit the studio of a potential client. But the prospect did not appeal to Aldous. Maybe it was the difficulty of his feelings about Agnès and her relationship with Julian, maybe it was just the sentimental angst he felt about revisiting that rather lost part of his life. He didn't want to go there again.

At the same time he was mesmerised by these images of Agnès's. When he phoned Julian back to tell him that he was interested but needed to see the photographs themselves and didn't want to travel to Ostend, Julian hummed and ha'd until Aldous suggested he have one shipped over by express delivery, and that he would pay for it himself.

It took a lot of organising. Aldous almost began to wish he'd gone to Belgium instead, it would have been much simpler and quicker, and even cheaper. Julian claimed he couldn't afford to send the parcel without getting the money first. He'd made enquiries and found it could cost a hundred and fifty pounds to post the parcel with guaranteed same-week delivery. He said he just didn't have that sort of money lying around. Aldous offered to post a cheque – but it would have taken a long time to arrive and a long time to clear. In the end Aldous had to set up a cable transfer bank to bank, which was very expensive and involved lots of phone calls and visits to Aldous's local branch.

The artwork arrived eight days later, the size of a dining table, not exactly a parcel but a solid wood container stamped and labelled with the carrier's details and lots of 'handle with care' and 'this way up' stickers. Aldous had to open the thing with a hammer and chisel. Balls of polystyrene tumbled out when he broke the seal. The artwork itself was wrapped in several layers of bubble wrap which had to be unsellotaped. When Aldous finally reached the framed X-ray at the centre of all this soft matter he propped it on the floor against the main wall in the front room (Gallery 1) and contemplated it for a long time. Two skeletons, one recumbent, the other squatting above it, leaning forward, the head bent down slightly. Impossible to tell at first that one was a man, the other a woman, or even that they were making love. After a long period of contemplation, however, there emerged a sense of extraordinary tenderness in the image. The hand of the male figure (Julian) lying on its back was raised slightly, the claw-like finger bones spread in a gesture that was almost like praying. Imagining the flesh that engulfed these bones in reality, Aldous realised that this hand must have been cupping the hanging breast of the squatting skeleton (Agnès). Looking closer he realised that what he'd previously thought of as simply a smudgy part of the X-ray was in fact the duct-filled tissue of Agnès's right breast. There was the gorgeous black nipple on which he'd once sucked, now appearing white against the dark. Herman Lorre was right, these images did acquire a strange erotic charge after prolonged viewing.

Having invested so much time and money already in Agnès's work, Aldous felt unable now to decline her the opportunity of a show in his gallery. Not that he really had any doubts now about the quality of Agnès's work. He was utterly enthralled by it. What remained, however, were qualms about how his own work would look in comparison. Perhaps he should just forget about showing his own work at all. Perhaps he should give both galleries over to Agnès.

When he next phoned Ostend it was to Agnès that he spoke. It was a moment he was rather dreading, unsure at all of how to handle a conversation with a former object of his obsessions, but Agnès spoke as if there had never been anything at all between them, was polite and businesslike and friendly.

'Did you like the piece we sent?'

'Like it? I thought it was utterly lovely.'

'What did you think was lovely about it?'

Her use of 'lovely' made his own seem ridiculous.

'What I love about it is the way when you first see it you think it is some kind of macabre image from a horror film, but then you realise that these are not frightening skeletons, but they are real living human beings doing something incredibly intimate and tender, and how it makes lovemaking look such an awkward, clumsy and even dangerous exercise. Stripped of their flesh you see people are not made for lovemaking. But at the same time that is all we are: sets of bones. But then they emphasise how the important bit of a human being is all to do with the few inches of flesh that surround the bones, and ultimately the surface – the skin. Without our skin what are we? Darkly comic, macabre, ridiculous things . . .'

'You've said it all. That's what I want to say.'

Suddenly Aldous felt an impending sense of responsibility. What had started out as an act of selfish frivolity was now becoming a socially important act. From later conversations with Agnès he realised how seriously she was taking this opportunity. She had tried getting shows in London before, but had never succeeded. She was pinning high hopes on this exhibition. After further phone calls a firm date was set, only a few weeks in the future.

So things began happening rather quickly with Aldous's gallery. He painted the ground-floor walls white. He bought stylish wooden venetian blinds to replace the grimy curtains in the front room. He laboured for ages to think of a name for the gallery. Habitude and Habile were two that came to mind, but he decided they sounded too much like trendy furniture shops. And then the word popped into his head out of nowhere, something left over from the almost forgotten Latin lessons of nearly sixty years ago, the one simple word with its terrifyingly abundant wealth of meanings: Amandus.

And he spent an afternoon carefully painting this word in bold in a carefully chosen font on to the wall in the hall that faced the front door, letters in a deep maroon colour.

Amandus

And then, contemplating the beauty and heartache of this word as it appeared so cleanly and elegantly lettered on the wall, he wondered if he should add as a subscript beneath this word in small lettering, a definition:

Latin – *deserving or requiring to be loved* . . .

The aptness of this word was so strong that Aldous couldn't help giggling, the lovely implications of its gerundive form conveying an urgency that had no single-word equivalent in English. But he decided to leave the definition out, and have just the word on display. The Amandus Gallery. It had a very pleasing sound. The Amandus Gallery in Windhover Hill. Agnès Florizoone at the Amandus Gallery, Windhover Hill, London.

Then followed the most difficult part, the part for which he felt himself least suited. Arranging publicity. The original plan of printing out a few linocuts to serve as posters would not now satisfy Agnès's ambition, and he felt he must invest more in order to do justice to the quality and strength of the work the gallery would show. He had to have proper publicity material printed, and this took a sizeable chunk out of Aldous's budget. He splashed out on advertising space in the quality art magazines and supplements. He even got on the phone and found himself in conversation with the art editor of *Time Out*. To Aldous's amazement the editor showed great interest, and already knew of Agnès's work.

'That'll be a great boost for your gallery, Aldous, showing the first UK exhibition of Agnès Florizoone. What a coup!'

The art editor of the *Observer* was equally interested, not only in the exhibition but in the notion of opening a gallery in a suburban London house. He asked if Aldous would mind if he dropped by sometime to see how things were coming along. Aldous said he wouldn't mind at all. The potential guest list for the opening was beginning to build. The local papers were interested as well, and one even decided to do an interview with Aldous before the gallery opened. And so the same paper that had previously borne the image of Aldous's bruised face now carried the story of his miraculous comeback.

SAD PENSIONER SET TO TAKE ART WORLD BY STORM – FROM HIS OWN HOUSE

There was a picture alongside, of Aldous standing outside the house, holding one of his paintings, and smiling stupidly. The article aroused the interest of neighbours who, to his surprise, seemed quietly approving of the project, although one woman with tinted hair and gold-rimmed spectacles did call and begin asking difficult questions – How many visitors did he expect at this 'art gallery' (she somehow managed to speak the quotation marks)? What were the opening hours going to be? etc., etc. Aldous was prepared and fobbed her off with half-lies: it would only be open to people by appointment, so there was no need to worry about crowds of art lovers clogging up the driveways.

It took two days just for Aldous to fix up the new lighting in the galleries, then several days were spent on framing his paintings. He'd decided to confine his own work to the kitchen office and give Agnès the two main galleries to herself. That was six walls for Agnès, three of which could take two big paintings, and one could take three smaller works, which meant that he could mount an exhibition of eleven pieces. Agnès also wanted a table where she could display her notebooks and sketchbooks. With Aldous's work in the kitchen that would make a decent show altogether, well worth a trip. To add further excitement Agnès was expecting to sell her work, and they needed to reach an agreement as to what commission Aldous would take. This they did over a series of phone calls, and Aldous realised he was expected to draw up a written contract. He had nothing to do this with, and in the end had to get Juliette to type it up on her newly acquired Amstrad computer. Aldous and Agnès agreed to a 50 per cent split of sales. Agnès was thinking of charging six hundred pounds for some of her pieces. If a few sales went through, Aldous could actually make some money out of her.

Shortly after the adverts appeared in the newspapers and magazines, Aldous was swamped by letters and packages arriving in the post. These mostly contained slides and CVs. Hopeful artists touting for exhibitions. But Aldous hardly had time to open most of these as the time for Agnès's exhibition drew near. Agnès and Julian were going to bring the works over themselves in a borrowed van just a few days before the opening. Aldous had already sent out the invitations for this. He'd posted nearly 150. He enclosed a letter with Maria's, which he sent care of the blind school.

Dear Maria,
Your idea has finally borne fruit. Thank you for suggesting it. I hope you can come to this opening. It promises to be a grand occasion, with people from the national press attending (confirmed) would you believe? I've sent invites to a few famous names – Euan Uglow, Francis Bacon, Graham Sutherland (you never know) also Melvyn Bragg, in the hope that he'll do a *South Bank Show*. The artist, Agnès Florizoone, is an old friend from Belgium. I really think you should see her work, it is

absolutely astonishing, but not for the faint-hearted (you're not that, are you?). Your idea was brilliant, but you were wrong when you said there would be hardly any expenses. This project is costing me a fortune and has just about emptied my bank account. I don't even have any money left for whisky, which is a good thing, I think you'll agree.

How are things in the Kingdom of the Blind?

Love,

Aldous

Aldous also enclosed a copy of the article in the local paper, and was amazed to get a reply from Maria within a couple of days.

Dear Aldous,

This really is a marvellous thing. I'd be delighted to come on the 19th. I always knew you would do something wonderful, and now you have. May I bring a friend?

Love and hugs,

Maria

Several others confirmed. Cliff Ashbrittle sent an icy little note saying he would 'try and make it, depending on trains'. It promised to be a big gathering. Aldous now had to sort out wine and food, plates, glasses, cutlery. Juliette offered to do this, and when she came round one evening, asked him if he needed any other help.

'You don't mind me saying, do you, Dad, but you look totally exhausted.'

'No, I don't mind you saying. I am totally exhausted, I keep getting dizzy spells.'

'You need to have a rest. Look what you've done, all this on your own, transformed the house, you must be shattered.'

'How can I rest? Agnès and Julian are loading up their van as we speak and I haven't even got the floor painted. They'll be here tomorrow afternoon. I still need some display tables –'

'I can get you some of those – there's a shop in Finchley –'

'And I've got to do labels for all Agnès's photographs –'

'Give me the wording, I can run it off on the Amstrad –'

278

'And I've just realised – the only toilet's upstairs, and the upstairs is a total mess. You've seen it. The landing's just full of junk, the toilet's all grotty, and the bathroom is just a box room, you can't even get to the sink –'

'But that's what it's all about,' said Juliette, 'the art gallery that is also a home, that's what's so special about it.'

'True, but it has to be a presentable home. I've just concentrated on the downstairs, I haven't even thought about the upstairs. What's Melvyn Bragg going to think when he wants to go for a pee?'

'Don't worry about Melvyn Bragg. I'm sure he's peed in worse places.'

Juliette left in the early evening, having promised to run a number of errands for her father, and having failed to persuade him that he needed any help with the final touches to the gallery.

'I'm going to paint the floor this evening. I want it dry for when Julian and Agnès arrive tomorrow afternoon –'

'But that's a big job, three rooms, you'll need help – what if I send Bernard over to give you a hand? He won't mind.'

'No, we'll just get in each other's way, or we'll both paint ourselves into different corners. Honestly, it'll be much easier for me on my own. And it's only painting the floor. All I need to do is to pour the paint on to the floor and spread it around with a broom – I'm joking.' (He added this last remark on seeing the alarm on his daughter's face.)

When she left, however, he was a little daunted by the prospect of the task he had set himself. Three big wooden floors, three two-litre tins of grey paint, one not very big brush. But he set to work anyway, in the front room at first. The floorboards here were dark around the margins of the room, having been varnished many years before. The centre, where the carpet had been, was paler, but the quality of the wood generally was very bad – splashes of paint, mottled stains, mismatching boards.

Juliette and Bernard were horrified when they first learned of Aldous's plans to paint the floorboards, since these features were making a comeback, it seemed, among the trendier young middle classes, who saw wall-to-wall carpeting as the height of bad taste. Aldous insisted they would be impressed once they saw the result, how like an art gallery it would look. The floor-boards could always be stripped at a later stage.

As Aldous worked, it dawned on him that this was going to be much harder than he thought. It was the pain he experienced in the knees, down on all fours as he was, paintbrush in one hand, slapping on the grey paint, having to shuffle along every few strokes to change position and cover more of the floor. After painting only a quarter of the front-room floor he had to stop for a rest, then found he couldn't get up, at least not at first. He had to think carefully. His legs felt numb from the feet to the hips, he couldn't raise himself up on his knees, it was too painful. He could do nothing for a while but stay as he was, breathing deeply. In the end, the only way of getting himself upright was to roll himself over on to his bottom, then push himself up. Sensation came back into his legs like champagne flutes slowly filling – the rising, bubbly surge of pins and needles. He hobbled to the kitchen and took a swig of whisky. It was the first drink he'd had for several days, and it took all the aches away instantly. He went upstairs to get some pillows off the bed and returned to the front room. Using the pillows as a hassock for his knees he got down again and resumed painting.

He managed a good stretch this time before the pain set in. Nearly three-quarters of the room done. It was now approaching midnight. He struggled upright with difficulty and took another drink. The blood seemed to fall away from his brain and he was momentarily dizzy. He punched the wall with a mild fit of anger at his own lassitude, decrepitude, for being yoked unwillingly to this unwilling body of his. One more session and the front room was finished. This time he felt the immense reward of having Gallery 1 finally complete. With the spotlights on and the door taken away and the slatted window blinds down, it looked just like one of those swanky Cork Street galleries.

It was getting on for one o'clock in the morning. He had to concede now he might not paint all three rooms this night, but as long as he had Galleries 1 and 2 painted, the kitchen didn't matter so much. He could leave that till later.

Gallery 2, which used to be the music room, was slightly harder to paint because of the piano. It had been a difficult enough job for those removal men to get the cream lino out from under the instrument, but at least that was gone and there weren't even any shreds left under the castors. They'd had to cut the lino away and then lift the piano up an inch while the remaining lino was pulled out – a perfect illustration, Aldous thought, of the phrase, 'having the rug pulled away from under one's feet'. That's certainly what it must have felt like for the piano. The instrument had stayed exactly where it was, in the same position it had occupied for nearly thirty years, while all around it everything had changed: the floors and walls had drained away, new ones had appeared, curtains had risen and fallen like the passing of eras, paintings had appeared on the walls, enjoyed a few years of notoriety, then had somehow disappeared into the walls themselves. How many light bulbs had it taken to keep this room illuminated for thirty years? Aldous wondered, often feeling that light bulbs themselves had become less reliable as time passed. In the old days it seemed a light bulb would last for years, but nowadays they seemed to expire every few weeks, giving one last threatening flash before their filaments snapped.

This was potentially the best room for an art gallery. Three big plain walls and an array of windows and glass doors that gave on to the tangled greenery of the garden. The piano stood sleek and black like a piece of modernist sculpture itself. Aldous spent a few minutes giving the floor one last sweep to remove the grit and dust that had built up since his last sweeping of the boards. Then he was on his knees again. In his tiredness he started painting the floor from outside the door, so that, once he'd realised his mistake, he had to get up and take a big stride across the wet paint in order to continue.

It was bound to happen. Just as he always thought it would. Slopping on the grey paint, the waxy smell of emulsion filling his nostrils and bringing on a headache. As the clock moved on into the small hours, and the ebb and flow of pain continued in his muscles and joints, she began talking to him.

'On your knees at last,' said the sweet, soft voice. 'How long has it taken to bring you to your knees?'

At first he couldn't see her. All he could see was the floor, disappearing under his tide of grey emulsion, and then the legs of the piano.

'Well, it's not the first time I've been on my knees. I've been flat on my face before now . . .'

'And will be again soon I shouldn't wonder . . .'

From his viewpoint near floor level the piano appeared like a great black canopy and seemed to cast an immense shadow. In fact, the whole piano felt like one solid shadow. Aldous looked sideways along the vista beneath the piano, his hand carrying on its slopping back and forth of grey paint unobserved. There were the thin black struts that housed the pedal mechanisms, at the bottom of which were the little brass tongues of the pedals themselves. And there, behind these black struts, a pair of human legs were placed. Graceful female legs, clad in white silk, ending in deep red velvet slippers. They were positioned rather primly together and at an angle offsetting the rigid verticals of the pedal struts. Exquisite female legs. There was a woman seated at the piano.

'Why are you bothering with all this?' she said.

Aldous raised himself on his knees. This didn't give him quite enough height to see over the top of the piano, but he could glimpse the crown of someone's head peeping just above the music rest. Glossy, dark brown hair, combed back and set in a braid.

'Why shouldn't I bother?' Aldous said. 'You might as well say why bother with anything.'

'It looks like a lot of work for nothing,' the sweet, soft voice said with such gentle insistence it was impossible to be offended. 'And who is this Alice Florizel anyway?'

'Agnès Florizoone, she's a fantastic artist –'

'X-rays of people copulating? You call that fantastic art? A year ago you would have laughed at such pretentious nonsense.'

At this Aldous had to stand up. He found it surprisingly easy, the pain in his knees seemed to have seeped away.

The woman revealed by this raised perspective was as he had expected. The white, marmoreal face, the conker-brown eyes under gently curving eyebrows, ovals within ovals. She even had the faceted jewels hanging from her ears, and the amber-beaded necklaces draped over a pale white bosom, itself partly revealed by the open white fur she had about her.

'What has become of you,' she said, 'on your knees for the sake of a little piece of female fakery? She wouldn't even let you take her alone to Amsterdam, and then ran off with your son, but still she has you on your knees.'

'I'm on my knees for the sake of the house,' said Aldous, leaning one hand on the piano for support, feeling giddy with the apprehension of beauty. Hendrickje Stoffels sitting on the piano stool. An illusion of course, and Aldous knew it, but what a pleasing one, what an extraordinarily generous gift of his own mind to itself to conjure this thing in his room.

'How long are you going to stay?' he asked, inching his way carefully along the side of the piano, gripping it with one hand like a banister. He was frightened that if he came too close the vision might disappear. He was near enough now to see the skin in detail. It was living, human skin, moving with life, but at the same time he could see the brush marks that gave a texture to its surface.

'How long?' the image replied. 'Well, I'm here for ever.'

'I'm glad,' said Aldous, 'but what will Rembrandt think? Have you left him all alone in whatever world you've come from?'

Here Hendrickje looked puzzled (Aldous was delighted that the emotion brought to the face a configuration never before seen by the world) and she replied, after some thought, by simply saying, 'Rembrandt?' as though she had no connection with the great artist whatsoever.

The genuine puzzlement on Hendrickje's face made Aldous realise that it wasn't Hendrickje at all seated at the piano. Perhaps it had never been Hendrickje who had been the object of his obsessions. Or rather, he now realised why he had been so attracted to the portrait in the National Gallery.

'Trust you to get me mixed up with some whore,' she said, taking a sip from the tumbler of Gold Label that was by her side.

'But the likeness – I never realised until now. The painting – it is you, but forty or more years ago. The young you.'

'So you say. I suppose there is some resemblance. More so

than with that ghastly Maria woman. What on earth were you doing with her? Juliette was absolutely right about her. Not your type at all.'

'Well, what's it got to do with you? At least she showed me some friendship, which is more than can be said for the other five billion people on this planet.'

'She soon took it back though, didn't she, once you'd over-stepped the mark?'

'Have you come here just to taunt me about my failed relationships?'

'Should I have another purpose?'

Aldous took his hand away from the piano and stood without support.

'Funny how we never argued like this in real life. But I suppose that's because you're not really here and I'm arguing with myself.'

'But then you could say you're not really here either.'

Aldous wondered what she could mean for a moment, watching her as she took a cigarette out of a packet of Player's No. 6 and lit it with a rather extravagant flourish of a match. She had become a most enticing variation of Rembrandt's portrait.

'Oh, I see. You've come here to cart me off to the life beyond, is that it? Just when I'm starting to get things done with my life, on the very brink . . . Can't you just let me finish painting the floor?'

'Don't be silly. How could you ever finish painting this floor?'

And it was true.

Aldous looked down and saw that the floor stretched away in all directions as far as the horizon, his painted patch a mere dot in the vast expanse of floorboards. As was the piano. Young Colette opened her arms, holding out another tumbler of drink to Aldous, and shuffling up on the piano stool to make space for him. He went over and sat down beside her, taking the glass, and they both drank.

27

'What the fuck's he done to the house?' said Julian, as he pulled the van up outside 89 Fernlight Avenue. Agnès, in the passenger seat, looked with interest through the window, ducking to take in the whole structure.

'Is it this one? The one on the end?'

'Yes, but some bastard's cut down all the trees. It used to look much nicer – now it looks sort of naked and exposed. You could hardly see the house before because of the trees.'

'There are still plenty of trees –'

'And there's something else wrong – the roof, it's got horrible orange tiles on, it used to be slate. I'm sure it used to be slate.'

The two climbed out of the van, approaching the house slowly, Agnès so that she could admire the charm of a typical London suburban house, Julian so that he could take in every detail of what was wrong with it, what was missing, what was new.

'Didn't your dad tell you he was having the house reno-vated?' said Agnès as Julian knocked.

'He did say something, yes. It's just a shock to see it, that's all.'

The knock went unanswered. There was a strong smell of emulsion paint, even from here.

'Haven't you got a key?'

'No. It's not a problem, you can usually get in round back. Dad should be here though.'

They walked down the narrow side alley and through the gate into the back garden. Here Julian experienced more horrors.

'Pebble-dash! Is he mad? He's gone and pebble-dashed the back of the house. The whole thing . . .' He walked backwards down the garden to get a view of the house. 'How can he have a serious art gallery in a pebble-dashed house? Oh God, what's he done to the inside? If the outside is anything to go by. D'you know what, I carved my initials on this bit here –' he showed Agnès the spot by the back door – 'we all did. Lovely old orange bricks. Now they're covered up by this cement porridge.'

He tried the back door. This was all new, and was locked securely.

'The old one used to open if you jiggled it about a bit. I suppose the same thing's happened to the music-room doors.' He walked across the cracked, weedy concrete to the French windows, also new and securely locked. 'This feels really weird, like it's not my own house any more. I feel like a burglar.'

'Perhaps your dad's asleep? You said he could fall asleep sometimes during the day.'

'Maybe. I don't know what to do. I've never been unable to get in the house before. And I can't see inside because of these stupid blinds that he's had put up.'

They hovered around the house for a while, back and front, knocking every now and then, tapping on the downstairs windows, throwing pebbles at the upstairs windows. Nothing produced any response.

In the end they walked to the phone box at the top of the road and phoned Juliette, who luckily wasn't at work.

'She sounded really worried,' said Julian, as he emerged from the damp space of the phone box. 'She said she'd been trying to phone him since lunchtime and there's been no answer. I said, so what, he's probably gone out, but she seemed to think something was wrong. So she's coming over with a key. She'll be about an hour, we might as well go and sit in the van.'

It was a long wait. Juliette looked very flustered when she arrived, dropping her keys on the path, fumbling at the lock, hardly noticing Agnès. Juliette's heaviness with child was the cause for a brief and oddly inappropriate round of congratulations, Julian and Agnès unable to contain their surprise at Juliette's pregnant form. 'I know you told us, but it just looks odd to see you that shape.' They followed her into the house but were held back by their admiration for the space that Aldous had created, while Juliette probed further into the rooms beyond the hall.

'This looks really good,' said Julian, 'brilliant.' They admired the bold calligraphy of the word Amandus, as it appeared on the opposite wall, and peeped into the pristine white space of the front room, with Gallery 1 lettered on to the wall in smaller lettering. Just then Juliette emerged from the music room, her face red and broken.

'He's dead,' she said.

Juliette had found her father's body lying face down on the floor of the music room, at the feet of the piano. His deadness was so apparent that she didn't need to approach closely. Neither did Julian or Agnès. They watched from the door of the music room, unable to enter. They didn't discuss with each other the peculiarity of being unable to enter the room. While they waited for the ambulance to arrive they felt unable even to stay in the house, but stood outside on the pavement, or sat in Julian's van. Agnès and Juliette made edgy, embarrassed conversation, trying to make themselves feel better by talking about babies. But they made themselves feel worse. Julian was shocked to find that he was frightened of going into the house in just the same way he was frightened, as a child, of going on the ghost train at Battersea Funfair. A primitive fear of the supernatural had unexpectedly asserted itself. His father had entered the realm of things that lurk in dark corners. Of things that give you a fright. This annoyed Julian. It was sadness he wanted to be feeling, not fear.

The ambulance people were in the house for a long time. They had taken a stretcher in, but after twenty minutes they were still in there. When they did emerge it was without the stretcher, or the body. They spoke in slightly embarrassed tones to Juliette.

'I'm afraid there's a bit of a problem. It looks as though your father was painting the floor when he died. Well, he collapsed into wet paint, and this has dried quite hard and we're having difficulty getting him off it.'

'It's like he's glued to the floor,' the other paramedic offered.

'We've tried some solvents that we usually use for oil-based paints and glues, but these haven't worked. We want to find a way of separating your father from the floor without damaging his body, but we don't have the equipment. I've called the fire service and they're sending an engine. They usually have all sorts of things for getting people out of sticky situations . . .' The ambulance man tested out a laugh when he realised he'd made a joke. It failed.

Juliette would have said just cut away whatever's stuck to the floor, if he's dead it doesn't make any difference, but the ambulance man wouldn't hear of anything that involved the unnecessary disfigurement of a body, even a dead one.

So a fire engine joined the ambulance outside Fernlight Avenue. A police car also appeared after a while. The firemen could do nothing to separate Aldous from the floor either.

'He's stuck by his face,' one of the firemen said, 'that's the main problem. And his face is getting more fragile by the minute . . .' For the first time that day Juliette felt impelled to ask someone to withhold information. The fireman apologised and returned inside.

Eventually a partial solution was reached. It was decided that the main priority was to remove the body from the house. He could be separated from it later. Juliette noticed a fireman strolling into the house with a large axe in his hand, then the thump thump thump of someone chopping through wood. Then, finally, the stretcher emerged, Aldous beneath a blanket, given a peculiar shape by the floorboard attached to his face.

After some discussion it was decided that the exhibition should go ahead anyway, and the opening should serve as a kind of memorial event for Aldous. Julian and Agnès worked at finishing the furbishment of the galleries (the replacement of one section of missing floorboard being their first task), repainting the floor, collecting catalogues and other printed matter. Juliette had helped Aldous with so much of the planning that she was able quite easily to pick up where he'd left off. This provided a useful distraction from the grim processes of organising Aldous's burial. His funeral was finally arranged for the same day as the opening of the Amandus Gallery, the party in the evening counterbalancing the burial in the afternoon.

Extract from the 'Around Town' column in *Time Out*, no.3012, 26 April 1986

So, when was the last time you were in Windhover Hill? Have you even heard of the place? While you may contend that the true Londoner would never venture further north than the Rainbow in Finsbury Park, or further south than the Rock Garden, you might in future feel the pull of this former haven of retired insurance salesmen and senior civil servants. Why? Because it has suddenly become home to the Amandus Gallery, which was itself formerly the home, and I mean a proper three-up two-down type home, to the gallery's creator, Aldous Jones. Yes indeed, Mr Jones has done for Windhover Hill what the Turners have done for Whitstable: he has turned an ordinary domestic house into a real, live and kicking art gallery. (Hey, if it's that easy, are we going to find these places springing up everywhere? Will it soon be a rarity for a house not to be an art gallery? Could be, especially if you can charge an entry fee – Amandus is free, by the way.) Anyway, 'Around Town' found itself with an invite to the 'press night' of the Amandus Gallery's first ever show, Agnès Florizoone, a Belgian (yawn) artist who apparently takes X-ray snaps of people having nookie (yawn suddenly replaced by look of salivating interest). So one naturally made one's way there. Machete in hand I ventured forth from Wood Green tube into ever thickening forests of lime and plane, I hacked my way through dense privet and overgrown laurel until, to my amazement, I found myself in one of the smartest-looking galleries outside Cork Street, rubbing shoulders with a surprisingly elevated crowd of London arty-literati. There was not just *Time Out*'s very own art editor (why didn't he tell me he was going, could have given me a lift), but several demigods of our cultural life such as Melvyn Bragg, Sir Roy Strong and even weatherman Michael Fish (at least it looked like him) admiring the transparent nobs and see-through knockers of Agnès Florizoone's X-rays.

How had such a tiny, unknown gallery attracted such a crowd of arty celebs? Then the evening took a poignant turn when speeches were made that announced the recent death of the gallery's founder, Aldous Jones. Mr Jones's paintings were on display in one of the three galleries – rather fetching little landscapes that were much more fun than the X-ray sex pictures. It was said that Mr Jones's children are going to take over the running of the gallery. By the standards of the party that followed (free booze in endless supply, and Vick's Synex on tap for Melvyn who looked decidedly shaky on his legs by the end), and the mixture of people (I met someone who claimed to be an Amazonian Indian, another who claimed to have shagged Hitler – a guy I might add), it can only be hoped that the Amandus Gallery thrives and thrives. I'll even use this column to make a special plea (and I don't often do that). Go to Windhover Hill and visit the Amandus Gallery. When should you visit? I will tell you. NOW! NOW! NOW!

The Amandus Gallery, 89 Fernlight Avenue, Windhover Hill, London. Galleries 1 and 2 – 'Ghosts', recent works by Agnès Florizoone. Gallery 3 – Landscapes, Aldous Jones. Both until 21 August. Mon–Wed 10am–4.30pm, Sat 10am–1pm. Other times by appointment.

Acknowledgements

I would like to thank Bath Spa University for allowing me the time to finish this book, and for supporting a research trip to Belgium and beyond, and also for providing me with somewhere to belong when I'm not writing. Staff and students at the university have helped me in ways they won't be aware of, and I'd especially like to thank Tim Liardet, Richard Kerridge, Richard Francis, Nikita Lalwani and Tessa Hadley for many interesting conversations in many interesting places about many interesting things, some of them to do with writing. I am very grateful to Zoe Waldie for her persistent, indefatigable help and support. Special thanks must go to Rebecca Carter for her brilliant editing of this book and its predecessors, and for being able to see what I was trying to do before I could. Finally to Suzanne for her love, to Corin for allowing me on the computer sometimes, and to Phoebe for her magicianship.

Lines from 'Abacus', by Peter Redgrove, are from *In the Hall of the Saurians*, published by Secker & Warburg in 1987, reproduced by kind permission of The Random House Group.